The Yellow Rose Mysteries
by Leann Sweeney

Dead Giveaway

A Wedding to Die For

Pick Your Poison

SHOOT FROM THE LIP

A YELLOW ROSE MYSTERY

Leann Sweeney

A SIGNET BOOK

SIGNET
Published by New American Library, a division of
Penguin Group (USA) Inc., 375 Hudson Street,
New York, New York 10014, USA
Penguin Group (Canada), 90 Eglinton Avenue East, Suite 700, Toronto,
Ontario M4P 2Y3, Canada (a division of Pearson Penguin Canada Inc.)
Penguin Books Ltd., 80 Strand, London WC2R 0RL, England
Penguin Ireland, 25 St. Stephen's Green, Dublin 2,
Ireland (a division of Penguin Books Ltd.)
Penguin Group (Australia), 250 Camberwell Road, Camberwell, Victoria 3124,
Australia (a division of Pearson Australia Group Pty. Ltd.)
Penguin Books India Pvt. Ltd., 11 Community Centre, Panchsheel Park,
New Delhi - 110 017, India
Penguin Group (NZ), cnr Airborne and Rosedale Roads, Albany,
Auckland 1310, New Zealand (a division of Pearson New Zealand Ltd.)
Penguin Books (South Africa) (Pty.) Ltd., 24 Sturdee Avenue,
Rosebank, Johannesburg 2196, South Africa

Penguin Books Ltd., Registered Offices:
80 Strand, London WC2R 0RL, England

First published by Signet, an imprint of New American Library,
a division of Penguin Group (USA) Inc.

First Printing, January 2007
10   9   8   7   6   5   4   3   2   1

Copyright © Leann Sweeney, 2007
All rights reserved

The Edgar® name is a registered service mark of the Mystery Writers of
America, Inc.

Ⓟ REGISTERED TRADEMARK—MARCA REGISTRADA

Printed in the United States of America

For the kids, in order of appearance in my life:
Shawn, Jillian, Jeffrey and Allison.
I love you all so much.

ACKNOWLEDGMENTS

In the writing of this book, I was fortunate to have two wonderful experts help me get things right. Any mistakes I've made are my fault, not theirs. I thank Officer Sheridan Rowe of the Houston Police Department and Joyce Gigout, a skeletal remains and cold case expert with the Harris County Medical Examiner's Office. These two women offered their expertise over and over. If this story rings true, it's because of them. I would also like to thank my husband for his unbelievable support. Also, my writing group regulars, Amy, Bob, Charlie, Kay, and Laura, as well as Susie and Isabella. These folks are the best at offering intelligent insights when it comes to writing a mystery. Thank you Patti Nunn of Breakthrough Promotions and Jeffrey Cranor, my webmaster. Lastly, I am grateful to Carol Mann, Tina Brown and my amazing editor Claire Zion, three very wise women.

1

My daddy used to tell me the biggest troublemaker I'd ever meet watches me brush my teeth in the mirror every day. If the folks I'd let into my house that Sunday in October had an ounce of Daddy's insight, they might not have come calling.

My first words after I opened my door were, "Please don't turn on that camera." I smiled like a politician at the two people I'd seen through my new small-screen security monitoring system—the young woman with her three-ring binder and designer sunglasses, the man with the big video camera. I don't ignore media people. I've learned it's better to face them, 'cause I sure as hell don't want them behind me.

The slim young woman turned to her older, balding companion and said, "We'll wait on any footage, Stu."

I searched beyond them, looking for their TV news van, but they must have arrived in the dark SUV parked at the curb. "What can I do for you?"

"A production assistant was supposed to call and let you know we were coming," the woman said.

"No one called. You sure you have the right address?"

"Abby Rose?" the woman said. "Yellow Rose Investigations?"

"That's me." I leaned against the doorframe, arms crossed.

She smiled and removed her sunglasses. "Great, Abby. Now can we talk inside? It's, like, *so* hot already."

Since most people in these parts know eighty-degree mornings in Houston aren't unusual this time of year, and I'd heard no familiar twang in her voice, I suspected they weren't locals. "First off, you need to tell me who you are."

She pulled a business card from the binder pocket and handed it to me. "Chelsea Burch. Venture Productions. And this is Stu." She turned to him. He still had the video camera balanced on his shoulder. "Stu . . . what *is* your last name?"

"Crowell," he said gruffly.

She arched her penciled brows. "Like Simon Crowell from *American Idol*? Are you kidding me?"

"Crowell, not *Cowell*," Stu said.

"Oh." She turned back to me, apparently unbothered by not knowing Stu's last name, something that obviously had pissed him off. "Anyway, we've seen pictures, have your bio. We're beginning production here in Houston." Before I could ask exactly what they were producing, she went on. "I'm an assistant producer working for Erwin Mayo of Venture Productions. He'd like to involve you."

Involve me? I didn't like the sound of this. The address on the card said Burbank, California, meaning Hollywood had come calling. If they had my so-called "bio," they probably knew that Yellow Rose Investigations didn't pay my rent; my inheritance did. Our adoptive father left my twin sister, Kate, and me buckets of money when he died. They no doubt knew plenty more about me, while I knew *nothing* about them. I definitely needed to find out what this was about—and quick.

But again, before I could speak, Chelsea said, "Listen, Abby, if you won't let us in, could I please have a paper towel before this sweat dripping from my scalp ruins my makeup?"

I widened the door. Wouldn't want Chelsea Burch melting like a theatrical witch. "Do me a favor and keep your finger off that record button, Stu," I said.

He nodded his agreement—air-conditioning *is* a powerful weapon—and I led them past my office, where I'd been finishing up the paperwork on my last case.

Chelsea glanced around my living room. "This is cute."

My living room is far from cute. Messy, eclectic and

coated with cat hair, maybe. Not *cute*. The vanilla candle burning on the table by the sofa used to be cute, but was now a smoldering glob of wax. Smelled good, though.

Chelsea moved aside this morning's *Houston Chronicle* and sat down on the sofa. Her blond hair had gone limp from the humidity and hung around her face in thick, product-laden chunks. She wore an embroidered peasant shirt with long sleeves and stretch denim jeans—not exactly the best wardrobe choice for today. Then I noticed the cowboy boots—baby blue and powder pink.

"You like?" She smiled and held up one foot. "Boots are so hot right now."

"Literally," I said under my breath. When it's this warm, you see girls wearing boots in Western dance clubs only in the evening—and those would be real boots—boots that do *not* look like they were first worn by some gaunt runway model at a Paris fashion show. "What production brings you to Houston?" I asked.

"*Reality Check.* You've heard of it, right?" Chelsea said.

"I think so." I noticed Stu had set the camera on the wood floor and was perspiring heavily. He, too, had chosen to wear blue jeans. I offered him water.

"Oh, me too," Chelsea said. "What brand do you have?"

"T-A-P," I spelled.

"Funny," she said. "No bottled?"

"I have Dr Pepper in a bottle, Diet Coke in a can and water from the fridge door. Take your pick."

"Just water, *thanks*." Bitchy edge in her voice. Clearly my Hollywood producer didn't like the beverage selection in my home.

I caught Stu's eye-roll as I left to get them their water. He had her number, too.

The trip to the kitchen gave me time to wrack my brain regarding *Reality Check,* the television show she'd mentioned. As I held glasses under the icemaker, I remembered they did home makeovers and cosmetic surgeries, gave scholarships, sent people on luxury vacations. Then I could hear the commercial's voiceover in my head: *Reality Check—the lifestyle makeover show. Turning American dreams into the real thing.*

What the hell did a show like that want with me?

When I returned and handed them their glasses, Stu was sitting cross-legged on the Oriental rug with my cat, Diva, in his lap.

Chelsea had apparently rediscovered her "California Dreamin' " attitude, because her tone was pleasant when she said, "Our research assistant learned about you through the local media, Abby. She said you arranged this wonderful reunion for a college basketball player. He was adopted and hired you to locate his birth family, right?"

"Yes." I sat in one of the armchairs, thinking, *That's how these people found me.* Several years ago, after learning that my daddy had illegally adopted Kate and me when we were infants, I'd taken a new path in life. Rather than spend all my time at the family computer business, which ran itself anyway, I chose to work as a PI and help adopted people locate their birth families. One of my clients, a college athlete with celebrity status, had recently appeared on a local morning program and, though I had asked him not to mention my name, the perky, way-too-eager host managed to get it out of him anyway.

I'd been swamped with calls since, folks hoping I could help them with their adoption issues, too. This had forced me to create two flyers—"Tips for Locating the Child You've Given Up for Adoption" and the other titled "So You Want to Find Your Birth Parents? The Beginning Steps." I was stuffing envelopes an hour a day now. Most people with a little computer savvy can locate who they're looking for without a private eye's assistance, and this seemed the best way to let them in on those secrets.

"Abby, we'd like you to sign on as a consultant to our program," Chelsea said. "Since we work somewhat like a documentary, I was hoping we could tape an initial interview later today—we will edit extensively, so don't worry about running on and on, or—"

"Taping?" I cut in. "When you've told me next to nothing? I'm not so sure about that. What does my being a private investigator have to do with consulting on a TV show?"

"In the story we're currently producing, plenty. Wait until you meet our makeover candidate and her family. In fact, let me show you." She opened her binder and slipped two photos from a plastic sleeve.

I took them from her. One was a Wal-Mart special eight-by-ten, the colors faded to blurry siennas and dull pinks. A teenage girl stood in the center of three younger children. The other was a four-by-six glossy snapshot of the teenager, but in this newer photo she was a dark-haired, hazel-eyed woman in her twenties with flawless nutmeg-colored skin and an expression that puzzled me. Fear? Anger? Sadness? Maybe all three.

Chelsea pointed to the snapshot. "You're looking at a real heroine. She's been raising her brothers and sister since she was sixteen. Isn't she Penélope Cruz all over again? The camera eats her up."

Stu said, "The family's nice . . . really a nice, deserving bunch of kids."

I looked at him. Here was someone I could relate to—sun-weathered skin, laugh lines everywhere and brown eyes that could tell you the truth without accompanying words. Plus the man had set his empty water glass on a coaster—unlike his companion—and he was making friends with my cat.

"Tell me more," I said, still wary.

"*Reality Check* receives referrals for the life makeovers we do on air—thousands and thousands of referrals, by the way—mostly via our Web site," Chelsea explained. "This particular one, however, came in through the mail. Unusual, but what a riveting, American dream story. That's why we're in Texas. We have our hands on a fantastic, heartwarming tale of courage and perseverance. You won't believe all that's happened to Emma Lopez in her short life."

"Why do you need my help?" *And why do you sound like you're rehearsing a script? But I suppose everything but getting up in the morning is easier with practice.*

"Problems, that's why we need help. We had everything set to go. Then we mentioned something to Emma about the referral letter and whamo! She's backing off all of a sudden. We can't have that. Not now."

"You've lost me," I said, shaking my head.

"This is Emma Lopez, our makeover girl." Chelsea tapped the snapshot with a cherry-colored nail. "Put herself through college and is doing the same for her younger brother, Scott. Anyway, their house, the only thing they own, is set for demolition by the city. The city would give them money to rebuild, but not nearly enough for the kind of home they deserve. Plus, the other kids are getting to be college age—"

I held up a hand. Jeez. This one could talk the ears off a ceramic elephant. "You're still not telling me what this has to do with *adoption*. I investigate adoption cases."

Chelsea raised her pointy chin. "Don't you think I know? Anyway, the referral letter mentioned a missing baby."

"Missing baby? Emma gave up a baby for adoption?"

"No, not Emma. Her mother. And that's why we need your help."

"Okay, Emma's mother gave up a child for adoption," I said.

"We're not exactly sure." Chelsea gestured as if she were giving a speech, hands palms out to me. "And there's the problemo, Abby. Emma got like, *so* whacked out when we mentioned her missing sister."

Stu looked at me. "I told Chelsea that Emma must not have realized we had the info on the missing kid before she signed on for the show. She was taken off guard, and now she wants out of her contract."

Chelsea flashed an angry glance at Stu. "She's not getting out of anything." She paused, took a deep breath, then smiled at me. "Production delays. Very frustrating. But Emma will have America in tears. She is *amazing*. *Reality Check* wants to pay her back for all the suffering she's endured in her short life. We plan to make magic for Emma and her family, Abby. Magic for the world to see. That's what we do. That's who we are." Broader smile, tooth veneers really gleaming now.

"Okay. You've got me as confused as Jennifer Lopez's ring finger. Could we start over, maybe in chronological order?"

Chelsea laughed—an unattractive snorting laugh that gave me a perverse sense of satisfaction.

"You are so *cute,* Abby," she said. "Everyone on the set will fall in love with you and that great Texas accent. I really hope you'll let us get you on tape."

Stu cleared his throat. "From what I hear about the referral letter, Emma's missing sister would be about fifteen now."

Thank goodness someone had taken their Ritalin today and knew how to stay on track. "And where's Emma's mother?" I looked back and forth between them.

"She disappeared in 1997," Chelsea said. "As I said, Emma has been raising this family, been doing the most fantastic—"

"Ah. *Two* missing people. Did the mother take the girl with her?"

"No," Chelsea said. "According to the letter, the child disappeared the day after she was born—in 1992. Our research people concluded the mother must have given her up for adoption. But they hit a roadblock. Did you know Texas won't let you look at anything that has to do with adoption or foster care? I mean, like, *nothing.* That's where you come in. You know the ropes here." She giggled. "Hey, Stu. Ropes? Texas? Get it?"

He offered a tight smile.

Meanwhile, I sat back and took a deep breath, considering all this. I had to admit I was interested, but I might not have any better luck than the TV researchers. Texas keeps the safe securely locked when it comes to adoption. And the thought of working with Chelsea Burch was about as appealing as sticking my hand in a bucket of leeches. Hell, I probably *would* be sticking my hand in a bucket of leeches if I met her entire production crew.

I said, "I don't think I can help you, Chelsea."

"But I *need* you. You specialize in this kind of investigation."

"Indeed, I do."

Chelsea stared at me, her contact-blue eyes shiny with anger. "But you're refusing to help me?"

"That's right."

She snatched up her notebook and shoved the pictures inside. Meanwhile, Stu stroked Diva one last time and picked up his camera.

"Come on, Stu," Chelsea said, marching past me. "I knew Mr. Mayo's idea was stupid."

"Where are you going?" I asked.

"Out the way we came in," she said over her shoulder.

"Too bad. Because I need more information."

She turned, her narrow jaw slack. She stared at me in confusion for a second. "But . . . I thought—"

"I won't help *you*, but I sure do want to meet Emma. What happens after that is in her hands."

2

Turned out, Chelsea Burch was far less annoying with her binder open in front of her. She told me Emma's story in more detail, and before she and Stu left, I made copies of Emma Lopez's home and work addresses, her history and all the photos in the file, not just the ones I'd already seen. Erwin Mayo, Chelsea's boss, gave a reluctant phone okay for these copies after I refused to sign a contract or be videotaped. I not only needed to talk to Emma before deciding to take the case. I needed their notes to get as much history as possible.

When they were gone, I made a pitcher of sweet iced tea, then took a big glass with me and sat down at my desk, ready to call Emma and set up an interview. But before I could pick up the phone, I heard Kate calling my name from the kitchen. She'd come in through the back door as usual.

"In the office, Kate," I shouted.

I could hear her coming, and that was what got me out of my chair to see what was going on. Sounded like she was wheeling in one of those flatbed carts from Home Depot.

Not a flatbed. Two suitcases. Big suitcases. But that wasn't what concerned me. My sister's swollen eyes and pale face grabbed at my heart. Her gorgeous shoulder-length brown hair was pulled into a tight ponytail, something she does only when she's cleaning ovens and toilets. Her border collie, Webster, was with her, and even he looked sad.

"What's wrong, Kate?" But I had all the clues I needed. Your sister does not arrive looking like she's been up all night listening to sad country tunes, suitcases and dog in tow, unless she needs a place to stay. And that meant trouble with Terry, the guy she's lived with for the last two years.

She bit her lip . . . looked at the floor. "Terry and I are done."

I hurried over and wrapped my arms around her, nearly stepping on Webster's front paw in the process. He had his body pressed to her leg and wasn't about to budge—not even after Diva appeared from some hiding place and sniffed him all over. My cat's buddy was here. At least someone was happy.

Kate released her suitcase handles and clung to me like a two-year-old to her mother after the babysitter arrives.

Things had been rocky between Terry and Kate for the last month—probably even longer. He wanted to get married and have kids. Soon. Like, tomorrow. Kate did not. She simply wasn't ready. And though Terry can be sweet and empathetic and all kinds of wonderful things, he can also dig in his heels when it comes to playing emotional tug-of-war.

I held her while she cried, and when she seemed done I sat her down in my living room and gave her a big glass of tea, tea too sweet for a health nut like her, but today she didn't complain. There is something to be said for the comfort of pure cane sugar.

Webster settled at her feet, and Diva cuddled by the dog like she used to do when we all lived together in our daddy's River Oaks mansion. Kate spilled her guts about the breakup while I sat next to her on the sofa, my hand on her knee. I'm usually the gut-spiller when it comes to stuff like a major boyfriend event. After all, she's the true listener in the family—a professional one. She's a shrink.

Kate had been telling me for a while that Terry was becoming more and more insistent about their getting married and starting a family. Apparently he wouldn't quit, kept up the marriage talk every day.

"Guess what he brought home from the drugstore yesterday afternoon," Kate said. "A *Modern Bride* magazine. I asked him if he thought that if I looked at wedding gown photos for an hour I'd change my mind. He didn't have a good answer, Abby. He got this strange expression, and I knew then that he truly believed I'd be swayed by pictures of dresses and cakes and flowers. Are you kidding me? It's like he forgot who I am in this freaky role-reversal game he's been playing."

"Terry has always been a very focused person. He has a plan for his life," I said. "And for yours, too, I guess."

"He's totally lost sight of us as a couple. We used to have fun. We used to talk about the movie we just saw, go to the museums, talk about our careers, discuss what books we're reading, but this? This is all he can talk about. What I need is a partnership with compromise and discussion, not a contract to have X number of kids in X number of years and then retire to a house in Arizona big enough to accommodate twenty grand-children."

I rested my hand on her cheek. Her face was warm with anger. "Charlie Rose's girls were raised to do their own thinking, thank you very much."

"He even had the nerve to give me an ultimatum. A *time line*. We have couples' therapy for three months, and then if I don't change my mind, we split. Well, guess what. He doesn't get to make that decision. So . . . can I stay with you until I find a place of my own? I won't get in your way with Jeff, I promise."

Jeff is my boyfriend, an HPD homicide cop I met when he worked on the murder of our yardman in River Oaks.

"Of course—you'll stay here as long as you want. And don't worry about Jeff. He took this mysterious trip to Seattle—where he was born."

"Mysterious how?"

"He won't tell me why he went, how long he'll be gone or anything else except that he'll be back."

"He *is* a man of few words. Does he have any family left there?"

"Not that I know of. Maybe something came up with his parents' estate. They're buried north of Seattle. Could be he wants to move their bodies to Houston. I mean, he does have a certain attachment to bodies."

"That's not something to joke about," Kate said.

"Sorry. You know me. If I can't figure something out, I make jokes. I simply don't get the secrecy thing, and it kinda ticks me off. Makes me feel like I should worry about *our* relationship."

"Because he doesn't trust you?"

"Right."

"Could be he's feeling vulnerable about family issues. Jeff would have a hard time with vulnerability."

I cocked my head, looked into brown eyes so much like my own—the only twin thing we shared, aside from our identical birth date. "Jeff does seem . . . nervous or something. I thought he clammed up because I kept bugging him before he left to tell me what was up. Maybe I should let him do what he needs to do and keep my insecurities to myself."

"Good idea. Now, can you help me take my stuff upstairs?"

"Sure. Then maybe you'll feel up to hearing about a new case," I said.

Kate does psychological assessments on all my prospective clients, just like the Texas Adoption Registry does for the state. The kind of adoption reunions I specialize in can be happy, heartrending, stressful or sad, and I don't take a case if Kate believes the client can't handle both good news and bad. Sometimes reunions don't work out the way the client fantasizes they will.

Kate almost smiled after I mentioned the possibility of a new client. "I would love to hear about a case, if only for the distraction. Can you believe that I nearly called up tomorrow's clients to cancel their appointments?"

"A day off might not be a bad idea," I said.

"No. That would only give me time to question my decision—and I don't want to do that. After this last argument, I had to make a clean break with him. Today."

I hugged her again. "You have great instincts. And you'll know in time this is the right decision." Despite her words, I had my doubts. Terry and Kate seemed perfectly matched—both shrinks, both generous and sweet people who had seemed very much in love for most of their three-year relationship. Maybe they could work this out.

But after I lugged one suitcase upstairs and into a guest bedroom, I decided my sister was serious about the split. She must have brought everything she owned, because the suitcase was as heavy as a bear rug with the bear still attached. I rolled the suitcase toward the closet, aware that there was hardly space for Kate in this room. I hadn't organized anything except to have clean linens on the bed. Both walnut dressers were piled with boxes, Christmas ornaments, stacks of framed pictures, and who knew what else.

I'd moved into this amazing old home in the West University part of Houston more than a year ago. The River Oaks house had been too big and too overflowing with memories of our late daddy for me to stay after he died. Kate had already moved in with Terry by then but agreed with my decision to sell the mansion. Maybe I hadn't unpacked because I was afraid I'd see too much of Daddy inside those boxes, get depressed all over again. God, I missed him, even though he'd been gone almost four years.

Once we'd moved several boxes into the closet so Kate could have her suitcases handy, she and I went downstairs to my office and I laid out the new case.

"Wow," she said when I was finished. "Very interesting."

I liked seeing the spark back in her eyes. Kate is always anxious to evaluate new clients. The adoption investigation business seemed like a good move for me after Kate and I learned Daddy lied to us about our own adoption—a way to work through my anger and a way to help others. But Kate's involvement in my cases was becoming almost as passionate.

She said, "Do you think this girl Emma will meet with you?"

"Not if I mention the production company. So . . . since you're in the market for a new home and since I've learned Emma Lopez is a Realtor, maybe we should check out some real estate."

"You think she works on Sunday?"

"I'll bet they do their best business on the weekend," I answered.

I felt like I needed to apply to Saint Peter for a passport after I'd called Green Tree Realtors, got Emma on the phone and arranged for Kate and me to meet her in her office on the pretext of a possible house hunt. I mean, the girl sounded plain nice.

Kate and I left Webster and Diva still sleeping and took off in my Camry. Green Tree Realtors was a small operation occupying the corner spot in a strip mall on Bellaire Boulevard. I recognized Emma immediately from her photo after Kate and I walked in. She was staring at a computer screen in a glassed-in office a few feet beyond the receptionist. True to the company name, we were surrounded by "green trees." Buckets of Norfolk Island pines were everywhere. The larger ones sat on the floor in corners and between the two simple leather chairs by the front windows. The houseplant-size trees occupied every desk and counter. This was like a trip to a miniature version of the East Texas piney woods.

"We have an appointment with Ms. Lopez," I told the smiling receptionist.

"Yes. Abby and Kate Rose, right?"

I nodded.

She turned and called to Emma, who'd already seen us. She came out offering a brilliant smile, her hand extended. The bottle-green summer-weight suit and matching shoes complemented her creamy brown skin.

We shook hands and I felt strength in her grip—strength and confidence, two assets, I imagined, that had served her well over the past decade. Once we cleared up which sister was which, we sat near Emma's computer. The chair arrangement was such that prospective home buyers could check out properties on the Internet.

"What can I show you two today?" Emma said.

Time to get real. "Though my sister may soon be in the market for a home, that's not why we've come. To be honest, I had a visit from a television producer this morning. Venture Productions asked me to work for them, and—"

Emma scooted her rolling chair farther away from us, eyes narrow, the dark brown irises going nearly black with anger. "Oh, my God. I can't believe you people."

"Hear me out, okay?" I said quickly. "I think you and I might have similar opinions of Venture. I enjoyed about all I could stand of Chelsea Burch."

"Oh, she's the *nice* one. What's this about, Ms. Rose?"

"Abby wants to help you," Kate said. "And so do I."

"You think I haven't heard that bullshit about a thousand times since I was stupid enough to sign a contract with them? Me with my degree from Rice—you'd have thought I'd know better."

"Smart people don't always make smart decisions, but we'll discuss that later," I said. "First, you need to be assured I haven't signed any agreement with Venture. After reading through the documents they gave me, I believe your story is important. I want to help." I pulled a card from my purse and handed it to her.

"Yellow Rose Investigations," she read aloud. She looked up. "You're a private investigator?"

"I specialize in adoptions, and from what Burch tells me, there *is* a missing child. Your sister, right?"

"They told you about her, too. Figures." She shook her head in disgust.

"Chelsea Burch mentioned they only told you they knew about your sister recently. Is that why you wish you'd never signed on with Venture?"

"You know something? I was absolutely on cloud nine when they first approached me several months ago. They were offering us the world on a platter. I should have no known there is no free lunch."

"You felt misled?" I asked.

"Lies by omission are still lies, so yes, I was very upset when I discovered the person who wrote the letter mentioned my missing sister. Anyway, Mayo thought bringing that out on the TV show would make me look even more sympathetic—his word, not mine. I think that's exploiting me and ridiculous and . . . and . . ." Emma bit her lower lip, her eyes bright with tears.

"What bothered you most about this?" Kate said softly. "The fact that they knew, the fact they didn't tell

you they knew, or that you realized this man wasn't as
sincere as you thought?"

Emma blinked away the sheen of tears, and considered the question for several seconds. "All those things,
I guess, but something even more important. I never
shared the information about Mom's last baby with
anyone—not even my brothers and sister. I had to sit
down and tell them one more piece of our mother's
sorry history. Had to dredge up things from my past that
I had almost blocked out because I never wanted to
remember. And Mr. Mayo, the producer who'd been so
nice to me up to that point? He could have cared less
how that affected my family."

Kate nodded. "You have good insights, Emma. How
did the kids handle this new information?"

"Amazingly well. They're great kids. And now I think
we're done here. I have no money to pay a private investigator, and if you let Mr. Mayo pay you to find out
about a secret better left buried, don't expect much cooperation from me." Emma grabbed at the dark wavy
hair that had slipped over the right side of her face. She
pulled a handful away from her forehead, her knuckles
white with tension.

Obviously a very proud woman. I'd seen this reaction
before when clients asked about my charges. Most
decent, honest people prefer to pay something, anything,
I'd learned. I said, "As far as my fees, my sister is in
the market for a new house. Maybe we could use the
barter system?"

Emma looked away, but at least she didn't say no.

Kate said, "Emma, I'm a psychologist. I work with my
sister on cases like this, and I can promise you Abby
will dedicate herself to your cause, whatever that cause
may be. She will be your advocate, not reside in the
pocket of a TV show producer. But first we need to
know—do you even want to find out what happened to
your sister?"

Emma turned to stare into Kate's eyes and softly said,
"To be honest, I want nothing more."

3

Since Emma had houses to show, we didn't have time to do much more than agree to continue our talk that night. She agreed to bring her brother and sister to my place in the evening so Kate and I could interview all three of them together. Her other brother was away at school, but Emma said she would call him hoping he'd participate via speakerphone.

For my part, I promised to send a copy of the contract Emma had signed with Venture Productions to a lawyer friend. Because she now mistrusted Erwin Mayo for failing to reveal up front that he knew about her missing sister, Emma was willing to give up everything he'd promised her in order to reclaim her privacy. Mark Whitley, my attorney friend, is a defense lawyer, not a contract specialist, but I was hoping he could get an opinion from a colleague, see if there was any way Emma could escape from the deal she'd made.

The minute we arrived home from Green Tree Realtors, Kate went straight upstairs for a nap. She probably hadn't slept a wink last night. Me? I was hungry, and PBJ sounded good. Either that or a pint of Ben & Jerry's Cherry Garcia. I chose the healthier option and I made the sandwich, spreading peanut butter on both slices of bread. I was already feeling Kate's holistic health presence and could only hope I wouldn't be force-fed organic bulgur wheat "meat loaf" or a tofu stir-fry for dinner. Diva jumped on the counter and sniffed my sandwich, offered me a look of disdain, then scurried away to parts unknown. But Webster? He was at my side, anxious as a kid on Christmas Eve for any crumbs to fall his way.

While I ate I called Jeff, and he answered right away—something that never happens when he's in town and working cases.

After our initial hellos, I said, "I miss you so much."

"I miss you, too," he answered.

I wanted to ask him what the hell he was doing so far away—he'd actually taken vacation time—but I decided to stick to my plan and not question him. We ended up talking about my new case.

When I was finished summing up, he said, "No murder victim?"

"What's that supposed to mean?" I was pacing in the kitchen, Webster shadowing me.

"You seem to attract those kinds of cases. PIs don't have to be involved in murder on every job, hon."

I smiled. He'd started calling me "hon" about a month ago and I loved it. My ex had always called me "babe," and I thought I'd never be a fan of sweet nothings again. "Jeff, I've done plenty of reunions without murder involved. And maybe you haven't noticed, but I pick my cases because they're challenging. Murder is pretty damn challenging—or at least you seem to think so."

"True. Guess I worry about being way up here if you run into trouble."

"I can get your advice on the phone, and believe me, I will."

"It's not the same," he answered.

He sounded down, and I was proud when I chose not to say, *Then get back here and help me!* Still, restraint was uncomfortable territory. Maybe I could learn from this experience. "Needing help doesn't always have to do with cases. You might have to talk me to sleep while I snuggle with Diva. She is a poor substitute for you, as much as I love her."

"I would very much enjoy talking to you while we're both in bed, if you know what I mean."

I could picture him with one of his rare grins, and I laughed. "Oh, I know what you mean. Glad we have a plan."

We talked for a long time, moving on to Kate's

breakup with Terry. Jeff was no more surprised than I was. The man's an ace detective who can read people in a minute. Apparently he'd assessed and formed an opinion about their relationship even earlier than I had.

I said, "There's some book called *He's Just Not That into You,* and I think the title should have included both sexes. No matter how many times Kate said she loved Terry—and I think she tried hard to make those feelings real—maybe she was never that into him. I had sensed resistance building in their relationship, this tiny hint of tension between them."

"I remember you telling me she didn't want to move in with Terry in the first place, but he kept bugging her, and she, being compassionate and sweet, gave in," Jeff said. "Yup, not that into him."

"I am very into you, by the way. Call me tonight?"

"Will do."

After we disconnected, I went to my office and called Mark Whitley at home. Without hesitation he told me to e-mail him the contract and promised to get someone on it. Mark is the go-to man for getting things done in a hurry. The lawyers at CompuCan, the company Kate and I inherited from Daddy, probably knew plenty about contracts, but if I gave them the job, I could join Jeff in Seattle for two weeks before I'd hear a word—and then the word would be a question and not the answers I needed.

After I hung up, attached the contract Emma had e-mailed me and hit the send button to Mark, I began researching Venture Productions and the two names that might help me learn more about the company—Chelsea Burch and Erwin Mayo.

Burch, I learned, had once been an evening anchor at a San Diego TV station, but there was precious little else on the Net about her life or career. Erwin Mayo's Google results turned into a résumé of all the shows he'd produced. I figured he probably owned a giant share of Coyote TV, the station that aired *Reality Check.* When my eyes grew tired of clicking from one Web page to the next, I quit. The man was obviously a seasoned veteran, probably knew every word in that contract Emma had signed. There would be no loopholes.

But that wouldn't stop me from working for Emma. A missing baby? A missing mother? Those problems were right up my alley, and I wanted to know more, wanted to help her. Every new case was unique, often filled with surprises, and I couldn't wait to get started.

Emma, her sister, Shannon O'Meara, and her brother Luke O'Meara arrived at seven o'clock that night. Emma brought a folder with more family pictures and her copy of the Venture contract. We all sat in the living room rather than cram into my office. Thank goodness no one was allergic to or afraid of animals, because Webster chose the eighteen-year-old, fair-skinned and blond Luke as his new best friend. Not to be outdone, Diva settled into Shannon O'Meara's lap. She was sixteen, freckled and red-haired. What a difference a father's genes could make. She was Emma's opposite. Scott O'Meara, the nineteen-year-old, was supposed to call in from college.

After all the introductions were done and everyone had a soft drink in hand, we'd visited for a while and Kate and I made sure all three had our cards with our cell numbers. Kate began the interview, starting with Emma.

"Your brother and sister seem like great kids," Kate said. "They're polite, sound like they take school seriously, and they have the clear eyes of sober adolescents. Seems like you've done a fine job raising them."

Emma had shed her business suit and was wearing khaki capris and a peach T-shirt, but she looked just as exotically gorgeous in casual clothes and with little makeup. "These kids made it easy. They're smart, they help me, they're . . ." Her voice cracked, and Luke, who was next to her on the couch, put an arm around her.

"Emma's way cool, too," he said.

Kate glanced at her watch. "It's a little past seven thirty. Can we get your brother Scott on the line, since he hasn't called us?"

But though Emma tried several numbers, she couldn't find Scott.

"He's probably mad," said Shannon, staring down at the cat. "He stays that way."

"Mad about what?" Kate scribbled something on the legal pad on her lap.

"How about everything?" Luke stroked Webster's head. The dog sighed and settled on the floor, his head on Luke's feet.

"He's had his problems," Emma said. "If he won't participate, does that mean we can't go on with this?"

Kate smiled. "Anger is a normal reaction to what you and your family have been through. He's been living away from the family for how long?"

"This is his second year at Texas A&M," Emma answered.

"That's a long time," Kate said. "Maybe anger is his way of separating, of being his own man. But don't worry. His reluctance to participate won't affect how Abby and I work with you."

Emma slowly nodded. "Being his own man. Yes. That makes sense."

"Okay, then," Kate said. "What we need now is a family history. What happened when. Before I make any psychological assessments, I think Abby can ask those questions. Then I'll get your feelings about possibly reuniting with a sister you never knew—that is, if we can find her."

"Can I ask something first?" Emma was looking at me. "What about the contract?"

I told her I hoped to hear something from Mark soon, then redirected the conversation. I was sure what Mark would tell me, and Emma didn't need to hear that now. "Emma, can you start with your father? Did you know him?"

"No. I wasn't even born when he went away. He was a soldier, died in Beirut in late 1983—the marine barracks bombing. His name was Xavier Lopez, and he bought the house we still live in. He left me the house along with a small trust to cover the taxes and insurance. My mother was so angry that he'd given her nothing, she made sure Scott, Luke and Shannon only had *her* last name, O'Meara, on their birth certificates. They don't know who their fathers are—but that's another issue, maybe for another time."

Hmm, I thought. *More missing information.*

"Scott is half black, we think," Emma said, "but as you can see, I'm half Hispanic, and Luke and Shannon are white through and through. Shannon looks a lot like Mom."

"Don't say that." Shannon said this loud enough to send Diva scurrying off her lap and out of the room. "I'm *not* her."

Kate jotted something on her pad while Emma said, "I'm sorry. You're nothing like her on the inside, Shannon. Nothing. She was selfish and mean and a drunken idiot."

"An alcoholic?" I asked, writing for the first time in my own notebook.

"Raging," Emma said. "A binger. She'd leave us alone for days at a time, then come back and sleep for hours and hours."

"How long had this been going on?" I asked.

"As far back as I can remember, but before the baby was born—the one who's gone—she cut back on the booze. But she still left us alone quite a bit, probably because she was working more. She kept saying how expensive kids were."

"Did you ever see this child? Or did your mother come home from the hospital empty-handed?" I asked.

"She never went to any hospital. I helped her birth the baby at home." Emma looked down at her hands, her long brown fingers intertwined tightly.

I tried to hide my shock. "She had her at *home*? How old were you?"

"About eight, I think. She had the baby in the bathtub. But the next day when I returned from school, she and the baby were gone. She'd left Shannon and Luke with the neighbor lady who had a home day care—they were just babies themselves. Mom came back that night—alone."

"Alone?" I said. "But—"

"I didn't ask any questions, if that's what you're wondering," Emma said. "I knew better."

"Knew better?" Kate said. "Help me understand what you mean."

Emma didn't make eye contact with Kate or me. "I could tell she was super drunk—probably to dull the pain from the baby coming—and when she was like that, well . . . she did things."

"Violent things?" Kate asked.

Emma nodded, and Luke squeezed her closer.

"And you . . . what were you? A third grader? You took care of your sister and brothers while she was gone?" Kate asked.

"I took care of them even when she was around, so it wasn't that hard." Emma had regrouped. She was in control of her emotions again.

Kate blinked several times, shook her head. "But you were *eight,* Emma."

"I was never really eight." Her voice was a near whisper. "When you have an alcoholic mother, you're never a kid and you never really have a mom."

"How true. If there's an upside to this, you've gained plenty of insight," Kate said. "I hope we can talk more in the future about these issues—that is, if you want to."

"That might be good. To talk. You both seem like you might actually care—unlike those television people."

"We'll get to them later." I looked back and forth between Luke and Shannon. "Do either of you remember the baby?"

They both shook their heads no. Not surprising, since they would have been very young at the time.

Kate said, "How do you feel about your baby sister's disappearance?"

"Sad. I want to meet her," said Shannon, "Hug her. Find out everything about her."

"And you, Luke?" Kate asked.

"Same thing. I sure hope she has decent parents. That would mean Mom did something good for once. You get what I'm saying?"

"You mean you hope your sister was adopted," Kate said. "But we may learn that's not what happened."

"You think I don't know how messed up this world is?" Luke shot back. "What scuzzes people can be?"

"Sorry, Luke. I just don't want you to get your hopes up." Kate's tone was soothing, sincere.

"Yeah, I know," he said quietly.

I focused on Emma. "Did your mother ever talk about what happened to the baby?"

Emma rested her hand on Luke's knee and settled back against the sofa cushions. "When she sobered up about a month later, she had a story. She figured I hadn't forgotten, even though I never said anything. She told me that Child Protective Services came once I'd left for school the morning after the baby was born. See, Luke had marks on his legs—from the switch Mom used to hit us with. She told me someone notified CPS."

"Who might have called them?" I asked.

"I didn't ask questions. Maybe the day care lady in the neighborhood. Anyway, Mom said that when the caseworker heard the baby crying, the worker took Mom and the baby to Chimney Rock Center—where the CPS headquarters are. She and the caseworker made a deal. If Mom gave up the baby and no more reports came in about abuse, they'd close the file on Luke's bruises."

"And the child was never returned to the family?" I said. "You three were never interviewed?"

They nodded.

Right then I knew this whole CPS story Emma had been fed was nothing more than a corral full of bullshit. This was *not* how CPS did things. All the children would have been taken to Chimney Rock, and Emma would have been interviewed. But then, this story was from childhood recollections. She may have forgotten facts or not been told the whole truth. Emma's mother, Christine O'Meara, could have simply given up her baby for adoption.

"You never mentioned this baby again?" I asked Emma.

"My mother told me that if I even hinted about her to anyone, CPS would take us all away. I'd be separated from Scott, Luke and Shannon. So I kept my mouth shut. And this may sound awful, but for a while, I thought I'd dreamed the whole thing."

Kate said, "Children often protect themselves from emotional trauma by blocking out events."

"But I felt terrible for forgetting." Emma bit her lip, looked down. "I had a CPS caseworker of my own when I turned thirteen, and she helped me understand that Mom probably sold the baby. Turns out there was no previous file on any of us. Luke's bruises had never been reported. It seemed too late to do anything after five years, and with Mom gone—"

"She'd left again?" I asked.

"Right. That's why CPS took custody of us. I tried to hold things together at home for more than a month when she split that last time, but Shannon missed a week of school with the chicken pox, and I missed the same week to take care of her. The truant officer came, quickly followed by CPS. Mrs. Henderson, my caseworker, was awesome, though. She got a placement for all of us in the same foster home, and that lasted about three years."

"How did that go?" Kate asked.

"Lots of kids coming and going, and our foster parents were pretty cold people. Mrs. Henderson suggested I become an emancipated minor at sixteen. I still owned the house, and we were able to move back in. She'd made sure I didn't lose it by helping me keep up the insurance and tax payments from the trust."

Kate said, "Mrs. Henderson sounds like a great person."

"She was the best," Emma said.

"Was?" Kate asked.

"She retired. Moved away."

"Bet you miss her," Kate said.

"Sort of," Emma said. "But foster care teaches you to never get too close. We saw about twenty kids come and go. Good-byes can be hard, so *you* get hard."

Kate nodded, and I saw her eyes fill as she looked down at her tablet. She'd had a rough day and was probably ripe for a crying session even without hearing this story.

I looked at Luke and Shannon. "I hear from Emma the baby part is new information for you guys."

Luke said, "When Emma found out that Mr. Mayo knew, she told us."

"But someone outside the family obviously was aware of the missing baby," I said. "The person who wrote that letter to the *Reality Check* staff. Could it have been the day care lady, as you called her?"

"Not her. She was almost as nasty as my mother," Emma said.

"Then who?" I asked.

Emma said, "I have no idea."

"Finding that person is important, because whoever it is may know what your mother did with the child," I said.

"I agree," Emma replied. "But I'd like to find out if there's any way I can get out of the contract first. Since the demolition is set for the day after tomorrow, I realize that's asking a lot."

"Day after tomorrow? I had no idea," I said. "The way I read that contract, once the city tears the house down, Venture sends their builder in immediately. Any chance we can delay the demolition to give Mark, my lawyer friend, more time? Meanwhile, I could start hunting for the person who wrote the letter."

Emma shook her head, looking discouraged. "Right after I found out Mr. Mayo knew about my baby sister, I asked for a delay from the city."

"The city?" Kate said.

"Yes," Emma said. "They'll be tearing the house down. They gave me one delay but said that was it. The house is a hazard—very old and structurally unsound. No cement foundation." Emma closed her eyes and looked down at her clenched hands again. "How I wish I'd taken the deal the city offered."

Luke said, "Emma's all stressed because of those TV assholes. They made their deal sound so sweet. On *Extreme Makeover: Home Edition,* you can tell they care. *Those* guys are decent."

Emma smiled at Luke. "I know you're upset, but please watch the language, okay?"

"Yeah. Sure," he mumbled, reaching for the dog again.

"Guess I should have a chat with Chelsea's boss first," I said. "Maybe I could convince him to give you more time, even if the house has to go down as planned."

"Don't count on *him,*" Shannon said. "He's like a human ice cube and smells like the Dillard's cologne counter."

"Worth a try," I said, making a silent vow not to fail them like their mother had.

4

The next day, a sunny Monday morning, I awoke with plenty of energy, juiced by all the information and leads to follow. I had to see Mayo, and I figured that since the demolition was set for tomorrow, he might be in town. I showered, dressed in shorts and a blue T-shirt, and went downstairs in time to hear the message Kate was listening to on the answering machine.

"Please, Kate," Terry's recorded voice said. "I'm sorry about how upset you were when you left. I don't feel any closure. I believe you want what I want, but you just don't know it. Can we get together someplace neutral? Talk this out? Because—"

Kate hit the delete button on the machine and said, "No way, Terry."

"Good for you," I said.

She sighed. "He'll make a great father and husband when he meets the right person. That's not me. Meanwhile, I have clients to see."

She was dressed for work: dark gray linen skirt and shirt with matching shoes. But despite the gorgeous natural-stone necklace that added some life to her appearance, this was a mourning outfit. Funeral attire. When she went back to her usual pastels, I'd be relieved. For now she needed to grieve, and I respected that.

"You booked all day?" I asked.

"Pretty much. I'll be plenty busy."

"Me, too. I hope to find Erwin Mayo, talk to him."

She looked me up and down. "Dressed like you're going to the mall?"

"Hey. I know you're having a hard time, but—"

She held up a hand. "Sorry. That was out of line."

I nodded. "You're right. And maybe now's a good time to set a few ground rules about our eating habits during your stay. I am not into organic brown rice and black beans. And I swear tofu is not real. It's produced by al-Qaeda and sent here to wipe out all the smart people like you."

She actually laughed. Good sign.

"Now get to work before you have to fire yourself." I headed for the fridge after she left and grabbed a yogurt, the kind that tastes like dessert.

Webster was whimpering at the door for his lost mistress, but Diva rubbed up against him, and pretty soon the two of them would be curled together to sleep the morning away.

Yogurt and spoon in hand, I went to my office, took out Emma's file and found Chelsea Burch's card. She answered on the first ring and must have seen my caller ID, because she said, "Abby. What's going on? Have you spoken to Emma?"

"I have. Now I'd like to talk to you. Where can we meet?" I left out my real purpose—getting to Mayo. Let her think I was her best friend. Bet she needed one.

"We have a trailer set up on an empty lot down the street from Emma's house. We'll be working out of here from now on."

"You never mentioned the demolition was set for tomorrow," I said.

"We don't talk about our schedule. I mean, like, you could say something to someone, and then we'd get all sorts of extra media attention. When we go to smaller towns it's no problem, but in a big city like Houston we can't have a huge crowd all wanting to be on TV."

"I'm with you on that." I sounded as pleasant as possible, considering she'd decided I couldn't be trusted with the schedule. "When can I come by?"

"I'll be here all day, preparing for the first taping."

"See you within the hour." I hung up. Just like her, I planned to give out very little information. And once I learned Erwin Mayo's whereabouts, I'd be done with Chelsea Burch.

*　　*　　*

Emma's neighborhood in northeast Houston had been crying for help probably as long as I've been alive. Peeling paint, damaged roofs, and houses tilting in the ever-shifting Texas soil told the story. A few small homes must have already been rebuilt, because they looked new and had cement foundations, unlike most of the houses on Emma's street. I found the trailer first, on an empty corner lot, but after I parked on the grass and got out, I realized something was happening down the street. Loud voices carried from very near where Map-Quest had told me Emma's house stood.

I thought I heard Emma, and sure enough, she and Chelsea Burch were standing in the street beside a small moving van. Chelsea's arms were crossed, and Emma was yelling and gesturing at a small clapboard house that hadn't seen a new coat of paint in maybe thirty years. Looked to me like the place might fall down even before they brought in a bulldozer.

I hurried their way, thinking that Emma and her family were lucky they hadn't all died under a collapsed roof. But before I reached them, my cell rang. I pulled my phone from my pocket and flipped it open. Mark's caller ID.

I slowed my pace. "Hi, Mark. What've you got?"

"No way out of that contract, Abby—not without a long, expensive legal battle. Venture owns Emma Lopez's story—even has all future rights. But the family will be getting plenty—a newer, bigger home and unspecified gifts valued at a hundred thousand dollars or more."

"No loopholes anywhere?" I asked.

"None that my colleague could find, and he looked long and hard. These folks have played this game many times. They know how to seal a deal."

"That's what I figured. Thanks for your help."

"Anytime. But can I ask exactly why she wants to give up a new house and a lot of money?"

"The TV producer is hinting that this story will turn out to be more like an episode of *Unsolved Mysteries*. They may focus on Emma's alcoholic mother and other things Emma doesn't want the world to know about."

"I get it. Venture pulled the old bait and switch."

"Exactly. Thanks again, Mark." I closed the phone and reached Emma and Chelsea a few seconds later.

"You *can't* make me do this today," Emma was saying. "I'm not ready."

Chelsea was wearing those same ridiculous boots from yesterday, along with a bohemian skirt and short jacket over a T-shirt. Her antiperspirant had to be working overtime.

I cleared my throat and they both turned my way.

"Um, Emma? Can I talk to you for a minute in private?"

Chelsea rolled her eyes with impatience. "What's this about? Because they've moved up the demolition to today and she still won't let the movers in to pack up their shit—I mean stuff. We have to get this done. We need all the daylight we can get for taping."

I ignored Burch. "Emma? Please? Let's talk?"

Emma turned to Chelsea and pointed her finger in her face. "You don't do anything without my say-so. Understood?"

Chelsea pushed Emma's hand away. "You know something? I'm getting real tired of—"

I grabbed the sleeve of Emma's lacy cream-colored shirt and pulled her toward me. "I need to tell you something. Let's go across the street. You can watch from there and make sure the movers don't sneak in."

Emma whirled and marched across the asphalt, high heels clicking. Then she stood with her arms folded across her chest.

I followed and in a calm voice said, "My daddy used to say you can't be angry and reasonable at the same time any more than a horse can buck and eat hay. I need the smart, reasonable Emma I met yesterday to reappear so we can talk."

Emma closed her eyes and sighed heavily. "It's happening, and I can't stop them, can I?"

"No, you can't. I've heard from the lawyer, and he says the cost of any legal action you take would be enormous and probably unsuccessful."

"Figures. I never realized how their digging around in my life would affect me when I signed that contract. I know the house has to come down, but I feel like I've sold my soul to the devil. Does that make sense?"

"Perfect sense, considering what I've heard about Hollywood producers. But there's no turning back."

Emma's jaw tightened. "I know. But I'm not kissing that woman's butt. All she cares about is her damn taping."

"Let go of the anger. You're stressed enough as it is. How's this? I promise not to turn over anything I learn about your missing mother and sister unless I believe doing so will help you."

She looked into my eyes. "You can't promise that. They have money, they wanted to hire you, and now that you're on my side, they'll find someone else to dig up dirt on my mother, even though giving away that baby was probably the best thing she ever did."

My turn to sigh. "You're right, probably because the worse she looks, the more sympathetic you and your family appear. I guess that makes some kind of sense."

"I only know I saw a big change in Erwin Mayo's attitude when I said I didn't want them talking about my missing sister," she said. "He got all arrogant and pushy. That's why I'm glad you're on my side. Trusting people is very difficult for me, but you're different. You seem to truly care."

"I've been on your side from the minute I heard this story. Now a simple 'Okay, do your job' to Chelsea might make the process easier on everyone."

"I can handle that. If I have to be nice to make this easier, be reasonable like your daddy said, then so be it."

Turned out Emma's shift in attitude worked well, with one small glitch. Chelsea came with us to watch the movers pack. She seemed to think we were all sorority sisters who had simply had a tiff, had gotten past the issue and were best friends again.

Emma maintained her cool, and I was proud of her. She didn't even flinch when Chelsea put an arm around her shoulders and said, "I know how hard this must be. But we will make everything all better. You'll see."

I could tell why Chelsea was behind the camera rather

than in front. She was a horrible actress, couldn't even fake sincerity.

The packers, already sweating from having to wait outside, worked quickly, starting in the kitchen. They had the room finished in about fifteen minutes. I was bothered by the small amount of food I saw being packed up, felt guilty as I thought about my overflowing pantry and overloaded refrigerator. Yet this family had managed to thrive in a small dark house with tilted floors and a musty odor so strong it overpowered the plug-in air fresheners. A worker picked up a couple of throw rugs, took the mop and the vacuum from a hall closet and laid them alongside several boxes on a dolly. He wheeled his first load away under Emma's watchful eye.

I followed her out of the kitchen, stumbling over the handle to the crawl space trapdoor that had been covered by the throw rug. Sometimes, I swear, I could fall *up* a tree.

Emma had eyes only for the two other workers, who had taken away the kitchen table and chairs and were now busy in the living room. We both stood beside the way-too-happy Chelsea.

"These guys are the best," she said.

"Where will Emma's things be stored?" I asked.

"We've rented an air-conditioned storage unit not far from here." She turned her beaming smile on Emma. "Emma, Luke and Shannon will be staying at one of the best hotels in the area. A suite, all the room service they want. We also have a little surprise about Scott's living arrangements at college, but that's the only hint I'm giving."

But Emma didn't appear to be listening. She was watching a worker carefully wrap framed family pictures. She walked over to him and said, "I need this one." She took one picture.

The man shrugged and went on with his work.

Emma returned to my side and showed me the photograph. "This was my father."

The picture was of a handsome Hispanic man in military dress uniform.

"Did you give that to our researcher?" Chelsea asked. "I don't have a copy."

"Too bad." But then Emma remembered she was supposed to be reasonable. "Talk to your researcher, because she *does* have a copy."

"If she lost it, we'll need another. Like I have time for this," Chelsea snapped. But she lost her snippy attitude almost at once. "We're almost done here. It wasn't so hard, was it, Emma?"

"No." Emma glanced around her nearly empty house. "Not for you."

Once the movers finished, we went back outside. I was relieved to be out of that house and breathing good old polluted Houston air rather than pure mildew. As the last piece of furniture, an old sofa bed, was loaded on the truck, a black Lincoln Navigator pulled up to the curb behind the moving van.

Chelsea ran over to the Lincoln and opened the back passenger door.

Hmmm. Bet the king has arrived without my having to hunt him down.

"What the hell happened, Chelsea?" the man said as he emerged from the backseat. "Why didn't I hear about this from you first?"

He was maybe five-foot-eight, completely bald and dressed in what looked like Ralph Lauren everything. And Houston now had a new pollutant—the cologne wafting my way on the late-morning breeze.

"Didn't the city call you, Mr. Mayo? They said they would." Chelsea tried for both a confused and contrite expression, but as I'd seen earlier, she was a terrible actress.

Erwin Mayo ignored her, turned his attention to Emma and smiled broadly. "Miss Lopez. What a pleasure to see you again. Lovely as ever, I see."

I whispered, "Reasonable," which had become our go-to word, and she responded by saying, "Hello, Mr. Mayo." She almost sounded polite, but there was still an edge to her tone.

He widened his arms and walked closer to us. "I'm so glad to see you again. Are you excited?"

"Oh, happy as a lottery winner," she answered.

No one could miss the sarcasm.

"Are you still upset about this baby secret of your?" Mayo said.

Emma said nothing.

"You are upset," Mayo went on. "I told you the mention of the baby during the episode will be brief, if it even survives the edits." He gripped both her upper arms and stared into her eyes. "We'll work our magic, and you'll discover that what we're doing for you is better than winning the lottery." He looked at me. "And who is this? A friend?"

"Abby Rose," I said. "Yellow Rose Investigations."

"Really? Chelsea brought you on board, then. Good. You have a wonderful face for the camera, and maybe you'll get some airtime. This is a big story, our two-hour sweeps special."

Not even my pinkie toe's on board your ship, I thought. Did anyone working on this project have an ounce of sincerity? You'd think Hollywood people would be better at pretending to care.

Mayo released Emma, and I could see the relief in her face, noticed how her shoulder muscles relaxed. I wouldn't want his hands on me either.

"I'm told the demolition is set for one o'clock," he said. "Why don't we do an early lunch, ladies?" He turned to Chelsea. "While we're gone, get the crew ready to roll by twelve thirty. The city has been jacking me around, and I wouldn't be surprised if they showed up early."

Chelsea nodded, turned and trotted back to the trailer.

"You know a good place for lunch, Abby?" Mayo asked.

"Um . . . listen," Emma said. "I don't think—"

"I do know a place," I said quickly. "*Reasonably* priced, too." I placed a reassuring hand on Emma's back.

But we didn't even have time to climb into the Navigator. A City of Houston truck barreled around the corner and pulled into Emma's narrow, cracked driveway, amber lights flashing. A public works pickup followed.

A thirty-something guy with a no-nonsense, beard-stubbled face got out of the first truck, walkie-talkie held close to his mouth. He said, "Let me check out the house and get back to you before we shut off the utilities."

The guy ignored Emma's "What's happening?" and started toward the house.

Mayo took off after him, calling, "Hold on. What do you think you're doing?"

The man turned, looking perturbed. "City-ordered demolition. I don't think your name's Emma Lopez, so you aren't the owner and it's none of your business."

Emma walked toward the men. "I'm Emma Lopez. I-I thought we had a few more hours."

The man smiled at Emma. "We have to work with the utility people, organize the electrical, gas and water shutoffs. They could do it now before lunch, so we're setting up."

"Okay," Emma said, a hitch in her voice. "Now or later. Doesn't matter."

Mayo bellied up to the city worker. "It matters to me. I had an agreement with the city to allow us to tape for my program. *We're* not ready."

The man said, "I heard something about your TV show. Didn't realize it was this particular demolition. Sorry, but we go on our schedule, not yours."

"Dammit." Mayo flipped open his cell phone. He speed-dialed a number, identified himself and, after listening for a minute, he said, "I need the mayor now, not this afternoon."

Meanwhile the city guy was walking down the drive to the house with Emma at his side.

Mayo flushed as he listened to more talking. Without saying another word, he closed the phone, reopened it and punched one number. "Chelsea, get everyone out here now. They're ready to bulldoze."

I don't think he even waited for her reply, because he pocketed his phone, then squeezed the bridge of his nose with thumb and index finger. "Good thing I showed up. I had a feeling they'd do this. Territorial bunch, these city people."

I decided to see how Emma was doing, but before I took two steps, she and the guy came out of the house and headed back toward me.

Mayo started for the Navigator. Where the heck was he going? Maybe he had a secure line to the White

House in the trailer and planned to call in some favors to delay the demolition for an hour or two.

Emma and the worker, who, now that I checked him out, was pretty hot—lots of muscles, expressive eyes—had stopped and were deep in conversation maybe halfway down the driveway.

She smiled when I met up with them. "Andrew was explaining exactly what will happen. He said the whole process will take about an hour. You know, amazingly enough, this feels like a weight off my shoulders. The fight is over."

Andrew spoke into the walkie-talkie. "Get the dozer down here. Utilities are set to go off in ten minutes."

Meanwhile, the film crew had gotten their act together and were setting up in the street. Then Mayo's Navigator came rolling back from the trailer, and he emerged wearing pressed jeans and a *Reality Check* T-shirt. Chelsea was with him, having changed into similar clothing. They were also wearing hard hats, and I wanted to laugh. This was all for the show. They weren't getting anywhere near the house and didn't need hard hats.

Emma and I stood about ten feet to the right of the TV crew until the bulldozer arrived. The dozer was soon followed by a dump truck and another piece of equipment that would scoop up the debris that had been Emma's home. Several men—mostly Hispanics—climbed out of the truck with shovels, what looked like fence cutters, and other tools I'm sure they needed for tearing things apart. When the cleanup crew was in place, we moved closer to the curb to watch.

I held Emma's sweaty hand when the bulldozer rumbled in. The temperature was rising, another warm afternoon before a promised cool front arrived, and everyone was sweating. It seemed so quiet, even the sound of heavy machinery was somehow lost in the humid air. Chelsea passed out cold bottled water to everyone, and I liked her for one brief second. Within minutes the small, already broken house toppled like stacked blocks.

The *Reality Check* people captured every moment with mounted cameras as well as handhelds, while Stu Crowell's attention was dedicated to Emma's reaction.

She seemed not to notice or care. Tears crept down her face, and I could feel her body trembling.

The job of clearing the debris began and the crew was almost finished when their work came to an abrupt halt after a worker shouted, *"Terminar . . . Stop . . . Terminar."* His voice was filled with an urgency that raised the hairs on the back of my neck.

This man hurried over to on-site boss Andrew, and then Andrew jogged after him to where the back of the house once stood. A few seconds later Andrew approached Emma and me.

He said, "This isn't a burial ground, right? I mean, we always check the plats and the city history, but something could have been overlooked."

Emma seemed too stunned to speak, so I said, "Burial ground? You mean . . . ?"

He looked at Emma when he answered. "Disposable diapers take about five hundred years to decompose. We find lots of them during demolitions. But this time . . . well, there's bones, too. Baby bones."

5

Baby bones. Could there any worse words for Emma to hear right now? Good thing I had a hold of her arm, because I felt her go limp for an instant before she regained her equilibrium. Confusion rippled across her face, but this was quickly replaced by a wave of understanding. A baby sister who disappeared fifteen years ago must have been lying dead beneath her house all along. That thought would buckle my knees, too.

Emma said nothing, just stared over Andrew's shoulder at the workers with their still shovels, their bowed heads. A few had their hats in their hands.

Meanwhile I became aware of cameraman Stu moving in, his lens fixed on Emma's face.

"Andrew," I said, "take care of Emma for a second." I stepped between Stu and his camera. "Know something, Stu? I can get as mean as an alligator in a drained swamp, so I suggest you give the girl time to take this in or you may wish you never brought that beautiful expensive camera to Texas."

His face was hidden, but within seconds the red light went off. "You got a job to do and so do I," he said. But I could tell by the look in his eyes that he, too, might believe that sometimes your job isn't the most important thing in the world.

I turned back to Emma. Her expression had turned stony, her skin pale green. I noticed Andrew had his cell phone to his ear.

"He's calling the police," Emma said, her gaze still locked on the mound of debris that was once her home. "I-I . . . never called the police back then, even when she'd leave us alone for a week at a time. I was too afraid. I should have called them, Abby. God, I should have."

"You don't know if what they've found—"

"I don't know? Come on. You're not stupid, and neither am I. They found my sister."

"Maybe. We'll talk to the police and—"

"No. I need you to get me out of here before then. I don't have time to talk to the police. They'll want to know things, and it could take hours. I have to pick up Shannon from school. She needs braces, and this was supposed to be her first appointment with the orthodontist. And Luke has football practice, and—"

I put a finger to her lips. "Stop and think what you're saying. You know this is a different kind of . . . interruption in your routine. This is serious business."

Eyes bright with tears, she took a deep breath and finally her wobbly legs gave out. She fell to her knees, made the sign of the cross and started praying. "Holy Mary, Mother of God . . ."

The rosary prayer, the one Catholics do penance with after a confession. Why should she have anything to feel guilty about? This wasn't her fault.

"Why aren't you rolling on this?" Chelsea said, poking Stu in the arm.

Where the hell had she come from?

Stu got in her face. "Don't you ever touch me again." But he did lift his camera and resume taping.

Chelsea took a deep breath and knelt beside Emma, putting an arm around her.

You phony bitch, I wanted to say, but instead I backed off. *Jeez.* I felt like I had my foot stuck in the stirrup of a runaway horse. Things were totally out of my control here. Maybe when the police arrived, it would feel less chaotic.

The police came pretty fast, but not before another *Reality Check* cameraman walked right onto the property to videotape what looked like a black garbage bag— I could see the torn pieces blowing in the afternoon breeze. He ignored the admonitions of the workers standing near what I assumed were the remains. But then Andrew intervened, and he and the cameraman got into a shoving match. Thank goodness a uniformed cop arrived in time to escort the photographer off the property.

Mayo had disappeared after the discovery, but he'd apparently been inside his Lincoln the whole time. When the cops showed up, he emerged from the backseat, a cell phone pressed to his ear. Something was up. I could tell by the hardness in his gray eyes. He stayed by the car, talking, looking like he was ready for Halloween in his hard hat and designer jeans.

With arrival of the police, more onlookers appeared. There had been a few curious neighbors watching the demolition, but sirens summon a crowd, and that crowd was quickly growing across the street.

I watched one officer set up a perimeter with crime scene tape, and another herd all the city workers off the property. They piled into Andrew's extended-cab truck and he tossed them the keys to turn on the air-conditioning.

Meanwhile, Stu kept taping until an officer who seemed to be in charge came over to us.

He said, "Sir, I have to ask you to stop filming until we determine what's gone on here."

"But we have an agreement with the city," Chelsea said. "A contract with the homeowner giving us the right to film. We have—"

"Ma'am. We know all that. The *Chronicle* ran an article about your little production visit to town this morning. No matter what deal you had with who, you're turning the camera off or I will confiscate it as evidence. Might do that anyway."

Chelsea's artificially bronzed face paled. "No way this was in the newspaper. You're lying."

The cop stared down at her, smirking and shaking his head.

"Okay, you're not lying," she finally said. "Syndicated or local piece?"

"I don't know and I don't care, ma'am. Now, this is your last chance. I want all your people to wait in the street. We'll be barricading this block so they won't have to worry about being in the way of traffic."

I liked this guy. Calm. Tall. And very much in charge.

"Oh, *whatever*." Chelsea tugged at Stu's sleeve despite his earlier warning not to touch him. He pulled his arm free and stomped away toward the other crew members.

Chelsea started to follow but stopped and turned back to me. She was hot, and not hot like her little boots. "You did this, didn't you?"

"Did what?"

"Called the newspaper. I know it wasn't Emma, because she was told not to talk to the local media. It had to be you."

"I didn't tell any reporter anything."

"Don't deny it, you little hick bitch. Don't you see? Now that this . . . this . . . *grave* has been discovered, every reporter in town will be digging around for information. And Mayo will blame me." She whirled and ran off in Stu's direction.

I smiled to myself, almost wishing I *had* called the *Chronicle*.

Meanwhile, Emma was sitting on the ground, knees to her chest, arms wrapped around her legs. Her face was buried in her drawn-up legs. I squatted beside her and put an arm around her shoulders. "Emma? Are you okay?" I asked.

She didn't answer.

The police officer cleared his throat, and I stood up. The name badge on his bright blue shirt read CLARK.

"Is this the homeowner, Emma Lopez?" he said.

I nodded.

She looked up then, her cheeks smudged with eye makeup, her eyes tired and red-rimmed.

"The city crew chief, Andrew McDonald, pointed you out." Clark looked to his left at Andrew, who was talking to a female officer holding a notebook and pen. "He said you've been pretty upset, that you've asked for delays on this demolition."

"He told you that?" Emma said. "Seems everyone knows my business."

"Officer Clark, do you have to do this now?" I said.

He turned his attention to me. "Your name, ma'am?"

"Abby Rose—Yellow Rose Investigations."

He looked puzzled. "Do I know you?"

"No, but you may know a friend of mine—Sergeant Jeff Kline. Homicide."

He nodded. "That's it. I've seen you downtown. Your Jeff's—" He caught himself, refocused on Emma. "I think you'll both need to talk to the homicide investigators, so I'll give you guys a break until they get here. Meanwhile, guess I need to deal with them." He nodded at the Venture crew, all standing in the street, listening to a Mayo lecture. Most of them looked hot, tired and disinterested in whatever he was saying.

"Yup," said Officer Clark, "my lucky day. You two stay right here until homicide shows up."

He strode toward the television people.

"Homicide?" Emma said. "Can they tell that she was . . . you know . . . ?"

"It's all routine, Emma. Any suspicious death belongs to homicide."

She offered an "Oh," then fell silent, staring at where her house had stood only hours ago.

The investigators who arrived minutes later identified themselves as Sergeant Don White and Sergeant Ed Benson. They looked close to retirement age and vaguely familiar—perhaps just as I had looked familiar to Clark. We'd probably passed each other on the homicide floor at Travis Center when I visited Jeff while he was working.

White grinned at me. "Your pretty-boy cop goes on vacation and where do we find you? At the site of a possible homicide. What's Jeff gonna say about that?"

He *did* recognize me. I extended my hand. "Abby Rose. I don't think we've ever been introduced."

"Hey. Don't get all formal on me," he said. "I'm just giving you a hard time. Jeff has nothing but good things to say about you, and believe me, he's the man. Guy knows what he's talking about."

Benson spoke up. "Uh, Don, how about apologizing for giving *me* a hard time for the last ten years?"

"Shut up, Bennie." White smiled again. "What are you doing here, Abby?"

I explained—and the explanation was long and detailed. Emma remained wrapped up like a ball at my feet, her shoes beside her. I wasn't sure she was even hearing what I was saying. Benson, meanwhile, had snapped on gloves and left with Andrew, the two stepping over the crime scene tape and heading toward the spot where the bones had been found.

White turned his attention to Emma. He knelt in front of her and in a quiet voice said, "Miss Lopez? Can we talk?"

He was a huge man with hands like spatulas, and he held one out to her to help her up, treating her like the frightened child she had become. My guess was that her mind had taken her back in time, maybe to the kitchen of that now-demolished house. Maybe she saw herself standing on that throw rug over the crawl space door and blaming herself for the death of her sister.

Emma ignored White's offer of assistance and instead drank from her water bottle, closed her eyes for a second, then said, "Yes, we can talk. But I want to see her. Can I see her?"

"We'll gather her remains, and the ME's office will take them to the morgue. I think that's a better place for you to . . . see her."

"No," Emma said, her voice rising. "I want to see my sister."

White used his church voice again. "We don't even know if that *is* your sister. The ME will figure all that out. For now, why don't you talk to me? I could use all the help I can get."

Emma's lower lip trembled. "Help you? What makes you think I can help you? I couldn't help her." Her gaze was fixed on the men looking down at that black garbage bag.

"Let's go to my car," White said. "We can talk there."

"I've already told you everything," I said. "Can't you see how upset she is?"

"I do see," White said. "And I understand. But I need the story directly from Ms. Lopez." He bent and cupped Emma's elbow, helping her up.

"Can Abby come with me?" she said.

White's tone was less pleasant when he said, "We can do this alone, can't we? I mean, I want to help you and—"

"But I need her with me." She stared at White with those intense eyes.

His shoulders finally sagged in agreement. "Sure, why not?"

"Thank you," she replied.

They started down the sidewalk while I picked up her forgotten shoes.

A minute later, the three of us were enjoying the air-conditioned comfort of White's unmarked car. Even the hum of the engine felt normal and nice, despite the presence of crime scene tape, hovering TV news choppers and the ever-growing crowd across the street.

Emma sat in front with White, and I was hunched forward in the backseat, my face inserted in the space between them.

"Can I call you Emma?" White asked.

"Please," she said, her water bottle held tight between both hands.

"Emma, you got any clue how this little body got under your house?"

"A clue? I can tell you exactly what happened. My mother put the baby there."

"You saw her do this?" White asked.

"No. But I'm sure that's what happened. Since you're a detective and Abby's told you everything about me, you should have figured that out."

Emma's anger had resurfaced, and I could only imagine what was going through her head. Nothing reasonable, that was for certain.

I reached around and put my hand on hers, noting that the water bottle was as hot as the air outside. That was when I saw Stu and his camera through the tinted glass of the front passenger window.

"Can you make him go away, Don? I think that would make Emma more comfortable." If I was Abby to him, he was Don to me.

"They won't get nothin'." White loosened his gold paisley tie. "This glass protects against bullets as well as other penetrations, if you know what I mean. Now, Emma, tell me again what year your mother had the baby and everything that happened afterward."

It was her turn to go through the whole story, reiterating everything he'd heard from me already. This time, though, he had a laptop sitting on his bulky legs and took notes.

"And you haven't heard from your mother for ten years? Not even a phone call?" White asked.

"No. She's probably drinking herself to death somewhere," Emma said.

"You had the city delay the demolition once," White went on. "Tell me again why you asked for that."

"Venture would take over my life once the house was torn down. I thought that if I delayed the demolition, I'd have time to get out of the contract," Emma said.

"Not that I watch the show all that much, but they're giving you a new house and a bunch of cash and gifts, right?" He feigned surprise. "Who in their right mind would give up major freebies?"

Emma sighed. "When I signed the contract, I had no idea they knew about my missing sister. The world doesn't need to know every detail of my mother's sorry life. I mean, what if my sister watched that show? Found out about her mother that way?" She drummed her fingers on the bottle and looked out the window.

"See, that's where I'm confused," White said. "Venture may have known plenty, but why would they want to air much about your mother? From what I know— through the wife, of course—this is a touchy-feely show about making people smile."

"I got the impression during my last meeting with Mr. Mayo that my sister's disappearance would up the sympathy factor when the show aired, and her disappearance *would* be mentioned," Emma said. "Erwin Mayo put on a good show before I signed on, but he got downright spiteful when I asked him not to air anything about my missing sister."

"But they never said for sure they'd use this information?"

"I've only seen the show for the first time recently, but anything they can use to make the life-makeover candidates appear pitiful is apparently standard operating procedure," Emma said.

"What about your mother? This Mayo guy indicated he'd be checking into her disappearance?" White was typing away as he asked the question.

"I don't think so. She abandoned her kids, made a baby go away, and that was enough. He seemed far more interested in the missing baby."

"Wait a minute," I said. "Maybe he wanted you guys to be reunited on TV."

Emma turned quickly and stared at me. "Oh, my God. That's why he was so evasive."

"What's more heartwarming than a surprise TV reunion?" I said.

Emma was squeezing the bottle now, her knuckles white with the pressure. "He was going to spring this on us? With no warning?"

"Makes for great TV drama," I said.

"That would be so wrong, at least for us. We would want a private reunion. But that's not going to happen now, is it?"

"I'm so sorry, Emma," I said.

"Yeah," White said. "Tough day for you, young lady."

Glancing out the window, I noticed that the medical examiner's assistant had arrived. She wore the baseball cap with HCME printed on the front, a T-shirt with the same logo, and cargo pants, and was staring down at the spot where the child had been found. Then she turned to the Crime Scene Unit officers and made a sweeping gesture that took in the entire lot.

This caught Emma's attention, too. "Something's happening. Can I go out there? I won't get in the way."

"Like I said before, I don't think—" White started.

"You've got her story," I said. "Let her go, Don."

"All right," he said wearily. "But we stay outside the tape." He turned to me. "I suppose you're coming, too?"

"Certainly," I said.

We all got out of the car, and they walked ahead of me while I speed-dialed Jeff. God, how I wished he were in town.

6

I hung back from Emma and White and gave Jeff a brief summary of this morning's events. He told me White and Benson were experienced investigators who'd solved plenty of cases. He also said he'd brief DeShay, his partner, and see if there was anything he could do to help Emma. After talking to him, I felt a little better. But though Jeff vouched for the investigators, Erwin Mayo still had me worried.

I had no idea what his next move might be, but his crew sure wasn't happy. I could tell by their faces as Sergeant Benson herded them back to the trailer. Benson walked side by side with a cameraman, his notebook ready.

The only people left on the street were Stu, Chelsea and Mayo, who were huddled, talking. I had a feeling Emma and I might not like their game plan. Then there were the onlookers held back by portable fences on the sidewalk across the street. You couldn't swing a dead rat without hitting someone; that was how much the crowd had swelled. The news vans had been kept a block away, but several reporters continually shouted questions to any cop who came close, hoping for an interview. Bet this had been breaking news on every local TV channel.

I joined Emma and Don White near Emma's driveway, and we watched the careful work of the ME's assistant. The folks working the scene were in no hurry. Heck, at the pace they were going they might be done by the second Wednesday of next month. After about thirty minutes, White left us to consult with the other cops, but kept glancing our way. Guess he thought Emma might make a run onto the property. Like I'd let her do that.

The only good thing that happened during the hour we stood there was the pleasant cool front that blew in. At least we weren't sweating like hogs anymore. Emma called a friend and made arrangements for her brother and sister to be picked up and taken to the hotel. With that settled, she seemed more relaxed and far more interested than I was in the activity going on in front of us. CSU officers, the Harris County Medical Examiner's assistant and cops doing their jobs. I'd seen it all before.

"Why do you think they're taking so long?" Emma finally asked. "What's left of her tiny body shouldn't stay in the dirt any longer."

I put an arm around her shoulders. "They have their protocols. And I'm guessing they're looking for more graves. You see the grid they've made?" I pointed at the small stakes and the strings connecting them. "The CSU officers are sifting through every inch of ground looking for more bones or maybe even more bodies."

Emma folded her arms and moved away from me. "More bodies? That's ridiculous."

"Like I said, they follow procedure. Any evidence from the scene is vital in a case like this. The city and state have an obligation to that baby, and they have to make sure no one else is buried there."

"You mean like my mother?" Emma said. "Does Sergeant White think I killed them and buried them in my yard?" She wasn't angry, just incredulous.

"I have no idea what he thinks. I'm certain the evidence will convince him of the truth—that you have nothing to hide. But count on being questioned again. Probably Shannon and Luke will be brought in, too."

"Why? They don't know anything."

"The police have to make sure," I said.

Emma returned her gaze to where the CSU officers were gathering small items impossible to identify from where we stood. "So everything they collect is important—like the bags of soil I saw them taking away. How can dirt from my yard help them learn the truth?"

"From what little I know about soil collection, the

earth around the spot where they found the bones will help establish when your sister died and maybe even when the body was placed in that spot."

Emma looked at me. "How long will that take?"

"I wish I knew."

We again turned our attention to the yard. The ME's assistant was carefully lifting the trash bag, supporting her bundle, ready to slide it into a body bag. What was probably left of that tiny skeleton could have fit in a giant Ziploc. But they needed that trash bag. It might hold answers. Answers Emma needed.

Emma made the sign of the cross and bowed her head.

I clasped my hands and stared down at the sidewalk in respect for the child who had died, had perhaps been buried alive under that house—a thought I would never share with Emma, but one that had been with me since that diaper and those bones had been discovered.

Then, before we could blink, the fab trio descended on us—Mayo, Burch and Crowell. My daddy always said that no matter how high or out of sight a bird was, it always came back to earth to eat. And these guys were ready to feast on Emma.

"If you could join us in the trailer, we have a few things to discuss, Ms. Lopez," Mayo said. He turned and left for his luxury ride.

Hmmm, I thought. She'd been "Emma" before, but now she wasn't getting the "we love you so much" treatment. It dawned on me then that no happily-ever-after program like *Reality Check* would want anything to do with dead babies. This was about business and possible lost revenue. Maybe Emma could free herself from them after all.

"What's this about, Mr. Crowell?" Emma asked.

"Just do what he says," Stu said. "It's now or later, and believe me, now is your better option."

"What are you talking about?" I asked.

"I know the man," he said. "The longer he stews, the nastier he'll get."

"You got that right," Chelsea said with an accompanying eye roll.

The Navigator started toward us before making a screeching U turn to travel the block to the trailer.

"Go," Stu said.

I took Emma's arm and we started walking.

Stu Crowell stayed back, camera again on his shoulder as he filmed the coroner van's retreat. Chelsea lagged behind on our trek to the trailer. The girl was limping. Seemed those pink-and-blue boots weren't meant for walking.

When we arrived at the trailer, the lot had been emptied of cars aside from the Navigator. The crew had either been sent to their hotel or taken to the police station on Travis. I reached up and gave a cursory knock on the trailer door. Then we ascended the two small steps and entered. Mayo was in the living area sitting on one of two leather couches that flanked a long table. Typed papers, scribbled notes and empty soda cans littered the surface in front of him.

The scent of new leather filled the small area, and Mayo gestured at the sofa across from him. "Sit."

I heard the door squeak open again, and Mayo yelled, "Chelsea, bring me the contract. Now."

I sat and slid over to give Emma room.

She said, "You're ready to let me out of the deal? Is that what this is about?"

"I don't know what you're talking about." He grabbed the contract from Chelsea, who had come hurrying in with the document in hand. "Get all this crap off the table so we can work here."

Chelsea gathered the papers and cans and took them to the kitchenette.

Mayo had changed back into his Ralph Lauren overpriced shirt, and I thought, *Work here? What's this jerk got up his designer sleeve?*

Mayo flipped pages in the document, and while he did this, Chelsea returned from trash duty and sat next to him. This was not the perky young woman I'd met yesterday. She was tired. We were all tired. And it was only four in the afternoon.

"Ah, here it is." Mayo folded the document to the page he wanted, pushed it across the table and pointed to several lines midway down the page. "Cutting through the legalese, this clause states that our relationship shall continue with you in other capacities and with other possible programming options should there be unforeseen events." He stared at Emma. "I'd say we had an unforeseen event, wouldn't you?"

Emma's face flushed. "What do you want from me?"

"Your full and heartfelt cooperation—or so it should appear on the air. You understand?" His throat and earlobes were red with anger.

Emma said nothing. She let her folded arms and stiff posture do the talking.

I, too, had about all I could stand of this guy. "Why are you being such a jerk, Mayo? No one's having the greatest day, if you haven't noticed."

"Let me clarify, then. I've lost a nice, happy story sure to be a ratings winner. But I plan on salvaging this, minus the nice and happy part. I'll have to turn this over to Kravitz. And believe me, that burns my ass." He swept the contract off the table and sent it flying toward the kitchenette.

"Paul Kravitz of *Crime Time*?" Now *that* show I did catch on occasion. Kravitz, the interviewer, always came across as tough but compassionate.

Chelsea said. "Isn't that way cool, Emma? And he'll be here tonight."

Mayo the Magnificent gave her a look that could wither a live oak.

Emma turned to me. "Who is this person?"

"An investigative reporter on a program that digs into past crimes," I said. "Another show that I assume is produced by Venture?" I looked to Chelsea, who seemed a safer person to talk to, since she was in a better mood than Mayo.

But he answered anyway. "Yes. I'm an executive producer. And though I am very upset and disappointed about what happened today, Paul will do an . . . *excellent* job. I'm turning Emma over to his very capable hands."

Emma bolted upright. "You're *disappointed*? Is that because a child died or because you lost your stupid program? But wait, no need to answer. And by the way, I'm not being turned over to anyone. I'm not your slave."

I rested a hand on Emma's knee and looked at her. "We need to get something to eat and talk this over."

"If you're thinking about ducking out on—" Mayo started.

"Shut up," I said.

Then Emma and I hurried out of that trailer before I kissed jerk extraordinaire Mayo in his eyeteeth with my fist.

Emma and I left in our own cars and met up at Houston's, a restaurant on Westheimer. It was early enough, a little past five o'clock, that the place wasn't crowded. We each ordered a very frosty, large margarita. Nothing better than Cuervo Gold to take the sting off a horrific day. After a few sips of her drink, I think Emma exhaled for the first time in hours.

Neither of us needed the menu. We both chose the best Caesar salads on the planet, then Emma said, "What can I expect to happen now?"

"For one thing, investigators will be crawling all over Houston. I'd be willing to bet the *Chronicle* will run a big piece in the newspaper. That means I need to research your father and your mother before they do. Is that okay?"

"My father? But he's been dead for twenty-three years. What could—"

"That might be one of the first places the *Crime Time* investigators and even other reporters will start. Do you know how much research they did on your father for *Reality Check*?"

"They knew he was a marine and died in Beirut. The researcher copied his photo and said they'd probably use it during the show's intro, sort of give my background through old photographs."

"That part may not change, but *Crime Time* is a who-what-why-when-where program. Rather than an entertainment approach, you'll be subjected to a harder news angle. Ever watch *48 Hours Mystery*?"

Emma nodded. "Once or twice."

"Expect that kind of production. They dig deep, probably tape hours and hours of footage and edit extensively. You may not know until the show airs how you'll be portrayed."

"What does that mean?" Emma rubbed salt off the rim of her glass, licked her finger and took a drink.

"If the mystery remains unsolved, you may end up looking like a suspect. They're real proficient at innuendo."

"You've got to be kidding me," Emma said, eyes wide.

"Or you could be portrayed as the victim, a child left to raise three other children, a child who went through hell, only to learn the sister she'd helped bring into the world was gone before she had a chance to live."

Emma looked left and right at the customers surrounding us before leaning close and whispering, "I'm no victim, and I'm no killer."

"I know that. Now you have to convince Paul Kravitz." I nodded, offering her a small, determined smile.

She exhaled, relaxed again. "I can do that. Besides, anything has to be better than dealing with Mayo. As for my father, I haven't been completely honest with you. My father, well . . . he had a family. He was . . . married."

I sat back against the leather booth. "Uh-oh. How do you know this?"

"Because I went looking for any extended family I might have about three years ago. I got as far as his obituary."

"And a wife was listed as next of kin?"

She nodded. "Figures my mother would shack up with a married man and then feed me all those stories about how much he loved her and how much he wanted to see me and never got the chance. I wanted to believe that fairy tale, and that's why I didn't tell you. I'm sorry, Abby."

"Don't be sorry. Do you want me to talk to your father's wife? Warn her about the TV investigators, and the possibility that reporters might come calling?"

"I think that's the right thing to do. I wanted to contact her before the show aired, but didn't know where to start." She studied the fingernails on her right hand for a second. "You know what I'm most afraid of? That after the Beirut bombing, my mother slapped Xavier Lopez's name on my birth certificate. Gave me a hero for a father when I'm probably the daughter of some dope addict she slept with one night."

"Come on, Emma. *That's* the fairy tale. You have a house and a small trust, right? Whose name is on the deed?"

"Mine and his."

"You think your mother was capable of manufacturing something like that?"

"No. You're right. It's just that I felt like my life collapsed when that house went down and my home gave up such a terrible secret."

"Listen, I know you feel like your luck is running muddy, but you have your father's eyes, his smile, and I'd say you've got his courage, too."

"Thanks, Abby."

"If his wife is still alive, I'll find her, explain what's happening." Hopefully before a *Crime Time* investigator dumped the truth on her first.

Emma tried for a smile and failed, then changed the subject to her brothers and sister, speaking about them like the proud parent she'd become.

We were nearly finished with our salads when my cell rang.

"Where the hell are you, Abby?" came a familiar voice.

"Hi, DeShay." DeShay Peters, Jeff's partner, is one of my favorite people and enjoys giving me a hard time—in a playful way, of course.

"Guess where I am, at Jeff's request," he said.

"Uh-oh. Emma's property?"

"Correct, for two hundred dollars. Next category. What might piss off a police officer more than a turd who leads us on a high-speed chase all over Houston?"

"Someone who's not where she's expected to be?" I said.

"The girl's a genius. Give her the million dollars. Are you coming to me, or do I have to navigate rush-hour traffic to get to wherever you are?"

"I'm on my way." I hung up, speared the last piece of lettuce and told Emma I had to meet up with someone who might help us. She had to be drained, so I told her to head for her hotel and her family, that I'd handle this meeting alone. She didn't argue.

I arrived back in Emma's neighborhood about thirty minutes later and parked a block away, since the street was still inaccessible. Onlookers lingered, hoping for a glimpse of . . . what? Maybe they thought this would be another case like the Dean Corll/Wayne Henley murders back in the seventies. I seriously doubted they'd find thirty bodies buried on Emma's lot. There wasn't enough room.

It was now after seven, and no one was working the scene. DeShay stood talking to the lone officer guarding Emma's property. I figured DeShay was off duty, since he was wearing his favorite baggy jeans and a Houston Rockets T-shirt.

"Abby, my girl, what's going down?" he said.

"Some nasty stuff. I take it Jeff filled you in?" I said.

"Yeah. He thought you could use some help." DeShay gestured to his right. "This here is Officer William Evans."

Evans nodded in greeting.

"Officer Evans tells me they're not done with this scene. They'll be coming back tomorrow to finish the grid." DeShay extended his hand to the uniformed cop. "It's been nice jawing with you, my man. You take care tonight. Don't go fallin' asleep on the sidewalk or nothin'."

DeShay and I walked down the block to his car, parked in the empty lot by the trailer. He drove an ancient T-bird, but it was in mint condition.

He said, "You want to talk here? Or go somewhere else?"

"I'd like to get away from the TV trailer, in case anyone hanging around gets nosy. Can I buy you dinner?" I said.

"No, thanks. Already grabbed a burger." DeShay unlocked the passenger door, and I sat down on the cream leather bucket seat.

He slid behind the wheel and offered me a huge smile, his perfect teeth bright in contrast to his dark lips and skin. "Let's take Lucille around the block, okay?"

"Lucille?"

"Named her after my granny. Seemed fitting to call the best car ever made after the best woman who ever walked the earth."

He started the ignition, the engine came to life and the headlights lit up the empty parking area. He drove over to the next street and curbed the T-bird in front of an empty house with a FOR SALE sign.

"First off," I said, "I can't thank you enough for showing up. You know me. I may think I know what I'm doing, but it's nice having someone around who'll steer me straight if I stray."

"You've handled your cases pretty damn good, from what I've seen. How's your client liking the limelight?"

"She hates it."

"Well, she'd better get out her sunglasses. Hollywood loves to shine their spotlights far and wide. She's a good woman, this client?"

"I am so impressed by Emma. She has an amazing spirit, DeShay."

"If you say she's good, then I know she is. How can I help?"

"I want to research Emma's mother's disappearance. If we find her, we might find that baby's killer. Her name was Christine O'Meara, and she abandoned her kids in 1997."

"Missing-persons inquiry ever filed?"

"Not by the family, but maybe a friend filed a report. I don't know. CPS probably didn't. Since I started working as an adoption PI, I've learned that in Texas, the courts have no obligation to hunt down abandoned children's parents. Sure, the social workers look for relatives to care for the kids, but those people are seriously overworked and overwhelmed. Their job is placement, not investigation."

"Cold-case disappearance. Sounds like a tough one."

"Let me run a few things by you," I said.

"Sure."

"That baby disappeared and was probably buried under the house in 1992. Why do you think Christine waited five years to split if she'd put a defenseless infant under her house? Wouldn't she want to get as far away as possible as *soon* as possible?"

"Maybe she was afraid a new owner would discover the body and she'd be busted. Either that or something happened to her—something she didn't plan on."

"She could have ended up anywhere, maybe even landed in an alcohol-induced coma in a nursing home. Or maybe was arrested and put in jail—but wait . . . there's another possibility."

"She's dead." DeShay smiled. "I figured you'd get to that."

"Yes. And that would be the easiest place to start. Can you help me get a list of all unidentified bodies from 1997?"

DeShay wet his finger and wiped at a smudge on the dashboard. "Sure, but I won't be sneaking around behind anyone's back. White and Benson ask me what the hell I'm doing, I've got to tell them."

"Fair enough," I answered. "Let me give you her description."

DeShay pulled out his pocket notebook and jotted down what I told him; then he said, "And now, can you help *me* out?"

"Anything," I said.

"What the hell is our man Jeff doing in Seattle, Washington? And why does he sound like a different person, all subdued and mysterious and, well, *weird*?"

"DeShay, I wish I knew. I'm sure he'll tell us soon enough."

"Just kinda worried. That's all."

"Me, too." Worried more than curious, especially since DeShay, who spent hours and hours with Jeff, thought he now sounded like a different person, too.

7

I arrived home about seven thirty to find a hungry dog and an aloof cat, but no Kate. Working late, I guessed. I fed Webster and Diva, wondering how this case had gotten so complicated in less than forty-eight hours. Not that complications bothered me. On the contrary, I was sure I'd have a hard time sleeping tonight as I inventoried all the possible tracks I could take trying to solve this one.

When I'd left DeShay, he told me he'd dig around in the 1997 unsolveds, see if he came up with anything. Meanwhile, I would try to find Xavier Lopez's widow and warn her of the impending media storm.

I'd have loved to get my hands on the anonymous letter, but I suspected Venture would never willingly let me see it since I'd refused to hire on with them. Paul Kravitz was probably holding it in his hot little hands this very minute.

I pulled a pint of Häagen-Dazs pistachio from the freezer and was heading for my computer when my cell rang. Luke O'Meara was on the other end.

His words spilled out so fast I had to ask him to slow down.

"Emma called about six," he said. "She told me she'd be at the hotel in fifteen minutes. But she's not here and she's not answering her phone and I was thinking maybe she's with you."

"No, Luke. Could she have stopped for snacks or sodas, maybe?"

"I-I don't know. That wouldn't take nearly two hours, would it?"

"No. Okay, maybe she got mixed up about which place Venture put you guys up at and—"

"No way. She told the lady who picked us up from school where to take us, and she called here, so she's not mixed-up."

His panic was contagious and I started pacing, trying to come up with some plausible explanation. "Maybe she's with a friend. Venture is planning some changes, and perhaps she wanted to talk to someone about it. Is that possible?" Since I had no idea what Emma had said to him, I didn't want to go into detail about this morning's events.

"She'd call us."

"An unplanned meeting with a client?" I said, not believing myself now.

"Same answer. She'd call. You're a detective, Miss Rose," Luke said. "You can find her, right?"

"Yes. Yes. Absolutely. I *will* find her. Meanwhile, are you and your sister okay?"

"We're fine, but we don't have money to get anywhere. If you need us to help you look, can you pick us up?"

"You need to stay put in case Emma shows up. She'd get all worried if she arrived at the hotel and you guys were gone. Let me take care of this."

"Please find her. I want to talk to her real bad."

"I know you do. I'll be in touch." As soon as I hung up, I called DeShay. He answered on the first ring.

"What's up, Abby? Think of something else you need?"

"No. It's Emma. She didn't show up at her hotel," I said.

"She's been gone a couple hours," he said. "Maybe she had a flat tire or—"

"But she didn't contact her brother and sister, and she would have done that."

"Abby, come on. She's a big girl. She can—"

"Would you mind checking with Don White or even traffic patrol? Meanwhile I'll start calling hospitals. My gut tells me something's wrong."

He sighed. "Hospitals won't tell you squat these days. I'll get back with you in a few minutes."

I was still pacing and chewing my cuticles rather than enjoying Häagen-Dazs when Kate came in through the back door.

"Hey," she said, which was immediately followed by, "What's wrong?" The shrink knew her sister.

"Probably nothing," I said. "The house came down early, some unexpected things happened and now Emma didn't show up at her hotel. She should have been there by now. Her brother called and sounded pretty worried."

"And so are you." Kate bent to scratch an excited Webster's head. He started barking, then ran over and pulled his leash from the hook on the wall near the back door, hoping for a walk. "Okay, buddy. In a minute. What do you plan to do, Abby? Because you aren't the kind to wait around."

"I called DeShay for help." My cell rang and I snatched the phone up from the kitchen counter.

"You were right," DeShay said. "Emma Lopez was taken by ambulance to Ben Taub. Her car hit a cement barrier on the freeway. That's all I got."

"Oh, my God. Thanks, DeShay. I'm on my way to the emergency room."

I closed the phone and grabbed my car keys and purse. "Emma's been in a wreck. You want to go with me?"

She didn't even need to answer. We took her 4Runner, and on the fifteen-minute ride I told Kate all that had happened today. She agreed we should wait on calling Luke until we knew Emma's condition.

We hunted for a parking spot for what seemed an hour but was probably more like five minutes, then made our way to the emergency room. Ben Taub Hospital is a county facility, and the waiting area was swamped with sick and injured people. Kate and I weaved through the filled chairs, and I thought, *This is where you come when you cannot pay. This is where you sit for hours to find out what's wrong with you or your loved one. This is where you cry when you learn that the bullet your son or husband or brother took in the chest killed him.*

The unhappy, pained faces only made my anxiety level rise. More than thirty minutes later, we finally convinced someone with access to the mysterious goings-on behind the closed double doors that we were friends of Emma's and that her brother and sister were minors who had no clue about their sister's accident. The convincing factor, unfortunately, was a call to the hotel where Luke and Shannon were staying. I'd hoped to be the one to call them, but it didn't work out that way.

They gave me the phone then, and Luke insisted we come get him and Shannon. He sounded close to tears. Kate agreed to be their taxi while I was allowed into the belly of the ER. Behind curtain number one I heard a woman squealing like a pig caught under a gate, and I was also engulfed by more smells and sounds than my brain could sort. The nonsorting was probably a good thing.

A nurse's aide pulled back curtain number four, where Emma lay, her gurney raised at the head. No hospital staff was with her, and the nice person who'd helped me left us alone. Emma's upper body was wrapped like a mummy, her left arm bent at the elbow and secured against her stomach. Other than looking like she could use about a week's sleep, she seemed in far better shape than I had imagined. She didn't even have a mark or a bruise on her face.

"Thank goodness you're here," Emma said. "They took my clothes and purse and put them in that closet next to you. I couldn't call anyone. Did Luke or Shannon tell you I was here?"

I explained about Luke's call, then said, "The kids are on the way here."

Emma's eyes flashed with anger. "But the policeman said he'd call them." She closed her eyes. "Oh, no. My fault. I think I gave him our old number, and with the house torn down . . . how could I—"

"It's been an awful day, Emma. Don't be so hard on yourself. What's the word on your injuries? Nothing serious, I hope."

"I have a cracked collarbone from the air bag. My car's totaled, and this little visit will cost me a fortune."

"Try not to obsess over things you can't control." I rested a hand on her knee. "Tell me what happened."

"I'm not sure. The car behind me was tailgating, I

think. I was distracted after all that happened today, not paying much attention to my driving. But the lights got so close and I thought that car might drive into my trunk. Then the headlights swung to my right, and next thing I know, I've got an air bag in my face and this serious pain in my shoulder."

"Kids, probably. Or a drunk driver."

"Funny, but the cop asked me if anyone was mad at me—mad enough to run me into that barrier. Could have been my own fault, though. I should haven't been in the left lane."

"The officer implied someone did this to you on purpose?"

"He asked a lot of questions. I think he was trying to understand why a woman who admitted to one margarita that didn't even register on the Breathalyzer would drive her car into an immovable object." She nodded with her chin toward her left shoulder. "Think this little problem will make Venture delay shooting their damn show?"

I smiled. "Wishful thinking. A broken collarbone may slow you down, but not them."

"I can't imagine they'd want the world to see me on TV like this."

"More bad luck to exploit for ratings," I said with a wry smile. But I wasn't sure this incident had anything to do with luck, and the thought sent a small chill down my spine.

8

The following morning I showered by seven thirty, made a pot of French-roast coffee and then took my mug and a muffin to my office, ready to hunt down Xavier Lopez's relatives.

Emma had been released from the hospital last night, not long after her brother and sister arrived with Kate. The kids were relieved to see that Emma could walk and talk. Before we all drove back to the hotel, my practical sister made sure Emma called her insurance company to inform them of the accident.

Then Kate took the phone from Emma and arranged to have a rental car delivered to the hotel—this over Emma's protests when Kate told them to bill her. After we'd arrived home, my sister and I were asleep within a half hour. It had been a long day.

Today I would search for any of Xavier Lopez's surviving relatives, and after devouring my blueberry muffin, I booted up my computer. Since Lopez had died at a young age, around thirty-three, his widow was probably still alive. The obituaries of fallen heroes, I soon learned, are easy to find, especially those related to a news-grabbing event like the marine barracks attack in '83. It was one in a string of terrorist bombings that year, which offered more than a hint of what we now faced in the twenty-first century.

When I found Lopez's obit, I sat back in my swivel chair and said, "Uh-oh. More surprises." The article listed the surviving relatives as not only his widow, Gloria, but his two children, Xavier Junior and Raul. Did Emma know about them, too? She had to if she'd read the same obituary I was reading. Yet she'd failed to mention them. I wondered why.

I also wondered if Sergeant Lopez had been divorced or estranged from his wife at the time of his death. Was that why he shared a house with Emma's mother? Or had he never even lived with Christine O'Meara? Emma had only her mother's side of the story to rely on.

Diva slinked into my office and jumped on my keyboard. I lifted her onto my lap before she had a chance to dislodge a key and carry it away and stroked her soft calico coat. I returned to work and learned that Sergeant Lopez had been buried in his hometown, San Antonio. That seemed like the logical place to look for Gloria Lopez.

"Diva? You settled in? 'Cause I'm about to take us on what could be a long ride on the Internet to find a woman named Gloria."

She closed her eyes and began to purr. This was her favorite part of my job.

By the time I heard Kate coming downstairs, ready to leave for work, I'd located Gloria Lopez—now Gloria Wilks. This particular Internet surf had taken only an hour. The woman was a prominent figure in San Antonio, active in charity work while playing a visible, supportive role to her lawyer and Texas senator husband, Neal Wilks. A politician's wife. Great. If she didn't already know about her late first husband's love child, she might feel like shooting the messenger when I called.

Kate poked her head in the door. "I'm off. Let me know how Emma's feeling after you talk to her."

"Sure. I'm hoping the TV people will leave her alone to recover." I then explained about Xavier Lopez's family and how I had Gloria Wilks's phone number on the screen in front of me and planned to call her.

Kate said, "You're delivering this information over the telephone? What if the woman has no idea Emma exists?"

"She'll be shocked, sure, but at least she'll be ready when *Crime Time* or the newspaper reporters show up on her doorstep."

"You should tell her in person. You can take a Southwest flight, be there in forty-five minutes."

"Kate, maybe face-to-face is a better way to handle

this situation, but I don't want to leave Houston even for a couple hours. Paul Kravitz was coming into town last night, if you remember."

She sighed. "I can see I won't win this argument. You have the protective instincts of a big sister—which you've never been, by the way, since I'm sure I was born before you."

I sat back and smiled at Kate. "I'm pretty certain the midwife who delivered us would tell us I came first. But I do feel like Emma's almost a sister. How did that happen so quickly?"

"Because she's a lot like you. Smart, kind, stubborn . . . but if I go on, your head will swell to the size of a watermelon. Time for me to get to work—and the same for you." She blew me a kiss and was gone.

I looked at my computer screen, wondering how to approach the problem of Mrs. Wilks.

Call her, Abby. See how she reacts and respond accordingly.

I picked up the phone and was surprised when she answered right away, sounding polite and warm as only Texans can over the phone.

"I'm not sure how to start, so I'll get right to it," I said. "My name is Abby Rose, and I'm a private investigator with Yellow Rose Investigations."

"Private investigator?" Polite turned to wary in a flash. "If this is about Senator Wilks, perhaps you should call his office."

"This isn't about your current husband." I tried hard to sound nonthreatening, or so I thought.

"Not about my *current* husband? Are you calling about Xavier?"

"Yes. Do you have time to talk? Or are you too busy?"

"I have time," she said. "But if you're a private investigator, someone hired you to make this call, correct?"

"Yes. A young woman named Emma Lopez," I said.

"Lopez? I'm guessing that last name is no coincidence." Her tone had gone way past wary. She sounded downright hostile now.

Why? But then I understood. "You know who Emma is, don't you?"

"I know my husband had a period of time when he was weak. He had a problem with . . . Well, you obviously don't need me to tell you what you already know. How much money does this girl want to remain silent about my late husband's indiscretion? Because I don't want his memory sullied."

"Trust me. This isn't about money." I sure didn't blame her for being upset, but she hadn't heard the worst yet.

"What do you want, then?" she said. "Because everyone wants something."

"To warn you." I continued before she could interrupt. "As I said, I'm a private investigator, but what I didn't say is that I specialize in adoption searches. I recently took on a case that I hoped would lead to finding a child who had either been placed in foster care or adopted out by CPS fifteen years ago. That child was Emma's sister. Events turned tragic very quickly, however, and Emma Lopez's life story will be on national television next month—due to a situation that has nothing to do with your late husband, by the way. But his name is certain to be mentioned, and the photo she has of her father will also be aired. She wanted you to know, wanted you to be prepared for the publicity."

Silence followed. A long silence. Finally I said, "Are you still there, Mrs. Wilks?"

"Why would she do this for me? We've never even met."

"Because she's a considerate, sensitive young woman," I said quietly.

"And she doesn't want more money?"

"*More* money? Now I'm confused."

Gloria Wilks sighed heavily. "Before Xavier was blown to bits by those contemptible terrorists, he sent me a letter, told me to take care of Emma should anything happen to him. He hated Beirut. With the violence escalating, I think he knew he'd die there."

"Take care of Emma how?" I'd assumed he bought the house before he left the country.

"He told me he bought her a house and set up a trust to cover the yearly taxes and insurance, but he'd only had enough money to purchase a place in a poverty-stricken neighborhood. He wanted her to have as much as we could offer. After he died, I sent what money I could to Emma's mother for her care. But about ten years ago, the checks stopped being cashed, so I stopped sending them."

"That's about the time Emma was placed in foster care and the house was empty," I said. "You see, Emma's mother abandoned her and her brothers and sister."

A small silence this time. "Th-that would have upset Xavier very much. Maybe I should have tried harder to find out why the money was returned . . . but—"

"You don't need to explain. But one thing you could do now might help Emma more than anything. Maybe she could meet her half brothers." Why I said this, I didn't know. Guess I'm a reunion junkie.

"B-but they don't know about her," Gloria Lopez said quickly.

I'd obviously pressed her panic button. "You never told them?"

"I foolishly thought I could keep this secret from them forever. Another mistake."

"They might like to meet her, too," I said.

"But if I tell them about Emma, that would mean they'd discover their father wasn't quite so heroic when it came to his family. He betrayed us. I forgave him before he died, but I don't want my sons to know what their father did. Can you understand that?"

"Not really. They're adults. And they'll probably find out anyway, now that Xavier Lopez's name and picture will be on national TV."

"You're right, of course," she said.

"You'll tell them, then?"

"I have to, don't I? Now please, if you would, tell me all about this television program and what's happened to Emma these last ten years. I'm really not as self-serving as you probably think."

Later that afternoon, I decided to check on Emma, see if she needed anything. When I arrived at her suite, I was recruited to take Shannon to dance class and pick up Luke from football practice. I was glad to help.

Thirty minutes later I returned to the hotel with a dirty adolescent who hardly fit in the front seat of my car—but since Luke had me laughing nonstop with his corny jokes, the grime wasn't an issue.

Their new temporary home was the Renault Hotel near the George Brown Convention Center. They had a huge suite with two bedrooms, a small kitchen and a roomy living-dining area. There were wood floors and Oriental rugs, not to mention a wet bar. Very nice, as Venture had promised.

Luke told me on the drive to the Renault that Shannon and Emma were staying in one bedroom, and he had a big room all to himself. He even had his own shower—a first. So after we arrived, Luke kissed Emma hello, grabbed four bananas and about ten granola bars from the kitchenette and retreated to his new sanctuary. Emma told me there was a television with an Xbox in there as well, and we knew we wouldn't be seeing him anytime soon.

Emma smiled from her spot on the reclining sofa after he shut his door. "Thanks for doing taxi duty. I wasn't even sure Shannon would make her class."

"One of the moms who saw us arrive at the dance studio said she'd bring her back here and drive her next week, if necessary. Nice lady." I sat in the armchair alongside Emma, a cushy chair I could really sink into. "How are you feeling?"

"Not as sore as this morning, and my shoulder only yells at me when I wiggle my hand." Her left arm was still restrained against her body by a wide elastic contraption that also crisscrossed over her good shoulder.

"Ouch," I said with a sympathetic grimace. "You taking something for the pain?"

"It doesn't hurt that much, Abby. I feel like I had a bad fall, that's all."

"If you say so. And no one from Venture has come by?"

"They've called three times. Paul Kravitz phoned. He said he'd be here at nine o'clock tomorrow morning. Can you come?"

"Wouldn't miss it. We caught a break, pardon the pun, with the accident. I've had time to get a jump start on the investigation. DeShay Peters, my boyfriend's partner, is already helping me with your case."

"What kind of help?" she asked.

"What should have been done by someone when your mother abandoned you. We hope to find your mother."

Emma paled, her skin taking on that greenish color I remembered from yesterday. "Did we talk about you finding her? I was so stressed yesterday I don't remember. I don't want her back in our lives, Abby."

"You may have no choice, Emma. The police can't forget they found those bones under your house. They have to pursue this and that means looking into her disappearance so they can ask her a few important questions."

"If you find her, you'll turn her over to the police?"

"Absolutely. If you don't want me to follow up on this, I can leave it to HPD. But I promise you, *Crime Time* will be searching for her, too—probably already is. She has to be held accountable, not only for abandoning you and your brothers and sister, but for what she may have done to that baby." *Held accountable even if she's incapacitated or dead,* I thought.

Emma rubbed her upper left arm, head bowed. "You think you can find her faster than the police or the television investigators?"

"I don't know about Paul Kravitz's team, and I'll need HPD's help, but I'll only be working your case, while the police will be dividing their time between who knows how many homicides? Police and PIs have to work together sometimes—not that they always like the arrangement."

"I-I'd rather you find her before anyone else does," Emma said.

"Okay. That's settled." For a moment I debated whether to mention my conversation with Gloria Wilks or my knowledge of Emma's half brothers. But she was already having a hard time with the information I'd just given her. Best to wait. Instead I said, "Anything else I can get you before we move on? You hungry? Need ice for your shoulder?"

"There is something, actually. I could use Kate's help telling Luke and Shannon about the . . . bones, because I don't even know where to begin."

"You haven't told them?" I tried not to sound shocked. The headline in the city section of the *Chronicle* this morning had been, "*Reality Check* Gets a Reality Check."

"They were awfully upset about my accident. Once they knew I'd be fine, they felt free to be excited about staying in such a nice place. I didn't want to ruin that for them."

"But someone else *will* tell them, Emma. Maybe they've heard already and are keeping quiet to protect your feelings." I checked my watch. Five o'clock. Kate might be between sessions right now. "Let me call Kate, see if she can drop by here on her way home."

I used my cell to call her office. Sure enough, she was available. "Hi, there," I said. "Need a favor."

"I will do anything but pick up corn chips for your Frito pie dinner."

She had her sense of humor back only three days after the split from Terry. Good progress. "After your last client, could you pay Emma, Shannon and Luke a visit? Emma needs to tell them about what happened yesterday and could use some support."

Kate didn't say anything for a few seconds. "Um, sure. I had dinner plans but I'll cancel them."

"Dinner plans? Is it business?" The only person Kate ever went out to dinner with was Terry, me or, on occasion, another therapist.

"No, not business, but Emma is more important. Tell her I'll be at the hotel at seven o'clock, if that works."

"Seven?" I said to Emma, who nodded. "Seven it is, Kate. Guess I'll see you tonight—unless you change your plans and have a late-night dinner?" I was probing.

She knew it and laughed. "If I'll be late, I'll check in with you first, Mommy."

She hung up and I folded my phone closed, still wondering what she was up to.

"Kate shouldn't have changed her plans," Emma said. "Now I feel guilty."

"Kate does what she thinks is right. I've learned not to argue with her, and so should you. Now, back to business. Exactly how did your mother support you when she was still around?" From what Gloria Wilks had told me during our long conversation, she couldn't afford to send much back in the nineties before she remarried.

"Mom cleaned houses. She advertised by posting flyers on telephone poles or trees and always got paid in cash, which I realized later was so she didn't have to report the income. I don't know how many times I helped her make signs and put them up. She hardly knew how to write."

"She have any other jobs?"

"Drinking. Kept her real busy, too," Emma said sourly.

"Probably be difficult to locate any of the people she cleaned for. She have any friends?"

"She did, but I never met any of them except the boyfriends—and they're a blur. After the baby, well . . . went away, she didn't bring men home anymore. That doesn't mean she didn't have men friends. I'm sure she did, but she kept them away from us. She still binged, though. After a while I wished she'd stay gone. Finally that's exactly what happened—and I felt as guilty as hell."

"Not your fault, Emma," I said softly.

"Intellectually, I understand that. But here?" She pointed to her heart. "Here I still feel I'm to blame for her screwed-up existence. Maybe if I'd never been born—"

"Hold on. Kate tells me all the time how kids take on their parents' problems, adult issues that have nothing to do with them. From what I know about alcoholics, they always promise to stop drinking, but they *never* promise to stop lying. And lying trumps everything."

Emma's gaze met mine for the first time since we started talking about her mother. "You're right. My mother was first and foremost a liar—she even lied to herself."

"You ever recall her being arrested?" I asked. "That might be a way to track her down."

She shook her head no. "But she could have been in jail some of those times she left for days and days. She knew how to raise all kinds of hell at home, so why not in public?"

"The freelance housecleaning angle will be a near-impossible trail to pick up, but a check on drunk-and-disorderly arrests might be a place to start."

"One more thing—don't know if it will help. She had some regular housecleaning customers over the years. Right before she disappeared, she told me she and a friend planned to save up and open their own cleaning agency. She said nobody with money stayed home anymore and they needed housekeepers. She even had a name for the new business—Happy Homes. Like my mother could create a happy home for *anyone*."

"But you don't recall this friend's name?"

"Sorry, no. But if I remember right, it was a woman, someone she teamed with on the bigger cleaning jobs."

"I could use a snapshot of your mother in case I get a lead," I said.

"I threw away most of her pictures. That sounds terrible, doesn't it?"

"Not to me. You do what you have to do to make peace with the past. You did leave a family photo with me. I'll scan it into my computer and use Photoshop, restore some color and get her headshot from that."

Emma closed her eyes, sighing heavily. "This is getting so complicated. Thanks for taking me and my problems on. This isn't exactly about finding the lost relatives of adopted people. That's the kind of work you usually do, right?"

"Let me explain something. Not long after my daddy died of a heart attack, and after my difficult divorce, my kind and gentle yardman was murdered on my property—while I slept away the day by my fancy swimming pool."

Emma's eyes widened. "How awful."

"That man's death was a huge wake-up call, made me realize I'd been a shallow, spoiled brat most of my life. I soon discovered that if I dug deep, a real human being resided inside, and that person could actually do a little bit of good for deserving people. I'm in this business for the long haul, for folks like you." Again I was tempted to tell her that this case *was* about finding lost relatives—that I'd already found two of hers, but she was tired and, despite her protests to the contrary, probably in pain. It could wait.

9

After I drove home from Emma's hotel, I fed the animals, nuked a frozen pizza and left the box on the kitchen counter so Kate could see I'd chosen veggie supreme over pepperoni—because she *would* notice. Then I undressed and slipped into one of Jeff's shirts from the dry-cleaning pile. I needed to at least smell him if I couldn't touch him.

Then I went to my office to Google Happy Homes and see if Christine O'Meara somehow managed to sober up and make her dream of opening her own cleaning agency come true. Not in this area, I learned after searching the online yellow pages. I did find companies by that name throughout the rest of the country, though, and printed the list thinking I might call up a few of the out-of-staters tomorrow during business hours. Maybe Christine O'Meara had made a new life outside Texas. Satisfied I'd put in a full day and more on the case—my gosh, was it only Tuesday?—I poured myself a glass of chardonnay, curled up on the sofa along with Diva and called Jeff.

He answered after the phone rang a long time. "Hi, Abby," he said.

"You sound out of breath. You busy?" I said.

"Can I call you back later tonight—say around eleven your time?" He was talking fast—a rare thing for him—and he sounded . . . what was a good word? Stressed. Yes. Stressed.

"Are you okay, Jeff?" I said.

"I'm fine. Talk to you later. Love you."

"Love you, too. Bye." But right before the line went dead I thought I heard a woman cry out.

I looked at the phone for a second, as if it could clue me in on what I'd heard. The cry had been guttural, unpleasant, and might still be going on up there in Seattle. *What the hell?*

I needed an escape from my own thoughts or I'd be obsessing all evening about this new mystery. I picked up the TV remote and turned on Animal Planet, but then I heard the back door open. I checked my watch. Eight. Kate hadn't spent all that much time at—

"Abby? It's me," called a familiar but unwelcome voice that did not belong to my sister. Aunt Caroline.

I hit the power button and dropped the remote, thinking, *Great. No escape to Animal Planet possible now.* I stood to greet her, knowing I'd be transported against my will to Meddlesome, Egotistical, Self-Serving Relatives Planet—somewhere most people are lucky enough to visit only during the holidays. Though deep down I loved my aunt, she had kept important secrets about our past from Kate and me—facts about our adoption. She thought this was best, but Kate and I still beg to differ.

Aunt Caroline looked me up and down. "Are you and Kate having a pajama party to celebrate her foolishness?" Her tone was angry, her face-lift-afflicted mouth attempting—and not succeeding in—a frown. Instead, she was left fighting a ridiculous half-smile.

"Good to see you, too, Aunt Caroline. Come in—Oh, excuse me. You already did that without even knocking."

"I'm in no mood for your sarcasm, Abigail. Now where is she?" She glanced past me in the direction of the front foyer and stairs, then marched across the living room, apparently ready to tear Kate out of a closet or some other hiding place.

"She's not here," I called after her.

Aunt Caroline faced me. "You're lying. Terry told me she came here and I—"

"She's working," I said firmly. But I cringed inwardly. If she'd talked to Terry, Kate had a passel of hassles coming her way.

"Shame on you, Abigail. You're trying to protect her

from me—from *me*. The person who gave you girls everything when you were growing up, the person your sister should have come to for advice before she made such a stupid decision."

"I'm not—"

"No more lies," she said. "After Terry told me what she'd done, I called her office. Her receptionist told me she has left for the day, so she is *not* working."

"I'm telling you, she's not here." I enunciated each word, thinking Aunt Caroline must have had one too many martinis before dinner, because she seemed to be ignoring what I was saying more than usual.

She flicked at imaginary lint on the sleeve of her jade silk warm-up. "Get her down here. Right now."

"She's seeing one of my clients at a downtown hotel, but go upstairs and check if it makes you feel better." I sat back down and showed great restraint by sipping my wine rather than downing the whole glass in one gulp.

"I see. Then I'll wait." She sat at the opposite end of the sofa from me, folded her arms across her chest and crossed her legs.

My seventy-year-old aunt is a woman who probably insists the doctor retouch her X-rays, so, as expected, every white hair was in place, her warm-up was fresh from the dry cleaners and her nails were newly manicured. But I could tell that right now she was a mess on the inside. I hadn't seen her this upset since Kate and I sold Daddy's mansion in River Oaks. Daddy had been her brother and the only man who could handle her— *ever*. I wished he were here now. I'd even settle for his ghost.

"Can I get you a glass of wine?" I asked.

"I thought you'd never ask. Then you can tell me what on God's green earth has gotten into Katherine."

I took several deep breaths on my slow walk to get her drink. I should have known Kate hadn't called Aunt Caroline and told her she'd broken it off with Terry— Terry, the most perfect man in the world for Kate, according to my aunt. As for my choice, Jeff? Though "extremely good-looking," in Aunt Caroline's estimation, Jeff hung around thugs and killers day and night. And I, Abby Rose, had been lured into a similarly unsavory profession. One day we would both fall victim to the consequences of "cavorting with criminals" if we continued our line of work.

On days like today, I'd like to cavort my aunt right out the door. But Kate and I are all she's got in this world—she's driven most everyone else away—so we're stuck with her. Besides, Daddy wouldn't have wanted us to abandon her. Your family *is* your family, intimidating personalities and all.

I deflected her questions for the next half hour, deciding that Kate would have to provide the details of her breakup. Then we were blessedly interrupted by the doorbell.

I checked the security monitor and saw a well-dressed man standing on the stoop. Probably some new Venture producer. I called out to Aunt Caroline, saying, "Would you mind answering while I run up and get dressed?"

She came out into the foyer, smoothing out the wrinkles in her warm-up pants. "Are you expecting someone?"

"No, but I probably need to talk to this guy." I wasn't about to explain my new case to Aunt Caroline. I always avoided talking to her about work.

Leaving her sputtering several *but*s, I ran up the stairs and threw on jeans and a T-shirt. Animal Planet seemed like a kingdom far, far away now.

When I came back down, Aunt Caroline was blocking a crack in the door and saying, "You must have the wrong address, and if you persist in—"

"Aunt Caroline, step aside, please." Had to be Venture.

The forty-something man in the charcoal business suit—a trim, *hot* forty-something guy—was no one I recognized from my few dealings with Venture.

"Can I help you?" I asked.

He smiled. Dimples. *Jeez.* Who knew dimples and salt-and-pepper hair could look so good together?

"My name is Clinton Roark, and I was supposed to meet Kate Rose here. But it seems I've made a mistake. Do you know if she lives on this block?"

I turned and gave Aunt Caroline the stink eye for

lying to this guy, then said to Clinton Roark, "Kate's not home yet. Are you a colleague?" He could be a therapist. He had those soft, probing brown eyes that shrinks use to their advantage—or at least, Kate does.

"Actually, we met this afternoon. I'm a pharmaceutical rep and—"

"Come in and wait for her. I'll call and see how long she'll be. I'm her sister, Abby, by the way, and this is Caroline Rose, my aunt." Aunt Caroline had recently taken back her maiden name, saying she never intended to change it again with three failed marriages and a half dozen dead relationships on her tab.

Roark entered the foyer and held out a hand to my aunt. "Nice to meet you, Ms. Rose."

Aunt Caroline crossed her arms over her chest and stepped back, ignoring his outstretched hand. "Are you here to take my niece on a date only three days after she's nearly destroyed the most meaningful—"

"Aunt Caroline," I said sharply, then smiled at Roark. "Will you excuse us for a second?"

I took Aunt Caroline's elbow, swung her around, pulled her into the living room and whispered, "What in hell do you think you're doing?"

"Kate's lost her mind, Abigail. We have to protect her from herself."

"No, we don't. You have no idea what this is about. If and when Kate wants to discuss this with you, then you can offer your opinion."

"But—"

"Think about it," I said. "Do you want to share details about Kate's private life with a stranger?"

Aunt Caroline pursed her lips, looking down at her gold-trimmed tennis shoes. "I suppose you're right." She pointed at me. "But you tell your sister she has a lot of explaining to do. And now, I'm sick at the sight of this man and worried about what Kate has done. I'm leaving."

She hurried off toward the kitchen, knocking her knee on the antique trunk that served as a coffee table. I think I heard a "Dammit all to hell" before she slammed the back door on her way out.

I returned to the foyer with another smile for Clinton Roark. Anyone who could send my aunt packing had already scored points in my book.

"Sorry about that. My aunt can't always weigh the facts because her scales are full of opinions. We're used to her, but I know she can be scary."

Clinton laughed. "She sounds protective, that's all."

"Right. Sort of like a scarecrow is protective. But you want to know about Kate. She's out on a case of mine and—"

"I know. She said you're a detective." He looked me up and down appreciatively. "I have to say, you don't look like any private investigator I could ever imagine."

My cheeks grew hot. "I don't wear the trench coat and fedora at home. Anyway, what time did she say she'd meet you?"

"Eight thirty." He glanced at his watch—a TAG Heuer. Drug reps must make good money.

"You want to come in and wait?" I asked.

"Do you mind?"

"Not at all." I led him into the living room, appreciating his cologne, which was subtle and probably cost as much as his watch. "Meanwhile, I'll call Kate."

He sat in one of the overstuffed chairs. "I tried her about ten minutes ago and got her voice mail."

Webster came prancing out from his spot under the kitchen table. He must have felt safe now that Aunt Caroline had left, and maybe the sound of a man's voice got his hopes up that Terry had arrived to take him home. Webster adores Terry.

Roark put out his hand for Webster to sniff, and when the dog's tail started wagging, he scratched Webster behind both ears.

I found the phone that had slipped between the sofa cushions and speed-dialed Kate. She answered right away.

"Hey," I said. "Your friend is here."

"I'm pulling in the driveway. But he was supposed to wait for me outside."

"Hmmm. I wonder why," I said.

"Don't start, Abby. I came to a realization today. Giving advice to others can sometimes make you see how you've boxed yourself in. Anyway, no time to chat. I'm starving."

I clicked the phone off and looked at Roark. "She's here."

The back door opened, and seconds later a flushed Kate was all smiles for Clinton Roark, who had stood to greet her.

"You said you'd drive, right?" she said, ignoring me.

"Yes." But Roark didn't ignore me. "Abby, would you like to join us for dinner?"

"Oh, no. I've already eaten. But thanks."

Kate couldn't get him out of the house fast enough, leaving me a little stunned and confused. What was the girl thinking?

When Jeff called me later, I told him all about Aunt Caroline's wrath and Kate's attempt to jump out of the box and into the fire. He said he wished he could have been here to see Aunt Caroline's face, since she always put on a good show.

"I wish you were here, too, but not for that reason," I said. "How much longer will you be gone?"

"I can't give you an answer. I'm not finished with what I came to do. And Abby, thanks for not asking me the million questions I know you've been wanting to. Your giving me this space and time without asking for details means a lot."

"Hey, no problem. You'll tell me when you're ready." I was glad I hadn't started our conversation with a question about the woman I'd heard cry out before he hung up last time. Who knows? Maybe he'd been in a wet Seattle parking lot and someone nearby slipped and fell.

He said, "How about your case? Any progress?"

I told him about my phone call to Gloria Wilks, my discovery that Emma had two half brothers and my plan to find Emma's mother.

"Sounds like you'll be busy," he said.

"What else would you do if this were your case, Jeff?"

"Hmm. The woman was a drunk and had to buy her drinks somewhere. Are there any bars or clubs in Emma's neighborhood?"

"I can check."

"Liquor stores are good sources of information. It

helps if you know what her drink of choice was. Many times liquor store clerks know their customers by what they drink."

"I'll ask Emma if she remembers. Thanks."

"Another thing. Since she wasn't homeless, I doubt she drank alone like a street drunk. She probably had drinking buddies. Club cocktails are expensive, but hanging out in the park sharing a bottle of Jack Daniel's isn't. Beer joints are an option, too."

"I would have never thought of pursuing leads in those places. Your job has made you quite the expert about what goes on in the streets."

"I chased a lot of drunks from under freeways and out of parks early in my career."

"Thanks. Now, changing the subject, are you tired, Jeff? You sound tired."

"Not from lack of sleep, but yes. I can't wait to get back to normal, climb into your bed after a night chasing badasses who think life is disposable—hold you, smell your hair, kiss your neck. I miss you, hon."

"I miss you, too."

"What are you wearing?" he asked.

The conversation went on from there and had nothing to with anything but us. A nice long conversation.

10

The next morning, before I went to the hotel for Emma's meeting with Kravitz, I scanned the family photo and used Photoshop to produce a decent headshot of her mother.

I had no idea what time Kate came in last night, but she'd showered and left for work without even sticking her head into my office to say good-bye. That told me she didn't want to discuss her "get back on the horse before nightfall" approach to her love life. She couldn't avoid me forever, though. We needed to talk. This was way out of character for her.

I put several of my new Christine O'Meara photos in my bag, bade farewell to the animals and left for Emma's hotel. On the way, I called DeShay and got his voice mail. I didn't leave another message. He'd get back to me when he had something on any unidentified bodies from '97 or arrest records for Christine.

When I arrived on Emma's hotel floor, Sergeant Benson was waiting for the elevator as I got off. He let the elevator leave without him when he recognized me.

The man was built like my daddy, short and stout, with a similar cheerful demeanor—like he owned a permanent smile. Nice if you can get it working homicide. He smelled like cigarettes rather than like Daddy's cigars, and had an unhealthy-looking ruddy complexion. Probably headed for a heart attack, too.

"How you doing, Ms. Rose?" he said.

"Great, Sergeant. You learn anything new to tell Emma?"

"Nope. They just finished processing the crime scene this morning. I came to check on her after her accident."

"A courtesy call?" He'd probably come for more than a medical report.

"Ah, you're a sharp one. Ms. Lopez needs to make a trip to the ME's office. I'd give her a lift but Don and I got a call. Maybe you can drive her over there."

"Did they find something identifiable about the baby's remains? Clothing, maybe?"

"Don't I wish. We gotta have an ID on the infant for court. Ms. Lopez needs her mouth swabbed for DNA to verify kinship. Has to sign up at the county morgue for the privilege or I'd take the sample myself."

"For court?" I wondered if progress had been made that he wasn't talking about.

"If we ever get there. Judges are happier when they know who the victim is for absolute certain. By the way, I hear you're working the mother angle for Ms. Lopez."

"She hired me even before the baby was found. Venture Productions may think money is all Emma cares about, but that's not true. She realized too late that they want to air information Emma would rather keep private, and I'm trying my best to run interference for her—find out about her missing mother before the production company does. Is that a problem?"

"Not for me. Girl can hire whoever she wants. But let me give you a heads-up. My partner? Very territorial. Don's got a heart of gold, but he pisses a ring around our cases. He might give you a hard time."

"That's good to know. I'll try not to step on any toes," I said.

"From what Ms. Lopez just told me, it's clear you want to help this family," he said. "But maybe you could share anything you learn with us."

"Sure. I worked with the police on a case not long ago." I held out my hand and we shook.

"Now go talk to your client," Benson said. "She was worried you wouldn't arrive before the reporter did. But he's running late—as you'd expect from someone *so* friggin' important." He grinned and jammed the elevator's down button.

A few seconds later Emma let me into her suite. She'd

switched to a simple sling to support her arm. She said, "Glad you got here first. Kravitz called and he's on his way up. Don't let me say anything I shouldn't, okay? Wink or clear your throat or do whatever you think is necessary to shut me up."

"He probably knows everything already." And probably knew about Xavier Lopez's wife and sons, too. I should have discussed this with Emma yesterday and—

My thoughts were interrupted by a staccato knock, and Emma opened the door.

I recognized Paul Kravitz at once, but he wasn't alone. Beside him was an older, petite woman, and behind them stood Stu Crowell.

Emma said, "I-I thought you were coming alone . . . to meet me first."

Nothing like a crowd of unwelcome faces when you were expecting only one. "She's not exactly up for a meeting that requires stadium seating," I said.

Kravitz smiled. "This is only a preinterview. Mr. Crowell is here to check sound and lighting as well as a number of other technical issues." Kravitz, a tall, lanky man, looked down at Emma. "Good to finally speak with you in person. I can't convey how sorry I am about the circumstances that brought this story to our attention."

"I appreciate that," Emma said, sounding wary. She nodded at me. "This is Abby Rose. She's a—"

"Private detective. I know." Kravitz held out his hand. The man was skeletally thin, and I was sure I felt all hundred-something bones in his hand when we shook. He wore a sports jacket, crewneck shirt and worn jeans.

I turned to the woman Kravitz had failed to introduce. "Nice to meet you. I'm Abby."

"Sandy Sechrest." She smiled warmly. Judging by the age lines on her square face, I'd say she was in her late fifties, early sixties. She carried a black suitcase—briefcase size, only thicker—that bore her gold initials.

Emma led the way into the living area.

Kravitz said, "Stu, where should we set up?"

Emma, who seemed bewildered by this invasion, said, "I don't understand. You said you wouldn't be taping today. You said—"

Stu cut her off. "The armchair will work. We can close the drapes, turn on the lamp. Create a nice soft look for Emma."

"Sandy, will that work?" Kravitz asked.

The woman nodded.

"Sandy is our makeup artist," Kravitz said. "We want to see how you'll appear on tape, but I have a feeling you won't need much help. Your skin is perfect and you won't wash out."

"You promised we'd talk first and tape later." Emma's jaw was tight, her words clipped.

"We won't use anything we tape today on the air," Kravitz said. "I have another story in Ohio to wrap up. I need an initial interview, will take the tape with me and go over your story. I'll only be gone a few days."

Emma lowered herself onto the sofa—not the chair Stu had chosen. "Why can't anyone be straight with me? You hide information from the beginning, say one thing and do another; then you come here after promising—"

"I wasn't the one who hid information from you." Kravitz took one of the leather chairs across from the sofa. Stu, meanwhile, was opening and closing the drapes, checking out the dining area, no doubt deciding if there was a better option than his first choice for the taping.

Sandy Sechrest took the other armchair next to Kravitz while I sat next to Emma, a glass coffee table between us. A white china coffeepot, three mugs and various pastries rested on a silver tray. The sweet cinnamon smell hit me in an unexpected way, reminding me how much I missed Jeff and his ever-present Big Red gum. How would Jeff handle Paul Kravitz?

"Listen, Paul—I can call you Paul, right?" I said, taking in Kravitz more fully. If I'd met this guy on the street, I might have thought he'd recently had chemotherapy. On the tube he looked distinguished and sharp. In person, without makeup and lights, he had charcoal shadows beneath his eyes and his posture spoke of fatigue. I guessed his ash brown hair had been dyed, because the stubble on his clefted chin was steel gray.

"I think first names are a good start toward building

a relationship." Kravitz looked at Emma. "Is that okay with you?"

She nodded.

I said, "Emma's interactions with Venture haven't gone well since she learned that her missing baby sister was mentioned in the anonymous letter *Reality Check* received."

"I heard about that from Erwin," Kravitz said. "I would have handled things differently, but from what he told me, not telling her the full contents of the letter was an oversight. He had no reason to withhold information."

Emma said, "I don't believe you. The man's a controlling, egotistical—"

I rested a hand on her arm. "An apology from Mr. Mayo would go a long way."

Kravitz laughed. "Erwin believes apologies might possibly be redeemable for cash in the future; thus he holds on to them. Never heard him apologize for one damn thing. But if it helps, I'm sorry you weren't fully informed."

Ah, the charming Paul Kravitz, the one I knew from TV, had appeared.

Emma repositioned her arm with a grimace and leaned back against the sofa. "I should have been told what was in the letter before I signed the contract."

Kravitz nodded. "You're absolutely right—but legally, *Reality Check* was under no obligation." He reached inside his sports jacket and pulled out a folded piece of paper. "Would it help if you saw a copy?"

I sat up straighter and held out my hand. "You're damn right it would."

He passed the letter to me and I unfolded it so Emma and I could read it together. Meanwhile, Kravitz motioned to Stu to come closer.

The letter had been written on lined notebook paper in a lefty back-slanting style. It read:

Someone good for your show is Emma Lopez in Houston. She's a good girl and works so hard. Her mother used to leave her to take care of everything lots of

*times. Then CPS took Emma and the other kids.
When she was sixteen Emma was raising her brothers
and sister herself. Still is. I been watching her and
she doesn't know about me. They have a little house
in Crystal Grove, this falling down place. Your show
helps strong, good people like Emma. She's so beautiful and puts everyone ahead of her. Her mother
had another baby that disappeared right after it was
born in 1992. Maybe you could find this other kid
for Emma, 'cause she'd want to know where the
baby went. You don't need my name. Please just
help Emma.*

I looked at Kravitz. "This is all they had to go on
when they decided to sign Emma for *Reality Check*?" I
noticed that Sandy had put her case on her lap and
opened it to reveal dozens of pots of makeup as well as
brushes, foam wedges, and Q-tips.

He said, "The research team does extensive work before they decide on a deserving family. We've learned
pretty much everything about Emma." His gray eyes
stared straight into mine. "*Everything*. We didn't antici-
pate the discovery of the bones, however. How could
we?"

"Do you think I did?" Emma said almost to herself.
She was staring at the letter I'd put down.

I poured myself a mug of coffee, thinking I understood Kravitz's unspoken message. He knew about Gloria Wilks and her sons.

Kravitz said, "This begins our preinterview, Emma.
First Sandy will dust you up with some makeup, enough
to take away any shine. Then Stu will roll—but again, I
promise you, none of this tape will be used by anyone
except me. I will study the preinterview and decide if
I'm going in the right direction. The actual interview will
be far more thorough. Our investigators are still working
in case the *Reality Check* researchers missed anything."

"Forgive my paranoia, but I want your promise in
writing not to use any of this preinterview," Emma said.

I swallowed my second sip of the truly disgusting coffee and set down my mug. "Good idea. I'll get some
paper."

While Sandy went to work on Emma, and Stu moved the chair she'd vacated to a different position with the lamp table beside it, I made up a minicontract on hotel stationery.

Kravitz, looking amused, signed it willingly. I served as a witness. Emma then moved over to the chair, looking more relaxed than I'd seen her all morning. Having a morsel of control seemed to have helped.

Kravitz told Stu to roll and said, "Emma, do you recognize the handwriting in the letter I just showed you?"

"No."

"We have a handwriting expert examining the original. The person who wrote this is either left-handed and uneducated or they were faking one or both of those traits," Kravitz said. "Does that information help you in any way identify the person who wrote it?"

"No," Emma said.

I probably wasn't supposed to say anything, but I did anyway. "Shouldn't the police be given the original? Maybe the letter writer knows more about the baby's disappearance. There could be DNA or fingerprints and—"

"Close to twenty people have handled that letter since we received it. I doubt there's any usable evidence." Kravitz didn't seem bothered by my interruption; in fact, he seemed to welcome it. "Besides, the police haven't asked for anything from us yet."

"Right," I said with more than a tinge of sarcasm. "And why give up anything without a request?"

"I was a print journalist before *Crime Time*. Forgive me if I've learned to keep information to myself. Offering to let Emma see the letter is a good-faith gesture," he said evenly.

"And I *am* grateful," Emma said. "Seeing the words in black and white is very different from hearing about this from Mr. Mayo. It seems much more real. Someone knew all about us. Someone was watching. But I can't think who that could have been."

"You have no clue?" Kravitz said.

"None. No one knew about the baby but me and my—" Emma's free hand flew to her lips. "Oh, my God. My mother."

Kravitz's satisfied smile told me he'd gotten exactly what he wanted by producing that letter.

"You think Emma's mother sent this?" I asked Kravitz. I was angry with myself. I hadn't seen this coming.

"Could there be a more logical person? She may have abandoned her family, but we're betting she hung around, checked up on you and your siblings, and when guilt got the better of her, she sent this to *Reality Check*." He gestured at the letter.

I nodded. "Makes for a great story. Doesn't quite explain the baby under the house, though."

"In my experience interviewing more than a hundred criminals, I've come to understand that many of them want to be caught—their conscience at work, when they have one. Emma's mother is probably no exception. She sent the letter, subconsciously hoping we'd track her down."

This wasn't working for me. Why did Christine O'Meara wait five years to disappear after the baby's death? And I didn't buy that she'd want to draw attention to a crime she may have committed, subconsciously or not. However, I decided not to question Paul Kravitz on these points. I liked him better than Chelsea or Mayo, but he sure hadn't earned my trust yet.

Emma looked at me. "If my mother wrote the letter, that would mean she cared at least a tiny bit about us, wouldn't it, Abby?"

"Do *not* get your hopes up about that," I answered. "Think about it, Emma. Are you ready for a reunion with her while America watches? Because that's what they're setting you up for."

Emma closed her eyes. "No, no—"

"Abby, Abby, Abby," cut in Kravitz. "You have no idea how we work. We're here to help solve a mystery."

Sandy, who had been watching us all carefully, looked at Emma and said, "I've done makeup with Paul for years. He wants the truth; that's all."

I could tell Sandy believed that. It was nice to have a normal, self-possessed grandmother type in the room. She was so un-Hollywood.

Emma said, "Can we finish this?"

"Tell me what you know about your father," Kravitz said.

Emma started right in, happy to talk about this subject.

"So," Kravitz said when she'd finished telling him how he'd left her the house and the trust, "you never tried to find your extended family?"

Emma's eyes hardened. "I did. But when I found out my father was married when he died, I took it no further."

"You know about Gloria Wilks, your father's widow?" he said.

"She knows," I said. "What does Mrs. Wilks have to do with any of this?"

"Don't know yet," said Kravitz. "Maybe nothing. But background is important."

"I didn't even know her new married name," Emma said. "I didn't want to know."

"You didn't want to meet Xavier Lopez's sons?" Kravitz said.

Despite Sandy's great makeup job, Emma's face paled, making the patches of color on her cheeks look like brush burns. But she recovered quickly. "Now that this story has become a hunt to find out what happened to my sister, I don't see how meeting my brothers has any relevance. My father died long before the trouble with my mother, and I'd like him left out of all this."

"I need every morsel of information I can collect, whether it turns out to be relevant or not," Kravitz said.

"But—" Emma started.

He held up one of those long, skinny hands. "Let me finish. We may never use this part of your history. But I won't put that in writing."

A short, tense silence followed, Emma's gaze trailing back to the letter.

Kravitz said, "Sandy, what kind of vibe are you getting from Emma? How do you think our viewers will receive her?"

Sandy smiled at Emma. "She's well-spoken, which you would expect from such an intelligent young woman, and you know as well as I do that the camera will love her.

She will come across as very sympathetic, because, well, she is."

"I agree," Kravitz said. "Now, I'd like to hear about your sister's birth, her disappearance and all that followed. Forget about the camera. Just start talking."

Emma had repeated the story so many times this week, her words ran together. She also lost focus more than once, and I had to help her get back on track. She was probably unnerved to have her half brothers brought up. I blamed myself for that. I should have felt her out before these people ever showed up.

When Emma was finished talking, Kravitz stood. "You're looking overwhelmed, but you've given me good ideas on how to present this mystery to the public. I'll keep you up to speed on the next steps, report anything new I might learn from the police."

Telling Emma not to get up, I walked them to the door and out into the hallway. Stu and Sandy went on to the elevator after I asked to speak to Kravitz alone.

"Why'd you have to bring up the brothers?" I said.

"All the facts should be on the table. That's the way I work. Did she even know about them?"

"I don't know, but wasn't it obvious she wants her father's family out of the loop? They don't need to be dragged into this mess."

"No promises on that, Abby."

"You're pushing, Paul. The girl's been traumatized enough in the last few days, and now you want to pile on something more?"

"No one tortured her into signing that contract," he said. "Remember that the next time you're feeling sorry for your client." He turned and strode off to join Sandy and Stu.

I knocked on the suite door and Emma let me back in.

"That wasn't as bad as I'd anticipated," she said.

Oh, yes, it was, I thought. "Did you know about your half brothers?"

"You probably read the same obituary I did," Emma said.

"Why didn't you say something?" I said.

"Discovering my father was married was bad enough. I didn't want to picture him with his family. See, I had this little private dream that if he'd lived, he would have come back to us and everything would have been different. No drinking, no babies born in bathtubs, no—"

"And maybe he would have rescued you, but you'll never know," I said softly.

"H-he never got the chance to tell me the truth, and for some reason, I believe he would have. A girl's got to have something to hang on to, right?" Her eyes were bright with tears. "Thanks for talking to Mrs. Wilks for me. The last thing I want is to intrude on her life. I can only hope Paul Kravitz agrees there's no story there and stays away."

I smiled, resting a hand on Emma's good shoulder. "You spoke your mind, and that's all you could do. You know, I'm learning a lot from how you handle things. You're tough. And now I believe you need a ride to the county morgue."

She smiled. "How did you know?"

"I'm a detective, of course."

11

After Emma signed a release at the morgue and had her mouth swabbed for a DNA sample, I drove her back to her hotel. I was on my way home when DeShay called and asked me to meet him at the House of Pies on Kirby.

When I walked into the diner—House of Pies isn't only about dessert—I was never so grateful for the combined odors of baking pies and greasy hamburgers. I'd always loved this restaurant, not only because they have about forty different desserts on the menu, but because the thin neon-red tube lights bordering the mirrored back wall, the mismatched Tiffany light fixtures and the sixties-style wallpaper were so gaudy and wonderful all at the same time. Open twenty-four/seven, this relic must be an ideal place for homicide cops who often worked nonstop on a case.

DeShay waved to me from the back of the small restaurant, and seconds later I slid into an ancient two-seater booth. "Feels like that morgue smell is still clinging to me like cobwebs," I said.

"All in your head, Abby, my girl. You smell like you always do. Delicious. Almost as delicious as this." He picked up his fork and dug into a humongous slice of fresh apple pie.

A maroon-clad waitress appeared and took my order. Her apron and the gray-trimmed uniform pockets and collar matched the retro atmosphere. I scanned the place mat that served as the pie menu and went with lemon meringue—even though strawberry cheesecake would have tasted oh-so-wonderful in all its twice-as-many-calories splendor. With Jeff not around to kick me out of bed and into my running shoes every morning, I hadn't been exercising, and reckless cheesecake intake requires plenty of exercise.

"Was that your first time at the morgue?" DeShay loaded up his fork again.

"Yes. Took us only a half hour, but that was about twenty-five minutes too long. Apparently they had a decomp and decomps stink up even the office areas."

"Indeed they do," he said, still attacking his pie and doing plenty of damage.

"When you told me to meet you here, I thought I'd be chewing Tums and not eating. But pie is a healing food, right?"

"Thinking like that, I'd say you're almost a cop, Abby." DeShay grinned.

My lemon meringue slice and a stoneware mug of coffee arrived and we ate in silence for a while, both of us lost in pie heaven. Once I'd wiped out half the dessert, I said, "I take it you found out something about Christine O'Meara?"

"We did," he said.

"We?"

"I told you this isn't my case," DeShay said. "The more I thought about it, I knew I had to talk to Don White, tell him what you wanted me to check on. Guy wasn't too happy, but that's nothing I didn't expect."

"Sorry," I said.

"Don't be. People like Emma hire PIs, and the PIs do their job. Simple as that. Fact is, he's more focused on the baby's death than the mother's disappearance right now. Even gave me the go-ahead to research Christine, though he grumbled long and hard."

"I apologize for putting you in that position. I realize you have to work with those guys every day."

"You think I care if that old fart White wants to whine?" DeShay said.

"Obviously you don't," I said with a smile. "What did you find out?"

He shoveled in several mouthfuls before he said, "Christine O'Meara was arrested once. Picked up for loitering along with several other *ladies*."

"She was a prostitute as well as a drunk?" I hoped Emma was unaware, if this were true.

"I don't think so. If she was a true pro, she'd have a distinguished rap sheet, but she was never arrested again."

"You're saying you got nothing useful from the arrest report?"

"She was picked up on South Main back when the city was trying to clean up that area. Astrodome-goers didn't appreciate their kids seeing women wearing postage-stamp skirts leaning into open car windows. Maybe her being there was bad luck."

"Or she had a friend who was a prostitute?" I said.

"Or she was waiting for a bus. Or she was hanging around and looked the part, got caught in the net. The report is sketchy. Us cops are experts at sketchy. She made a deal for jail time served—a couple days—and that was it."

"You don't know who she was with when she was picked up?" I said.

"That would take some serious cross-checking of old records, use lots of my time for a questionable lead," he said.

I couldn't hide my disappointment. "Gosh, where do I go from here?"

DeShay reached into his jacket pocket and took out one of his business cards. "All is not lost, Abby girl. I did get two case numbers. Unidentified female homicide victims from 1997 who fit Christine O'Meara's description."

He held up the card and I snatched it, though I really wanted to throw my remaining pie in his face. "You always have to play around, don't you?" Along with the case numbers, I read the name he'd written on the back of the card—Julie Rappaport. There were some numbers, too.

"I love to see you when you don't get what you want," DeShay said. "Great expression. You could do movies."

"I will never so much as *visit* Hollywood," I said. "Not after meeting some of the players. What do I do with these case numbers?"

"Julie works at the ME's office, and you can talk to her about the unidentified corpses. But here's the deal. White wants whatever you get as soon as you get it. I think he was secretly grateful you'd be going there instead of him. I've heard he and Benson switch off on morgue visits and it was Don's turn. He hates that place."

"I don't blame him," I said.

"Added to that, they landed a fresh case right when I was leaving Travis. They'll be plenty busy today."

"Julie Rappaport, huh? You're sure she'll talk to me, even though I'm not a cop?"

He nodded. "Yup. She's waiting for your call. Nice little lady. Smart as hell."

"You could go with me," I said sweetly.

"I have a witness interview in about twenty minutes," he said.

"I have to go back to that place alone?" I said.

"I got one word for you. Vicks."

"What?"

He rubbed under his nose. "Right here. Vicks. Before you go in the building."

"Ah. Gotcha," I said.

I called Julie Rappaport right after I left DeShay and she told me to come to the ME's office straightaway. Turned out Julie was a skeletal remains and cold-case expert, the HCME investigator who'd worked on Emma's property when the bones were found. Not only was she the person who could help me learn whether Christine O'Meara was one of the unidentified corpses from 1997; she was working the baby case as well.

The receptionist behind the glass at the front desk remembered me from when I'd signed in earlier. Rappaport must have let her know I was coming, because she picked up the phone and made a call.

Julie came out and got me. Can't say I recognized her from the other day, maybe because she wasn't wearing fatigues. She was small—looked like a kid—and wore a black baseball cap with FORENSICS in white letters on the front and a denim jacket that had seen better days. Her dark hair was pulled back in a ponytail and brought out through the back of the cap. She smelled like bleach. I'd bet bleach was the chemical of choice in this place.

Once we were seated in her cubicle, I said, "I can't

thank you enough for agreeing to talk to me on such short notice." I hadn't had time to pick up Vicks, so I'd slathered Burt's Bees raspberry lip balm under my nose. It wasn't working. Even though this part of the building was shut off from the morgue, the smell of death hung in the air.

"No need to thank me," she said. "I got excited when you called. Any chance I can put a cold case to rest is a great day for me. We get PIs in here on occasion, but none so highly recommended. DeShay thinks a lot of you."

"That goes both ways. What have you got for me?"

"I pulled the tracking sheets on the two unidentifieds DeShay mentioned," she said.

"What are tracking sheets?"

"They tell us what's been done so far on a cold case to identify the remains, what avenues we've pursued, any subsequent evidence that was unearthed. In addition, since DNA from all unidentified bodies is entered into CODIS, we document when the DNA profile was done and submitted. What's great is that today your client, Ms. Lopez, gave us DNA for the infant bones. But we can also match her DNA against these two cold cases, see if she's related to either woman."

I nodded. "You mentioned CODIS. That's a police database, right?"

"Yes. Used all over the country. The Combined DNA Index System."

"How long will it take to see if there's a match to Emma in either case?"

"If this were a TV show, five minutes. In reality, cold cases aren't a priority when you've got fresh homicides piling up."

"Even the infant bones won't be a priority?"

"Oh, yes. We're already feeling the publicity heat on that one. The police need a positive ID to pursue leads, so we'll run a mitochondrial DNA comparison against Emma Lopez pretty quickly. Fortunately, our facility is one of very few in the U.S. that does mitochondrial. I extracted the DNA from the baby's femur myself, and we should have the results tomorrow."

"I take it that's a super-special DNA process?"

"That's right. It works only through maternal lineage."

"If the baby is Emma's sister, would that hurry up the testing on the unidentified corpses?"

"Maybe, if there was enough pressure on us and on the police, but not necessarily. Every detective, constable, Texas Ranger or DEA agent wants their DNA case to be high priority. We can't always do that. But wait." She fingered the silver wolf pendant she wore. "We would have done facial reconstructions on both of the unidentifieds." She looked down, scanned her tracking sheets. "Yes, we did. I don't know how old Emma was when her mother disappeared. Does she remember her?"

"Oh, she remembers."

"Good. Then she could look at the photos we took of those two reconstructed skulls. You have no idea how much I love a well-preserved skull. A good reconstructionist can work miracles—bring the dead to life. I see on the tracking sheet that one of the victims was murdered, shot in the back of the head, but we still had a decent specimen."

I opened my bag and took out my photo of Christine O'Meara. "Can we compare the reconstruction to this photo of Emma's mother?"

She smiled as wide as the skulls she loved so much and accepted the photo as if it were a holy artifact. "This is *great*. But I'll have to dig around and find the original files—and that won't happen until the end of the day, if I'm lucky."

I glanced at the wall of filing cabinets across the aisle from Julie's cubicle. "Looks like you have a slew of records."

"We keep everything on the cold cases and save all unidentified remains. Most people are unaware that HPD has no cold-case squad. Those men and women on the force are amazing and do what they can to solve every case, but this is a huge city with a lot of homicides. Sometimes they have to let PIs like you help. I really thank you for coming."

I hadn't expected a thank-you. In fact, I was used to resistance during my investigations, especially from government or police people. But Julie wasn't territorial

or controlling or withholding. She seemed to want answers for those left behind as badly as I did.

She went on, saying, "Heck, I just thought of something, Abby."

"What?"

"Photos of the reconstructions went to the newspaper.
The police send them to the press and to other local
police agencies. If you go to the downtown library
annex, you could research the 1997 *Houston Chronicles*.
You know the regular library is closed for remodeling?"

"Right. Can you help me narrow my search with the
dates of those deaths?"

"Sure. The tracking sheets indicate that one of these
women was found in May, the other in September. Apparently the location of the head wound on that one woman
was never released to the press. Check the Crime Stopper
columns for exactly what was printed. Searching the newspapers yourself will really speed things up."

I stood. "I'm on my way."

"If you think your picture matches one of the reconstructions, call me right away and I'll send this back to
HPD as a new lead in a cold case after I take a look
myself. With the TV show in town, identifying one of
these women as Emma Lopez's mother could move the
case up on that priority list."

Geeky little Julie Rappaport was a gem. No wonder
DeShay sent me here. I wondered if folks had a clue
what forensic investigators were *really* like. She wasn't
showing off maximum cleavage like they do on TV, and
her battered ID hung around her neck rather than her
having a shiny badge clipped to low-riding jeans. But
her heart was where it should be. At least they got something right on *CSI*. Yeah. I liked Julie. A lot.

I left and drove straight to the library, parked and
went to the research area, my jeans pocket packed with
quarters for the copier. Though the *Houston Chronicle* is
archived and easily accessible online, any accompanying
photos are available only here. I felt my heart skip a
beat when I finally found what I came looking for.

The photo I held next to the newspaper picture left
little room for doubt. There she was—Christine
O'Meara—the woman who'd been shot in the head in

September of 1997. I was amazed at what the artist had done. I didn't know whether to feel happy or sad for Emma—happy because she would know where her mother was or sad because on top of everything else, Emma might have to arrange a burial or cremation now. I swear, if that girl started selling lightbulbs, the sun would stop setting.

I sent the Crime Stopper article to the printer, still shaking my head at all this bad luck. Several minutes later, as I headed to the library parking lot, several copies of the Crime Stopper article in hand, I called Julie Rappaport.

The receptionist put me through, and I said, "Julie, it's Abby. One unidentified corpse has a name. The gunshot victim who died in September."

"That's great. Now we'll need a CODIS comparison to Emma Lopez for a positive ID—which I'm certain the police will want right away. I'll call Sergeant White, since he's the lead investigtor," she said. "Thanks so much, Abby. I would have done this myself but—"

"Don't apologize. You people have to be swamped in a county this heavily populated." After I disconnected, I decided to drop by Kate's office and once again recruit her to help me break this news to Emma, Shannon and Luke. How much more could those kids take?

The drive to the medical center took about twice as long as it should have, thanks to early rush hour. But when I found a parking spot in the lot next to Kate's building I forgave all the buses, the broken-down cars and the jerks who had to be from somewhere other than Texas because they loved to lay on their horns.

Minutes later, I walked into Kate's comfy waiting area and found Clinton Roark chatting up Kate's receptionist.

What the heck was going on? I never thought I'd weigh in on Aunt Caroline's side, but Kate needed time to get over Terry, and a new man in her life didn't seem like the best way to do that.

"Hi, Abby," Kate's receptionist said. She'd been here only a couple weeks. What was her name? April or May or June?

Roark turned and smiled at me. "We meet again. Good to see you."

I pointed at him. "Back at ya." Then I addressed springtime girl. "Is Kate still in a session?"

"She'll be out in five minutes," she answered.

I took a seat on the mauve sofa—Kate's latest icky color choice. She tells me pastels are soothing for her clients, but I could only think of Easter eggs when I walked in here, and I'm not a fan of the hard-boiled egg unless it's deviled with plenty of mayo.

I was tempted to pick up a magazine and pretend Roark wasn't there, but of course that wouldn't work, so I said, "Does Kate know you're here?"

He walked over and sat on a chair adjacent to the couch. "No. Thought I'd surprise her. I heard about this vegetarian Chinese restaurant on Westheimer and was hoping we could try it out. She's helping me convert." He patted his chest. "Heart disease runs in the family."

"She's helping you with your diet? Last I heard Kate was a shrink, not a dietician."

He laughed. "True, but I came in here yesterday by mistake—I was supposed to deliver pill samples to a doctor named Ruston. But on the board in the lobby, I saw the name Rose first, and my brain decided that's who I was supposed to see."

"Kate doesn't prescribe drugs. She's a clinical psychologist."

"I learned my mistake soon enough. Kate was out here with April and we got to talking. When I heard April was heading to some vegan place to pick up their lunch, I told Kate how interested I was in getting healthier. She offered to help me."

I nodded. "Ah, so my sister's a regular Pied Piper when it comes to luring wannabe vegetarians over to the dark side. Learn something every day." But I wasn't exactly sure who the Pied Piper was in all this—Kate or Clinton Roark.

He said, "She told me you'd be skeptical about us making this connection right after her breakup with Terry. But we're just friends, Abby."

Yeah. Friends. That was why Kate wouldn't even face me this morning. "Hey, you don't have to explain anything to me." This conversation was making me uncomfortable. I walked over to April, who was busy behind the glassed-in counter. "Tell Kate I'll talk to her later."

I started for the door, but Roark blocked my path. "Are you leaving because of me? Please don't. I can catch up with Kate another day."

"Thanks, but I have something important to do, and she seems to be running over with her client." I maneuvered around him, the scent of his cologne still with me as went to the elevator and punched the down button.

He did smell damn good, seemed nice enough. Now that I thought about it, if I got all negative about Roark to Kate, that put me squarely in Aunt Caroline's court. I shivered at the thought. If Kate liked this guy, more power to her.

The elevator dinged and the doors opened. The compartment was almost full, and I hesitated.

"You coming or what?" a woman asked.

"Go on without me." Dammit, I didn't want tension between Kate and me. Besides, I needed my sister today, needed her beside me to offer comfort to Emma and her family.

I turned around, went back to her office and found her talking with Clinton in the waiting area.

"You're back," Kate said. "Clint and April said—"

"Listen, I don't want to interfere in your social life, but I need your help tonight. I've discovered Christine O'Meara was murdered in 1997. I don't want to take this news to her family alone."

"That's awful." Kate looked up at Roark. "Do you mind if I take a rain check?"

"Of course not." Roark looked at me. "Glad you changed your mind and came back."

"Yeah, well, sometimes I'm as dumb as an unplugged computer. A cold case warmed up, and I need my sister's help before this makes the late news."

"I'll get my purse, Abby." She looked at Roark. "Call me?"

"I will." He strode across the waiting room and out the door. Kate didn't take her eyes off him until he was gone, reminding me that I never take my eyes off Jeff's backside, either. Maybe there is such a thing as love in two days—even for shrinks who should know better.

12

"Mom's dead?" Emma sat in the center of the couch at the hotel, flanked by Shannon and Luke. Luke was looking at the article copy I'd handed to Emma with the photo of their mother's reconstructed face. Kate and I sat across from them.

"Yes. She was shot," I said.

"Did she do it to herself?" Shannon said. "Because if she was drunk she could have—"

"No," Kate interrupted gently. "Abby tells me the ME's office determined from the wound location that she couldn't have killed herself."

"That's a detail they left out of the paper," I said. "Probably on purpose. They'll compare Emma's DNA to the DNA they took from your mother when her body was brought to the morgue in 1997. But as you can see, the woman in the newspaper looks exactly like her."

"I'm glad she's dead." Luke's gaze remained on the photocopy.

"Why's that?" Kate had moved the coffee table aside to be closer to them, and her knees nearly touched Emma's.

"I'm glad because she can't come back," he said. "Emma doesn't have to be afraid of that happening anymore."

"I was never afraid for myself, Luke," Emma said. "I was afraid for you, Shannon and Scott."

"Yeah, whatever," he said with a shrug. He switched his stare to the Dr Pepper can held between his knees.

Kate leaned forward. "You're looking out for your sister and I think that's really cool, but how do you feel about your mother dying in such a violent way?"

His head snapped up. "You want me to cry? 'Cause that's not gonna happen."

"I only want you to know that I care, that I'm here for you. Anytime. No one should have to deal with what's been dumped on you your entire life."

Shannon said, "Emma always says that what doesn't kill you makes you stronger. We're pretty tough, Dr. Rose."

Kate smiled. "Oh, yes. Tough and great and three of my new favorite people."

"I have homework," Shannon said. "Is it okay if I go?"

"Sure," Emma said. "How about you, Luke? You want to stay?"

"No." He jumped up and hurried to his room.

When they were gone, Emma said, "What happens next?"

"Your mother's death will become an active homicide investigation again once a positive DNA ID is made. When the ME's office is finished with her remains, you'll have to decide what to do with her."

Emma seemed to draw herself in. "I can't afford a casket or—"

"What about cremation?" I asked.

Emma didn't speak for a few moments. "The church allows it, as long as I don't deny that she'll be resurrected. That's hard to think about—her being resurrected."

Kate said, "You don't have to decide tonight."

"Mr. Kravitz and Mr. Mayo will find out about this tomorrow, won't they?" Emma said.

I nodded. "I don't know how they learn about things like this. But they'll know."

"I'm not sure I want to find out who killed her." She looked at Kate. "Does that sound crazy?"

"Not at all," Kate said. "Learning details about her murder will bring back more unpleasant memories—and you've had enough of those for a lifetime."

"I'm not afraid of the memories." Emma fell silent for a moment, her forehead creased in thought. "She must have made someone very angry."

I nodded. "Or scared them."

Emma took a moment to think before she said, "You know something? Every time I think of her I'll always have questions. I want to put an end to that for good. Abby, will you help me find out what happened?"

My reply was interrupted by my cell phone. I looked at the caller ID and saw it was DeShay. "You mind if I take this?"

"Go ahead," Emma said.

I answered the phone with, "Hey," and walked into the kitchenette. "I planned to call you after I left Emma's hotel. I met with Julie and—"

"Abby, bad news. Ed Benson had a stroke earlier today. He and White pulled a jewelry store case, and the homicide victim turned out to be a young security guard, a guy Ed knew who couldn't make it in the academy. Guess Ed's blood pressure went sky-high at the scene, and next thing you know they're calling the paramedics. He's in intensive care."

"That's awful, DeShay. Will he be okay?" I leaned against the counter.

"We don't have many details. Guess Benson was conscious but couldn't talk after he went down. Scared the shit out of Don White."

"I am so sorry. I'll send flowers tomorrow."

"I'll be filling in for Benson, and that's not exactly my dream assignment," DeShay said. "White is no Jeff Kline. He's old-school. But I was the logical choice, since I'm already up to speed on the baby case."

"What about Christine O'Meara? Because I found out—"

"Julie called me. Good work, Abby girl. Course, we have to wait on a positive ID through Emma's DNA."

"What I don't understand is why no one checked her fingerprints back then," I said. "Even if she didn't have a driver's license, you told me she'd been arrested once."

"Yeah, well, there's a reason. I just pulled the initial HPD report filed after they found her. She was a meltdown. Discovered in a field and had probably been lying there in hundred degree heat for a couple days. The corpse was no more than bones in a puddle, Abby."

I swallowed, glancing Emma's way. She was deep in conversation with Kate. "Thanks for the image. I don't think I'll be passing that along to Emma."

"When Julie called she also updated me on the infant

bones. She said there's no evidence the child suffered any traumatic injuries, at least to the bones they collected. Could have been a natural death after the home birth."

"You're saying Christine's only crime may have been not reporting the child's death?" I said.

"We don't know. But the O'Mearas' case has become a priority. We had some jerk-off TV *journalist* all over our asses today. Did he care we have a brother hanging on in the ICU? I told him where to get off, but I'm betting he's not leaving this train, Abby."

"Paul Kravitz?"

"That's him. I thought Don White might have a stroke himself when this guy showed up."

"You didn't tell Kravitz anything?" I said.

"No way. But he'll go to the higher-ups, and then we'll have the local news crawling all over us, too. I gotta say, this is a nightmare, Abby. A damn nightmare."

"Emma wants me to stay on the case, find out why her mother was murdered. I hope that's okay."

"Okay? Of course it's okay. White might not be thrilled, but it's not like this is the first time a private eye's been investigating while we're doing our thing. He'll get over it."

"He did seem a little testy when Emma wanted me with her during that first interview," I said.

"Don't expect an improvement in that area now that Benson's down, and don't be surprised if I don't get back to you right away if you call. I still have my own twenty-some cases, plus I gotta study up on Benson and White's load."

We said our good-byes and I returned to Kate and Emma.

"That was DeShay." I put my phone back in my bag and told them what we'd discussed.

Emma said, "I am so sorry about Sergeant Benson. He was nice to me, seemed to really care that my baby sister was dead, said he'd help me find answers."

"Now you'll have DeShay on your side," I said.

"You didn't get a chance to answer my question," Emma said. "Will you keep helping me?"

"You betcha. Think I'd throw you to the coyotes?"

*   *   *

Kate drove home while I stopped at Beck's Prime and picked up our dinner. They do have an acceptable black-bean burger that Kate will eat. I went for the cheddar burger and added grilled onions so I could say I had a vegetable today. I skipped the fries, promising myself to get into those running shoes tomorrow. God, how I missed Jeff.

Once we were seated at the kitchen table and had started eating—Kate was drinking something thick and carrot orange from the blender while I enjoyed a Diet Coke—I brought up Clinton Roark.

"Tell me what's going on, Kate. You just broke off a serious relationship, and you're dating someone else only days later. That's sounds like something I would do, not you."

"We aren't dating. I'm, well, helping him."

I shook my head. "You think I don't know my heinie from a hard drive?"

"He wants to become a—"

"A vegetarian. Sure. You know what I think? I think 'Oh, my God, we were both born in the Year of the Rat' would have probably worked just as well."

She closed her eyes and took a deep breath before speaking. "Okay. Maybe I feel an attraction. Is that so wrong?"

"How would the shrink who resides in the thinking part of your brain answer?" I said.

"That's just it, Abby. I don't want to think and rethink every decision. That's what Terry tried to do for both of us; that's what totally turned me off."

"Bet Roark's at least fifteen years older than you." I swigged my Diet Coke.

"Fourteen."

I had my burger halfway to my mouth and froze. "He's forty-four?"

"How old is Jeff?"

I raised my chin. "Thirty-six." We sounded like we were back in junior high school having a boyfriend war like we used to—*mine's better than yours*. I took a deep breath. "Sorry. I guess his age doesn't matter. I'm worried about you, that's all. You had one big cry and now you're over Terry? I don't think so."

"I'm moving on, Abby, and it's not my fault if someone walked into my office and seemed like exactly the right person to help me do that. We have chemistry."

"Yeah. So did my ex and I, even after we got divorced. Chemistry experiments can blow up in your face."

Kate knew this was true. No reply needed. She drank her orange concoction and it left her with a neon mustache. She looked downright ridiculous when she said, "This is all your fault, you know."

"My fault?" But I couldn't muster any conviction. She looked too funny.

"I watch how you and Jeff interact. There's all this passion between you, so much—"

I was unable to hold back the laughter another second.

"What?" she said.

"You look like you should do a billboard for 'Got Carrots?' "

She swiped at her lips and then we were both laughing.

13

The next morning I managed to find my running shoes and spent an hour walking and jogging near the Rice campus. We were blessed with a perfect October morning, cool and bright, and I felt energized by the exercise. By the time I arrived back home, Kate had left for work, and the cell phone I'd forgotten on the kitchen counter must have been making noises while I was gone. Diva was sitting and staring at the thing as if it were a mouse hole.

When I picked up the phone, I saw I had a message from DeShay. I listened to him say, "Hey, Abby. The DNA comparison on the baby is in. After I talk this over with White I'll get back to you."

I closed the phone, thinking how Emma might have two sets of remains entrusted to her now—the baby's and her mother's.

But it was Emma, not DeShay, who called me after I'd showered and dressed. She said the police were coming to her hotel to talk to her. "Sergeant White sounded so serious, and he wouldn't tell me anything over the phone. I don't want to face him alone."

"DeShay told me they have DNA results on the baby," I said. "That must be what this is about." I told her I was on my way, then checked to see if DeShay had left me a voice mail message while I was in the shower. But he hadn't. Maybe he and White were shutting me out.

I made the drive to Emma's hotel in less than fifteen minutes, but not soon enough. When she let me into her suite, White and DeShay were there. Room service coffee and a plate of fruit and croissants sat on the glass coffee table. White was holding a jam-loaded roll in one hand and a mug in the other. DeShay stood as I came around the sofa to sit next to Emma. White took a giant mouthful of croissant and nodded at me in greeting.

"I asked them to wait until you got here." Emma took my hand and squeezed. "Go ahead, Sergeant White. I'm ready now."

White had a mouthful of food, so DeShay started to speak.

"Hold on, Peters. Let me handle this," White mumbled.

DeShay was seated directly across from me and rolled his eyes. "Sure, Sergeant." Then he mouthed the word *Sorry* to me.

White swallowed, gulped coffee and picked up a napkin from the coffee table. He slowly wiped every millimeter of skin around his mouth. I decided this was his way of saying, *You make me wait for this bimbo PI to show up, I'll make you wait, too.*

He gripped his lapels and straightened his one-size-too-small sports jacket. "According to the DNA comparison between Ms. Lopez and the female infant found on your property after the demolition, you and this child are not related."

Emma seemed too stunned to speak. *I* was too stunned to speak. We leaned back against the sofa cushions simultaneously.

Finally I managed, "That sure tears a plank off the wall."

"Yeah, it does," DeShay said. "We need to take a formal statement, Ms. Lopez, and since you've been a little banged up by your accident, we can do it here." DeShay picked up a laptop case from under the coffee table and took out a computer and a small tape recorder. "Sergeant White will ask the questions; I'll take notes. We'll also make an audio recording."

"I-I don't get it," I said. "Emma saw her mother give birth."

White said, "You're here only because Ms. Lopez asked for a favor. I'd appreciate it if you'd stay out of this." White looked at Emma. "I understand from Sergeant Peters that an unidentified woman found deceased in 1997 has tentatively been identified as—"

"Hold on," I said. "Does Emma need a lawyer?" White and I traded angry stares.

"For crying out loud, this is only a witness statement," White said. "But if you want to hold up the investigation, go right ahead and call up a suit." He started to get up, but DeShay put a restraining hand on his arm.

"Hang on," DeShay said. He looked at Emma and me. "We know from the forensic report that this infant was buried under the house about fifteen years ago. That would have made you around eight, Ms. Lopez. We don't consider you a suspect. We just want to find out what happened."

"Thanks for the clarification." I looked at Emma. "You okay with this?"

"I'll help any way I can," she said.

White was sitting again, but I could tell by his body language that he was mad enough to eat nails and spit rivets. He addressed Emma. "Since you've hired Abby, you had every right to invite her here today, but you need to know that HPD can handle this case, get to the truth."

"Like they handled the identification of my mother's body? Let's see . . . that only took ten years." Emma was having none of White's attitude, and I wanted to smile.

White's ears reddened. "I understand your, um, unhappiness. I can assure you the ME's office is comparing this dead woman's DNA to yours maybe right this minute. Isn't that right, Sergeant Peters?"

"Yes," DeShay said. "We hope to have a positive ID as soon as possible. And we're very sorry it's taken so long."

"I didn't mean to sound critical, because I'm very grateful to the police," Emma said. "But Abby's the one who went to the morgue. She's the one who showed me the reconstructed face of my mother. She's helped me in other ways, too, and I want her to have access to everything you learn. Is that possible?"

White sighed. "Yeah. I guess that's possible."

Emma smiled. "Good. Now, what do you need from me today?"

"We'd like you to tell us again about the home birth. Tell us everything you recollect from the events that followed," White said. "We need to figure out what's real and what's not—decide, if we can, whose baby this was."

DeShay rolled his eyes again. White sounded condescending, but Emma had already shown she could hold her own with him.

"Decide what's *real*?" she said. "I'm not delusional."

"Sorry," White said. "I'm sure you don't doubt what you saw, but, well, the forensics say that baby was not your sister."

I said, "But Emma saw her mother give birth. If the baby under the house was the child born in the tub, doesn't that bring into question whether Christine O'Meara was Emma's biological mother?" As soon as the words left my mouth, I knew I shouldn't have said them. Not yet, anyway.

Emma said, "Oh, my God. She's right."

DeShay shot me a look, gave a slight shake of the head to shut me up. He looked at Emma. "We won't know until that other DNA comparison between you and the woman in the morgue is complete. For now, can you tell us what you remember about the time period surrounding the baby's birth?"

"I don't know anything more than I've already told you," she said.

"Tell us again for the tape recorder," White said.

Emma told her story once more, while I tried to make sense of this unexpected information. If the baby wasn't related to Emma, was she related to Shannon and Luke? That question would have to wait, too. Or perhaps the police didn't care. But Emma would. She did resemble Xavier Lopez—same eyes, same smile. Could she have been born outside Lopez's marriage and he placed her with Christine to hide her existence from his wife?

Wait. No. Christine was supposedly pregnant with Emma when Lopez died. Or so Emma's date of birth indicated. But no one knew better than I did that birth certificates can be changed or forged or outright manufactured. I'd already seen it happen with previous clients. DeShay was right. Until the DNA comparison came in, we couldn't assume anything.

White was saying, "You're sure the baby was gone the next day? That you didn't see CPS come and take her away?"

"All I know is that if the baby had been in our house for any length of time, even one day, I would have held her, I would have fed her, I would have changed her diapers, like I did with Shannon and Luke. None of those things happened."

"You did all that when you were only eight?" White's voice was generously laced with skepticism.

"Emma raised her brothers and her sister," I said. "She's been their legal guardian since she was sixteen. I think she'd remember if there was another baby for her to care for."

White was apparently still simmering, and every time I opened my mouth he almost boiled over. Ignoring me, he said, "Most of those old houses have a trapdoor that leads to the crawl space under the house. Was there one in your place and did you ever open it?"

"The door was nailed shut," Emma said. "I never had any reason to remove those nails. I didn't want to know what kind of bugs and rodents were crawling around under there."

"Nailed shut, huh? Now you're telling me something. Seems your mother didn't want you kids snooping around. She had something to hide."

DeShay said, "I'm not sure we can draw that conclusion yet. A trapdoor to the outside wouldn't be safe for a houseful of little kids. Maybe Ms. O'Meara—"

"Yeah, right, Peters. Thanks for pointing that out. Why don't you do something useful, like call up your friend at the ME's office?"

"But Julie said the DNA results—"

"Call her," White said. "Put some pressure on those people."

"Can I talk to you, Sergeant?" DeShay put the laptop on the coffee table, stood and walked to the window.

"Excuse me, ladies." White followed, again adjusting his sport coat.

Though they'd stepped away, I could hear every word. It wasn't like they were behind a closed door.

"I am not your slave," DeShay said in an angry stage

whisper. "You treat me with respect, because for now, I'm the only partner you've got."

"Didn't mean to rub you the wrong way. I'll be more sensitive to your needs in our *partnership*. Sounds to me like you'd rather be partners with your little detective friend."

A tense silence followed. Then I heard DeShay say, "We've got a job to finish." He came back, reclaimed his chair and picked up the laptop. "Sorry about that."

White resumed his questions, and the answers hadn't changed from the last time he'd interviewed Emma and me. They left fifteen minutes later, and DeShay said they'd be in touch with any developments.

"I don't understand, Abby," Emma said. "How could my mother not really be my mother?"

"You were her oldest child. Maybe someone left you with her."

"Who? My father?"

"Listen, I know you've had several big surprises today. Let's wait on the DNA. Then we'll know exactly what we're dealing with."

"Guess you're right. I'll know the truth soon enough," she said quietly.

I could tell this had hit her like a heavyweight's punch. What else could happen? We talked a few minutes longer; then I took off and returned home to research Emma's neighborhood, hoping to use the ideas Jeff had suggested to find anyone who might have known Christine O'Meara back in the nineties.

Diva was happy to have me at the computer, and once we were both comfortable, I tried the Houston City-search Web site, used all sorts of query combinations using Dogpile.com, one of my favorite search engines, and combed the online yellow pages for bars and liquor stores in Emma's neighborhood. There were plenty of stores and bars, but after a dozen calls I learned that most places had turned over ownership time and time again. No one would remember a woman from ten years ago. I did come away with the names of two places that had kept the same ownership for longer than ten years, one bar and one liquor store. But a short list was better than no list at all. Time to hit the streets.

The liquor store was on Cavalcade, a good distance away from Emma's house. I decided to try Pedro's Beer Garden first. *Interesting name. Maybe I'll find Wolfgang's Cantina around the corner,* I thought, as I pulled into the empty lot next door to the bar. There was no parking lot.

Tejano music blared from speakers at the back of the building, where I could see a few rusty wrought-iron tables on a patio. The bar was a run-down shack made of metal sheeting. I noted only a few cars besides my own, or should I say pickup trucks, not cars. Three of them.

Since I was alone in an unfamiliar part of town, I considered sticking my gun in my bag—but bringing a firearm into an establishment that sells liquor is a big no-no, and I do want to keep my PI license. I put on a confident smile and walked through the screen door.

The sunlight was so intense that when I entered the dark interior, I had to pause while my eyes adjusted. The music was even louder inside, but the wonderful smell of cilantro, hot peppers and refried beans more than compensated. It was past one o'clock and I'd skipped lunch. My stomach knew it.

The place had a few mismatched tables and chairs as well as a bar with five stools. I could make out the silhouettes of two men seated there wearing cowboy hats. Both of them were eating, and as I got closer I saw they were also drinking longneck bottles of Dos Equis.

The bartender looked about forty, with dark hair slicked back in a ponytail. He wore a grungy once-white canvas apron. "You lost, *señorita*?" he said.

I practically had to shout over the music. "No. I'm hoping you can help me."

The two men who'd been eating lunch switched their attention to me and offered raised eyebrows and smarmy smiles to the bartender. To his credit, he ignored them and offered a welcoming expression.

I had a business card ready and handed it to him. "My name is Abby Rose. I'm investigating the death of a woman who lived in this area in the mid-nineties. She disappeared in 1997 and I've learned she was murdered."

The bartender stepped back. "I don't know nothing

about no murder. I'm a Christian man and run a good place. And I keep it good. No fights. No gangs. No killings."

I swallowed, a little scared at his sudden switch in temperament. "I'm only trying to find anyone who knew this woman, saw her—anything." I mustered as much sweetness as I could, still feeling the stares of the two customers. "Can I please show you her picture? Her name was Christine O'Meara."

The man stared at my card and then back at me. "You're not no cop? They come in here with the wrong idea every time a new one gets this beat. Who knows? Maybe they're sending women now."

"Do I look like a cop?" I set my purse on an empty bar stool, held out my arms and twirled. I was wearing tight jeans and a T-shirt. "I'm not carrying, as you can see."

That brought a laugh from all three, and the customer with a tattoo of a Bible verse on his bicep said, "Oh, you're carrying. Just not no weapons."

I held out my bag. "You want to look inside? You can check my ID. I promise the most dangerous thing in my purse is a Snickers bar."

More laughter, and the bartender yelled over the music, "Show me this picture."

While the bartender examined the photo, I decided I might need an eardrum transplant if I stayed in here much longer.

He placed the picture on the bar in front of the customers, shaking his head. "I been here fifteen years and I can count on my fingers how many white women come in here, and that's with counting you. This lady in the picture, I don't know her. I never seen her."

The two customers shook their heads no, too, and returned to their nearly finished lunches of tamales, beans and rice.

"If you've been here fifteen years, then you know the area." I sat at the bar. "Is there anywhere else a woman who, well, enjoyed her liquor might go to spend time around here?"

"Ah. She was *una borracha*, yes? A drunk?"

I nodded.

"I don't let that kind stay around my place. But a couple streets over, there used to be an icehouse. People could hang around all day if they wanted. Guess the woman who owned it didn't care, you know? She was something. Drove a motorcycle to work."

Thank goodness the current song was a simple Spanish guitar solo and I could hear better. "You said there used to be an icehouse. It's not there anymore?"

"Closed about five years ago, I'm thinking. Some of those customers—mostly gringos—they tried to come over here. Me and my brother, we had to keep throwing them out. They wanted to stay all day, take up my tables, sneak their own bottle in to fill their glasses after only buying one drink."

"Do you remember the name of this place?"

"Oh, *sí*. Rhoda's. It's not there no more, but maybe somebody on that street knows something." He wrote directions on the back of my business card and gave it to me.

"Thanks so much—is it Pedro?"

He nodded.

"One more thing," I said.

"*¿Sí?*"

"Can I get a few tamales to go?"

But Pedro convinced me to stay for lunch. Seemed his mother had just dropped off homemade flour tortillas. They were still hot. Besides enjoying delicious beans and tamales, I spread two tortillas with butter and rolled them up to enjoy with my meal. There is nothing in the world better than a homemade tortilla dripping with butter. Since the key ingredient in a good tortilla is lard, I was glad I'd exercised that morning.

Then I drove several blocks to where the icehouse used to be. The only structure anywhere near where Pedro had told me to look was a strip mall housing a pizza outlet, a dry cleaners, a manicure shop and a place that offered eight-dollar haircuts.

Okay. Wouldn't learn anything from the pizza place. Kids usually worked there. The cheaper hair salons probably had a high employee turnover. I parked in front of the manicure shop—Nails by Suzi—and went inside.

The pretty Asian woman was alone, and no matter what question I asked, it was always answered with, "You want French manicure?" Or "You want pedicure? We do nice pedicure." When I offered my card, I was directed with a smile to a fishbowl on the front counter loaded with other business cards, phone numbers inked on the backs. "We have drawing once a month," I was told. "Free manicure."

I backed out quickly, hearing, "It's okay you come tomorrow. I be here."

Please, dry-cleaner person, know something, I thought.

The man behind the counter said, "Ticket," and held out his hand even before I was through the door. In the background, a huge circular rack held plastic-draped clothes, and a giant gray laundry bin was overflowing with recent acquisitions.

"I don't have a ticket, I—"

"No ticket. Hmmm. And you're not a regular customer, because I certainly don't recognize you. What *shall* we do?" He clasped his hands in front of him and cocked his balding head. His pants were belted high, and his starched shirt was buttoned all the way to the neck. I guessed he had to be about sixty, maybe older.

"My name is Abby Rose, and I'm not here to pick up dry cleaning." I handed him the card the manicurist wanted me to drop in the fishbowl. "I hope you can help me with a case."

He took the card and stared at it for a second; then his eyes grew wide with delight. "You're a detective? How fun."

"Right. Fun," I said. "How long have you worked here . . . um . . . sorry. What's your name?"

"How rude of me." He held out his hand. "Herman. Herman Bosworth. I opened in 2002."

We shook, and I had to pull my hand away when he kept holding on.

"You own the place, Mr. Bosworth?"

"I do—or should I say the bank and I do. What would life be without mort-gag-es?" He practically sang the word, and followed this with a snorting laugh.

This guy's crosshairs definitely weren't lined up. "Okay, then. Would you by chance know who owned any of the properties bought up to build this strip center?"

His eyes grew brighter, and he supported his elbow with one hand while the other hand rested on his cheek. "I might. What's this about, Abby?"

"I'm hoping to talk to a woman named Rhoda who once owned a bar around here. I don't have a last name."

"Why do you need to find Rhoda?"

"As I said. I need to talk to her," I answered.

"You're being e-va-sive. About what, Abby? You can tell me."

I could research real estate records and might find out what I needed—probably should have done that to begin with. But I had a feeling this guy knew something. He could save me time if he'd quit fooling around. "You want money, Mr. Bosworth?" I started to open my purse.

But Herman Bosworth was shaking his head vigorously. "No-no-no-no. No money. I'm simply interested. Dry cleaning is, well, rather *dry*. Dirty clothes in, clean clothes out. But you're dealing with something important, and I can help you. So do tell, Abby. Please?"

I sighed and, without naming names, I told him I hoped to locate anyone who may have known a cold-case victim, hoping that would be enough information to satisfy him.

"*Cold Case*. I *love* that show. You don't look anything like that blond actress. But you're doing what she does, and that is *so* awesome."

"Will you please tell me Rhoda's last name now?"

He folded his arms, leaned toward me and whispered, "I can do more than that."

But before he could say another word, Paul Kravitz walked in. "You're sure taking a long time picking up your dry cleaning, Abby."

Damn. I thought he was leaving town, yet here it was Thursday and he was still lurking around. He'd found me even though I'd been watching for a tail. Probably had someone helping him who knew Houston streets.

"Do you work with Detective Rose?" Herman asked.

I said, "He does not—"

"*Detective* Rose," Kravitz said. "I like that. You could say we work together. Exactly what part of the case are you helping her with?"

"Don't answer that, Herman," I said. "I don't work *with* him. I don't work *for* him. He followed me here."

"You were followed?" Herman clapped twice. "Oh, my goodness, wait until I tell my partner, Robert."

"That's great," I said. "You can tell Robert all about it. But this guy—"

"You're *him*. You're Paul Kravitz from *Crime Time*." Herman's eyes had grown wide behind his glasses, and he was pointing at Kravitz. "Get over here. Let me have a good look at you."

Kravitz gave me a smug smile as he approached the counter.

I was certain celebrity status outweighed detective status and I wouldn't get what I needed.

Meanwhile, Herman was studying Kravitz. "I have to say, you look far better on TV. Are you ill?"

Paul laughed. "No, sir. Healthy as a horse. How are *you* a part of our story, Mr. . . . ?"

"Bosworth." He looked at me. "Am I connected to the story?"

Only in your mind, I thought. "Listen, Herman, I can't tell you what to do, but you promised to help me, not him. You have my card. You decide."

I walked out knowing I was taking a risk. Now I had to wait.

14

I waited a better part of the day for a call from Herman Bosworth, and waiting is not my strong suit. I felt as edgy as an armadillo at a monster truck rally as I paced in my kitchen. Adding to my agitation, the promised DNA comparison hadn't come in. I knew this because I'd bugged DeShay so many times he told me to stop calling him.

I'd done the property-records search for the strip mall, and this produced more than a dozen names of people who'd sold their land or businesses before the center was built. No one named Rhoda appeared on that list.

Finally, though I knew what had probably happened between the dry cleaner and Kravitz, I called Bosworth around seven that night. He told me he'd given Rhoda's last name to Paul Kravitz in exchange for studio-audience tickets to a talk show. When I asked if he'd do me the same favor for, say, Houston Rockets or opera tickets, he said that if he gave me any information, Kravitz's offer, which included money for a nice stay in Hollywood, would be withdrawn. Herman hung up with one long "Sorr-eeee."

Great. I'd lost out to Kravitz and also wasted precious time. I had to do something productive, and was headed to the computer to search the Internet for anything—a Web site, an ad or even a sentence containing the word Rhoda—when someone knocked on my door.

I checked the security monitor. Paul Kravitz. What the hell did he want? A chance to gloat?

I opened the door and said nothing.

He smiled. "Can we talk?"

"I thought you were going away. Far away. On an airplane." But I widened the door to let him in. I could take anything he wanted to throw at me. I might not have Hollywood connections, but I had something he didn't: a connection with Emma and a burning need to obtain the answers she wanted so she and her family could have a future without sorrow and regret haunting them for the rest of their lives.

I led him into the living room, and he accepted an offer of wine. He chose red, I took white and then we sat down across from each other.

"I think we've gotten off to a bad start," he said.

"What would make you think that?" I tried to sound like I didn't give a rat's ass and failed.

"Don't you understand? I can help your client find the answers she needs about her past and her family. Venture has the resources to do what you probably cannot."

Now, *that* really pissed me off, but I managed a smile. "You think I can't do the job?"

"Did I—"

"If I'm so worthless as a detective," I said, "how come you followed me today?"

The tips of his ears burned red. "That's the reason I came. I didn't realize Houston sprawled twenty miles in every direction. You know these streets and are obviously following a lead that has to do with this Rhoda person. If you share the information with me, maybe we could get answers for Emma sooner rather than later."

"Let me guess. What you learned today is not quite fitting together for you." I had to smile. I was betting he'd also gone to see Pedro. But from what little I knew of the cantina owner, he probably hadn't told Kravitz or his buddies anything. Yup. Kravitz had no idea why Rhoda was important and didn't want to talk to her until he did. I held her piece of the puzzle.

He said, "I'm willing to share what Mr. Bosworth told me if you agree to work with us on solving this mystery."

"I already got that offer from *Reality Check* and passed. I'm getting to the bottom of this and I don't need your help."

He raised one eyebrow. "Your client is legally committed to our production. What we learn needs to be complete. We want to tell the story from her perspective, but we can't do that without the facts. You can have a hand in making sure we get it right."

I hadn't thought of it that way. "Before I cooperate with you, you need to tell me what Bosworth said."

Kravitz sipped his wine and then stared straight into my eyes. "Then you'll tell me why Rhoda is important?"

"Yes. But I'm not promising anything else."

Kravitz considered my terms for a second. "I can accept that—but only if you agree not to talk to the press. If they get in the middle of this, I'll have one giant headache."

"They're already in the middle," I said.

"Yes, but they aren't camped outside your house like they are outside Emma's hotel. You're almost anonymous, unlike the rest of us."

"Ah. Now I get it. A sensational story makes for a crowded work environment. I have no plans to tell the press anything." I drank my wine, noting how much better it tasted all of a sudden.

"The name you want is Rhoda Murray," he said. "Bosworth says she owns Murray Motorcycles now. We don't want to question the woman until we know why she's important. Seems all Bosworth heard from you is that you're investigating a cold case. Which cold case are we talking about, Abby? The baby or the mother?"

"See, there you go, asking for more information before a minute has passed," I said.

"Why are you being so stubborn? We both want the same thing. The truth."

"Oh, I am stubborn, but my daddy used to say that the way to deal with a stubborn person is like you'd deal with a mule. You don't try to whip him into the corral. You leave the gate open a crack and he'll go in all by himself."

Kravitz smiled. "That's why I'm here, I guess. To crack the gate and hope you'll come in."

"Problem is, I can't have you or your investigators

thwarting my every move like what happened today. I want to talk to this woman alone."

"You won't allow one of my detectives to go with you?" he asked.

"You can't ask me to tag-team with someone I don't know. I'm pretty good at getting information out of people, but I'd feel awfully uncomfortable with another investigator there. Rhoda Murray might not like it much, either."

"Can you record the interview, then?" he asked.

"Not without the woman's permission," I said.

Kravitz took a deep breath, clasped his hands between his knees and leaned forward in the chair. "But you'll share what you learn?"

I didn't answer right away. But the truth was, we were on the same page. Finally I said, "We can't be tripping over each other on this, Paul. You let me do this my way and you'll get what you need."

"I like to be in control, you know," he said with a smile. "This is killing me."

"I prefer hanging on to the key to the gate myself."

"Looks like I'm not taking it away from you, either."

"You got that right." I smiled.

Kravitz stood and offered his hand. We shook and he said, "I'm glad we came to an agreement, and I hope you'll soon realize that I do what's right. We'll continue to work with the police, follow any leads we turn up on our own, but Rhoda Murray is all yours."

"Good." I wanted to believe this guy, but he probably knew how to say all the right things.

"I have an early flight tomorrow—yes, you'll be happy to know I *am* leaving town," Paul said. "Could you stay in touch with me should anything break on this story?" He pulled a small leather holder from his jacket pocket, scribbled a number on the card he removed and handed it to me. "That's my personal cell number on the back. Very few people have it."

Wow. What a privilege, I thought as I took the card. "Rhoda Murray may be a dead end," I said.

Kravitz said, "I'm aware of that. Time for me to get out of here now."

But before he could take a step toward the front door, voices came from the kitchen. Kate. I assumed the male voice belonged to Clinton Roark—unless the girl had gone as crazy as a goat at mating time and hooked up with someone else.

Kate came into the living room, Roark behind her. "Abby, whose car is— Oh, hi." She smiled at Kravitz. "I'm Kate Rose, and this is my friend Clint Roark."

As the men shook hands, Roark spoke before Paul could: "Aren't you Paul Kravitz from that program . . . what's it called?"

"Crime Time." Kravitz's TV smile appeared.

Roark pointed at Kravitz. "Yes, that's it. Nice to meet you. Love your show."

"Thank you." He turned to Kate. "It's Dr. Rose, correct?"

Kate nodded, and I could tell her radar had gone up.

"Paul was just leaving." I tried to clue Kate with my tone, reassure her about Kravitz, since I'd complained about all the Venture people to her more than once.

"Yes," he said. "I'm taking a plane at six in the morning. I bid you all a pleasant evening."

I led him out, then picked up the empty wineglasses on my way back to the kitchen, where I found Kate and Clint. She was showing him her refrigerated omega-3-6-9 oil and the container holding the flax flakes she sprinkles on her cereal. How romantic.

"What was *he* doing here?" Kate asked. Webster sat at her feet holding his leash, but she didn't seem to notice.

"Making deals. That's the Hollywood way. Anyway, I'm glad to report he gave me a piece of information I needed. Now, you guys go on exploring the amazing world of fatty acids while I take the dog out."

Webster and I took a walk up the block and back. The night would be cold—we'd gone from eighty degrees to fifty in the last four days—and Webster seemed wound up by the sudden change. Me? I would have enjoyed the humidity-free night better if I weren't bothered by Clinton Roark.

Kate had that glow women get when they've found a new guy, and for some reason I didn't like it. I was used to seeing her with Terry, and even Roark's dimpled, warm smile couldn't compensate for the loss I felt—a loss I seemed to be experiencing more than Kate. I would miss Terry's presence—he'd been a good friend— but she seemed to have erased him like a mistake she'd written on a paper. That seemed wrong.

I made sure to come in through the front door to avoid the two of them, and released Webster, who bounded toward the kitchen and the smell of what I thought was broccoli cooking. I went upstairs, did the whole triple-step face-cleansing thing and climbed into bed with the cat. Diva was surprised by this—it was early—but she settled in next to me. Then I called Jeff.

"Hey," he said. "How are you?"

"Missing you."

"I could be home in a week." He sounded more tired than when he worked a case for forty-eight hours straight.

"That's the best news I've had all day." I summarized what had happened since we last spoke.

When I'd finished, Jeff said, "You think you can trust Kravitz, hon?"

"For now, I have to. Besides, what's the alternative? Fight Kravitz and then trip over his investigators every step I take?"

"I'm betting they'll still follow you to that motorcycle shop tomorrow. Do you remember what I told you about ditching a tail?"

"Take the side streets, double back at times, stop and let the tail pass. Did I miss anything?"

"Never stop at yellow lights. Your tail might be four cars behind, and that's your chance to lose them. Of course, some guys know how to tail without being noticed. Hope you don't get one of those kind."

"You can do that, right? Tail without a suspect knowing?"

"Usually."

"What's your secret?" I asked.

"Anticipation of their next move, sometimes a gut feeling. Having a clue where the target is going is the best help of all."

"Kravitz will tell them where I'm going, won't he?"

"Probably. Maybe you can fool them. Follow some other lead or stay home."

"Is that what you'd do? Stay home? I don't think so, Jeff."

"You're right," he said. "Now, can we talk about something else? This time I want to know what you're *not* wearing."

15

The next morning I called Murray Motorcycles and asked for Rhoda. The man who answered told me she wasn't in, but he expected her soon. I asked for directions and hung up. The shop wasn't far from where I'd been yesterday, and I hurried out the back door, anxious to interview Rhoda.

Unfortunately, fifteen minutes later I found myself in a giant traffic jam on Highway 59. *Damn.* When I have a plan, a traffic mess like this is sure to happen. I tried a Josh Groban CD to calm down, and when that didn't work I picked up my cell. I hoped to reach DeShay rather than his voice mail, and prayed he'd forgiven me for pestering him yesterday.

"Peters," he answered.

"It's me. Did you hear anything on the DNA yet?"

"I'll call you in five minutes," he said. "White will be out of here by then."

"Gotcha." I closed the phone and in those seemingly endless five minutes the Camry and I moved about a hundred feet.

Finally the phone rang.

DeShay said, "Sorry, but Don's having a bad day, and you know how he feels about your working this case. Thought I'd better not antagonize him by giving you information while he was around."

"Sergeant Benson told me White was territorial, but his reaction to me seems way beyond that. Am I that annoying? Wait, don't answer that. What's this information?"

"You won't believe this, Abby."

"Try me," I said.

"The dead woman's DNA does not match the baby but *does* match Emma. She's Christine O'Meara for sure."

"Wait a minute. The baby under the house wasn't Christine's? And wasn't Emma's sister? Hell, do you even know if it was a boy or a girl?"

"Girl. They did mitochondrial testing to figure all this out," he said.

"That's right. Julie said you can only use female samples for that. What do we do now?" I said.

"Now we have a different unidentified victim. White's been busy pulling files to see if anyone reported a kidnapping or a baby snatching from a hospital in 1992. Thing is, we checked the *Chronicle* archives first and found nothing. Something like that would have been big news."

"White's focus is still on identifying the baby first?" I said.

"It's a good place to start, but— Wait. Hang on."

I heard White in the background say, "Who you talking to?"

DeShay must have covered the phone, because I couldn't hear his response. When he came back on the line, he said, "He came back for something. Anyway, he's on his way to the hospital. Ed's not doing so hot, and I think that's part of White's attitude problem. They've been partners a long time."

"Oh, no," I said. "Sergeant Benson seems like such a nice man, from the few times I talked to him."

"He had another small stroke."

"I sent flowers, put you and Jeff on the card, too."

"Thanks for thinking of Ed. Women are good at remembering shit like flowers and cards."

"And cops are good at giving their blood and their lives for the rest of us. As for the case, while White's doing his thing, are you following up on Christine O'Meara's murder?"

"Don't I wish. White jawed all morning that since Emma hired you for that job, you could take O'Meara while we focus on the bones. I sorta get that. Lots of media people have been asking questions about how a baby could die without anyone knowing. I wonder myself."

"I'll keep doing what I'm doing then."

"Yup. Find out anything you can on O'Meara and pass it on to me. And by the way, that asshole Mayo has pulled strings, gotten the okay for Paul Kravitz to talk to us about the investigation into the infant's death. Like I got time for that."

"Kravitz left town this morning. You won't be seeing him today."

"That's the best news I've had since I woke up. I've got something for you to follow up on concerning O'Meara."

"Shoot."

"I found out Crime Stoppers had a call in ninety-seven about the then-unidentified body of a woman. According to the report I found, this guy who phoned said he recognized her from the reconstruction photo in the paper."

"The police had a lead?"

"Not exactly. This guy wanted the reward, but when the investigator on the case interviewed him, the man flipped, said he'd made a mistake. Said he didn't know the woman."

"That's weird. Was he some kind of attention seeker? Just wanted to talk to a cop?" I asked.

"You mean like the attention seekers who've been phoning in useless clues all morning? I don't think so. Doesn't fit the personality of our regular callers. They prefer higher-profile cases like the infant bones. Some nameless woman found dead in a field wouldn't have grabbed their interest."

"But Christine's murder will draw plenty of publicity once people know her connection to the bones— whatever that connection is."

"Right," DeShay said. "That's why, besides you, only Emma and her family will be told about the O'Meara ID. We don't have any hard evidence to connect the baby's death and her disappearance and murder yet. I'm hoping something CSU collected will show that Christine killed that baby, or at least put her in the ground."

"Christine's death came five years after that baby died. Maybe her murder's not related," I said.

"True. But I'm not expecting answers anytime soon. White's not real into this case. Along with hating my guts because I'm not Ed Benson and being pissed off at you because he thinks only cops should work homicides, he's distracted by Ed's illness. Jeff got an earful about all this when I talked to him this morning."

"You talked to Jeff?" Even though we'd spoken less than twelve hours ago, I felt a little flutter in my stomach when I heard his name.

"Yeah, I told him he needs to get his damn ass back here."

"He doesn't have a damn ass. He has one of the nicest—"

"Some things you can keep to yourself, Abby girl. Anyway, I told him White's got me screening the crackpot calls, people telling me it was their baby under that house or they know someone who knows someone who might know something about the case. Stupid stuff that will probably lead nowhere. Jeff told me I should cut White some slack, so I'm trying."

"I guess I should try, too," I said. "Did Jeff say anything else?"

"No hint about coming back, if that's what you're wondering."

I smiled. "You read my mind." Just then, a kid in the back of the car ahead of me must have thought the smile was for him, because he began playing games with me—hiding and then popping back up. I said, "I'll follow up on the Crime Stoppers lead, see if this guy really did know Christine O'Meara and for some reason backed off on the ID."

"Go for it. It's probably a dead end, but it's all we've got. Guy's name is Jerry Joe Billings. No rap sheet—which would have helped, but— Wait a minute. The O'Meara woman was a drunk, right? If this guy knew her, maybe he was a drunk, too. He might have been arrested for public intoxication."

"But I thought you said he didn't have a rap sheet," I said, confused.

"Anything less than a Class A or Class B offense isn't

listed in our criminal database, but there's somewhere else I can look for minor violations. If I do find out he was arrested, then we'll have his social."

"I can do plenty with that," I said.

"I have a copy of his driver's license, but he's not living at his last known address. You want me to fax you the copy so you'll have a picture of him?"

"Send it as an e-mail attachment straight to my computer phone." I gave him the number. I always keep the new BlackBerry with me, but found I liked my smaller cell phone with the camera for regular use.

I'd moved only about a city block during our entire conversation. Up ahead I could see a car being moved to the side of the road. The flashing lights of about ten wreckers glittered in my rearview. Up ahead the little boy was still playing his jack-in-the-box game.

And that game suddenly brought it all together when I realized that there were two boys, close in age but one with darker blond hair and different clothes from the other. When one went down, the other popped up.

That was why there had been no report of a kidnapping in '92. Since Emma's sister had been born at home, there was no official record of her birth. No record would make a switch far simpler. That had to be it. One baby—Christine's—had been exchanged for another. Evidence or not, I had little doubt that if Christine hadn't put that tiny body under her house, she knew who had.

I clenched my fist and banged the steering wheel. She'd given up or sold her own newborn for another child, a baby who may have already been dead or about to die. A child was left under a house—hidden, nameless and forgotten. It made me sick. And where was Emma's sister? Continents away? Or still in Houston? With what little I had, finding her might be impossible.

16

If Kravitz's people hoped to follow me to Murray Motorcycles once the highway clog cleared, I disappointed them. I pulled off the freeway first chance I got and went to a coffee shop with wireless access. When I checked my computer phone, I discovered I'd been sent more than Billings's driver's license. DeShay e-mailed the man's arrest records—the ones he hadn't found when he checked his computer earlier. Billings had nine arrests for public intoxication.

I would need access to one or more of my person-locator databases now that I had Billings's social security number from the arrest sheet. I wanted to find out where he was—and I sure hoped he was a local—but I wanted to tell Emma about the latest round of DNA results before anyone else did.

I sat at a tiny table with my extra-large latte, double shot of espresso, and called her hotel. No one picked up in her room. I then tried her cell. When she answered, I was surprised to learn she was at work.

"You drove?" I said.

"Yup. The rental car company delivered a Cadillac, Abby. I couldn't believe it. I have to thank Kate for doing that. I've never even *sat* in a Cadillac before. It will be so nice for taking clients to properties."

"What about your shoulder?"

"Doesn't hurt much. But the reporters? Now, those people are harder to deal with than a cracked collarbone. They followed me. I told them if they came inside my office I was calling the cops. But then the cops called me instead. Sergeant White."

"Why did he phone you?" I asked.

"They got the new DNA report. Neither my mother—and she is my biological parent—nor I is related to that baby. I'm supposed to keep those results to myself. But I told him I was telling you. He didn't like that much. He's worried the whole world will find out."

"DeShay already gave me the news. That's why I was calling. I'm sorry you had to hear that over the phone from White. He's not the most sensitive man I've ever met."

"It's okay. Really. This means my sister could be alive. We're back to the beginning, back to why you agreed to help me in the first place—with one added problem."

"What's that?"

"The other baby. She belonged to someone, Abby. She didn't deserve to be buried under a house, left in a hole like trash."

"Yeah," I said, nodding. "That's the part that's given me a lump in my throat. I want to find out who she was and why this happened."

"Me, too," she said quietly.

"This means that learning everything about your mother is more important than ever. A dead baby about the same age as your sister is no coincidence. I—"

"Don't say it. My mother had something to do with this. She would have given up anything for money to keep her drug of choice in plentiful supply—even her own child. She'd certainly given up the rest of us for alcohol, though in a different way."

We talked for another minute, mostly about Emma's schedule and how she was supposed to do her job with people following her all the time. After I hung up, I turned to my BlackBerry and the matter of Jerry Joe Billings. Wherever he was, I would find him.

First I checked his driver's license photo and decided Billings must have fallen from the ugly tree and hit every branch on the way down. All DPS photos are gruesome, but Billings had wild hair, half-open eyes, a day's growth of beard and a mouth that made me think he might have left his teeth in a jelly jar by the bed. He couldn't possibly look like this every day, and I worried the photo might be worthless. Would I recognize him if I saw him

in person? Then I noted he was an organ donor. I hoped
he had decent corneas, because his liver was probably
pickled.

I checked the arrest record. The last offense had been
in 1998, which could mean he was either dead or he'd
gotten sober. If sober, he probably had a job. I hit a few
keys with my computer pen and opened a person-locator
database, a very expensive but trustworthy tool. I entered Billings's social security number, and within a minute I knew where to find him.

The man who answered the phone at the warehouse
discount store in the NASA area where Billings worked
was happy to tell me he'd return my call after he finished
mounting a set of tires. I didn't bother to leave a number, just packed up and left the coffeehouse to find him.
Trouble was, when I arrived I was told that since I didn't
belong to the club store, I'd need a membership to enter.
When you live alone—except for frequent and wonderful Jeff sleepovers and extended visits from sisters
who've dumped their boyfriend—you don't need a hundred of anything. Besides, where would I store that
many rolls of toilet paper?

Once I'd filled out the application and been approved,
it was my turn to have a truly awful photograph saved
for posterity on my brand-new plastic member card—
my ticket to overconsumption on a massive scale. I had
to admit, however, that the places I shopped could take
a lesson from the bare cement floors and unfinished ceil-
ings. Might bring the price of a little black dress down
to within reason.

Getting around to the tire section took me about a
week, or so it seemed. But if I thought I wouldn't recognize Billings, I was wrong. I spotted him leaving through
a back door that led out to the garage area, where I
assumed tires were changed. No one could miss that
hair. His considerable long fuzz was sticking out from
his cap like a clown wig.

Okay. There had to be an entrance for the cars somewhere around the building, and I hurried back the way
I came, unswayed by the lure of hot pretzels, pizza or
fresh popcorn. In my rush, I practically knocked over a

poor woman who must have been seventy years old who was trying to offer me a mini sample of peach cobbler.

Another senior citizen was standing guard at the exit, checking people's purchases. I didn't know if I had to show my card to get out of this place, so I held it up like it was an EZ Tag as I rushed through the automatic doors. When no alarms went off, I figured I was okay.

I briefly considered walking around to the back of the building, but decided that might seem odd. No one bought tires on foot. Better to look like a customer. I jogged to my car—another long trek, since I'd had to park about a mile away. *At least I got my exercise for today,* I thought as I slid behind the wheel.

I'd just made it around the building when I spotted Billings climbing into a battered navy Pontiac. I pulled my car behind his, blocking his way. I didn't want to chase him on the freeways. If he was going home, no problem, since I'd also learned where he lived, but if he headed anywhere else I could easily lose him.

I got out, calling, "Mr. Billings?"

He went from looking pissed off to looking confused. The DPS photo might have actually been complimentary, now that I saw him up close.

"Do I know you?" he said.

"My name is Abby Rose, and I'd like to talk to you."

"Not on my lunch break. Get your car out of my way."

"I only need a few minutes of your time."

"Are you some nut wantin' to convert me to your crap religion? 'Cause the bosses here don't let none of you people on the—"

"I'm a private investigator, and I'll make it worth your while."

He almost smiled. Now I was speaking his language. "I only get thirty minutes."

"Fifty dollars," I said. "And I'll buy you lunch."

He squinted at me, fighting the late-morning sun. "You got yourself a deal." He climbed in beside me and directed me to the Sonic Drive-In on the other side of the huge lot.

A moment later I pulled into an angled parking spot. Billings shouted his order into the speaker and had to

lean close to me to do this. Though I smelled no alcohol
on his breath, it might have been better than his halito-
sis. Didn't he know they sold mouthwash by the gallon
right where he worked?

I checked out the menu and skipped the Tater Tots
smothered in processed nacho cheese that I *so* wanted
and settled for a cherry limeade.

Then I handed Billings my business card. "As I said,
I'm a private investigator."

He stared at it and said, "What's this about?"

"You tipped the police back in 1997, said that you
recognized a woman whose picture appeared in the
paper—an artist's reconstruction of a murder victim's
face."

"You're here about *that*? I didn't get a penny, if
you're coming to take it back—but wait . . . that don't
make sense, since you said I'd get fifty bucks. Were you
lying about the money?"

I removed two twenties and a ten from my wallet, but
held on to the cash. "You knew that woman, didn't
you?"

"What if I did?" he said.

A teenager roller-skated up to the car window with
Billings's order and my drink. I paid and tipped her generously. Anyone who could skate and hold a tray of food
at the same time deserved a few extra bucks.

Billings picked up his foot-long chili dog with both
grimy hands.

"Tell me who you thought she was or you only get
the free lunch," I said.

"Christy O'Meara," he mumbled around his mouthful
of food.

I wanted to smile. He *did* know her. "Why'd you back
off on the identification, Mr. Billings?"

"It *was* her, wasn't it?" He jammed three onion rings
into his mouth.

"Why didn't you tell the police you recognized her?"

It seemed to take an eternity for him to suck down
half of his Brownie Blast milk shake. "When you're
drinking as much cheap wine as I was back then, hard
to tell if seeing is believing."

"I'm not buying that, Mr. Billings. I compared a photo

of her to the picture that appeared in the *Chronicle*. The resemblance was remarkable."

He eyed the money in my hand, maybe worried I wouldn't pay up if he didn't come clean. "So?"

"Then why not claim the reward?"

He crammed more onion rings into his mouth and chewed for several seconds. "My stupid ex, that's why."

"Your ex-wife told you to keep quiet? Why would she do that?"

"You don't get it. She wasn't getting anything from me. Not then, not now. But I had my dumb-ass kid for the weekend and he heard me talking about the reward, so he calls and tells her. Then she turns around and tells me she's taking every cent for back child support. Said the police would be happy to turn the money straight over to her." He sucked on his straw, then added, "Bitch."

"You allowed a dead woman to remain unidentified rather than let your ex have a few dollars you owed her anyway?" I couldn't hide my distaste for Jerry Joe Billings.

He dropped his half-eaten hot dog into its paper boat swimming with chili. Some splashed onto me, onto him and onto my car upholstery. His sallow skin had flushed with anger. "Christy was dead, wasn't she? Nothing I said was gonna raise her up. Now take me back to work. I got nothing more to say."

I'd let my feelings about Billings contaminate the interview. Big mistake. Time for damage control. I calmly said, "A hundred dollars more if you'll tell me everything you knew about Christine O'Meara."

He wiped mustard off his chin with a knuckle—made me wait. But I could tell he was hungry for more than fast food. His gaze never wavered from the fifty dollars in my hand. "You mean tell you more than she was a drunk like me?"

"You two hung out, right? You were friends?"

"Yeah, you could say that. We were both down on our luck, you know? World don't give you no fair shake when you got a problem. They just throw you in jail every chance they get."

"She talked to you about her problems?"

"Maybe." He checked his watch. "I need some time to think about it."

"You mean time to fabricate a hundred dollars' worth of information? I prefer we finish this conversation now."

"That's a risk you gotta take. I'm in the program, and lying ain't my thing no more. Right now I have to get back to the job, 'cause I can't afford to get fired. And you know what? I'm thinking a hundred isn't enough. I got debts to pay off. I say five is more like it."

"Sorry, that's a little much for someone with a faulty memory. I can do two-fifty—but only for something I can use to help me find out what happened to Christine."

"What about the baby? You want to find out what happened to the kid? Is that what this is about?"

He had me now. I held out the fifty. "Tell me."

Billings took the money and stuffed the bills in his overalls pocket. "Show me the *rest* of the money."

I didn't have that much cash, and I was sure he didn't take MasterCard or Visa. "There's an ATM in your store. I can—"

He licked his lips, glanced across the parking lot. "I'll get my ass fired if I don't get working again, and I can't afford to lose another job. You bring me four hundred dollars later and you get everything I know."

"You say where and when."

"My place. Gotta meeting tonight, so it will have to be around ten."

"Give me your address." I didn't want him knowing that I knew where he lived.

He recited the street and apartment number that matched what I already had.

I drove him back to the store and he got out, patting his overalls pocket and smiling. I dumped his trash at the adjacent gas station, then used a sample bottle of Clinique makeup remover I found in my purse to clean chili off my upholstery and my shirtsleeve. Then I took off for my next stop, Murray Motorcycles on Houston's north side. I checked for a tail often, but freeways are tough. Every car looks almost the same at sixty miles per hour.

On my way there, I called DeShay and told him about Billings.

"I don't like this, Abby," he said.

"I don't either. That's why I hope you'll come with me tonight. But not with your badge on your belt or your gun bulging. I get the feeling he won't say anything if he knows you're a cop."

"I'm your boyfriend then, or I'm your brother—no, that won't work, will it?"

We both laughed, and I said, "Not unless I spend the rest of the day at a tanning bed. But seriously, can you wait outside?"

"Only if you're wired, and that would take some paperwork and the agreement of one irritable, temporary partner named White."

I sighed. "Okay, you're my boyfriend, but you'd better be good at playacting. I mean, Billings tells me you cops threw the poor man in jail time after time when all he needed was a little love to get over his problem."

DeShay said, "Then please give me a chance to apologize for the entire department and the city of Houston after he spills what he knows about Christine."

I laughed again, and DeShay said he would pick me up at nine thirty that night.

17

I arrived at Murray Motorcycles forty-five minutes later. First I noticed the sign saying Murray's was in the repair business, but they offered used sales as well. On the door of the storefront, the words THESE PREMISES PROTECTED BY SMITH AND WESSON were painted on the glass. I peered inside, but the small showroom and sales counter were deserted. The door was locked, too, but the garage doors were raised and I walked in there. A man with braided gray hair and massive muscles knelt by a bike in the garage.

He greeted me with "Are you wanting a new ride?" without getting up.

"I'm looking for Rhoda."

"Did you talk to her on the phone about a bike?"

He didn't take his eyes off whatever he and his wrench were doing.

"Um, no. My name is Abby Rose and I'm a private investigator. I'm hoping Rhoda can help me with a case I'm working on."

The man stood and focused amazing blue eyes on me—eyes almost as wonderful as Jeff's. Then he stared past me at the street. "I'm Larry Murray, her husband. She's out test-riding a bike I repaired. Did you bring a partner in another car?"

"What are you talking about?" I said.

"The person who seems to have followed you here—Oops. They're gone."

I turned to check the street, thinking how this man's perfect grammar and soft-spoken manner were smashing some of my "biker guy" stereotypes—though he did have the leather vest, tattooed arms and multiple ear piercings.

"No one followed me." I sounded defensive and hated that I did. I'd been constantly checking my rearview and side mirrors. Besides, for some unexplainable reason, I didn't want this man thinking I learned to wave good-bye only yesterday.

"I'm commenting on what I observed," Murray said with a smile.

He was probably right, too. I remembered Jeff's words: If a follower knows where his target is headed, tailing someone is pretty easy. Kravitz did have me followed.

"White Ford Focus," Murray went on. "Driver wore sunglasses and a cap. Hard to tell gender." His demeanor was in no way condescending. He wasn't showing off, just offering information. I decided I should be grateful, not defensive.

I smiled. "Thanks for telling me."

He grinned. He grabbed a filthy rag and wiped his hands. "Let's go into the office, see what this is about."

I followed him, saying, "Rhoda's who I need to talk to."

He opened a door smudged with oily fingerprints, allowed me to enter the store first and said, "After thirty years together, Rhoda's business is my business. But if you'd rather wait on her, have a seat."

A row of connected molded chairs sat against one wall. Two shiny motorcycles took up most of the floor space—those and a stack of tires.

"Maybe both of you can help me," I said.

He went behind the counter, picked up a container of waterless hand cleaner and squeezed some into his palm. "I'm an agreeable person and am more than happy to answer your questions. Rhoda is a horse of a different color. You might test your luck with me first."

"Okay. I'm working a cold case. A woman was murdered in 1997 and her body was identified only this week. Her name was Christine O'Meara and—"

"Christy was murdered? That's terrible."

"You knew her?" I said.

"She came into the icehouse we owned every day for

years. Rhoda had a soft spot for a few of her regulars like Christy. But one day the woman stopped coming in. I think Rhoda told me Christy's friends quit the place, too."

"Friends?"

"Rhoda will have to help you with the friends. I only knew Christy because she made herself known when I would come into the icehouse after work. She always had a greeting, was always so . . . : *present,* so loud and lively. Rhoda said she felt guilty for supplying Christy with Old Number Seven all those years. She decided that when the woman disappeared, a bottle of Jack was probably all she took with her."

Always so present? Her friends quit the place? Who was this guy? "I have to ask. What planet are you from?"

He laughed. "Academia. I took the next outbound rocket as soon as I figured out there was life on earth." Then his smile faded. "You've brought sad news."

I walked over to the counter, the strong scent of the hand cleaner tickling my nose. "Mind if I make sure we're talking about the same person?" I pulled out a photo of Christine O'Meara.

"Yes. That's her," he said.

"She was found murdered, left in a field off Highway 290. I guess neither of you recognized her from the photo in the paper back then."

"Her picture was in the newspaper? I never saw it. I was too busy writing papers to read anything, and Rhoda sticks to cycle magazines. If we'd seen the picture we would have made sure she was identified. I suppose with all the time that's passed, the police will have a hard time finding out who killed her."

"Yes. But I'm hoping—" The roar of an approaching motorcycle startled me, and I turned to look out the window. A shiny blue-and-chrome machine came to a skidding halt. A large woman parked the bike and came into the showroom, shaking her white-blond hair after freeing it from her helmet.

"Hi, there," she said, nodding at me before addressing Larry. "Smooth ride. Nice job, baby. I'll call the customer to pick her up." She put her helmet on the counter and kissed her husband.

Rhoda's raspy voice and the lines around her lips spoke of heavy tobacco use, and when she passed me to go behind the counter I smelled smoke clinging to her hair and clothes.

"Rhoda," Larry said, "this young woman came to talk to you about Christy O'Meara. She's a private detective."

"Don't tell me Christy's asshole husband finally decided to hire someone to find her after all this time."

"Her husband?" I said, surprised.

"Yeah. Lopez, I think his name was."

"Xavier Lopez?"

"That's the guy."

"Um, no, he didn't send me. I'm sorry to tell you that Christine O'Meara died in 1997."

"You're kidding, right?" Rhoda said.

"Sorry, no," I answered.

"Did that jerk beat her to death?" Rhoda's voice had risen, and anger hardened her weathered features.

"I'm not sure what Christine told you, but Xavier Lopez died in 1983, and they were never married," I said quietly.

"No way. She was pregnant with his baby the year we first met. Then right after she delivered, he stole the kid and took off. Christy didn't have the money to find him and—"

"I promise you, Mrs. Murray, Xavier Lopez was in the military, and he died in the line of duty. The baby you're talking about couldn't have been his. He only fathered Christine's first child, Emma."

Rhoda looked at Larry. "Is she telling the truth?"

"I think she probably is, sweetie," Larry replied.

How did soft-spoken academic Larry and tough-talking Rhoda ever hook up? Looking at them, seeing their obviously strong and loving bond, I felt a little guilty for questioning Kate's attraction to Clinton Roark. When people follow their heart rather than do what's expected, sometimes they hit the jackpot.

"Do you have time to talk to me, Mrs. Murray?"

"Rhoda. Everyone calls me Rhoda." She still seemed bewildered by the news I'd delivered.

Larry said, "Rhoda, take Abby—you said Abby, right?"

I nodded.

"Take Abby to the office, pour both of you a shot of that bourbon your father sent us for our anniversary and then you two sit and talk."

Rhoda looked at her husband, a straight-on gaze, since they were both the same size—six feet and about two fifty. "What people told me at the bar was private stuff. Shouldn't I be quiet about all that?"

"Not if you were fed a pack of lies, sweetie," Larry said.

I was liking Larry more by the minute.

"You're saying I should talk to her?" Rhoda said.

"That's what I'm saying," he answered.

He kissed her briefly on the lips; then Rhoda said, "Okay, let's do it," and led me through a door behind the office.

The small room with its old yellow vinyl sofa and ancient oak desk was tidy, the tile floor newly buffed. But black fingerprints marred every surface the couple had touched, and the smell of smoke hung in the air. A piece of construction paper had been tacked on the wall over the desk and read, *My prayer: May your camel infest your enemies with a thousand fleas and may their arms be too short to scratch their crotch. Amen.*

I smiled thinking this had to be Rhoda's sense of humor at work.

I passed on the bourbon but Rhoda didn't. She took the desk chair and swiveled to face me on the sofa. After she'd fortified herself with several sips of her daddy's bourbon, she said, "If Christy is dead, what's that to you?"

I gave her the short version, how I was working for Emma to find Christine's killer and how infant bones had been found under the house.

"You're saying Christy killed her baby?" Rhoda said.

"Not exactly. It wasn't *her* baby they found, and we're not sure what happened."

"Don't this just beat the band? You listen to people

pour their hearts out, think you know them and then wham! A slip of a woman comes around ten years later and whomps you upside the head with a whole new reality. Yeah, that's what Larry would call this. A whole new reality."

"A reality check," I said, smiling to myself. "What else can you tell me about Christine? Did she have many friends?"

"She hung out with a guy named Jerry Joe Billings. Serious drinker, that one. I swear, there were times he left the icehouse and had to hold on to the grass to lean against the ground."

"I met him. He doesn't drink anymore," I said.

"He's a solid citizen now?" She laughed derisively. "Never knew why Christy stuck with him. Mean SOB. Maybe she liked him 'cause he laughed at her jokes and their mutual friend was Jack Daniel's. Christy really made people laugh once she had a few whiskeys in her."

"Who else did she hang around with?" I asked.

Rhoda swirled her drink and stared at the amber liquid. "Well, there was Bob—but I heard he died last year. She mostly sat with Jerry Joe and Loretta—when Loretta wasn't working."

"Loretta have a last name?"

"She was just Loretta—and I never let her do business in my place. Tried to tell her more than once I'd help her get rid of that asshole who pimped her. I can be a pretty convincing woman, and pimps are all cowards anyway."

"Loretta was a prostitute?" I said.

"She hated what she was doing—or at least, that's what she said. The drinks numbed her, and I didn't feel all that guilty providing the anesthesia, even if I knew her ID was fake and she was under twenty-one."

"I'd like to find Loretta. Christine may have fed you lies about the baby she was carrying, but I'm hoping she told someone the truth."

But Rhoda was distracted. She lifted the sleeve of her Harley T-shirt and patted one of several nicotine patches she was wearing. "These are crap." Then she shouted, "Larry, you owe me a million dollars."

Larry stuck his head in the door. "Yesterday it was a Ducati 749."

The couple smiled at each other and he left.

She pulled her sleeve back down. "I'm always wishing someone would bring a Ducati in here for repair and then not pay the bill so we can keep it."

But I was wondering about her nicotine intake. Wasn't one patch supposed to be enough?

"Yeah, yeah, I know what you're thinking," Rhoda said, "but I figured I needed one patch for every pack a day I used to smoke. I only quit day before yesterday, so the days are tough."

"Loretta?" I hoped to get her back on track.

"Loretta. Right. Young, gorgeous, blond hair—the opposite of mine." She picked up a hank of her dried-out, bleached-out hair. "Is peroxide addictive?"

I smiled. Tough interview. The lady was distracted, probably because she was coming off a more serious addiction than peroxide. Her foot was bobbing, her finger was tapping the glass of bourbon she still held and her eyes were darting everywhere.

"Sorry. You didn't come here about me," Rhoda said. "Let's see. Loretta and Christy were pretty tight. Christy mighta told her something about this whole baby thing. You know, her lying about the kid really pisses me off."

"Maybe she'd apologize if she were alive," I said.

"Christ, she'd dead and I'm bad-mouthing her. That's pretty wrong. Sorry. Go on with your questions."

There I went again, nearly alienating a person who could help me. Jeez, when would I learn? "Did Loretta pick up johns near your bar?"

"Tell you the truth, the less I knew about that subject, the better I felt. Larry finally helped me understand that owning a place like the icehouse wasn't good for me spiritually or emotionally—and Loretta was one of the reasons. She was just a kid, for Christ's sake."

Spiritually or emotionally? Obviously Larry's words. "Larry sure looks out for you, doesn't he?"

"He's the best."

"Back to Loretta. Is there anything you can remember that might provide me with the information I need to solve this murder?"

"Okay. I'm thinking hard here." Rhoda squeezed her eyes closed. "I remember that pimp came and dragged her out of the icehouse one afternoon." She looked at me. "Actually she and Christy were sitting outside—we usually kept the garage door up and folks would sit a long time, especially the regulars. Anyway, he was all sweet-talking Loretta at first and he called her by a different name . . . what the hell was it?"

"Maybe there was something special about that day? Something that might jog your memory?"

"Nah, I . . . Wait." Rhoda thumped her head with the heel of her hand. "What the hell is wrong with me?"

"You remember something?"

"Loretta had a diamond ring tattoo on her finger— you know, on the left hand. That's what he called her. Diamond. Shit, I was doing so much weed back then it's a wonder I could put on my panties with the label in the back."

"Maybe that was her street name," I said, half to myself.

"Yeah. Makes sense, doesn't it?"

"It does."

We talked for several more minutes, but Rhoda couldn't pull anything else from her memory. Finally I rose and said, "You and Larry have been wonderful." I gave her a card. "If you think of anything else, call me anytime."

She stood. "This place, doing the motorcycle thing? We love it. It's totally selfish. The icehouse wasn't. I felt like I helped people by letting them talk, by being there all the time, standing behind that bar. I kinda miss that. Will you let me know if I helped Christy one last time, whether she deserved it or not?"

"Sure. If anyone else besides the police comes around asking questions about Christine O'Meara, do me a favor and don't tell them anything."

"Deal," Rhoda said with a smile.

I drove home, watching for the white Focus Larry had mentioned. I saw a few—they're probably the most rented car in the country—but none of them followed me.

As I turned the corner onto my street, I noticed an unfamiliar Honda parked at the curb in front of my house. I pulled into my driveway, and got out, heading for the back door. The woman who'd been waiting in the car immediately came after me.

"Are you Abby Rose of Yellow Rose Investigations?" she called.

New client or the press? The press, I decided. She confirmed this by saying, "Mary Parsons, investigative reporter for K—"

"Sorry," I said, stopping to face her near my back gate. "I can't help you."

I didn't expect this to deter her, and it didn't. "Is it true Emma Lopez has hired you to learn the truth about the infant found under her demolished house?"

"I said I can't help you."

"But she is your client?" Parsons said.

"I suggest you leave, because I have police friends who—"

I was interrupted by Kate's 4Runner pulling in behind my car.

"Hey, Abby," Kate called as she got out.

Before I could warn Kate, she walked right up to the reporter and held out her hand. "Kate Rose. You new in the neighborhood?"

"She's a reporter. I've politely asked her to leave. A few more minutes and polite is off my radar."

"I only have a few questions, Ms. Rose," Parsons persisted. "Just a minute of your time. Please?"

She was resorting to *please*? Must be new on the job. "Kate, let's go inside." I opened the gate and walked through, Kate on my heels.

"I'll be around," Parsons called before we were inside the house.

I wondered then if Larry Murray had mistaken a white Focus for a pale gold Honda earlier today. But I doubted he'd make an error like that.

While Kate fed Webster, I took a Dr Pepper from the fridge and popped the top. The sugar and caffeine hit me almost immediately, and I realized I hadn't eaten all day. "Want to do Chinese?" I asked Kate when she came back into the kitchen from the utility room.

"Let me make a call first." She took her cell from her skirt pocket and punched in some numbers.

"Hi," she said into the phone. "We on for tonight?"

I watched her lose her smile as she listened. Then she said, "I understand completely. You need to straighten things out with your ex. A teenage boy needs as much time as he can get with his father."

After she hung up, I said, "Did you know before now that he has an ex and a kid?"

She raised her chin. "Yes, I did. I asked about his family and he finally told me about his son."

I sipped my Dr Pepper. "*Finally* told you?"

"Clint was reluctant to talk about his son at first. He was worried I'd run for the hills, I guess."

"Smart guy. You just left Terry because you didn't want kids, and Clint knew that, right?"

"I told him. Yes."

"Does this change how you feel about Clint?"

"I-I don't know. A half-grown child is different from a newborn, and—"

"I'm glad you're giving this some thought." I could tell this was the wrong time to discuss her choices. She needed to sort this out in her mind without my interference.

"I'll give it plenty of thought. Now, how about that Chinese? I'll drive," she said.

"Can we pick up and eat here? I'll be out on the case tonight, and before I leave I should document what I've learned today."

"What's going on, Abby?"

I told her about Billings.

She opened a kitchen drawer and removed the take-out menu. "I'm glad DeShay will be with you. I hate when you deal with people like this Billings guy in the daytime, much less after dark."

"I know how to protect myself, Kate."

"Why? Because Daddy taught you to shoot? That doesn't mean I'll stop worrying."

I smiled. "Yeah, I know." I wanted to tell her I was worried, too—worried about her getting her heart broken. But I kept my thoughts to myself. I was getting better at that, thanks to Jeff.

18

DeShay picked me up at nine thirty for our meeting with Billings. As I slid into his T-bird, I patted my jeans pocket. "Got the money."

"How much are you paying him?" DeShay said.

"Four hundred," I answered. "I hope what he's got is worth that much."

"You're worried about money? Is that company you inherited in trouble all of a sudden?" DeShay turned onto Kirby and headed for the freeway.

"No, but that doesn't mean I don't spend my money wisely."

"I hear a lot of you rich people are penny-pinchers. Now, tell me everything you know about Billings. Then we need to plan our cover story for why I'm with you. Don't want Billings to get suspicious of me."

By the time we reached Billings's apartment complex on the southeast side of town, DeShay knew everything I did. We decided he'd pretend to be a partner in my detective agency. Seemed simple and believable.

DeShay pulled into the pitch-black parking lot. All the lights had either burned out or apparently been used for target practice. The overflowing Dumpster, the burglar bars on some of the apartment windows and the fact that one section of the complex had obviously burned down at some point and never been rebuilt brought the word *slum* to mind. Yup, I was glad DeShay was by my side.

As we walked toward building D, I noticed Billings's battered car parked near the cracked sidewalk. I slid my hand into my pocket and clutched the cash. Holding on to my ticket to the truth with one hand, I slipped my other arm through DeShay's.

Billings's apartment was on the second floor—apartment D-2320. When we started to climb the outside iron stairs, a Hispanic man in an apartment on the first floor stood in his window watching us. The man appeared angry, and I wondered if that was how he always looked. I sure wouldn't be too happy living here.

Billings's place was the first door we came to and directly above the angry guy's apartment. DeShay knocked while I stayed in line with the peephole. No answer. DeShay knocked again and I called, "Mr. Billings? It's Abby Rose."

Still nothing.

"Maybe he's not back from his meeting," DeShay said.

"I saw his car . . . but maybe he got a ride with a fellow ex-drinker."

"Or maybe he used that fifty bucks you gave him on a bottle of Scotch and—"

"We need some quiet," came a voice from below.

DeShay leaned over the railing. "Sorry about that, man. We're friends of the guy in 2320. You know if he's home?"

"I seen you two, and you don't look like no friends of anyone lives in this place," the guy called back.

DeShay went down the stairs and I followed.

Same guy from the window. He wore a T-shirt advertising Corona beer but hadn't bothered with shoes. Since I'd already stepped around several broken bottles I didn't think that was too smart.

"Okay, we're not friends. We're business acquaintances," I said. "You know if he's up there?"

"What's it to you, lady?" The guy took a step toward me, frowning.

DeShay put an arm in front of me and pulled his badge from his pocket with his other hand. In a quiet but menacing tone he said, "This is what it is to us, man."

Mr. Corona lifted his hands in surrender. "Holy Mary, good. I thought you were . . . I don't know what I thought. I just know all the noise on the stairs, it keeps waking up my baby."

"Noise on the stairs?" I said.

"You a lady cop?" the man asked.

DeShay said, "You don't need to know. What's your name, man?"

"Rodolfo Aguirre."

"I'm Sergeant Peters, HPD. Tell me what you heard tonight."

"I heard two people go up a little while ago. Maybe more than two, even. They pounded those stairs and then I hear them walking around up there. Stupid paper ceiling. The baby starts crying and then I'm in trouble, 'cause I leave for my shift as soon as my wife gets home in the morning—she's a nurse and works at night—and I gotta get some sleep, you know?"

"What's a little while ago?" DeShay asked.

"Nine thirty—right in the middle of FOX News. Then I hear someone come down, but by that time the baby, she's crying real hard and I'm trying to get her back to sleep."

"One person came down?" I asked.

"Yeah, one. Believe me, I learn the sound of just one—and they was going fast, making plenty of noise."

"Thank you for the information, Mr. Aguirre," DeShay said.

"We need more police around here," Aguirre said. "Could you tell your cop friends?"

DeShay nodded. "I will."

After he'd gone back in his apartment, DeShay and I climbed the stairs again, trying to be as quiet as possible.

DeShay whispered, "Two or more go up, sounds of activity in the apartment, then one person comes down. Our guy's home."

"He could be asleep," I said.

"Maybe. But trying to get anything out of a passed-out drunk will probably be a waste of time." DeShay knocked again.

Meanwhile, I put my mouth near the door seam. "Jerry Joe, it's Abby. I have your money."

Nothing.

"Okay, that's it," DeShay said. "We'll have to do this another—"

I reached for the knob, unwilling to leave without learning anything. The door opened.

"Abby, are you trying to get my ass fired?" DeShay whispered harshly.

But he was looking at me, not inside the apartment. He didn't yet see the body on the floor near the kitchen entry.

"Oh, my God." I started inside.

DeShay saw now and held me back, pulling a gun from his ankle holster. "My cell is in my right pants pocket. Use speed dial number six and you'll get dispatch. When they answer, hand me the phone."

I did this, staying behind DeShay while he crept toward the body—definitely Billings, lying facedown. DeShay pulled a latex glove from his pocket, and I told the woman who answered the call to hang on for Sergeant Peters.

DeShay traded the glove for the phone. "Put this on and check for a pulse, Abby."

While he asked for backup, I snapped on the glove and lifted Billings's hand, felt his wrist. I found a faint beat beneath my fingertips. "He's alive."

DeShay went around to the kitchen, phone to his ear, being careful not to step in the bloody trail that seemed to lead there. I heard him ask for paramedics; then he disappeared down the hall.

I wasn't sure where all the blood near Billings's neck was coming from, and felt helpless kneeling next to him, knowing he might be dying and I couldn't do anything.

DeShay returned to my side and said, "Apartment's clear."

Billings hadn't stirred. I felt for a pulse again. This time I couldn't find one. "I-I think he's dead."

DeShay knelt and rolled Billings over.

I saw the wound, saw where all the blood had come from. His throat was cut.

DeShay bent over Billings, his ear close to the man's open mouth, checking for any sign of life.

All I could do was gag and turn away.

"CPR won't do this dude any good. From what I saw he ran out of blood in that kitchen." DeShay leaned back on his heels. "Maybe God kept him alive to carry him those last steps to this spot."

The backup police officers and paramedics arrived not

long after DeShay led me to a filthy couch and told me not to move or touch anything. By the time Don White arrived, CSU must have already taken a hundred pictures, and bright circles of light blurred my vision. Now the videographer was finishing up.

When White saw me, my skin no doubt the color of a fried egg white, he said, "I should have known you'd be here."

DeShay was in the kitchen, where apparently Billings had been attacked, and called, "She came with me."

"That figures." White turned his attention to the body. Keys, wallet and rolled-up cash that probably once belonged to me had been bagged in plastic by the HCME assistant who'd arrived a few minutes ago.

White knelt by Billings's body and stared at the neck wound. "That's a jagged mess. What'd the killer use? A fucking butter knife?"

DeShay came around into the living area. "No weapon found. Probably took it with him. I've got a few uniforms searching the shrubs, drains and Dumpsters. Whatever he used didn't kill Billings right away."

The ME's assistant said, "You found no arterial spray, Sergeant Peters?"

"Nope. Just blood in the kitchen where he first fell, then the trail in here. Looks like he crawled to this spot and collapsed."

The young man nodded. "Killer cut several veins rather than the carotid. The victim probably bled for a good while."

I said, "Could we have saved him if we'd gotten here sooner?"

White gave me his "why don't you shut up?" look.

The assistant said, "I can't answer that."

"Any footprints other than the victim's?" White asked, scanning the dark gray carpet.

"No," DeShay answered. "No sign this was a burglary, either. Like this guy would have anything worth stealing."

His life was worth stealing, I thought. Probably because he knew something, maybe tried to sell information to a higher bidder than me. But he paid with his life.

White addressed me. "Explain how you and Peters ended up here."

"Sure, but somewhere else, if that's okay. You guys may be used to a dead man in the middle of the room, but it's making me kind of sick." My mouth felt wiped dry inside, but I didn't want even one sip of water from this horrible, dirty apartment.

"Somewhere else," White said with a smirk. "Sure, princess. Wouldn't want you to have an upset tummy."

I had no idea why he'd taken such a dislike to me, but it had all started when Emma asked for me to be with her during his first interview with her.

White left DeShay to interview the neighbors who had gathered on the second-level cement walkway bordering the apartments. Maybe someone besides Rodolfo Aguirre heard or saw something tonight. Meanwhile, White and I went down to his unmarked car.

The moment I sat in the front passenger seat, my phone rang. I checked the caller ID and showed the display to White. "It's Jeff."

"By all means tell him what you've been doing tonight."

I opened the phone and put it to my ear. "Hey."

"You getting ready for bed?" he asked.

"Not exactly. I'm sitting in Sergeant White's car at a crime scene. Hang on." I looked at White. "Can we go to speakerphone, Sergeant?"

"Why?"

"I think Jeff would like to talk to you." God knows I needed his help.

"Sure, princess. I'll talk to a real cop."

"What happened?" Jeff said. "Are you all right?"

"I'm fine. Speaker okay?"

"Yes," Jeff answered.

I pressed the speaker option. "I'm about to tell you and Sergeant White why I'm here at a murder scene."

And I did, talking too fast at times—Jeff had to ask me to slow down more than once—and finishing with, "I hope it's not my fault this man is dead."

"Your fault? I don't think you wielded that knife tonight, Abby," Jeff said. "Don, you there?"

"Yeah, I'm here."

"I heard about Bennie. I'm sorry, man. How's his wife doing?"

"You know what she said? She said all these years neither one of us got shot in the line and then he goes down on the job anyway. Fucking bad luck, you ask me."

"You're there for them both, though. And that's *good* luck. Bet you can't think about much else," Jeff said.

"That's the God's truth. I guess no one can call your girl off this case, Kline? Not even you?"

"She's working for a client and has a license to do it. You know that, right?"

White sighed heavily. "I know, but she's probably the same age as my daughter. She's gonna get hurt. Then I got these TV assholes to deal with. And your partner? You can have him back the minute you show up. Wants to tell me how to do—"

"Don? If you trust DeShay and if you let Abby do her thing, I promise you they'll work as hard as any of us. You can spend more time with Bennie that way."

"I'm still on the job," White said defensively. "I'm still—"

"Listen to me. Abby and DeShay are the good guys. They're smart. They can help you."

White bowed his head. "I never thought anything would be more important than the job. Never. Not until Bennie went down."

I think I'd been holding my breath through the entire conversation, but I felt like I could relax a little now.

Jeff said, "Abby? You there?"

"Yeah," I said quietly.

"Work *with* Don, not against him, okay?"

"Sure. Of course. I'll call you later."

I disconnected and looked at White. "I've told you all I know. I'm worried about the tail, the one Larry Murray picked up on. Someone could have been following me all day, and that's how they got to Billings."

"See, that's the kind of stuff that worries me, Abby." At least, thanks to Jeff, all his anger and sarcasm seemed to have dissipated.

"What do you mean?" I asked.

"You're saying a murderer probably followed you around," he said. "Doesn't that scare you?"

My turn to be defensive. "Sure it does, but that's part of my job."

He smiled. "Tough girl, huh? Who besides the TV company would want to tail you?"

"An investigative reporter from a TV or radio station was sniffing around my house this afternoon. Mary Parsons. She seemed to know I'm working for Emma."

"I know her. She's nothing to worry about. Anyone else?"

"I was seen all day with Emma on Monday—the day the house was leveled. Our pictures were even in the *Chronicle*. Then, after her accident, I made plenty of trips to her hotel. I've also had a little publicity of my own in the last few years. Guess it wouldn't be that hard to figure out who I was and what I do if someone decided to check me out."

He said, "Who you are, yes, but maybe not what you're doing for Emma Lopez. The TV crew knew, though. One of them could have been approached by or spoken to the wrong person when everyone was standing around watching after the baby bones were found."

"I never thought about that. Did the HPD videographer catch any crowd footage?" I asked.

White raised his bushy gray eyebrows. "You want to see if you recognize someone you've never seen from crowd footage?"

Guess all the sarcasm *wasn't* gone.

He went on, saying, "All we know is that someone was real interested in what you've been up to. I'm glad you were smart enough to ask Peters to come with you tonight."

"Hey, I may have been born at night, but it wasn't *last* night. And so you know, I have a thirty-eight in my glove compartment and I know how to use it."

"Somehow, that doesn't surprise me, Annie Oakley." He closed his eyes, shook his head. "Figuring out how all these cases are connected will be tough. Billings died because he knew something. Either that or he got too honest at that meeting he went to and pissed somebody off. Christ, we'll have to find out where he was and who he talked to. And the *anonymous* don't much like talking to us. Maybe because we put so many of them in jail before they decide to get sober."

"You actually believe it was a coincidence that he was

murdered on the day I talked to him? Or that one of his AA—"

"No, I don't believe he was murdered by one of his AA pals. But I always try to think about all the possibilities."

"Billings knew Christine O'Meara and mentioned her baby to get me to offer him more cash. Someone had to shut him up before he talked."

"Duh, yeah," White said.

"You think Christine's murderer and Billings's killer are the same person?" I asked.

"We can't jump to that conclusion yet," White said. "One thing I do know: Someone's out there with a major secret, and they've been covering their trail for years—piling on layers while all we've got are dried-up leads."

"Then a TV show comes to town," I said. "And shines a big, bright light on a buried child."

"Yeah." White nodded. "That's what drew this turd out of the shadows. The publicity."

"The *Chronicle* ran a piece before Emma's house went down. I didn't see the article, but Chelsea Burch was pretty upset that the paper printed a story about the reality show in advance. If the demolition hadn't been moved up, all the local TV stations would have been there Tuesday morning."

He laughed. "Ain't that too bad they missed out."

"But that doesn't mean the killer wasn't there later on," I said. "He or she could have arrived on the scene once the story about the baby bones was bulletined across every television screen."

We were both silent for several seconds. White finally said, "We can guess all we want, but we need evidence. I gotta go help Peters with that. Your car around here?"

"DeShay drove."

"Then I guess you're stuck until I can find you a ride home."

I could have called Kate, but decided I'd rather hang around a little while, maybe learn something more. But I hoped that didn't mean I had to sit with the corpse.

19

The following morning, a Saturday, I awoke feeling like I hadn't slept at all. The same question kept invading my dreams, waking me over and over: What did Billings know that got him killed?

As I lay under my quilt with Diva purring beside me, possibilities rolled around in my brain. Billings may have lied about why he declined the Crime Stoppers reward. Perhaps he'd figured out who killed Christine and was blackmailing the murderer. But judging from his low-rent apartment and his job mounting tires, he sure hadn't received much of anything for keeping a very big secret. I suppose he could have lost the blackmail money somehow—or maybe the ex-wife took everything for child support. I had no idea.

Billings *had* mentioned the baby to me, and from what Rhoda said, Christine was hanging out at the bar while she was pregnant with Emma's sister. Maybe Billings knew that Christine lied about Xavier Lopez stealing the child and he planned to sell me that piece of information. Perhaps that was all he knew. But the killer might have feared Billings knew more. Leaving him alive to tell me anything was too big a risk.

I squeezed my eyes shut at the thought, regret welling up in my throat. Despite what Jeff said last night, I still blamed myself for the murder. I'd probably led a killer to where Billings worked. When I left, my tail either stayed behind or followed me to the motorcycle shop. No matter what, he knew where to find Billings and followed him home. From my own experience with Billings, if he'd been offered cash, he would have allowed Hannibal Lecter inside his apartment.

No wonder I'd hardly slept a wink. Even though Jerry Joe Billings would never have been my best friend, he was still a human being who deserved better. But getting lost in guilt wouldn't help anyone. All I could do now was what I did best—find answers. Find out what happened to him, to Christine O'Meara, and to those innocent babies.

Something came to me then, something I should have realized as soon as I learned that Christine O'Meara died in 1997. She couldn't have written the letter to *Reality Check*. Then who did? Who watched Emma's family and cared enough to write to a TV show? I needed to quiz Emma more thoroughly about this, and over breakfast, when Kate told me Emma had a few houses to show her, I decided to go along.

Emma's rented cream-colored Cadillac arrived outside my house around noon, and the first house we drove to was only about four blocks from mine in West University Place. Kate decided not to tour this first place because it was too big. Although the lots in this part of town were small, recent buyers had taken to tearing down the original average-size houses and replacing them with huge new homes that left no room for a yard—and Kate wanted a yard for Webster.

When we started out for the next place, Kate's cell rang. By her flirty tone, I knew who had called.

She said, "We're leaving one house not far from Abby's place. You want to catch up with us?" Kate asked Emma for directions to the next property, still in West U, and repeated them to her new best friend, Clint Roark.

Five minutes later we pulled up to a curb less than a mile away. Kate's eyes lit up. It looked like an English cottage: redbrick, peaked roof, and small enough that it was probably the original structure, and thus had a backyard.

Emma glanced in the rearview mirror and said, "Your friend's here."

Kate got out to greet him.

I introduced Emma to Roark and said, "Thought you were tied up this weekend."

"My son had a movie date. Funny, I never had a movie date when I was that young." He laughed. "Anyway, I dropped them off at the theater and had a couple of hours to kill."

Kate said, "I told Clint about our house hunt."

Emma led us up the walkway, and I realized that maybe I was feeling jealous. I feared Roark might monopolize Kate's time, something Terry had never done. Today was proof of that. He couldn't spend two hours without her.

I should be happy for her, I thought. *Am I that selfish?* Daddy always said I was a real foot stomper when things didn't go my way, and I guess when you get older, foot stomper turns into "control freak."

After Emma pressed a four-digit code into the lockbox, opened it and retrieved the key, we all went inside and stood in the small foyer that offered a view into the living area. The stairs were to our right, and a small angled room, a study or office with French doors, was on our left. The layout looked similar to mine, but this house appeared older on the outside.

Reading from a sheet of paper, Emma said, "Two baths and three bedrooms, master downstairs, two upstairs. New furnace and air conditioner, wood and tile floors throughout, kitchen redone two years ago."

Roark smiled. "What are we waiting for?"

"Kitchen first." Kate grabbed his hand.

I mumbled, "I'll bet the son's movie date was Roark's idea so he could hook up with Kate."

"What?" Emma said.

"Nothing. Can we talk when we're done, or do you have to get back to the office?"

"I have another client. Then I plan to go over to my own property before dark. The foundation has been poured and they're framing today. I can't believe they're still giving us the house."

"They have to stick to the contract, just like you did, and it clearly stated you would get the new house and gifts no matter what. Besides, you still have to appear on one of Venture's programs."

"Don't remind me," Emma said. "I'm amazed at the progress they've made on the house. They said from the beginning it would only take a couple weeks, but I guess I didn't believe them," she said. "They bring in all these people and work long hours."

"Maybe I can meet you there this evening?"

"That would be great, but I hope you don't feel the need to protect me. The house seems like a small thing after everything that's happened."

"And something else *has* happened. That's what I wanted to talk to you about."

"Tell me," she said.

"A witness has been murdered."

She drew in her breath, covered her mouth with her hand. "Is it someone I know?"

"No—at least, I don't think so. We can talk about all this later. There's something more I want you to think about, even though we've been over this before. Your mother obviously didn't write the letter to *Reality Check*. Finding out who did could help us. That person knew the baby was missing. Think about counselors or teachers or neighbors who took a special interest in you. Maybe one of them decided to disguise their identity by making the letter seem like it came from an uneducated person."

Emma sighed, tucking strands of silky hair behind her ear. "I'll try, Abby, but I've already gone over this a hundred times since we were chosen for the show."

"Revisit it for me again, okay?"

"Sure. I should be over at the property by five. Can you tell me the name of the person who . . . died?" Today she'd been free of the worried expression I'd seen all week, but now it had returned.

"Jerry Joe Billings," I said.

Her eyes widened. "J.J. I remember my mother mentioning someone named J.J. Was it him?"

"Since she and Billings were definitely friends, the answer is probably yes. See? You do remember more than you realize."

She smiled sadly. "When prompted by terrible events, yes. Now I need to get to work."

When she walked into the living room, she reverted to Realtor mode—probably her *safe* mode. "Drapes are old, but the floor is in excellent shape." She walked over and pulled aside the heavy fabric that covered the window. "New windows, too. That's a plus."

Kate and Roark's laughter echoed through the empty house, and Emma and I joined them in the kitchen.

Emma stopped in the entryway, her hands on her hips, and scanned the large room. "This is different. Haven't seen a house with this layout in West U." She glanced down at her paper. "No dining room. I'll bet they knocked out a wall to enlarge the kitchen."

I took in the room, then swallowed, hoping to get rid of the lump in my throat. One end of the kitchen, beyond the breakfast nook where a bay window offered a view to the backyard, was a second cozy living area with fireplace. This arrangement was unbelievably similar to the house we grew up in River Oaks. How I had loved that kitchen.

Kate glanced at me and smiled. "Isn't déjà vu wonderful?"

More love at first sight, I thought. "Maybe, but knowing you, you'll look at about a dozen other places before you decide."

"If the upstairs and the bathrooms pass muster, I doubt it." She took Clint's hand and they went off to explore the rest of the house.

What had happened to her? The new Kate would take some getting used to.

While Kate and Emma went to Emma's office to draw up a contract—she was absolutely crazy about the house—Clint left to pick up his son, and I went home. I'd already started separate files for each case—one for Billings, one for Christine and one for the two babies—hoping that organizing them this way would give me better clarity. I planned to work on them, but there was a message on my phone, which Diva pointed out with loud meows and much pacing on the counter. It was Jeff.

"Didn't want to call you on your cell and disturb you if you're working your case, but I'm home now. When you get a chance, give me a call."

Didn't want to disturb me? When I got a chance? Had everyone I loved gone nuts?

Speed dial is the best thing ever invented, and he answered on the first ring.

"I'm home, so get your butt over here," I said. "I can't wait to see you."

"Can you come here instead?"

"Sure, but—"

"Is Kate there?"

"No. Why?"

"I prefer if no one knows I'm back yet."

"Okay, sure." This was strange.

"And Abby, do something for me first. After we talked about the Billings murder with Don White and you were feeling all guilty about leading the killer to Billings, I got to thinking. My five-hour flight offered plenty of time for thinking. You need to check your car for a GPS tracking device."

"You mean the thingie I never use? You've seen it. It's right on the dash—"

"No. I mean someone may have put a monitoring device on your car."

"You think?" I'd never even considered the possibility.

"Get a mirror and look under your bumpers. If it's there, the device might be hard to find, could be smaller than a deck of cards."

"I'm on it. And then I will see you very soon." I hung up and realized that my heart was beating ninety to nothing. There was no doubt I had a grade-A-pasteurized passion for that man.

The cool fall air had remained, and I ran upstairs and changed into low-rider jeans and a new scoop-neck sweater that Jeff hadn't seen yet. I considered wetting my hair and restyling it, but didn't want to waste the time. I grabbed my makeup mirror, the kind that magnifies on one side, and also took an old beach towel outside to lie on.

Turned out the magnifying side only made all things dirty under my bumpers blend together. Using the regular side, I began my search again, going too quickly at first, impatient to get to Jeff's place.

I stopped and took a deep breath. "Slow down and do this right, Abby."

I hit pay dirt on the back bumper, driver's side. I found

a small black rectangular case amid the filth. I pulled it free and slid from beneath the car. "Damn," I whispered.

How do you shut this thing down? I wondered. I turned it over and saw there was a battery case, opened it and dumped out the double-As. I gathered everything up, used the baby wipes I keep in my car to clean my hands and took off to see Jeff, thinking, *follow me now, whoever you are.*

With Saturday shoppers out in force, getting to Jeff's apartment took more than thirty minutes. I kept a watchful eye for a tail, but no one seemed to have followed me into his complex. I even parked by the manager's building for five minutes and waited for anyone else to drive in. Nobody did.

Jeff's car was parked in the first spot near the sidewalk leading to his building, and again my heart sped up. I hurried to his door and knocked my special knock.

When he opened the door we were in each other's arms at once. Our kiss was getting better by the second when a woman's voice interrupted us.

"Jeffy? You got a girlfriend, Jeffy?"

I pulled away and peered around his shoulder. A short, chunky woman wearing blue sweats stood in the center of Jeff's mostly barren living room.

I blinked, not quite believing what I was seeing. No mistaking: This woman had Down syndrome.

"This is Abby," Jeff said. "She *is* my girlfriend."

With Jeff's arm around me, we came in and he kicked the door shut.

"I'm Doris." The woman grinned, opened her arms and ran to us, capturing us both in a bear hug.

"Really nice to meet you, Doris," I said after she let us go.

"Jeffy took me on the airplane. I want to do it again."

"Not for a while." Jeff looked down at me. "Doris is my sister."

"I-I . . . Wow," I said. "You have a very cool brother, Doris."

"Cool?" She picked up his hand and pressed his palm against her chubby cheek. "I don't think so, Abby. Jeffy feels warm."

I smiled. "Sorry. You're right. He *is* warm, and I've missed him a lot since he was in Seattle with you."

"Linda lives in Seattle. But she went away and Jeffy came. He says Linda's not coming back, that she's visiting God."

"Linda took good care of Doris." Jeff's voice was soft, almost a whisper.

"Was Linda related to you two?" I asked.

"Not by blood," Jeff said. "But she loved you, didn't she, Doris?"

Doris averted her narrow eyes. "Can I have a Coke?"

"Sure." Jeff walked toward the kitchenette, Doris on his heels.

I followed, wondering why in hell Jeff had kept this from me. But the more I thought, the more I understood. He had a mentally retarded sister twenty-five hundred miles away from Houston—and not once since I'd known him had he visited her. He was a workaholic homicide investigator who'd put his family on the back burner. Talking about Doris to me or anyone else would not come easily to him. In fact, it would probably be harder for him than staring down at a corpse covered in blood.

"This isn't the red can, Jeffy." Doris was holding a Diet Coke and pouting.

Jeff said, "I know, but—"

"I want the red can. Linda always gave me the red can." Doris's happy demeanor had vanished, and I got the feeling I was about to witness the kind of tantrum that produced the wail I overheard on the phone the other night.

I stepped toward Doris. "This is my favorite kind of Coke. Texas Coke."

Doris looked at me, frowning, then glanced at the can. "They had red Coke on the airplane."

"But the airplane isn't part of Texas," I said. "This is what I drink all the time."

"Your girlfriend drinks Texas Coke, Jeffy. And so do I." She held out the can to Jeff. "Help me?"

After he popped the top, she reclaimed the soda and took a long drink. "Texas tastes kinda good."

I smiled, and Jeff looked plain relieved. No way was

he equipped to deal with this situation if a soft-drink issue made him this tense.

Doris, meanwhile, had something else in mind, because she walked by us, her Texas Coke in hand, headed for the TV. That was when I noticed the stack of DVDs—it looked like all Disney titles. She sat cross-legged on the floor, set her can beside her and started rummaging through the titles.

I said, "Does she need help with—"

"She can work the DVD player and remote like an expert. In a minute, she'll be so into her cartoons we can talk."

Jeff was right. Shortly after *The Little Mermaid* started, Doris seemed transfixed.

Jeff and I sat at the card table in his small dining area. I vowed not to say what he expected, like, *Why the hell didn't you tell me about Doris?* But before I could come up with an adequate response to learning something new and very unexpected, he spoke first.

"I'm sorry, Abby. I couldn't—"

I put a finger to his lips. "Don't be sorry. I understand."

He took my hand and kissed it. "When my parents died, it seemed right to leave my sister with Linda. Linda cared for Doris for years. Structure and routine are important for Down people. When I got the call after Linda had the heart attack and died, the doctor wanted me to put Doris in a group home."

"But you couldn't do that," I said.

He shook his head, lips tight.

"Do you plan to find someone like Linda here?"

"Yes, but that won't be easy. That's why I don't want anyone to know I'm back, or they'll be calling me out on cases. I need time. Does Kate have contacts in social services? I can't exactly put an ad in the paper and hire the first person who shows up."

"I'll ask. In the meantime, how are you?" I put my hands over his.

"I won't lie. This has been harder than any homicide I've ever worked. At first I planned to do what the doctor said. But it seemed wrong to send her off to live with strangers."

"How functional is she?" I asked.

"She can't fix her own meals—unless you call opening a package of cookies fixing a meal. But she can take care of herself in every other way—dressing, the bathroom, you know." His ears colored with embarrassment and his hands balled into fists.

I rubbed those white-knuckled hands, trying to ease his strain. "I'll help you any way I can."

He leaned forward and kissed me. "Thanks." He reached into his jeans pocket and pulled out a crumpled pack of Big Red. When he had two sticks of gum working, he said, "Did you look for the GPS device?"

I picked up my purse, took the thing out and placed it on the table. "You were right."

"Ah. Easy to tail someone with this." He picked up the little box and turned it over several times. "No identifying marks—looks like the manufacturer's label has been removed. This thing sends your location to a satellite and—"

"Oh, I know," I said. "Then someone picks up the signal on their little handheld computer loaded with fancy software. This spy stuff doesn't come cheap. Why did I ever trust those TV jerks for a second?"

"You think they're the ones who tracked you?"

"They have the money," I said.

"If it was them, how did the killer find Billings?" The smell of his gum filled the space between us, and I was finding it hard to concentrate on anything but him.

I sighed. "I don't know. Maybe the killer was the one who put that thing on my car. Or followed the Venture investigators who were following me. I probably had my own motorcade."

"Come on. I think you would have noticed."

"The idea that a murderer could put this under my bumper is scary. Without any identifying information, can we find out who bought this thing?"

"Give it to DeShay," he said. "Our tech guys might recognize the brand, or might be able to activate it and find out where the signal is being downloaded."

"I don't think that will work, Jeff. When I disabled it, I probably clued in whoever was receiving my location information. They know I pulled the plug."

"You're the computer whiz, so I don't doubt you're right, but it can't hurt to turn it over to DeShay and Don, see what the department can do with it."

"Will do." I checked my watch. "Wish I didn't have to go, but I promised to meet Emma. Can I do anything for you? Pick up groceries, maybe?"

"Yeah. That would be good. Taking Doris to the supermarket would get her all revved up—something that's not hard to do. Linda was great with her, but from the number of empty Coke cans I found at the house where they lived, I'll bet Doris drank at least a six-pack a day. Maybe you can convince her that there's a better Texas Coke—one without caffeine as well as sugar."

"Mind if I ask her what she likes to eat—so we can at least wean her off her bad habits slowly? I mean, who better for the job than the queen of bad habits?" I grinned.

"Sure," he said. But when I started to get up, he gently grabbed my wrist, gave me one of his intense blue-eyed stares. "You were great with her. I can't tell you what—"

"Shut up," I said.

He nodded, chewing his gum like crazy, and wearing the saddest smile I'd ever seen.

I blinked back tears as I went to talk to his sister.

20

Emma was waiting for me outside the production trailer when I arrived in her neighborhood. She'd had plenty of energy earlier, but now she held her left arm close to her body, and her eyes showed her fatigue.

"I didn't want to talk to Mr. Mayo or Chelsea alone, and I can't get near my house without their approval. I thought I'd just wait on you."

"Let's go for it," I said.

She climbed the two steps to the trailer door and knocked. I was right behind her.

Chelsea let us in with a "Hi, y'all." Besides her new-found and very bad Texas accent, she'd really taken to Nuevo Western wear and wore a straight denim dress, braided belt and new boots that were red, white and blue.

Emma said, "I'd like to see the house, but the workers at the barricade said I have to get a badge or something."

From beyond the curtain that separated the front of the trailer from the back, Mayo called, "Chelsea, who is that?"

"Emma and Abby," she shouted.

Then came the dreaded, "Send them back here."

I rolled my eyes and Emma whispered, "Great."

He was sitting on one of the couches watching what looked like an episode of *Reality Check,* a remote control in hand. By his ruddy cheeks and angry expression, I had a feeling he didn't like what he was seeing. He turned the TV off and looked at us.

"I'm very glad you two turned up." Mayo smiled, his flush fading.

Uh-oh. He'd flipped too fast, sounded way too nice.

Emma beat me to my own question, saying, "What do you want?"

"First off, things have been very tense this past week, and I'd like to put that behind us. Sometimes I lose sight of the fact that most people have no clue what it takes to be a show runner, to be the person who makes certain a program is produced on time and within budget."

"Is that a long-winded apology?" I said.

"You could say that. My job is to see that the construction and the interior design are done, that we have drama in our episodes that touches America. The unfortunate discovery under your house has eclipsed any thought I might have had of making your story our sweeps winner in November. I lost a very wonderful story to Kravitz."

"Are you whining, Mr. Mayo?" I didn't like this guy one bit—even when he tried to be human.

"Maybe I am. There's no circumventing the effect a dead child would have on our demographic."

I started to respond, but Mayo held up a hand. "Let me finish. Paul's program with Emma's story will draw better Nielsen numbers than the episode of *Reality Check* we now must air that same week. He'll have the superior show because of the work I did. Now, this goes no farther than this room. I will pay you, Ms. Rose, pay you whatever you want, to make sure Paul is . . . shall we say, *hindered.*"

I stared at him for several seconds, not believing what I'd heard. "I don't get it. Aren't you executive producer of both shows?"

He cleared his throat. "In name only. We have all sorts of titles in Hollywood, some of them meaningless. Paul has almost full control of his program, but that's not the point. Those higher up than myself have gotten into the mix. They've told me to finish Emma's house giveaway as we promised, give it plenty of local attention. A crime discovered during the filming of an entertainment program like *Reality Check*? That's the program they *don't* want from me, but they do want it on *Crime Time*."

I was beginning to understand. Egos. Turf. Nielsen numbers. First Kravitz wanted my help and now this guy. "How am I supposed to *hinder* Kravitz?"

"I'm sure you'll think of something," he said. "You've certainly made things difficult for me—and for him, too, from what I've heard."

"Won't you get in trouble for trying to ruin his show?" Emma asked.

"Not if no one but us knows," he said.

"Not to burst your bubble-slash-ego the size of Minnesota," I said, "but I won't do anything differently. And I'd certainly never take a penny of your money."

A tense silence followed; then Emma said, "Could we please have visitor badges?"

Mayo smiled then, tenting his hands. "It was worth a try." He called for his gofer, Chelsea, and soon Emma and I were walking down her street wearing *Reality Check* hard hats and paste-on paper badges.

At first the house couldn't be seen, because trucks were parked everywhere, but when we got closer Emma sucked in her breath and stopped dead in her tracks. "Oh, my gosh. It's bigger than I thought." She grabbed my hand and pulled me along to where the driveway used to be. The newly turned earth and discarded two-by-fours made me wish I'd worn work boots.

The framing was complete, and the insulated walls were up. Before we could go inside, Stu Crowell met us coming out, his ever-present camera with him.

"Hi, there," he said. "Did the big man leave town and you two snuck down here somehow?"

"Mayo gave us the hard hats himself," I said.

"He must want something," Stu said. "How about a tour?"

"No taping, right?" Emma said.

"Nope. I'm keeping track of the work for budget purposes."

Stu led us through framed-in rooms on the new cement, and Emma seemed able to visualize what everything would look like. She guessed the square footage at around twenty-four hundred. I supposed Realtors could do that. As for me, it was all beams and pipes and wires. Emma wanted to walk through again on her own, so Stu and I waited in what would be the foyer—at least I could figure that much out.

"I was hoping to see you while we were here, Stu," I said. "Have you had more than one interview with the police about what happened Monday?"

"Nope. I talked to a Sergeant Benson that day, but he only wanted to make sure he had my name and phone number in case he had more questions later. They did that with the whole crew."

"Did everyone know why I was with Emma that day?"

"Not everyone, but a few people asked after they made the find. Why? What's this about?"

I debated whether to tell him. Stu *had* impressed me as an honest, genuine man since day one. "Someone has been following me while I've been investigating the death of Emma's mother."

He looked at me, surprised. "Her mother's death? I thought this was about—"

"It's a long story. Can you recall specifically who asked you questions, aside from the police? Strangers in the crowd? Crew members? City employees?" Saying this made me realize how vast the suspect list might be.

"I don't remember. Sorry."

Damn. "Maybe there was someone who stood out to other production people, someone who seemed overly curious?"

"No one said anything to me," he answered.

I sighed. "If you get a chance, could you ask around and see if anyone else noticed or talked to someone like that?"

Stu nodded. "I can do that. There was a lot of mumbling in that crowd behind the fence. But we're used to people watching us, wanting to get on camera."

I smiled. "Emma and I would be grateful for anything anyone remembers."

"Sure. She's special, that one. I've done plenty of these shows and helped a lot of nice people. People like Emma are why I keep coming back when Mayo calls. He may be there to take the credit when the e-mails roll and the ratings are out, but it's the researchers, the directors, the film editors, the builders, the craftsmen, the decorators, the shoppers, the banks that give scholarships, the companies that— Hell, I could go on and on. Those are the real heroes."

"Them and you," I said. "Without you catching true emotion on tape, *Reality Check* wouldn't be the hit it is."

"I didn't finish. Mayo's an ass, but he's a true show runner. You gotta have someone like him to put it all together. He does that well."

I nodded. "You're probably right. Thanks for reminding me you can't judge a car by the sound of the horn."

The call from DeShay came while I was in the grocery store trying my best to balance boxes of Cocoa Puffs with equal parts broccoli. It took everything I had not to blurt out the news that Jeff was back in town. Especially when DeShay's first words were, "You hear from the man today?"

"Have you?" I was hoping to avoid an outright lie.

"Voice mail. Guess he's busy."

"I talked to him last night." At least that much was true. "He seemed to hint that he'd be home soon."

"That's good. Listen, I got a lead on our pro, Diamond. I decided to try a shortcut first and it worked. Remember Christine O'Meara had that one arrest?"

"Yeah." I realized where he was going with this. "Did she get picked up because she was with her friend Diamond?"

"You got it. Diamond had lots of names, but funny thing—her fingerprints never changed. Her real name was Fiona Mancuso. Had multiple arrests for solicitation."

My stomach sank. "You're speaking of her in the past tense. Is she dead?" I'd stopped my cart in front of the Pop-Tarts and realized a woman with a toddler was staring at me, her mouth open. I guess the words *Is she dead?* don't go over well in the supermarket.

"She's dead to HPD," DeShay went on. "No arrests since 1998. I'm running a print check through DPS to see if she's still around, and then I'll check the NCIC database. Maybe she relocated and is still in business."

"And if she's not?"

I'd maneuvered my cart over to a less trafficked area and stopped.

"Don't get discouraged, Abby. Your boy DeShay has been on this all day. Last time she was brought in they also hauled in her pimp on drug charges, a guy named James Caldwell. We know he's still around because he was recently released from prison. His next scheduled visit to his probation officer is Monday, and White and I plan to be there."

"Would he know where to find Diamond after all this time?" I asked.

"Maybe not, but he might be able to give us a few names of friends, relatives, you know."

"By the way, I know why someone tailed me so easily last week. Guess what I found stuck under my bumper?" I told him about the GPS device.

"Could be Kravitz had it put on your car."

"That's what I thought," I said.

"White's been dealing with the *Crime Time* jerks. He could ask one of them, but he took off today and tomorrow to spend time at the hospital, I guess I could call him, see if he wants to make a call."

"Don't bother him with this yet. The good news is, I found the stupid thing, so—Wait a minute. What about Emma? Could she have one on her rental car?"

He sighed. "She might. I'm on my way out of here. I'll stop by the hotel and check her car. What's she driving?"

I gave him the description.

"Are you home?" he asked. "I can pick up the device you found, turn it over to the tech people. We may be able to find out who bought it."

"Actually, I'm not home. I-I'm shopping for a friend who's not feeling well." More skirting the truth. I hated this. "I could meet you in the hotel parking lot and give the thing to you—say, in about thirty minutes?"

"That'll work."

"Another question. Did you talk to Billings's family?

Ask if he came into any money around the time he changed his mind about his Crime Stoppers tip?"

"I did, as a matter of fact. If he had any extra cash, the ex didn't know about it or she would have taken everything she could for back child support."

"Hmm. Maybe he didn't blackmail anyone, then. See you soon." I hung up and hurriedly finished shopping.

When I pulled into the hotel lot a half hour later, I spotted the rented Caddy right away, but DeShay wasn't there. I found him on the other end of the parking lot, and as I handed over the GPS device, he told me he'd spotted someone he thought he recognized—a local PI named Louie Tillson—sitting in a car with the window down, and smoking.

"I think Louie and I need to talk. Want to come?" DeShay said.

I smiled. "I would love nothing more."

I climbed in the T-bird and we made the short trip. DeShay didn't bother to find a parking spot. He just braked when we reached Tillson's car. DeShay got out and rapped on the driver's-side window, which was now rolled up.

Slowly the window came down, revealing a man with the perfect face for PI work. If I had to describe him to someone else, the only word I could think of would be *ordinary*.

"Hey, Peters. What's going down?" Tillson said.

"Nothing, man. You working?" DeShay said.

"You wouldn't be knocking on my window if I wasn't. Who's the lady?"

I was leaning against the T-bird and planned to keep my mouth shut, as DeShay had suggested on the drive across the lot.

"I'll bet you've seen her before, isn't that right?" De-Shay said.

"Me? No way." He laughed.

But all three of us knew this was a lie, and I wondered if Louie Tillson had followed me to that dry cleaner with Paul Kravitz in the passenger seat.

"Louie, I'll pass on your bullshit," DeShay said. "Why are you hanging around here? No, don't bother answering. Emma Lopez, right? And if she finds out, she might have to resort to that nasty stalker law."

"You know that ain't gonna fly, Peters. Public streets are a PI's domain."

"But see, this isn't a public street, man. This here is a private parking lot, and I don't think you've rented a room at the hotel. Or am I wrong?"

Tillson's face colored. "You running me off? Is that it?"

"Depends on who hired you and why you're here."

"You know I can't tell you that," Tillson said. "I'll go park in the street if that's what you want."

"From what I saw on the drive here, you won't find a metered spot unless you go about five blocks."

"I can do my job without any help from you, Peters."

"Sure. That's right." DeShay turned to me. "Abby, you got your phone handy?"

I pulled it from my pocket. "Right here."

"Take a picture of my friend Louie, would you?"

I flipped open the phone, hit the camera button and pressed capture before Louie could blink. I didn't even get his ear in the shot, but I nodded, saved the worthless photo and closed my phone with a satisfied smile.

"Thank you," DeShay said. "Now here's the deal, Louie. You tell me why you're here—not who hired you, 'cause I know you got your ethical standards to uphold—and maybe I won't show this picture to hotel security and tell them they've got a pest on their property. If I do that, I'm thinking they'll throw your ass out of here every time you show up."

"She's an investment, a reluctant one, they say," Louie replied. "They want her protected, want to see where she goes and with who."

"And what about my friend Abby? Are *they* protecting her, too?"

"Nah. They're just interested in what she's up to. I don't know if anyone's even on her anymore."

DeShay walked over to the T-bird for the GPS device. He then brought it back to Louie and held it out. "This belong to you?"

"What the hell is that?" Tillson asked.

"Don't play dumb, Louie."

Tillson squinted and then said, "A GPS monitor?"

"If I look under Ms. Lopez's rental, am I going to find one like it?"

"You think I need GPS to tail someone, Peters? What do you figure me for, some kind of amateur?"

DeShay laughed. "And do you figure me for some kind of stupid? Tell me you've never used one of these things."

"Okay, I've used them, but not one like that, and not on this case. Go ahead. Check her car if you don't believe me."

And that was exactly what DeShay did. He found nothing.

Before we parted ways with Louie Tillson, DeShay pointed at the phone still in my hand. "If I find out you've lied to me about anything, I'll make sure you lose your nice fat paycheck from those TV assholes by getting you kicked out of this lot."

"What the hell would I lie about, Peters?"

"That's the problem. I don't know."

I thanked DeShay, left the GPS device with him and drove on to Jeff's apartment. He and Doris helped me carry the groceries inside. Putting away the food was like Christmas for Doris. Every box of cereal, every vegetable, every piece of fruit was like a prize. Then I showed her the *other* best Texas drink: caffeine-free, sugar-free Dr Pepper. I thought it would be an easier sell than something with the word *Coke* printed on it. Then I realized I didn't even know if Doris could spell. Gosh, Jeff and I had a whole new learning curve ahead.

The Dr Pepper was a hit, and we shared a late dinner of deli rotisserie chicken, potato salad and fruit. Doris seemed to savor every bite and had better table manners than me. She even offered a halting, "May I leave the table?" when she was finished eating. Dr Pepper in hand, she went straight to Jeff's ancient recliner and used the remote to turn the DVD player back on. Once Jeff and I tossed the paper plates and loaded the dishwasher with glasses and silverware, we could hear Doris snoring loudly.

"Been a long day for her." Jeff pulled me close.

I tossed the sponge I'd wiped the card table with into the sink and wrapped my arms around him. "Long day for you, too. DeShay was asking about you."

"I called him about five minutes before you got here. I had to tell him I was back, Abby. I couldn't lie to him."

"I know the feeling, but I wish you would have done that earlier. I was dancing all around the topic of Jeff Kline. Or should I say *Jeffy* Kline?"

He smiled down at me. "When Doris was little, she couldn't say Jeffrey—that's what my Mom always called me. I became Jeffy."

"You're taking on a big challenge, but I'm glad you brought her here."

"Nothing else felt right. But my place is too small. I'll have to find a bigger apartment, get her bedroom furniture and—"

I put a finger to his lips. "Kate put a contract on a house today, and she'll be moving out. We can stay at my house while you hunt for apartments and find Doris a good caregiver. At least then everyone will have a bed to sleep in."

"Abby, I can't ask you—"

"You don't have to ask. Now do something better with your mouth than talk. She's asleep and we need to make good use of our time."

21

The following morning, Kate and I ate breakfast on the back porch. She'd made a bagel run and as promised brought home cinnamon raisin as well as the two-ton, whole grain, generously seeded kind she prefers. Kate wasn't in when I got home the night before, so at least I didn't have to lie about being at Jeff's place. In fact, both of us avoided the subject of the previous night altogether, instead focusing on the house she'd fallen in love with and how she hoped they'd take her cash offer.

"Who wouldn't?" I said.

"I'm afraid the owner will change his mind or something," Kate said.

"The house is empty, Kate. Why would he change his mind?"

She grinned. "If I don't have something to worry about, life seems so empty." But despite the joke, she and I both knew who the pessimist in the family was.

She said, "The armoire and the bedroom set I let Aunt Caroline keep when I moved in with Terry will soon have a new home."

"I picture her being completely shocked that you would take back furniture you'd given her."

"She knows they're mine, Abby."

"Hey, I'm preparing you, okay?"

She looked out at the cloudless sky. "Buying all new furniture would be cleansing, wouldn't it? A brand-new start?"

"You don't want to ask her for your stuff back, do you?"

Kate smiled. "Not really."

"Coward," I said.

I heard the doorbell ring through the open porch door, and Webster started barking—seemed he was already getting protective of my place. Kate and I went inside the house, and while I went to the foyer to see who was there, Kate took our plates and coffee cups to the kitchen.

DeShay's smiling face appeared on the security monitor when I turned it on. I opened the door and let him in. He wore a navy sports jacket and striped tie.

"You coming from church or are you working?" I asked.

Before he could answer, Kate joined us. "Hi, DeShay. Bet you're missing Jeff almost as much as Abby."

"Hey, Kate. You are looking particularly gorgeous this morning." He avoided the Jeff question, as I had yesterday.

"You're between girlfriends again, I take it?" she said.

"You think I'm hitting on you?" He looked at me. "Abby, she thinks I'm hitting on her."

We all laughed. DeShay does like the ladies.

"What's up?" I asked.

He'd brought a manila folder with him and opened it. "Check this out."

It was a mug shot of a woman with blond hair, smeared makeup and lifeless eyes.

"This is the woman I told you about. Fiona Mancuso, aka Diamond Monroe, aka Loretta Mancuso—I won't bore you with all the other names she's used. This has to be Christine O'Meara's friend."

"I'm sure Rhoda could tell us for sure, except I doubt the motorcycle shop is open on Sunday," I said.

Kate was staring at the mug shot, and I could tell she'd switched to therapist mode. "I hate seeing someone that young look so empty."

"If it helps, she hasn't been arrested in nine years." DeShay looked at me. "I checked the databases and there's nothing recent. She's never had a driver's license using any of the aliases we know about. Either she died or she went down the straight and narrow into oblivion."

"What about her social security number?" I asked.

"You don't exactly need one of those when you turn tricks for a living. No number was ever recorded on any of her arrest reports."

"Great. All we've got is a pimp to help us. And why should he do that?" I asked.

"If he knows anything, he'll cooperate. Not hard to dig up a reason to send a lifelong criminal back to jail."

"Ah," I said, nodding. "What about Emma? If this was her mother's friend, maybe she saw her at least once. There were parties at the house before the last baby was born."

"Can't hurt to show her the mug shot, I guess," De-Shay said.

"I'll give her a call right now," I said.

I learned Emma, Shannon and Luke were headed for Mass, and she said she'd stop by when the service was over. DeShay had no problem with this arrangement, as there were bagels and cream cheese to enjoy. I put on a fresh pot of coffee and had just poured three mugs when the doorbell rang. I checked my watch and was thinking they went to the shortest Mass they could find, but the monitor showed Clinton Roark's smiling face.

I called for Kate, then let him in.

"Good morning, Abby. Is Kate— Oh, there you are." His smile grew wider, and they had eyes only for each other.

I left them eyeball-to-eyeball and heard Kate say, "You feeling better about your family problems this morning?" as I walked away.

Roark said, "If my son doesn't want to spend time with me, I can't force him."

Bet Kate was loving this. She could rescue this guy from his *pain*.

A minute later, as DeShay and I were enjoying some damn fine coffee, I heard Kate call out that she and Clint were going for a drive.

DeShay said, "She's already found a new man? And you think I'm bad?"

"I'll admit I'm a little worried."

"Rebound," DeShay said. "I've done it myself, especially when a girl had that extra something. I saw Terry moping around Travis Center once this week on a psych consultation. Wonder how the good shrink is getting over her?"

"I should call him," I said. "But I'm afraid I'll be tempted to ask if he knows about Clint Roark."

"Call him. He's still your friend. Anyway, while we've got a minute, what's with Jeff? I assume you've seen him?"

"Yesterday. He told me he had to tell you he was in town, but right now he doesn't want anyone else to know. He has business to take care of first."

"What kind of business?"

"The details have to come from him, but I can tell you it has to do with his family."

"But I'll help him with anything. He knows that." De-Shay sounded hurt.

"You do know him, which means you understand he has to do things his own way, in his own time."

"Yeah, but—"

"DeShay, I don't doubt for a minute that when he's ready, he'll sit with you in that bar you two go to, and spit out more words than you ever thought he could. For now, I think we have to respect his wishes."

"You're sure he's okay?" he said.

I nodded and changed the subject, asked if they had any new leads on the Billings murder.

"Before White took off yesterday, he found out where Billings's AA meeting was. A church. Nothing unusual happened there, according to the janitor who cleans up when the meeting is over."

"Did anyone besides Mr. Aguirre hear or see anything at the apartment complex?"

"I bet they did, but since half the complex is filled with illegals, no one's talking. The preliminary autopsy report came in. Billings was cut from behind, left to right. There were hesitation marks, and you saw that ugly wound. The weapon may have come from the kitchen, a dull knife."

"Could the attacker have been a woman?"

"Unless we're talking domestic violence or gangs, women don't try to overpower a man with a knife, Abby. They prefer guns or blunt objects."

"I trust your experience, but Billings was a skinny, small man, and—"

"According to the report, the attacker was taller than the victim. They'll probably be able to figure out exactly how tall, but that will take time."

Before I could ask more questions the doorbell rang.

When I let Emma in, she hugged me with both arms— a good sign that she was almost mended.

"Where are Shannon and Luke?" I asked.

"Youth group meeting."

"Good. They probably don't need to hear about this anyway. Come into the kitchen for coffee."

While she greeted DeShay, I poured her a mug of French roast. She took it black and smiled after the first sip. "Now, this is some good coffee. You need to give the hotel a lesson."

"I have a photograph for you to look at, Ms. Lopez," DeShay said. "We believe this woman was a friend of your mother's, and perhaps you can confirm that."

"Like I've told Abby, aside from her parties, my mother never brought her friends home unless they were male."

We sat at the kitchen table, and DeShay reached for the folder. "I understand. Maybe seeing this face will jog a memory." He removed the photo and slid it in front of Emma.

She stared for several seconds, and her wide eyes told me she did recognize Fiona Mancuso. "Oh, my God," she finally said. "That's *her*."

"She came to your house?" I asked.

"No, no, she's the bus stop lady."

"The bus stop lady?" I echoed.

"Yes. I haven't seen her in the last couple of weeks, but to save gas, sometimes I leave my car at work if I don't have to drive a carpool for the kids. I take the bus, and this woman"—Emma tapped the mug shot— "she was at the same stop pretty often. We talked a lot. Really nice person."

"She tell you her name?" DeShay asked.

"No, but I must have told her mine, because I remember once she called me Emma. That's strange, isn't it? That I would give her my name without asking for hers?"

"Unless she knew who you were," I said.

"This woman was my mother's friend?" She glanced back and forth between us.

"We think so," DeShay answered. "Anything in particular you remember about her?"

"She's small, has a really bad dye job—jet-black—and I know she works for a maid service. She wears a turquoise uniform with a logo—I can't recall what it says, something about maids, though. And she has this odd tattoo on her hand—on her left ring finger. A diamond."

DeShay slapped the folder and grinned. "That's our girl."

"You're thinking she talked to me because she knew who I was?" Emma said.

"Probably," I said. "How long since she first approached you at the bus stop?"

"Probably five years ago—even when I was in school, I worked part-time at Green Tree Realtors and took that same bus."

"And she always wore a uniform?" I said.

"No, not always. She dressed like she needed help as much as we did. She always steered the conversation away from herself, though. Funny, I shared my whole life story and I don't even know her name."

"Her name is Fiona Mancuso," I said. "Remember how the letter to *Reality Check* indicated the writer had been watching you?"

"Yes—oh, my God. *She* wrote to them?"

"She knew your mother. I don't think it was a coincidence she found you at a bus stop," I said.

"And because she knew my mother, she knew my baby sister had disappeared."

DeShay said, "We need to find this woman. The logo on the uniform. Think hard, try to picture it."

Emma closed her eyes for several seconds. "I-I can't remember."

We turned for help to Houston's two-volume yellow pages, searching under *maids, housekeepers* and *house-cleaning*. We found no ads that conveniently offered photos of what their employees wore to work, and the sheer number of companies made it impossible for Emma to pick out any name she remembered.

While we were still perusing the yellow pages, Kate and Clint came in through the back door.

Kate introduced DeShay to Roark and then explained that they came back to get Webster and take him for a run at the dog park. Now he wanted to bond with the dog? This was getting serious.

"It's a beautiful fall day. Why are you cooped up in here?" Kate asked. "At least get out on the porch."

I said, "We're hoping Emma can remember an important detail about something she saw. Not having much luck."

Kate bent and fastened the leash onto Webster's collar. "Remember, Abby, I do hypnotherapy in my practice. Let me know if I can help."

Then she and Roark were off again while DeShay and I exchanged smiles.

22

Monday held the promise of leads on Fiona Mancuso from both her ex-pimp and the hypnosis Emma had agreed to. I awoke way too early, had three cups of coffee before eight a.m. and my second breakfast by ten. I called Jeff but he couldn't talk long, as he'd phoned a few home health agencies for information and was awaiting return calls.

Emma was more than willing to be hypnotized, but Kate and Emma couldn't clear their schedules until this afternoon. DeShay and White were meeting with the parolee-pimp around lunchtime. I'd asked if I could go along and had been given a firm "No way."

I tried answering mail, paying bills and finally decided the best thing might be to work off my extra energy. I plugged in my iPod and off Webster and I went. But even our fast walk came to an early end when it started raining. Webster loved splashing around on the way home as one of Houston's lovely unexpected downpours hit hard and filled up the streets almost at once. At least I knew what I would do next—take a long, hot shower.

By the time I got behind the wheel of my Camry and headed for the congested streets of the medical center, I felt like I had a stomachful of bedsprings. The slick streets slowed everyone down, which made me even more anxious and impatient.

When I entered Kate's office, she and April were in the reception area talking.

"Kate, I need therapy for acute Houston Traffic and Parking Syndrome. Is there any hope?"

She smiled. "Not with your personality. Emma called

and she's having a hard time finding parking, too. I'm ready to start as soon as she gets here."

"You're sure it's okay that I'm present during the hypnosis?"

"She wants you here. She has a very strong and positive connection with you, and I can't think of anything that would make her feel more comfortable."

I smiled. "Really?

Before Kate could respond Emma walked through the door with a cheerful, "Hi, everyone."

Kate led us through the reception area, door and down the hall past her family therapy area, the only therapy room I'd been in before today. We entered a room set up like a cozy living room. A matching green pastel sofa and love seat were separated by a rocking chair—the glider kind. There were lamps on two end tables, and both lights were turned on, spreading a soft, warm glow over the room. An afghan Kate had crocheted was lying across the glider.

"Let's all sit—Emma, take the rocking chair if you would—while I explain what will happen," Kate said.

Emma placed the afghan across her knees after she sat down. I chose the love seat, and Kate sat across from me, adjacent to Emma.

"First," Kate said, "let's clear up any misconceptions about hypnosis. I won't put you to sleep, though you may feel more relaxed with your eyes closed."

"There's no trance?" Emma asked.

"Actually, there is one, but not like a stage show trance. Think about when you daydream. Does the daydream sometimes block out the rest of the world?"

Emma smiled and nodded. "Oh, yes, and I've had plenty to block out."

"That's all a trance is, a state of intense concentration. I'll help you get there with guided imagery. Abby, would you turn off the lamp near you?"

I did, then leaned back against the love seat cushions into the shadows.

"Emma," Kate said, "I'd like you to rock the chair slowly and at the same time think of yourself as resting on a huge, fluffy pillow."

Emma closed her eyes and moved the chair back and forth.

Kate whispered, "Clear your mind. Think of something that soothes you—a warm bath, a day in the sun, a good book . . . anything. It's your decision. Everything is in your control."

"Okay," she said.

Kate repeated, "Clear your mind," several times, and even in the dim light I saw Emma's body melting into that chair as her rocking became more rhythmic.

"I want you to ride on your pillow into the clouds. Can you do that?" Kate asked.

"Yes." Emma's eyes remained closed, her voice calm.

"Take yourself above the streets, above the bus stop you told Abby about."

"Okay," came Emma's reply.

"Tell me when you're there," Kate said.

"I want to go slow. Slow is better."

"Take as long as you want." Kate had been leaning forward whispering to Emma, but now she sat up without taking her gaze off her subject.

I swear it took an hour, but was probably no more than a few minutes before Emma said, "I see the roof of the covered bus stop. See the streets and the tops of the cars."

"Good. When you're ready, float down until you see the people sitting there."

"It's better up here." Emma's voice sounded a little slurred, like she was talking in her sleep.

"Safer?" Kate said.

"Yes. Much safer."

"Abby and I are watching out for you. You can look at the people's faces. Nothing will happen."

"Abby's here. Kate's here. On the pillow."

"That's right. When you're ready, Emma."

More silence as Emma rocked and rocked for another eternity. "I see," she finally said. "It's me, waiting for the bus, and she's there, too."

"A woman?" Kate asked.

"Abby. She's on the bench sitting with me. We're talking."

I saw my sister's eyes narrow, saw her shoulders tense. "Okay. What are you wearing, Emma?"

"The gray suit I found at Goodwill. Only cost me ten dollars."

"You're going to work?"

"Yes. Then I have class. Scott will have to cook dinner, and he hates that. But it's okay. Abby says everyone has to pitch in sometimes."

Kate leaned forward. "And what's Abby wearing?"

Emma laughed. "That funny-colored uniform."

I saw Kate's shoulders relax and she almost smiled. "What else does she have on?"

"The black shoes with the thick soles. She says she's on her feet all day. I'm lucky I don't have to be someone's maid."

"She's a maid?"

"You can tell she works really hard. Her hands are always chapped, and she looks tired, even though she's young."

"What else do you know about her?" Kate asked.

"She smokes, but when I sit next to her she always puts her cigarette out right away. I never ask her to. She just does. She cares about other people."

"What color is the uniform again?"

"Turquoise. White collar. The letters on her pocket are white, too."

"Are you close enough to see what the letters say?" Kate's tone was even, her voice soft and soothing.

I wanted to get up, shake Emma and tell her to spit it out. This whole deal was like sucking peanut butter through a straw. But I had to give my sister props. I could never do this job.

Emma went into another long, agonizing silence before she said, "I need to get a little closer."

"However long it takes is fine," Kate said.

I wanted to scream, "No it's not fine!" but I remained silent, sitting on my hands to keep them still.

At last Emma said, "Purity Maids. Those are the words embroidered on the pocket."

I must have sighed audibly, because Kate held up her hand and gave me a look that would freeze a jaguar. I mouthed, *Sorry.*

Coming out of the trance was almost as slow a process as it took to get her to that pocket embroidery. Kate brought Emma back above the bus stop and allowed her all the time she wanted to return to reality. Even when she opened her eyes, she still seemed to be somewhere else.

"Turn the light back on, would you, Abby?" Kate said.

I pressed the switch at the base.

Kate said, "How are you feeling?"

"I could live in this chair." Emma was smiling, her face content in the lamplight.

"I plan on having one like it for my new house," Kate said.

Emma quit rocking, sat upright. "How could I have forgotten? The owner took your offer. You got the house, Kate."

Kate grinned. "That's great. When can I move in?"

"Pending inspections and title searches, I'd say a couple weeks. Cash transactions really speed things up."

"I think we've both had a good day—and Abby, too, right?" Kate looked at me.

"Yes. Do you remember what just happened, Emma?"

"Remember you in a maid uniform? I don't think that's an image I'll ever forget." She laughed. "But why didn't I see the woman's face, Kate?"

"The human mind will always seek to protect the psyche from harm—sometimes even in unhealthy ways—but that's a whole other lecture." Kate smiled. "By putting Abby's face on this person, you felt safe enough to get close and to stay long enough in the trance to find what we needed."

"I did it right?"

"There is no right or wrong in my office, Emma. There's only your reality."

Emma nodded, understanding. "Without the two of you, I-I don't know where I'd be right now. Probably locked in a rubber room."

"I doubt that," I said. "Our daddy would have said you've got grit."

"I have a feeling I would have liked your father,"

Emma said. And then a sadness filled her eyes despite her smile.

I guessed any father at all for her would have been a bonus.

Once Emma left the office and I thanked Kate for her help, she immediately went into session with another client. I called DeShay after I emerged from the parking garage and told him we got the maid service name. He said he was glad to hear that, since they got nothing from the pimp except what a neat freak Fiona Mancuso had been and that he considered her stupid. All his girls had been stupid.

"I'm glad I wasn't there," I said. "You know how I shoot from the lip."

"I'm certain you two wouldn't have gotten along. Tell me the name."

"Purity Maids." I maneuvered around what had become standard fixtures on Houston city streets—orange construction cones.

"You can bet Fiona picked out a new name when she went straight. Can you work the maid angle? Try to find her?"

"Because you don't want to scare her off?" I asked.

"Right. If you can get to her without telling anyone who you are, that would be great. We've already got one of Christine O'Meara's friends in the morgue."

"Don't remind me," I said.

"Quit with the guilt. You didn't cut that guy."

"That's what Jeff said," I answered.

"You probably won't be able to reach me for a while," he said. "We just got called out to a murder-suicide. I hate fucking Mondays. I've learned people are damn selfish. 'I don't want to go to work or pay my bills or make up with my wife, so I'll kill myself—and maybe take someone with me so I won't get lonely in hell.' "

"DeShay, come on," I said.

"I know, I know. But suicide scenes are the worst. Usually messy, and then you got the crying relatives. Why do suicides have about ten times more relatives than other victims? That's what I want to know."

"Maybe that's the reason for the suicide," I said. "Too many relatives."

"Yeah. There you go." He laughed. "I gotta run. Keep in touch." He hung up.

Ever alert for a tail, I'd driven home wishing there weren't so many damn Ford Focuses on the road.

I sat back in my desk chair a half hour later, stroking Diva and wondering how to learn whether Fiona Mancuso still worked for Purity Maids. Seemed a safe bet, since Emma had talked to her two weeks ago. But I needed to be sure. A simple check of the yellow pages showed an ad that proclaimed Purity had been in business since I was three years old. They must be doing something right. But what if the recent publicity concerning the reality show that had come to town, not to mention the murder of her old bar buddy Jerry Joe Billings, had sent the woman running scared? If so, all I could do was try to pick up her trail.

Like DeShay said, Mancuso probably used an alias to get hired and had a fake or new social security number attached to that alias. Reputable housecleaning agencies required their employees to be bonded, and a rap sheet in your background showing multiple arrests for solicitation wouldn't get you a job with an agency like Purity. I wouldn't be asking about Fiona Mancuso, but rather a woman who had a very distinctive and visible tattoo.

How should I approach this? I couldn't call up and say I was a PI. The agency would get their back up, want to know if there was a problem. I decided I'd be a customer. Since someone cleaned my place every couple weeks, I knew the drill. When I called, they'd send someone out to evaluate my house, determine exactly what I wanted done, how often and at what charge. Which would take about a week. We couldn't afford to waste time. I needed to be a customer in a desperate hurry for a housecleaning—definitely not a stretch for me.

I dialed the Purity number, hoping I could convince them I needed help right now.

"Purity Maids, this is Randy. How may I help you?" the man answered.

"My name is Abby Rose, and your agency was recommended to me. I understand you do good work, and I'd like to get my house cleaned as soon as possible."

"Thank you for calling, Ms. Rose. As the manager, I'm authorized to give a free cleaning to the customer who recommended us. Was it a friend or relative?"

Uh-oh. Think fast, Abby. "Um, actually, neither. A friend and I were in line at Panera Bread and I was talking about how I didn't like my current maid service. This lady behind us mentioned Purity."

"Too bad. She missed out on her freebie. Anyway, we can get an evaluation done by tomorrow and—"

"But I *really* need the cleaning done tomorrow—I'm having guests, and the place is a mess. This lady mentioned a specific maid, said she didn't have her name but that you'd know her because of her tattoo."

"Unless she works your area, we can't promise that a certain maid will be sent to your house—and certainly not on a rush job. Tomorrow will require me to do rescheduling, and I'm afraid that will cost extra."

Damn. I gave away too much too soon. "Maybe she works in my area. This tattoo is on her left ring finger."

"Ah. Loreen. She's quite popular. Where do you live? I'll see what I can do."

My heart sped at getting a first name. I thought, *Where do I need to live?* But I had the feeling that if I asked too many questions—like Loreen's last name or her territory—he'd get suspicious. Nope, I saw no way around giving the manager what he wanted. "I live in West U."

"Sorry, Loreen works in The Woodlands four out of five days a week, and her other houses are in the Memorial area."

"Darn," I said. "Could I get her another day this week?"

"That would take a massive overhaul of my schedule. I have an excellent pair assigned to West U—Angela and Dolly. I can fit you in at, say, ten a.m. Tuesday, depending on your square footage. I'm seeing on my job chart that they only have until noon to do the house."

"My home is small, maybe twenty-one hundred square feet. And ten is fine," I said.

After he gave me a quote and took my credit card info, I gave him my address and hung up. At least they were coming tomorrow. I sure hoped Angela and Dolly liked to talk, and that one of them knew Loreen, or at least her last name.

I left my office, which ticked off Diva and sent her scurrying up the stairs to find a warm place in my bedroom. I wanted to swing by Jeff's apartment and check on how he and Doris were doing, maybe join them for dinner. But before I could gather my purse and an umbrella, the doorbell rang.

I closed my eyes and whispered, "Damn," when I saw Paul Kravitz in the monitor. Couldn't he have stayed away longer than a weekend?

I let him in.

"Hello, Abby. Looks like I need to be brought up to speed—especially since you didn't call me when a certain significant event happened after I left town." He strode past me into the living room and sat down on the sofa.

I followed him and said, "Hi, Paul. Come on in and have a seat."

"A man was murdered, a man connected to the Christine O'Meara case," Kravitz said.

I lowered myself onto the farthest chair from him. "I figured you'd be back soon and I'd tell you then. How did you find out?"

"HPD is communicating with us—but I thought you and I had an arrangement to cooperate with each other, for Emma's sake."

"Yeah, well, maybe when I found the GPS tracking device on my car, I decided cooperation is a one-way street for you—and goes in your direction."

"What are you talking about?" He looked truly surprised.

"And," I went on, trying to keep him on the defensive while he was a little confused, "what's with the guy you put on Emma? You never mentioned him."

Kravitz rubbed at a few drops of rain on his suit jacket shoulder. "It never came up, did it?"

He had me there. "You should have told me."

"We put someone on Emma because we don't want her talking to other reporters. Now, what's your explanation for not telling me about the murder? I want to know about this man and his connection to Christine O'Meara."

"I thought your police friends already told you," I said.

He pointed at me. "*You* are pissing me off. If you'd called me, I would have sent our own guy to the murder scene to tape. Now we can't even examine local news footage, because going to any of your TV stations would tip them off that the infant bones and the Billings murder might be connected."

"Listen, *Paul.* I don't care whether you got to tape or not. And if you or one of your yokels like Louie put that thing on my car, don't expect anything more from me."

He took a deep breath, his stare never wavering from my face. "I did *not* put a GPS device on your car, and I specifically told my investigators to leave you alone. Since someone else is obviously on to your investigation, did it dawn on you that you led a killer straight to Billings?"

"Oh, yeah. It *dawned* on me." I felt an unexpected burning behind my eyes and fought hard to avoid the tears. I succeeded.

But Kravitz saw. He was an experienced interviewer and could read the emotion in people's faces. "Sorry. That was unfair."

"No, it's the truth. What do you want from me?" I asked.

"I want you tell me how you found Billings and what you learned about his connection to Christine O'Meara."

"Like I said, sounds like you already got everything," I said.

"Not exactly. I want your take, with every detail you can remember. We're already doing a background check on this guy, but you were one of the last people to talk to him. It's the details that make a good story, Abby. The telling details."

23

I was watching from my office window when the Purity Maids minivan pulled into my driveway Tuesday morning. The van was turquoise, like their uniforms, and the logo on the vehicle was white with darker turquoise letters. I realized I'd seen vans like this in the neighborhood before, but they blended into the background, like so many other things that weren't important at the time.

Last night, after I'd told Kravitz all those telling details he so desperately wanted, I'd spent the evening with Jeff and Doris. Jeff had made plenty of calls Monday and scheduled interviews with two home health care agencies today. When I left them to drive home, I felt a sudden sense of loss. Jeff and I had a comfortable routine that would have to change. Though I didn't resent Doris, I realized we'd have to come up with new ways to spend time together. She was a part of our lives now. A new challenge—but maybe a reward, too.

The two women who'd gotten out of the van, one black, one white, dragged to my doorstep a vacuum, mops, and two plastic pails filled with cleaning supplies. I opened the door before they could ring the bell and welcomed them inside.

"I am thrilled you could do this on such short notice. I'm Abby, by the way."

The older woman set down her vacuum and pail in the foyer and pulled a folded paper from her uniform pocket. "Ms. Rose, right?"

"Yes."

"I'm Dolly, and this is Angela. You understand that

'cause this is a rush job your credit card's already been charged in advance?"

"Yes, and I'm sorry if I've inconvenienced you."

"One dirty house is the same as any other," Dolly said. "Don't make no difference to me. How many bathrooms you got?"

"A powder room down here and two upstairs." I smiled at Angela, hoping she might be someone I could chat with, because Dolly was already wheeling her vacuum into my living room. From what I could tell, she was all business.

"Angela's gonna do the upstairs, and I'll—" Dolly stopped talking when Webster loped into the living room to greet my visitors. The woman's stiff posture indicated that she wasn't happy to see him. He sat patiently in front of her, waiting to be petted. I knew he wouldn't get his wish. "I didn't get no alert about animals. You got any more?"

"A cat. But they're both really sweet and—"

"I don't care if they got angel wings; you gotta put them up. And if they've made messes anywhere, we don't touch animal waste."

"I understand. I'll put Webster in the utility room." I turned to see if Angela felt the same way about pets, but she'd disappeared up the stairs. I didn't blame her.

After I bribed Webster with a rawhide bone and closed him in, I decided to try to endear myself to Dolly one more time, hoping she'd open up, but she was muttering about cat hair as she unloaded her supplies onto my kitchen counter.

"The cat's probably upstairs. I'll have to find her," I said as I passed her.

Once upstairs, I saw the guest bathroom rugs neatly folded in the hall and heard water running. I walked to the bathroom and leaned against the doorframe. "Hi."

Angela was on her knees cleaning around the base of the commode. She returned my "Hi" and held up the canned bathroom cleaner. "You want me to use something different? We bring our own, but the customer can always—"

"No problem. I didn't get to say hello to you down there. You been doing this long?"

She went back to spraying and wiping. "Couple years."

"How many houses do you clean in a day?"

"Maybe five. Sometimes six if we have a few small places."

"Sounds like a tough job," I said.

Angela looked at me. "She's gonna come up here and get on my case if you keep talking to me. You saw what she's like."

"Sorry, I always chatted with my former cleaning lady. But she wasn't with a big agency like Purity. How many people work there?"

"About thirty." She pulled a wand from her pail and attached a disposable toilet brush, then flushed the commode and began to scrub the bowl.

"You always work in pairs? Because I think that's a good idea. You could—"

"Ma'am." Angela sat back on her heels. "What do you want from me?"

"I'm a talker; that's all." She was wearing rubber gloves, so I couldn't tell if she was married, but asking about kids might make her more talkative. "You have children?"

"Two." She was back to scrubbing. "I don't mind if you like to talk, but Dolly gets all over me if I don't finish on time. You're making that kinda hard."

"Okay. I'll leave you alone." But I wasn't about to quit without getting any useful information. I took a few steps toward my bedroom but came back and stuck my head in the door. "You look young to have two children. They must be little."

This time Angela laughed and shook her head. "You can't help yourself, can you?"

"You got me pegged. How old are they?"

Pretty soon I knew all about Angela. How her husband worked on an oil rig and was gone for months at a time, how some days she had to work as late as eight at night, even though she started at seven in the morning, but I mostly learned how much she loved her husband and kids and how every penny she made went into a savings account for the children—so they could go to college and not be cleaning houses when they were twenty-five.

By then, we'd moved through my bedroom and into the master bath. "Lots of women in the same boat at Purity?"

"Most are worse off. At least my husband's got a steady job."

"There was another cleaning woman recommended to me before you two were assigned. Her name was Loreen, I think. Is she worse off?"

"The only thing I know about Loreen is that she's got some monster houses on her schedule. She's been around a long time and makes more money."

"You wouldn't know her last name? My sister had a team of cleaning women about eight years ago. One was Christine or Catherine or something like that, and the other was Loreen. I was thinking maybe Loreen's the same person."

"Why you asking about Loreen?" came Dolly's unexpected voice from my bedroom doorway. She'd climbed those stairs as quiet as a coon stalking a crawfish.

I turned. "No reason. Just making conversation."

She stared past me at Angela, who looked like she wanted to jump into the shower and hide. "Angela, you haven't even changed the sheets. What the heck have you been doing all this time?"

"She's been doing a very thorough job on my bathrooms," I said. "They really needed attention."

"Right." Dolly looked at her watch. "Not much time, and you got three bedrooms and a hall to clean. I know you don't want to miss lunch, Angela."

Dolly gave me a look like I had a houseful of manure that had to be cleaned up—but no. She wouldn't touch "animal waste." Had to be me.

The plan to get anything out of the maids seemed to have hit a roadblock, but I wasn't defeated—not yet. I had another idea. They drove company vans, and that meant they had to drop them off at the end of the day. Fiona Mancuso must do the same, and since I had her mug shot, a stakeout at the Purity agency might work. A stakeout. I'd never done one of those before. I'd like being the follower rather than the followee for once.

After the maids finished and went on their way, I got busy. Since I didn't know Mancuso's schedule, I couldn't risk waiting until later in the day to show up at Purity. Though it was unlikely, she could be working a short shift. Besides, I was too antsy to wait around. We were having a real fall day after yesterday's rain, so I changed into cotton drawstrings and a long-sleeved T-shirt, packed up a few Diet Cokes in a small cooler and took along a package of potato chips. I remembered how Jeff said stakeouts were boring as hell ninety-nine percent of the time while you waited for something to happen. I almost forgot the binoculars and had to go back for them. What was a stakeout without binoculars?

The agency office was north, off Shepherd Drive, and I soon realized there was more to a stakeout than I planned. You had to find a place to park. *Duh.* Stakeout equals parking. I finally chose a busy Mexican restaurant, but my first spot did not offer a view of Purity's fenced-in lot, where several minivans sat. This made me anxious. I might miss Loreen coming and going. But I shouldn't have worried. I found a parking place facing the street fifteen minutes later—a good five hours before I needed to.

By the time Purity vans started arriving to end their day, I'd used the restaurant bathroom twice, and both times felt obligated to buy takeout, waiting and watching outside while it was prepared.

Tex-Mex is not user friendly, and I figured this stakeout had cost me about two thousand calories by the time I picked up my binoculars to watch as each van drove into the lot. I was tired after doing nothing for hours. Even the excitement of finally seeing action seemed dulled by the day's inactivity and the fatty food I'd eaten.

If I'd had to rely on the mug shot alone at this distance for an ID, I would have been out of luck, but Emma's description of the bad dye job paid off. I spotted the raven-haired Mancuso leaving the passenger side of a van about five thirty. Emma mentioned she was small, but I'd say *gaunt* was a better adjective.

She went into the office with her partner and soon came out alone, purse slung over her shoulder. She lit a cigarette and started walking, probably toward the bus stop I'd noticed when I arrived, just beyond the Shepherd intersection. *Damn.* I *knew* she rode buses. Why hadn't I anticipated that she would today? Now I had a problem: I couldn't see the bus stop from where I was parked. The best solution was to follow her on foot and get on the bus with her before she disappeared.

But then I'd have to leave my car, and it might be towed by the time I got back. I pulled out of the lot and idled on the side of the road, watching up ahead for a bus to pass through the intersection. I waited ten minutes for this to happen, and when it did, I quickly put the Camry in drive and pulled out in front of a driver who made sure I knew I'd pissed him off.

The light favored me, and I made a right onto Shepherd just as the bus lumbered away from the stop. Mancuso was not sitting on the bench, and I could only hope she was on that bus and hadn't decided to do a little shopping at the gas station/convenience store on the corner. Following Metro would be a new challenge—especially for an impatient person like me. But if I had no luck today, I could always come back tomorrow—and I'd wait on Shepherd to make sure she climbed onto the bus.

The bus couldn't have traveled more than two miles before Mancuso got off. This surprised me. I had it in my mind that she lived in Emma's neighborhood because of the bus stop visits, but we were more than ten miles away. I followed the bus through the next intersection and merged into the left lane, but I kept her in sight in my rearview, thinking maybe she might wait for another bus.

But no. She'd lit another cigarette and was waiting for the light to cross the street. I made a U-turn as soon as possible. She had already disappeared when I made it back. I turned right and saw her walking down the sidewalk, cigarette smoke in her wake. I drove past her, thinking how Houston can switch from commercial to residential in the blink of an eye. We were in an older neighborhood, the houses small and close together. I parked near the next corner and fumbled in my purse for a mirror and lipstick. As she walked by me, I pretended to be engrossed in applying color to my lips. She didn't seem to notice.

I watched her walk another two blocks and then turn left at a stop sign. I followed, and when I reached the sign, I looked in the direction she'd gone and saw her standing at the door of a gray house halfway down the block. She took one more drag on her cigarette before putting it out and unlocking the front door. *Wow.* She'd gone out of her way to make the bus stop visits to Emma if she lived here.

A few seconds later I pulled up to the house, noting the number painted on the curb by the driveway. I slid from behind the wheel, then felt a tiny surge of adrenaline as I walked up the short cement path.

I rapped on the door, reminding myself that this woman wanted anonymity. She would need reassurance, and I hoped I could deliver—if she agreed to talk to me at all.

She didn't open the door, just called out, "What do you want?"

"I need your help, Loreen," I said.

A short silence followed; then she said, "Do I know you?"

"We have a mutual friend who sent me here— Angela." Mentioning Emma's name first might be the wrong thing to do.

I heard the dead bolt turn and she opened the door a crack. "Angela sent you?"

"Yes."

"I hardly know her. What's this about?" Her door was open a little more now.

"My name is Abby. Can I come in and explain?"

"Not until you tell me how you know Angela."

"She cleaned my house, said you were one of the best employees at Purity."

"You need my help cleaning? 'Cause we're not allowed to do private jobs. We had to sign a paper that we wouldn't."

Even though she hadn't shut the door on me, I could tell this wasn't working.

"Okay, here's the straight scoop. I work for Emma

Lopez, and I think you know her, even if she doesn't know who you really are. She needs your help."

Loreen slammed the door so hard I think the house shook. I heard the dead bolt turn.

But I had another idea on how to get her attention, even though I wouldn't enjoy using this tactic. "Fiona," I said loud enough for her to hear—and maybe loud enough for the neighbors, too. "I know you don't want me talking out here about your past for everyone in the neighborhood to hear."

A few seconds passed; then she opened the door. "Get inside," she whispered harshly.

I stepped into a tiny foyer, shutting the door behind me. "Sorry I had to do that, but there are things you need to know and things I hope you can help us with."

"What'd you say your name was?" She crossed thin arms over an ample chest that didn't match her tiny physique. Were those implants a gift from James the pimp?

"Abby Rose. I'm a private detective, and I know you wrote a letter to a television show about Emma Lopez. I work for her."

She cocked her head, staring at me. "Work for her how?"

"I'm trying to find out what happened to the baby under the house—you've heard about that, right?"

"Who hasn't?"

"You wrote that letter to *Reality Check* to help your friend Christine's children."

She said, "That's a lie." But she was about as convincing as a FEMA official.

"Listen, can we sit down and talk? You're justifiably concerned about publicity, but I'm helping Emma just like you wanted to help her."

"Lotta good I did. Her baby sister's dead."

"But you did help. The show is building them a new house. I saw it myself." I wasn't ready to tell her that the baby in the news wasn't Emma's sister. She still seemed on her guard and might not believe me.

"A new house can't bring back a dead baby," Loreen said. "I'm done helping."

"Even if I promise to keep your name out of this?"

"How can you do that when there's a stupid TV show

in town? If they find out who I am, I'll lose everything. My job, my house . . . everything."

I took a risk and approached her, resting my hand on her shoulder. "I *won't* let that happen."

I felt her tremble under my touch. She said nothing.

"You were very brave to do what you did for Christine's children, but there are things you need to know."

"Like what?"

"Like what happened to your friend."

"She split. That's what happened. Left those kids to fend for themselves. I was so pissed at that stupid woman I promised one day I'd make things right." She paused. "And now I've screwed that up, too."

"You've got it wrong, Loreen. Let me tell you what I've learned, okay?"

"So I can feel more guilty? Okay. Bring it on, 'cause I'm an expert at guilt."

She turned and walked down the hall. I followed, thinking how she'd escaped a miserable existence and now had this little house and a steady job where no knew about her former profession. Heck, she might even have a husband or a boyfriend. My showing up probably felt no different to her than if I'd broken in like a kick burglar holding a gun.

She led me into a living room with old-fashioned dark paneling. Between the paneling and the double window covered by heavy drapes, I felt claustrophobic. But the carpet seemed new and freshly vacuumed, and if there was a speck of dust anywhere, I couldn't have found it. The house didn't smell of tobacco, so she probably smoked only outside.

I chose an armchair with a clean towel tucked carefully over the floral cushion, and she sat on the edge of a mismatched plaid sofa, her hands clenched in her lap.

"There's no easy way to tell you, so I'll start with what you thought you knew. Christine didn't leave town. She was murdered."

Loreen gasped, covering her mouth with her hand. "She . . . she's dead?"

"They found her body in 1997, but she remained unidentified until the TV show came to Houston and Emma asked me to investigate what happened to her baby sister and her mother. I discovered a cold-case death, and the victim turned out to be Christine."

"I didn't hear nothing about that on the news," Loreen said.

"You will soon enough. Anyway, I'm hoping you can help me learn why she was murdered. I'm not sure if it's connected to the baby's death, but I suspect so. And here's another important piece of information that hasn't been reported in the press. That baby they found last week wasn't Christine's."

Loreen shook her head vigorously. "You're talking crazy now. I went through all nine months with her. Even knew the guy she was sleeping with when she got pregnant."

"Who was the father?"

"A teenager who lived across the street from her—kid who had to be ten years younger. He liked to drink, and she was happy to supply the booze and drink with him. One night he drove drunk smack into a hill full of bluebonnets off Highway 6. Christy and me went there and left flowers by this white cross his parents put where he died. I was the one who cried. She didn't."

I swallowed. I already knew Christine O'Meara had led a life filled with mistakes and tragedy, and here was more of the same. "Emma was present when her mother gave birth, but the infant found under the house belonged to someone else. That's what I need help with."

"Maybe it was there when Christy moved in. Maybe it's just chance that—"

"There are no coincidences when it comes to murder, Loreen. Somehow Christine's baby was switched for the one found under the house. I truly believe that's why Christine was killed—because she made a deal with someone. Could she have been in contact with a trafficker in black-market babies?"

"I don't know. She told me she gave the baby to CPS, and that's why I mentioned the kid in the letter. I thought Emma should know she had a sister out there somewhere."

"She never mentioned a baby broker, and she didn't give you the story about the husband who beat her and ran off with the child?"

"That?" Loreen laughed scornfully. "The beating story was only for the people we hung with at the bar we used to go to. She wanted everyone to feel sorry for her 'cause then they'd buy her drinks. But us two were close, and I thought she was telling me this big secret about CPS because we were friends. That's what friends do, right? Tell each other important shit?"

I nodded, thinking, *But friends do not share that they have buried a baby under their house.*

Loreen went on, saying, "Christy talked all the time about not wanting the kid, how she couldn't handle the ones she already had, how they got in the way and how Emma always needed money for some crap at school. Those were her words, 'some crap at school.' But she never said she'd sell the baby. That's what you're saying, right? She sold her?"

"Maybe. I'm not sure. But you stayed friends with Christine for years afterward?"

Loreen hung her head, twisting a silver ring on her pinkie finger. "I was only seventeen when we met, and she let me work with her cleaning houses. I was trying to save enough money to get by without Jimmy selling me every night to whatever slobbering jerk walked down the street. Course, I never got away from him until he went to jail."

"Bet that was a relief." She'd been abused, treated like a slave, probably most of her life.

"Yeah, but this isn't about me. I still don't understand why you think Christy was killed because of the baby thing," Loreen said. "She disappeared five years after the baby came and went."

"That bothers me, too. Did she have extra cash after the baby was born? Or a new TV? New clothes? Anything?"

Loreen sat in thought for probably a full minute. "A few times Christy had money to throw around—nothing big, a couple hundred bucks, maybe. Once when I asked where she got it, she said Emma's family. But the father was supposed to be dead, so I didn't get it, you know? Did she lie about him, too? Is he still around?"

"No, he died before Emma was born." But I knew Xavier Lopez's widow sent money for Emma. Maybe she also sent Christine money in exchange for her silence. "Were there any other times you remember she had cash to burn?"

"Only that time she went to Vegas to make her million—that's what she said, make her million. She wanted me to go with her, said she'd pay my way, but I couldn't. Jimmy would have killed me."

"Jimmy is James Caldwell?" It wouldn't hurt to remind her I pretty much knew her whole life story.

"That's right." She crossed her legs and one foot began to bob.

"When was this trip?"

"You know, I think it was the same year she had the baby—yeah, it had to be, because I remember her saying she wanted to get rid of the leftover baby weight before she took the trip."

"Did she leave town often?"

Loreen sat back. "That's the only time I remember."

"How did she get to Las Vegas? Did someone take her?"

"Who would do that? It's not like there was all these rich dudes hanging around the bar." Loreen squinted, seemed to be thinking. "She was only gone for a couple days, if I remember right, and when she came back she went on this giant binge, told me she lost almost every penny playing the slots."

"But she'd had enough cash for a plane ticket and a vacation before she gambled away most of her money. Think hard. Are there any other times you recall her having extra cash?"

"She always had money for booze, even if it was just beer, but I thought that was because she was working more, spending less time at Rhoda's—that was the place we drank together. Christy could clean a house like nobody's business when she wasn't on a binge."

"And you'd been helping her with the cleaning? Maybe took up the slack when she was too drunk?"

"Yeah, but she wasn't as much of a drunk that year before she disappeared, and you probably think this is weird, but Christy and I? We worked good together. Drunks and whores can do *some* things right. We were a team."

"Such a good team you decided to go into business together?"

Loreen tilted her head. "How did you find out all this stuff?"

"I'll explain later. What about your business plans?"

"I thought she was serious, but then she split . . . sorry. That's not right, is it? She got herself killed."

"How did you plan on getting the money to start up? You'd need more than the flyers Emma made that you stuck on telephone poles."

For the first time since I'd arrived, Loreen smiled. "Emma made those? Christy always said Emma was the real mom in the family. That's why I called CPS when Christy didn't come back."

"You called CPS? I thought they showed up because Emma was missing school."

"She was. I went to Christy's house to see if she was sick or something, 'cause she hadn't been around. This kid answers the door and she's covered in chicken pox. I asked where her mother was, and she said she'd been gone a long time. She said her big sister, Emma, went to get milk but she'd be right back. So I left and called CPS. It's anonymous, you know. You can call and no one checks on you or anything."

I nodded. "How did you find Emma again after CPS took custody?"

"I was still living around there when the kids moved back into the old house. People talk. I heard. I watched them, sorta looked out for them, you know? I'd found out I could never have kids. Too many infections. Anyway, Emma took this one bus all the time, so I went to the stop. Talked to her. Got to know her. Christy was such an idiot to miss out on Emma and the other kids." She smiled again, but it quickly disappeared when Loreen's attention switched to the window. "Did you hear that?"

"Hear what?"

"That sound. Someone's out there." She hurried to the window and peeked through a crack in the drapes. "Did anyone come with you?" she whispered.

"No." But I got this sick feeling inside and thought, *No one that I know about, anyway.* "Do you see anyone?"

She carefully pushed open the drapes a tiny bit wider. "Maybe it was a bird or a squirrel in the bushes." She returned to the sofa but didn't take her eyes off the window.

"There's something else you need to know," I said. "Christine had a friend named Jerry Joe Billings."

"Him? A *friend*? Pure scum, drunk or sober. When I'd come into Rhoda's and sit next to Christy he'd always say, 'The whore is here. Let the party begin.'"

"Mr. Billings was murdered last Friday—killed after he promised to give me information about Christine. I think he knew something about her murder, and—"

"What?" Loreen closed her eyes for a second, then wrapped her arms around herself and began to rock. "If he got killed because he knew something, that means . . . you *know* what that means."

"I can protect you, Loreen."

"Did you promise to protect Jerry Joe, too?"

I took a deep breath. "I had no idea that if I talked to him, he'd . . ."

"End up dead? But you have an idea about me, right? You figured out I know a whole lot more about Christy than he ever did."

"And there may be other things you know that are important and—"

"Important enough to get me killed. Why in hell did I ever let you in here?"

"We have to catch this killer, Loreen. That's the only way you'll ever be safe. And you may need protection for another reason. James Caldwell was just paroled. The police asked him questions about you."

Her face paled. "Oh, God, no." She stood and started pacing in front of the sofa. "That's who was outside. He found me just like you did. I gotta get out of here."

She started to leave the room, but I went after her, gripped her shoulders and turned her to face me. "Don't you want to stop hiding?"

She struggled a little, but she couldn't weigh more than a hundred pounds, and I had no trouble hanging on to her.

"I have to get away. I have to—"

"Listen to me, Loreen." We were practically nose-to-nose, and I could smell the tobacco on her breath. "I'll help you if you let me—but first I need more information."

"I've told you everything I know." But she didn't shrug me off. She kept staring over my shoulder at the window, looking as frightened as a rabbit in a trap.

I shouldn't have told her about Billings, at least not until I'd probed for more information about the possible baby switch. I released my hold on her. "You want me to see if anyone's out there?"

"No. I don't want anyone to know you're here."

I guessed she didn't realize my car was sitting in front of her house. "I can take you to a safe place. I have police friends and—"

"No police." She was shaking her head vigorously. "Jimmy will find out. He can find out what the cops are doing as easy as that." She snapped her fingers.

"All right, what about my place?"

"Are you crazy? I'm not going anywhere with you. You said yourself you led a killer straight to Jerry Joe."

I sighed. How the hell could I make sure she felt safe? My gut told me she knew more than she realized and I needed to keep picking her brain. But she wouldn't be much help while she was this afraid.

"I have a suitcase to pack," Loreen said, jerking me back to reality.

"Wait," I said. "Let me think about . . . No, I've got it. I have a friend. He's my boyfriend, as a matter of fact." She didn't have to know that he was a cop, too. "He's big and strong and he'll protect you."

She took a pack of cigarettes from her uniform pocket and stared at them, licking her lips. "I don't know. That's a short-term thing. Besides, how would he get me out of here without Jimmy finding out?"

"See, that's the problem, Loreen. You need help getting away, and I'm willing to do that."

"How?"

"You have a fence in the backyard?"

"No."

"You could cut through the yard and hit the next block. Jimmy can't be watching the front and the back of the house at the same time, right?"

She was turning the cigarette pack over and over. "Then what? This guy picks me up over there?"

"That's right."

"But he won't know me, and Jimmy could be—"

"I've got my gun in my car. I'll walk with you. My friend's name is Jeff, and he can take you to his place."

She stared at me while she considered this. It seemed as if shadows had formed under eyes in the last few minutes. With her too-thin face, the uniform hanging off her like she was a kid wearing her mother's dress and those dark circles, she looked like she belonged in a concentration camp. But then, maybe that was what her whole life had been like.

Her gaze returned to the window, and she started pacing again. "I've had hundreds of strange men use me, and you want me to go ride off with another one to God knows where?" She'd gotten a cigarette out of the pack and was rolling it between thumb and index finger. "I don't like this."

"It won't be just you two. His sister lives with him. She'll come with him to get you."

She bit the side of her lip. "For real?"

"For real. Now let me make the call, okay?"

She carefully returned the cigarette to the pack and looked at me. "Guess I have no choice. But don't bother getting your gun. I'm taking mine."

24

When Loreen went to her bedroom to pack a bag, I called Jeff and explained the situation, emphasizing that Loreen did not know he was a cop and would probably shut down on me if she found out. Without asking any questions aside from directions, he said he was on the way. Bless the man. He was as reliable as the sunrise.

Once Loreen was ready, we went through her tiny, immaculate kitchen and out the back door. I'd noticed the shuttered windows and understood even better how paranoid Loreen was about her past being exposed or Jimmy showing up on her doorstep.

I took the overnight bag and she held the gun. It was a Smith & Wesson .22—very much like my own .38 Lady Smith. By the way she'd checked the ammo and handled the small handgun, I figured she knew how to use it.

It was dark when we left the house. I used the flashlight on my key chain to guide us through several yards to the next street over. I heard nothing except a few cooing doves and the distant sound of an ambulance, but Loreen looked over her shoulder and whispered, "Did you hear that?" over and over.

We reached the sidewalk without drawing attention, and I searched for Jeff's car. I spotted his sea green Altima parked at the end of the block. We hurried to the car and I opened the back door, since Doris was sitting next to Jeff. Loreen climbed in and I breathed a sigh of relief. She hadn't balked, as I thought she might. Maybe she was too scared.

"Hi, Abby. Jeffy says we're having Pizza Hut pizza when we get home. Get in quick."

"I have my own car, Doris. I'll be there in a little while. This is my friend Loreen. She'll ride with you."

"Hi, Loreen. Jeffy already has Abby for a girlfriend, and you know what that means." Doris smiled.

Loreen actually returned the smile. "I do know what that means. I'll be very careful." She looked at Jeff then. "Where are we going?"

He gave her the general location of his apartment, then looked at me. "Abby, remember that problem with your bumper the other day? I know you got it fixed, but check it again before you drive through traffic. I don't trust that body shop you used."

I hadn't thought to check for *another* GPS device. "I'll do that. Now you guys get going. I'll catch up with you at the apartment."

Loreen handed me her gun. "Take this. You shouldn't walk back to your car without protection. I know Jimmy's out there."

I started to protest, but she insisted.

I was surprised she didn't want to keep the gun, since she wasn't exactly thrilled about this whole arrangement. Must be that some part of her trusted us, and that was a good sign. I stepped back, closed the car door and watched Jeff drive away.

Rather than take the shorter route through the grass, I chose to stay on the sidewalk to go around the block. I kept the gun tucked into my waistband. Loreen's paranoia seemed to be contagious, and I stayed alert for any indication that someone was watching or following.

I made it to the Camry without any trouble. But when I checked under the bumper, I kept the gun ready in my right hand.

A minute later, damned if I didn't find another little black box, this time stuck beneath my front bumper. It was different from the other one. Smaller. I wanted to stomp on the thing, smash it into a million pieces, mostly because I'd been played for a fool again. Guess I'd have to put a mirror on a stick and check under my car every time I went anywhere. At least I'd partially learned my lesson by sneaking Loreen out the back way. Good thing I had Jeff thinking for me, since I'd totally screwed up.

Still steamed, I got into the Camry, locked up and

removed the GPS device's batteries. When I turned the ignition I decided that beating myself up wouldn't help. I took a few deep breaths and pulled away from the curb. Time to see if I'd learned my lesson about dumping a tail. It would be side streets and running every yellow light for this trip. I wasn't about to lead a killer to another victim.

On the way to Jeff's apartment, I pushed my anger about the tracking devices as far to the back of my mind as possible. I had no clue who had put them on my car, and until I knew, they were only a distraction. Instead, I thought about what I'd learned from Loreen and what it could mean. Where had the extra money for Christine's trip to Vegas come from? A baby sale? Probably.

The other money, the cash Christine always seemed to have to buy booze, most likely came from Gloria Wilks—money intended for Emma. But it wasn't enough to start a new business. Christine had probably gone to whoever took the child she'd given up and asked for the start-up money for the cleaning business. What if that person figured out her requests would never end and killed her? A child you'd raised, probably loved with all your heart, would be a powerful motivator, especially if the child had no idea she was bought or adopted.

Then there was the infant found under the house. An exchange had obviously been made. But how had this deal been brokered? I didn't know the answer. I was hoping Loreen had more to share about her relationship with Christine O'Meara, some small something that would piece all this together.

I arrived at Jeff's apartment about thirty minutes later than if I'd taken the freeway. Good thing I knew Houston streets. I rapped on the door and Jeff let me in. The smell of pepperoni and pizza crust filled the apartment.

"I don't think I've ever been so happy to see a pizza box in my life." We joined Loreen and Doris at the card table.

Loreen had changed out of her uniform into jeans and a T-shirt, Doris had pizza sauce at both corners of her mouth and Jeff must have finished eating, because he was chewing gum.

I took the GPS device out of my purse and showed Jeff. "DeShay has another toy to play with."

"What kind of toy?" Doris said. "Can I see it?"

"No, Doris, it's not that kind of toy," Jeff said. "After Abby's done eating, we can set up that jigsaw puzzle we bought today."

I picked up one of the three slices left in the box and took a bite.

"What is that thing?" Loreen nodded at my purse, where I'd returned the GPS device.

"A piece of equipment our friend DeShay—"

"I know Jeff is a cop." She glanced at him. "An ex-pro like me can smell a cop a mile away. What is that?"

"You can smell Jeffy because he smells nice," Doris said. "He smells like our dad."

We all had to smile, and I said, "He does clean up good."

"Loreen has a pretty smile like yours, Abby. She said she had a friend like me when she was in school a long time ago. Can you be my friend now, Loreen?"

Loreen blinked several times and then slowly reached out to Doris, her palm up. "Yeah. I'll be your friend."

But Doris wasn't about hand squeezes. She got up and wrapped the miniature woman in one of her hugs. Jeff had to put an end to this affectionate gesture or risk Loreen ending up with a few broken ribs. *Time for the jigsaw puzzle,* I thought, hoping Loreen had forgotten her question. Knowing about the GPS device, knowing I may have been tailed to her house, would make her feel like she'd sat down in a bear trap.

Loreen did seem to forget, and after only an hour of puzzling, something we discovered Jeff's sister was quite good at, Doris wanted to watch *The Little Mermaid* again. She abruptly left us for the DVD player. I guessed her attention span was limited. I'd have to get used to that.

With Doris occupied, I took Loreen's gun from my purse, unloaded it and handed her the weapon and the ammo. "Thanks."

Loreen put everything in her own bag. She looked tired, but I had been patiently waiting for a chance to finish questioning her about Christine and hoped she didn't fade on me. Jeff offered her a drink, and while the two of them broke into a bottle of Scotch, I had a Shiner Bock. Hard liquor isn't for me, and I usually have beer only at Astros games, but I'd forgotten to pick up wine when I did the shopping.

"Loreen, you've been so helpful, but I need to pick your brain a little more," I said.

"Yeah, well, I gotta call in sick for tomorrow first. Believe me, that won't make my boss happy." She gulped her Scotch. "Phone?"

"On the kitchen wall," Jeff said.

She left us to make her call, and Jeff leaned close. "She's scared for the wrong reasons, thinks her ex-pimp is the biggest threat. Get that GPS box to DeShay in the morning."

Loreen came back to the table. "Guess who's fired if she's not at work day after tomorrow?" She took another long swallow of her drink. "Why in hell did I ever write that letter?"

"Because you wanted to right a wrong," I said. "Usually that ends up paying off in the end."

"Yeah, well, I'm not seeing any nice payoff about now."

"You can still help Christine's kids," I said. "On the drive back here I was thinking about who Christine could have met who had the money to buy her baby—because the cash she had for Vegas could have been payment. You've said no one at Rhoda's seemed like a good candidate, but what about the people you two cleaned for?"

"Some of them were rich, yeah."

"Longtime customers?"

Loreen rested her elbow on the table and held her head with her hand. "I think so." She was sounding more tired by the second. "She had this list. Tuesday regulars, Wednesday regulars. She never worked on Fridays or the weekend. Those were her drinking days, and no one interfered with that."

"You remember any of these people?" I asked.

"Everyone we cleaned for worked in the daytime. They left a key and we usually didn't see them."

"How did you know where to go and when? The list?" I asked.

"Christine kept a notebook with phone numbers, too. I remember because I saw these doodles in there, and I asked Christy if she'd drawn them. She said yeah. She drew people's faces. Even me. I asked her for the page, but she said she had stuff she needed on the back side. She drew me another one later but I lost it."

I thought about the boxes moved out to storage the day of the demolition. Had Emma thrown away this notebook along with the photographs she'd mentioned? "You're sure you never met any of the clients?"

"I was helping with more houses by ninety-two, and every now and then someone was home sick or . . . Wait. There was this one lady who quit working when she was so pregnant she could hardly walk. I did see *her*. Vacuumed right around her for three weeks in a row."

My heart sped up, and I was thinking how long it had taken me to get this one morsel of information, something Loreen had no way of knowing might be important enough to pull everything together.

Jeff knew its importance, though, because he said, "Do you remember if you cleaned for this woman around the same time that Christine was pregnant?"

Loreen looked thoughtful. "She coulda been pregnant, too, now that I think about it. And you know, Christy never took me with her if she went back there, so I never saw that lady's baby. You think the kid under the house belonged to that woman we cleaned for?"

"Could be," I said.

"And maybe Christy did something to that kid so she could sell her own baby to that lady?" Loreen shook her head vigorously. "I wasn't there if she did that. You better make sure the cops know—"

"Chill, Loreen," I said. "I don't think you had anything to do with the baby or you never would have written that letter to *Reality Check*."

"Yeah. That's right," she said, nodding. "But why didn't the woman send Christy to jail if she hurt their kid? That's what any normal person woulda done. I went to jail plenty of times for a lot less than that."

"We don't know if Christine hurt any baby," I said.

Jeff nodded his agreement. "Your friend and this woman could have made a baby deal for reasons we haven't yet figured out, and Christine agreed to keep the secret. Then later she decided to earn some extra money to continue to keep that secret."

"Oh, yeah. She'd do that. She was always looking for the big jackpot that never came." Loreen closed her eyes briefly, then pointed past me. "I'm sorry, but I need to do what she's doing."

I turned and saw Doris lying on the floor in front of the TV. She was sound asleep.

"Take the bedroom," Jeff said.

"I'm not gonna argue," Loreen answered. She picked up the overnight bag she'd left near the hall entrance and left us alone.

Jeff took out several sticks of Big Red, then offered me the pack. I accepted, needing to rid my mouth of the taste of beer.

After he'd chewed his gum for several seconds, he said, "Tell DeShay everything you've learned tomorrow. I doubt this notebook is still around, but you said they stored everything from the house, and a search is worth a shot. Maybe Christine kept names as well as phone numbers."

"And I could find out if any of those people in the notebook had a baby around the same time as Christine by checking birth records from that year."

"Good circumstantial evidence, but that won't promise a happy reunion for your client. A lot can happen in fifteen years."

I put my hand behind his neck and pulled him close so our lips were almost touching. "You are such a pessimist, you probably never put anything away for a rainy day, 'cause you're always expecting a drought."

He smiled, and we were about ready to exchange gum when my cell rang.

I saw from the caller ID that it was Aunt Caroline, and groaned.

"Bet I know who that is." Jeff picked up our glasses and headed for the kitchen.

"Better answer or she'll fill up my voice mail box." I opened the phone and said hello.

"Abby, where are you?" she said.

"Um . . . someplace."

"I know that much. But you're not at home, because I've driven by three times. You need to get over here now."

"It's late. What can I do for you?" I asked.

"I have something of dire importance to share with you. Please come over."

Everything with her is always of dire importance, but I tried to sound nice when I said, "Can we do this in the morning?"

She was silent for a good ten seconds, and I knew I'd pissed her off. "If you don't care about your sister ruining her life, then fine."

"What are you talking about?" But, of course, this had to be about Clint Roark.

"This man she's seeing is not who he says he is, and I have proof."

She'd hired a detective to follow Jeff when I first started dating him, and this sounded like she was up to her old tricks. "If you're talking about the man's ex-wife and son, Kate knows about them."

"It's not a son. It's a daughter. And his name is not Clinton Roark. It Harrison Foster."

Now she had my attention. "What have you done, Aunt Caroline? You haven't told Kate about this, have you?"

"No, nothing like that. We need to face her with the facts together. Two voices are better than one, wouldn't you agree?"

"Let me sleep on this and come over to your place tomorrow morning around ten and you can tell me what you've got. Then we can talk to Kate." That would at least give me a little time to find out about this man myself and why he chose to use a fake name—if, in fact, Aunt Caroline had this right.

"That would work. Yes, I like that idea." The line went dead, and I stared at the phone before I snapped it shut.

"That your aunt Caroline?" Jeff said when he rejoined me at the table.

"Yes. Seems the man Kate is dating may not be who he says he is. This might mean trouble if Kate gets all defensive about Clint Roark. Gosh, my sister is dating—"

"Not who he says he is? What does that mean?" He'd slipped into detective mode as easily as if he'd put on an old slipper.

"Aunt Caroline says his real name is Harrison Foster. You think he might be some kind of con man? Or maybe someone with a criminal record who changed his name?" I was getting nervous now, and was anxious to get home and find out what I could about this guy.

Jeff said, "Maybe he's both. Or it could be he stole someone's identity—not good news any way you look at it. But, of course, you're talking to a police officer. The pessimist with a dark view of the world."

"My picture was in the paper right after the bones were found. The caption identified me as 'Heiress-turned-detective Abby Rose.' Someone may have seen that word *heiress* and plugged my name into a search engine. That search would quickly bring Kate's name into the mix."

"True," Jeff said. "It's no secret that thieves and predators read newspapers looking for vulnerable victims, although usually they check the obits, not the headlines."

"Why didn't he come after me?"

"Maybe you're a little too visible right now."

"True," I said. "And his endgame is to get money out of Kate?"

"I think you've already figured that out, hon."

"Dammit. I should have checked up on him myself." I grabbed a napkin and spit out the now flavorless glob of gum.

"My opinion? Aunt Caroline was the best person for that job," Jeff said. "You should be grateful."

"For once, I am. And now I plan to find out everything I can about this guy before I walk into Aunt Caroline's house tomorrow."

When I arrived home, I went upstairs, peeked into Kate's room and found her already asleep, with Webster curled at her feet. I was hoping that meant she hadn't been out with Roark or Foster or whoever the hell this man was. I shed my clothes, put on one of Jeff's T-shirts and headed back down to my computer, shushing the meowing Diva, who followed me.

I booted up and used the database I rely on when all else fails. I had two names, a city, an approximate age and a line of work for Roark. I immediately learned that the only Clinton Roark in the area was retired and lived in Huntsville. Harrison Foster, on the other hand, had two known addresses in Houston—one an apartment and one a home in the Memorial Park area. I was able to learn some of this because his wife had filed for divorce two months ago, and initial divorce filings are public record. Her name was Beth, and she was seeking sole custody of their child.

I also learned that Harrison Foster was not a drug rep, but owned his own software development company specializing in medical office and hospital products. If Aunt Caroline had Foster followed, it would have been easy enough for any PI to find all this out. He was probably living in the apartment, since the lease was signed around the same time Beth Foster had filed for divorce.

I sat back and considered why this man would want to con Kate. My guess was that he would take a financial beating in this divorce and wanted to hook up with someone who could help him continue to live the lifestyle he'd grown accustomed to. And Kate could certainly do that.

Had he planned to cheat her out of a generous chunk of change and split? I smiled. Yeah, he must think Kate was as dumb as a box of rocks and that she'd invest in whatever fake new drug or nonexistent business he'd enthusiastically told her about. But he'd hit on the wrong girl if he thought that would work. Even if she'd fallen with a thud for this guy, she was too smart to buy a black cat with a stripe down its back from anyone, Mr. Dimples included.

I felt better now, even though telling Kate wouldn't be easy. And making sure Aunt Caroline didn't tell her first might be like trying to drink out of a fire hose. But I'd deal with that tomorrow, after I found exactly what Aunt Caroline had on Harrison Foster.

25

The next day I overslept and had time for only a quick shower. Kate had long since gone to work by the time I left to hand over the newest GPS tracker to DeShay, and I was relieved not to have to face her this morning, knowing what I now knew.

I checked under my car bumpers before I pulled out, but found nothing. I decided it was long past time to organize the garage so I could actually fit my car in there. Leaving the Camry in my driveway had obviously created serious problems. It really boiled my water that someone had been lurking around and stuck those things on my car whenever they wanted. I still suspected Kravitz, no matter what he said to the contrary.

I drove downtown, and DeShay was ready for me, since I'd called ahead—if *ready* meant a morose man sitting in his cubicle up to his hairline in paperwork. I was a welcome distraction. He wore a navy suit, a silver-and-blue tie and a starched shirt. I guessed correctly that he had court today.

"This afternoon," he told me.

"Bummer," I said. The one thing DeShay hated about working homicide was the dress-up part. I gave him the plastic grocery bag containing the second GPS device.

"You think you can find any prints on this besides mine?" I asked.

"Doubt it, but we'll try. Even the batteries had been wiped clean on the other one. I talked to tech this morning, and they said whoever planted the thing buried the e-mail address they used to connect to the Internet and watch where you went."

"Having both devices might be more helpful, especially if tech can find a common link," I said. "E-mail is very tricky, yes, but if you search—"

"Abby, what did you call me and Jeff once? Luddites?"

I laughed. "Yes. You remembered the lingo. That's a step in the right direction."

"I know how to write reports, check databases and stuff like that on my computer, but I'm still a Luddite and don't plan on changing until the bosses make me. Jeff told me something I've never forgotten. He said technology is a great tool, but us homicide investigators have to deal with the people first. Murder is a people problem, and you learn the most from the humans, whether they're dead or alive."

"Jeff's right. Now, get ready to hear some good news in the people department. I found Christine's friend— the ex-prostitute." I summarized yesterday, told him Loreen, aka Fiona, was holed up with Jeff. I also gave him the info on the notebook. "After I deal with my aunt, who is probably feeling very neglected since I started working this case day and night, I'll call Emma, see if she remembers any notebook like the one Loreen described."

"White can handle that," DeShay said.

"No, I can do it. I'll go over to the storage unit with Emma and—"

"Abby, handing over the GPS monitor is one thing, but that notebook could lead us directly to whoever might have killed Christine. We could use it in court, and we don't want to mess with the chain of evidence."

I knew he was right. "It's just that I promised Loreen no police. If White does find the notebook, then—"

"Let's not play what-if. You got us a lead. That's what's important."

I checked my watch. "I've only got ten minutes to get to Aunt Caroline's house—not enough time. You can bet I'll pay for this by having to endure an extra dose of hostility. Gotta run."

"The *real* drama queen in your family is your aunt?" He grinned.

"Are you implying I'm a drama queen, too?"

"Nope. You are the busiest, most headstrong person I've met besides my granny. Now get out of here."

I nodded, hurried out of the offices to the elevator and jogged to my car.

My aunt lives in an older, established neighborhood with big, expensive houses, where she knows everyone on the block. And they probably know her better than she knows herself. This time of morning, the streets were wonderfully quiet compared to the frenzied freeways. But when I turned onto her street, a good twenty minutes past the time we agreed on, I saw that the chaos of an emergency had disrupted the peace.

An ambulance, a patrol car and my aunt's open door and shattered front window made my stomach lurch. A uniformed policeman tried to wave me away, but I called out the window that my aunt lived at the address where obviously something very bad had happened. He told me to pull over to the curb.

"What's your aunt's name?" he asked when I met him on the sidewalk.

"Caroline Rose. Is she okay?"

Just then the paramedics pulled a stretcher out the front door and onto the walkway.

My hand went to my mouth and I pushed past the cop, starting to run toward them. Aunt Caroline's neck was immobilized, and I could see blood on her forehead.

But when I heard her shout, "Abigail, you're late!" I almost laughed with relief. She sounded strong, not to mention as furious as a bear with a sore ass.

The stretcher had been pulled into the ambulance before I could get to her. Then the cop caught up with me and took me by the arm.

"Please, ma'am. Your name?" he said.

"Abby Rose. I need to go with her."

"I'm Officer Rowe. First off, they don't much like riders in the ambulance, plus she only has minor injuries—bruises and a cut. Because of her age—"

"What about my age?" I heard Aunt Caroline shout before the smiling paramedic closed the back ambulance door.

"Anyway, you understand. We could use your help here for a few minutes. Then you can catch up with her in the ER. We need to figure out what went on here."

"I don't get it. She can talk. She must have told you." Aunt Caroline may be the most irritating woman on earth ninety percent of the time, but I felt an urgent need to be with her now. She *was* the closet thing to a mother I'd ever had.

"Your aunt wasn't exactly making a whole lot of sense. Maybe you can tell us if anything is missing. She kept saying, 'He took it,' over and over, but she never said what *it* was."

I tried to clear my head as I watched the ambulance drive off. Coming upon this scene had hit me like a two-by-four upside the head, and I had trouble forming any coherent thoughts.

"Ma'am?" the officer said.

"Sorry, what?" I answered.

"Can you come inside the house?"

"Sure, yes." But I had no idea if I could give him a clue as to what might be missing. My aunt's goal in life is to collect as many expensive material objects as she can before she dies. She has three sets of English china, lots of silver, figurines from Germany, oil and water paintings, antique spoons—hell, antique everything. And then there was the jewelry. Diamonds and emeralds, pearls from the Orient. One of her Prada purses was probably worth a couple thousand dollars alone.

When we walked into the foyer, an older man wearing a yellow polo and khaki shorts who looked vaguely familiar was sitting on one of a matching set of padded antique benches. A female patrol officer had her notebook in hand.

Rowe said, "This is Mr. Desmond. He lives two doors down. And this is Officer Price."

I walked over to them, nodded at the other officer and said, "Hi, Mr. Desmond. Remember me? Abby?"

He stood and took both my hands in his. "Abby, they say Caroline will be okay, so don't you worry."

Officer Price said, "Mr. Desmond is our hero. Sent the burglar packing."

"This was a robbery, then? And you guys came because of an alarm?" I couldn't imagine my aunt opening her door to a stranger. There must have been a break-in.

"Actually, Mr. Desmond called nine-one-one," Officer Price said.

"I'm confused. What exactly happened?"

Mr. Desmond said, "Paperweight came flying through a front window while I was taking my walk. I heard Caroline scream, 'Get away from me.' I went to the window and saw her fending off this man using a crooked walking stick. She had blood on her head, and I yelled, 'Hey!' That's when he took off—came barreling out the front door and ran down the block."

I gestured to the left of the foyer. "This happened in her study?"

"Yes," Rowe answered. "But Mr. Desmond doesn't remember if the man had anything with him when he ran off. If so, it wasn't large. I'm thinking jewelry, maybe? We found a safe in the study. You don't happen to have the combination?"

I wanted to say, *In your dreams,* but settled for a simple, "No." I walked toward the study, but Rowe said, "We've got a print unit coming. Please don't enter the room. You can observe from the door—see if anything jumps out at you as missing."

What jumped out at me was the utter disarray—the broken window, the overturned desk chair, the scattered papers, the lamp on the floor and the gnarled walking stick—a souvenir from my aunt's trip to Ireland.

I swallowed, feeling horrible that I hadn't been here to prevent this. Aunt Caroline had fought hard to protect herself. "Any other rooms look like this?" I asked.

"No, ma'am. Nothing else seems disturbed. I asked Ms. Rose if she disabled the alarm, and she said yes, but after that all she kept saying was like I mentioned before—that the guy took something."

"She let this person in? Is that what you think?" I said.

"Seems that way, yes," Rowe answered.

Officer Price said, "I'll walk Mr. Desmond home, then head to the hospital. Maybe your aunt can tell us more once she's calmed down. I'll be back."

Rowe nodded while I took Mr. Desmond's spot on

the bench. My legs felt rubbery, and I was still having a hard time making sense of this. "I don't know if anything is missing, but I can tell you that the wall safe in the study is for things like her will, her deed. She keeps her jewelry in her bedroom safe—and that's well hidden in her closet."

"Anything of value in the study?" He nodded in that direction.

"Nothing. The desk is ornamental. She has a built-in desk in the kitchen where she keeps her checkbook and bills."

"Yeah, I noticed that. Her checkbook is still there, and so is her purse with all her credit cards."

"Maybe the robbery had just started when Mr. Desmond interrupted," I said, half to myself.

"Unless your aunt was totally confused when she talked to me, whatever this guy took got her very upset."

I didn't want to disappoint him by pointing out that if the burglar took so much as a paper clip, Aunt Caroline would be upset. Before I could say anything more, the print unit arrived.

"Do you need me for anything else?" I asked as the two newest officers shuffled in and waited for Rowe's instructions.

"Not now. Get to the hospital." He told me Aunt Caroline had been taken to Methodist.

Before I left, I grabbed her purse from the kitchen, thinking she'd need her insurance card. I considered calling Kate, but I decided to wait until I had a better idea about Aunt Caroline's condition.

I shouldn't have worried about her health. When I was led to Aunt Caroline's curtained cubicle in the ER, I found her as feisty as ever, complaining about the *service*.

She had a few strips on the gash near her hairline, a wound that had rusted her snowy hair. The hospital gown couldn't hide the purple bruises on her arms or the dried blood streaks on her neck. Good thing there were no mirrors in here.

Officer Price was with her, and I recognized the look on her face. I'd probably worn that same frustrated ex-

pression more than once after an hour with Aunt
Caroline.

Price stood. "Glad you're here. Your aunt isn't willing
to talk, and the longer she remains silent, the harder our
job gets. Of course, perhaps she doesn't remember
much."

"What do you think I am? Senile? I remember. But
I will *not* speak of this incident in a public arena. And
let me tell you both, there is nowhere more public than
this place."

I closed my eyes, sighing heavily. "Please tell the officer everything you know."

Aunt Caroline folded her arms across her chest. "No."

"That's it," Price said, clearly irritated. "I've offered
to interview your aunt in a more private area, and she
is an unwilling witness at this time. She wants to file a
report, fine. She's got my card."

She walked out, and God, how I wanted to go with
her. "That woman was trying to help you."

Aunt Caroline closed her eyes, and I could tell her
demeanor had completely changed. "I know. The police
and the paramedics were wonderful, but I had to make
her leave."

"What?"

"You don't understand. I'm being released. When that
girl with the clipboard comes back with my paperwork,
take me home and I'll explain."

"Are you crazy? You're not going home. You can stay
with me until—"

"If you want to find out what happened and why,
Abigail, you will take me home."

"What in hell is wrong with you?" I practically
shouted. "You could have been killed today."

"You have a gun. You can protect us. I have something very important to discuss with you."

"Does this have to do with the person who hurt you?
Because we can have that discussion at my house." I
could be as stubborn as she was.

She crossed her arms over her chest. "Take me *home*
or I will call a cab. I won't be intimidated into leaving
the house I've lived in for more than thirty years."

The girl with the clipboard, who happened to be a

nurse about my age, arrived with a cheery, "Ready to get out of here, Ms. Rose?"

That was when my aunt said yes and to call her a cab, because her niece didn't want to be bothered with her.

I choked down my anger and said, "Have it your way. I'll take you home. But not before I get someone to guard your house."

"Don't bother. That stupid, deceitful man won't be back, if he knows what's good for him."

Uh-oh. The only deceitful person on her radar right now was Harrison Foster. Had he *attacked* Aunt Caroline?

The nurse, meanwhile, was going over the discharge instructions, but neither of us was listening.

"Have you called Kate?" Aunt Caroline asked.

This was worse than I imagined. How could I tell my sister that she was involved with—

"Have you called Katherine?" Aunt Caroline repeated.

"I wanted to wait until I had more information on your condition. Now I can tell her that even a blow to the head doesn't knock you off course."

"Very funny, Abigail. They wouldn't let me use the phone or I would have called her myself. You must tell her to come to my house straightaway and not waste a minute." She then turned to the nurse, who'd given up on trying to talk to either of us. "Now, young woman, where are my clothes?"

Once we were in my car, I tried Kate's office and got the answering service. They were gone for lunch. I left a message for Kate to come over to Aunt Caroline's if she could, that there had been a little mishap. I repeated the same message on Kate's voice mail. Meanwhile, I had to somehow convince Aunt Caroline that I should be the one to tell Kate about Foster's scam—but only after I made sure my aunt was protected.

"We're not leaving this parking garage until I make certain you're not attacked again." But as soon as I called DeShay and got *his* voice mail, I remembered he would be in court today. There was White—but he might be following the notebook lead, and besides, I couldn't see him agreeing to babysit an obstinate old woman. Jeff had more than enough on his hands, and that left only one person with the manpower I needed.

Aunt Caroline interrupted my thoughts. "Can't you get that policewoman to sit outside the house?"

"You haven't exactly been cooperative, and besides, the police are too busy to park outside your house for your convenience."

When she didn't snap back at me, I glanced at her. She had a thumb on her cheek and two fingers on her forehead.

"Are you all right?" I asked.

"After they scanned and X-rayed me, they gave me Tylenol for this headache, but it's coming back with a fury."

I grabbed my purse and a bottled water from the backseat. I found the Advil and handed her two tablets and the water. I also pulled out Kravitz's card. "One more call and I think we're in business."

"Do you have call waiting if Kate phones?"

"Yes, Aunt Caroline." I was sure she'd much rather have the sympathetic niece with her now, instead of me.

"I need a favor," I said when Kravitz answered.

"Which means you have something to offer in return, I take it?"

"Yes, but this favor has nothing to do with Emma's case."

"You expect me to believe that?" He was mocking, condescending, heck, pick your favorite unpleasant adjective.

I was tired of arguing with people. "I need one of your guys—Louie might work. My aunt was the victim of a burglary and assault today, and I'd like a deterring presence outside her house."

"I like that. Deterring presence. What do you have for me in return?"

"When I see your man in place, I'll call you back." I gave him Aunt Caroline's address and disconnected.

As I pulled out of the parking spot, I turned to her. "How's the headache?"

"Splitting. If you've finished playing detective, could you please get me home? I'm sure your sister will be waiting for us."

But we soon learned Kate hadn't arrived yet. The print unit was just leaving, and Price and Rowe met us in the driveway. They again asked Aunt Caroline for a statement. She again refused. In her oh-so-effective dismissive tone, she said she had a headache and might feel up to reporting this crime later.

They both shrugged and Price said, "It's your call." Then they left.

Whoever Kravitz was sending hadn't shown, so I took my gun from my glove compartment, then held Aunt Caroline's elbow as I led her up the walkway. She didn't protest. I noticed someone had been nice enough to board and duct-tape the broken window. Maybe Mr. Desmond or Rowe. Certainly not Officer Price, who was probably counting her blessings that Aunt Caroline wasn't *her* relative.

"Please get me an ice pack, Abigail. A ginger ale, too. I have mixers under the wet bar. . . ." She put a hand to her head and closed her eyes. "But, of course, you know that."

"Yeah," I said quietly. "I know where everything is."

I helped her into the living room after we both removed our shoes. Why she opted for white carpet was beyond me. The living room was directly across the large marble foyer from the study.

Once Aunt Caroline was settled on her gold sofa, her feet propped on a matching ottoman, and I'd fetched her the ice and the ginger ale, she said, "Are you sure your phone is on? Kate should have at least called by now."

"Relax. You should—" But then my cell did ring. "Not Kate," I told her, then answered.

Kravitz said, "My man is outside. Your turn."

"Hang on." I looked at Aunt Caroline, who was holding the ice pack at the back of her neck. "I need a minute."

Before I walked into the foyer, I glanced out the front window and saw a car parked across the street. Once I was out of Aunt Caroline's earshot, I said, "I'm getting closer to the truth. There may be a notebook with valuable information stored with Emma's household things. The police are looking for it, probably as we speak."

"That's all?"

"We may learn the name and address of Christine O'Meara's killer from that notebook. I'd say that's big news."

"You *may* learn the name? You're not sure?" he said. "And how did you find out about this notebook?"

"Can this wait? I just brought my aunt home from the hospital."

"What does this assault on your family have to do with the case, Abby?"

"Absolutely nothing." I was trying to keep my voice down, but Aunt Caroline must have heard me.

"Abigail, who are you talking to?" she called.

"I have to go, Paul. Thanks for the help." I closed the phone. Back in the living room, I sat on the matching love seat across from my aunt. "Time for your story." I wasn't about to admit I'd learned everything about Harrison Foster. That would only make her horrible day worse. The one thing that made her happy was being in possession of disturbing information.

"I know you will be very perturbed with me, Abigail, but what I did was out of love. Please remember that."

"Okay. Go on."

"Your sister has made a horrible mistake, and I have the proof to help her understand how foolish she's been."

"Apparently you've been checking up on her new friend Clint."

"I have. He's married and has a child, and—"

"Like I said last night, she knows all that, Aunt Caroline."

"Let me finish. His name, as I told you, is Harrison Foster, he does not work for a pharmaceutical company and he was the one who attacked me when I confronted him this morning."

"That's unbelievable," I said. *Damn.* Foster *was* her attacker. Kate was a shrink, for crying out loud. Couldn't she tell this guy was a major creep?

"I learned the hard way that he's a very violent man.

Your sister has gotten herself into serious trouble, Abigail."

"Why did he attack you?"

"Because he could. You were supposed to be here, remember? But he was early and you were late. When I showed him the report my investigator had given me, he went into a rage. I fought him off as best I could, but he grabbed the report and ran when that old fart Desmond showed up."

"That old fart might have saved your life, Aunt Caroline. What else did your investigator learn?"

"He's getting a divorce and has his own apartment. The wife and girl live in the house—somewhere in the Memorial area. All the details are in the report, which he stole from me."

I took a deep breath, becoming increasingly worried that Kate hadn't called. Was she with this guy right now? Would he go nuts like he had earlier and hurt my sister? "Before he went off the deep end, did he offer any explanation for why he lied about who he really was?"

"I didn't ask questions, Abigail. I knew everything there was to know. I simply told him he was a charlatan and that he needed to stay away from Kate. Don't you see this is about her money? He planned on swindling as much as he could from her and then disappearing."

"Oh, I understand." I'd come to the same conclusion. Foster's game was up, and I could only hope he'd decided to disappear as quickly as he'd entered Kate's life. "What detective agency did you use, Aunt Caroline? I keep duplicates of anything I generate for a client, and I'm sure they do, too. I'd like to read everything they learned." There could be more information than I had, more than Aunt Caroline remembered.

She gave me the name and said their card was on the bulletin board over her kitchen desk.

"Good," I said. "We can have them e-mail that report to your computer and—"

"What computer?" Her expression reminded me of a lying child caught red-handed.

"The one I gave you. The one I set up for you in your family room."

"The lack of a computer is rather a long story." She

avoided eye contact. "All you need to know is that I do not have one."

"Great. Let me think about this." She could have them send everything to my e-mail account, but though I could pick up the message on my BlackBerry, the print on the download would be small. It seemed far easier to print out everything at home and be back here within twenty or thirty minutes. Besides, I'd then have time to make an important phone call without Aunt Caroline asking questions about what I was doing and why.

I told her the plan and had her make the call to the agency and give them my e-mail address; then I left. The man watching the house wasn't Louie. He was younger and seemed less than thrilled with this boring job. I gave him Foster's description and took off for home.

I called Jeff as soon as I was on the road and told him about the attack and how I couldn't get hold of Kate even though I had tried several times. He didn't like the fact that Kate wasn't returning my calls any more than I did. He said he'd call in Foster's description as Aunt Caroline's assailant. She might not be willing to file charges, but they might be able to pick this guy up on something else.

I said, "I'll call you back as soon as I get the Foster report—maybe in the next fifteen minutes." I hung up and glanced at my phone. The current wallpaper on my display was a picture of my sister sitting on my couch holding Diva. "Where are you? Did you somehow find out the truth and are licking your wounds somewhere?"

I closed the phone and concentrated on my driving. The sick feeling in my gut that had begun last night when I found out my sister had been used and lied to was growing larger with each passing minute. But if she did know about Foster, maybe she was at my house hiding out, embarrassed and angry, not wanting to talk to anyone.

She wasn't at home. With Diva and Webster following on my heels, I'd checked every room before I went to the computer. I accessed my e-mail, and the message from Aunt Caroline's PI was waiting in my in-box. I saw there was more than a report. JPEG files were attached. Pictures. I saved the attachments to my desktop and printed them out. The report came first, and I was already reading how they had learned Foster's true identity as the pictures slowly filled the printer tray.

Their investigation had been as easy as shooting cans off a fence, and I wondered how much Aunt Caroline had paid them to follow Foster for a day and then probably run the same computer search I had.

The last picture was still printing, but I picked up the others. One was a grainy shot of Foster entering an apartment, the next a better picture of the entrance to the complex with the name prominent—Garden Grove. Then a photo of a brick home with well-tended landscaping and a Lexus in the driveway. This one was obviously taken with a telephoto lens, and so was the next—Foster leaving the car. Next came a shot of the front door and a woman standing there. Foster was leaving, a teenage girl by his side. The daughter. He'd even lied about her—told Kate he had a son. Her head was turned as she waved good-bye to her mother, and I couldn't see her face. But the last picture, the ink still wet, had a full shot of Foster's face as well as his daughter's.

I blinked . . . blinked again, and then I almost strangled on my own heart.

That girl could have been Shannon O'Meara's twin.

26

My hands were shaking when I called Jeff this time. "I'm e-mailing you a picture of a woman standing in the front entrance to her house. Please show it to Loreen and tell me if she recognizes her. I'll be waiting."

"Abby, what's happened?"

"I'll explain after she looks at the picture and you call me back, okay?"

"I'll be online in a sec. Take it easy. I'll get back to you as soon as I can."

He hung up, and all I could do was walk in circles, matching the swirl in my brain with my feet. Harrison Foster didn't scam my sister to get her money. He scammed her to get close to an investigation that threatened to open up his ugly box of secrets. Took advantage of her so he could hang around and put tracking devices on my car, show up anywhere I went as I followed the clues. Hell, I'll bet he even pumped Kate for information, and did it all with his dimpled, guileless smile.

He probably couldn't get to Emma's house fast enough once the TV stations and radio news programs had broadcast their breaking story about city workers finding baby bones under a demolished house. The photo of Emma and me had appeared in the *Chronicle* the next day, and Harrison Foster was in business. When he searched the Internet and learned I had a sister, he must have felt like he hit the jackpot.

But the only real proof was a photo of a girl who looked like Shannon. What if Loreen didn't recognize Beth Foster as the pregnant woman she and Christine

had cleaned for? What did I have then? *Jeff, come on.*
Call me back.

And then I remembered the notebook. Had White
found it, or had Emma tossed it? I grabbed my purse
and fumbled through all the useless things I insist on
carrying around until I found Don White's crumpled
card, the one he'd given me the night Jerry Joe Billings
had been murdered.

I called his cell, and he answered right away with a
brusque, "White here."

"It's Abby," I said. "Did Emma let you look in the
storage unit for the notebook?"

"What's going on, Abby? You sound in a panic."

"I am. The notebook?"

"I'm looking at it, so you can cool your jets. Checking
out all these names might take us—"

"There are names?"

"Oh, yeah. But like I said—"

"Can you look for one name in particular?"

"Sure. But what have you got?"

"I think a man named Harrison Foster might be who
we're looking for. Can you check and see if he or his
wife, Beth Foster, was a client of Christine's?"

"Sure, but how'd you find this out, Abby?" he asked.

I wanted to scream at him to shut up and just do what
I asked, but I managed to say calmly, "Please, Don.
Look for the name first. It's important."

What seemed a decade later he said, "It's here. She
cleaned for a Mr. and Mrs. Harrison Foster on
Wednesdays."

There it was. Proof. And I suddenly wanted to
throw up.

"Tell me what's going on, Abby."

"This man almost killed my aunt this morning. He's
been dating my sister to get close to us. You need to
find him. Now." I gave White the addresses from the PI
report, and he said he was on it.

I hung up and the other phone rang. The landline.
The caller ID read HEWITT BANK AND TRUST, where we
have our CompuCan accounts—the computer business
that Daddy left us. What the hell did they want? I
couldn't deal with company business right now. But

when the answering machine offered the caller a chance to leave a message, I heard a voice I recognized. "This is Jane Edgar from Hewitt Bank and Trust. It is urgent that I speak with Abigail Rose immediately concerning—"

I snatched up the phone, knowing that Jane Edgar wouldn't use the word *urgent* if she didn't mean it. "This is Abby. What is it, Jane?"

"This concerns a transfer of funds, Abby. Can you please verify your address?"

"Transfer of funds? Verify my address?" I said, confused.

"I must verify—"

"You *know* me. You know where I live. What's this about?"

"I have to go through standard procedure on this, check your passwords, everything. You'll understand soon enough. Please, let's go through the steps so I can document that I followed bank protocol."

I gave her what she wanted, even had to bring up my accounts online and look for a specific account number.

When I was finished with her "standard procedure," Jane said, "We have a request to transfer five hundred thousand dollars from the joint account you share with your sister, Katherine Rose. It's to go to a numbered account in the Cayman Islands. As per this account agreement, we must have your authorization to do this for any amount over ten thousand dollars."

I couldn't speak. I felt like I was listening to a radio not tuned in to any station, one just giving off static.

"Abby? Are you there?"

"Um . . . can I check into this and get back to you? Meanwhile, don't move any money, okay?"

"I think that's wise," she said solemnly. "Please ask for me when you call back." She disconnected.

I slowly replaced the handset in its cradle. I felt like I was drowning, struggling in a current that threatened to suck me under. There was only one reason Kate would need that kind of money.

Foster. He had her.

And she'd done the one thing she could to send me a message. Rather than transfer money from any of her private accounts, she chose the business account, knowing the bank would call me.

Yes. He *had* her. But where? How could I find her? What would happen if I didn't okay the money transfer? What would happen if I did?

A cold sweat dampened my forehead, and I tasted blood. I'd bitten my bottom lip without even feeling any pain.

My cell rang, and I started before I grabbed it up. Jeff.

Before he could say a word, I said, "He has her. Foster has Kate, and we have to find her before it's too late. But I don't know how to find her and—"

"Hold on, hon. Slow down and explain."

I did, but the words came out as a halting, jumbled mess, and I thought I'd have to say everything all over again, but Jeff got it.

"Okay, I understand. We're going to find Kate. Right now, you need to take a few deep breaths—get some oxygen to that very fine brain of yours so we can work on this together."

I closed my eyes and inhaled, but when I exhaled, the release of air was shaky, and my jaw quivered. "What in hell do we do, Jeff?"

"I'm calling this in to SWAT as a possible hostage situation. The report you sent me has enough information about Foster to offer plenty of leads. Loreen recognized the woman in the picture as the pregnant client she and Christine cleaned for. Must be Foster's wife. She's probably in on this, knows the kid she's been raising isn't her biological child. We'll have to get someone out to her house."

"Could Kate be there?"

"It's possible."

"Can I go? I won't get in the way. I just need—"

"What you need to do is sit tight. If Foster can't get his money through Kate, if he figures out she's alerted you, he may call you for ransom."

"He's trying to get away, isn't he? And that means he wouldn't need to . . . to *harm* her. He could take the money and go away and Kate could come home. Can we make that happen, Jeff?"

"Abby, do *not* okay that transfer. For now, he may

be unaware there's a problem with the account, and we can catch him off guard."

"Catch him off guard *where*? I mean, what if he's not at his house? What if she was forced to get the money another way or he got angry with her and—"

"Please, hon. Don't do this to yourself. We *will* find her. But I need to make a few calls to set things in motion. DeShay and White will probably come to your house, perhaps bring a SWAT commander."

"I already talked to White and asked him to look for Foster. He found the notebook, and Foster's name was there."

"Good. Try to stay calm. I wish I could be there, too, but I can't leave Doris. Bringing her along wouldn't—"

I heard Loreen in the background say, "Go. Doris and I have girl things to do, and we don't need you around watching us."

A short silence followed, and then Jeff said, "I'll be there as soon as I can."

I closed my eyes and felt tears coming. I managed to mumble, "Thank you," before ending the call.

Webster's head rested on my feet, and he looked up at me with questioning eyes. "She's coming home, buddy. I promise you."

And then I couldn't hold back any longer. Good thing I was done with my cry by the time Don White and DeShay arrived. I sure didn't want to come across as a basket case, too emotional to help find my sister.

We'd gone into the kitchen because I needed water, hoping to somehow swallow the lump in my throat. The three of us remained standing there to talk—standing because you didn't sit around in easy chairs when someone you loved was in trouble.

I said, "If that bastard has broken even one of my sister's fingernails he's going to pay."

"SWAT is on standby," White said. "They can't roll until we know where they need to go. An unmarked unit is checking out the Fosters' house, and another squad is looking at Foster's apartment."

"Foster stole the PI report," I said. "He's probably figured out at least a few cops know where he lives. I doubt he'll go to either place. But . . . Oh, my God.

Why didn't I think of this sooner? Kate's office. He could be—"

"We stopped at her building on the way here," De-Shay said. "The receptionist was busy canceling patients. Said Kate was a no-show after lunch."

"And April never called me? What's wrong with her?" I had to direct my anger somewhere, and Kate's receptionist, whom I hardly knew, seemed as good a candidate as anyone.

White answered, "She says she's new. Says she thought maybe Kate had an emergency. The young woman felt like the doc would want her to cancel the patients. That was her priority."

"She was pretty upset when we showed up, Abby." DeShay's voice was calm.

But I was not calm. I was angry with myself for not even thinking about Kate's office earlier. That was where Foster must have gone after he ran from Aunt Caroline's. He'd certainly hung around there long enough to know Kate's routine. I started pacing in front of the refrigerator. "I feel so helpless. Isn't there something else we can do?"

"The bank's cooperating, and we've tapped a line in case Kate calls in. We also have a tech investigator monitoring the computer there if she tries another online transaction."

"She attempted the transfer online?" I said.

"Right," DeShay said.

"Bank Web sites are very secure," I said. "Your tech guy can get the e-mail address she used to access the account and—"

"He's working on it, Abby. You need—"

Jeff came in the back door and interrupted the rest of what DeShay had to say—probably something on the order of, *Stay out of this*. But I wasn't staying out of anything.

White and Jeff shook hands, and White said, "Good to see you back."

Jeff and DeShay did this masculine half embrace, followed by what I assumed was their own special handshake, and DeShay said, "We need you on this one, man."

Jeff was ready, too. He wore his holstered gun and had his walkie-talkie and badge on his belt. No words were necessary to convey what Jeff and I were both feeling. I saw a little fear in his eyes before he hugged me, but also the steely resolve I had come to know when it came to his work. He gripped my arms. "How you holding up?"

"Waiting around for something to happen is making me crazy. I feel like someone poured battery acid into my gut." I gnawed on my thumbnail rather than cry again. No more tears. They wouldn't get Kate back.

"Give me your cell phone," Jeff said.

I pulled it from my jeans pocket. "Why?"

He held up what looked like a small battery. "I stopped at the bank, picked this up from our tech investigator. It will make it easier to triangulate any calls that come in, find the caller's location quicker." He attached the little button near the antenna.

"You think Foster will call?" I said.

"I'm counting on it. You all charged up?"

"Yes. But what if he doesn't call? What if he gets impatient and—"

"This guy needs to get out of town in a bad way, Abby. He needs that money. When he calls, you know what to do. TV is right about a few things, and you should keep him on the line as long as possible."

Just then DeShay's cell rang and the noise made my heart skip. I must have jumped, because Jeff put an arm around me. "Hey, it's okay. We're on this."

I watched DeShay's face while he listened to the caller, hoping I'd see relief in his eyes, but he gave away nothing. When he finished the call, he said, "No luck with the wife. Her house was clear, and she said she hasn't seen Foster since last Saturday. She was pretty freaked out, asking all kinds of questions. The officer told her Foster had missed paying a few speeding tickets, but he didn't think she was buying it."

"Where the hell do you take someone you've kidnapped?" I asked. I started pacing again, thinking out loud. "With cell phones, there's no need for a landline, but if Kate accessed the Internet, there has to be Internet availability where she is. Foster would need a computer to make sure he got his money transferred to the right place."

"Keep talking. This is good stuff," Jeff said. "Would he need a phone line? Or what?"

"A laptop with integrated wireless would do the trick—and that means he'd have to be somewhere he could pick up a signal." For the first time in an hour, I felt like I could string a few logical thoughts together.

"What? Like an Internet café or a Starbucks?" White asked. "Hard to work with a hostage to get your money in one of those places."

"These days you can pick up a signal in plenty of locations," I said, "and if Foster knows anything about computers he could—"

"He's a software designer," DeShay said.

"That's right. Then he knows plenty," I said. "He could steal the signal and log on. Best place to do that is in residential areas. Coffee shops and other businesses require a security key to tap into their wireless networks, and though you could hack through, that would take longer."

"Okay, where do people have wireless networks like this?" White asked.

Jeff said, "Upper-middle-class and wealthy neighborhoods are more likely to be equipped with that kind of technology in their homes, right, Abby?"

"Yes," I said. "When people set up wireless networks at home, they often aren't adequately secured. A computer with wireless capability could pick up and use their signal."

White nodded. "I get it. You're saying people set up home networks themselves and don't realize someone in the house a few doors down could steal their signal and surf the Net all day and night—and this turd would know that."

"That's right," I said. "Can that information narrow down your— Wait a minute." An image flashed through my mind—Kate, Emma, Foster and me, standing in Kate's new house.

"What is it?" Jeff asked.

"Kate just bought a house not far from here. I'll bet

there are home networks up and down that street."
Being able to contribute to the search was helping to
quell the fear that had threatened to shut me down. But
I still felt like I had a dancing bobber in my stomach.

"Let's get a unit to check out the house," DeShay
said. "Where is this place?"

I started to speak and then stopped. "Damn. I don't
know the street or the house number. I'll call Emma.
She sold Kate the house."

"Do it," Jeff said.

But I couldn't reach her. Her voice mail message said
she was showing properties and would get back to the
caller as soon as possible. I left a message telling her I
had an urgent situation and needed her help. Then I
called the real estate office, but no one answered there.
"Now what?" I said to Jeff.

"We invite the West U police to help us," he answered. "You told me the other day the house is in West
U, right?"

I nodded. "I can get their number."

White said, "Don't bother. Dispatch can patch me
through." He unclipped his phone. "But this is a long
shot, you know. Tell me who Emma works for."

"Green Tree Realtors. The 'For Sale' sign may still
be up." I gave him the approximate location and a description of the house. Knowing the West U police, they
could find the place even with that small amount of
information.

While White was talking to the our local police, my
landline rang.

Nothing had been done to trace calls on this phone
yet, but it didn't matter. The caller ID displayed Aunt
Caroline's number. I'd promised her I'd be back and
hadn't even phoned.

I picked up before the answering machine could take
over, knowing I couldn't tell her over the phone that
Kate was missing. She'd freak out. "Hi. Sorry I got tied
up and didn't get back."

"Abigail, can you please return?" She sounded like
she was crying—which never happened.

"Are you okay?"

"I'm in so much pain, and if you could help me get settled in bed, then . . . then you can go about your business again."

She sounded absolutely pathetic, which was probably partly an act, but that didn't matter. I already felt guilty for leaving her alone after what she'd gone through today.

"I'll see what I can do, Aunt Caroline."

"What does that mean?" she said.

"I'm thinking I'll call your friend Martha to come over. She can help you out until I can get away."

"Martha is in Europe. Does this mean you won't come? You won't help me?" But there was none of her usual indignation. She sounded like a different person. Yeah . . . maybe an old woman who'd been in a fight with a killer and lived to tell about it. Now I felt even guiltier.

"Okay, I'll be there in fifteen minutes. But then we'll pack a bag. You're staying here with me—and don't bother arguing." She did need to know about Kate, especially if— No, I wasn't going to think about that. And despite Kravitz's man on guard duty, I'd feel better having her here with Foster on the loose.

Amazingly enough, she didn't argue. She simply said, "Thank you, Abigail," and hung up.

I looked at Jeff, who'd been talking to DeShay. I'd heard the word *trace,* and I was guessing he wanted to make sure any calls to all my phones could be traced. "I have to pick up Aunt Caroline. She's alone, she's been hurt and I think what happened today is finally penetrating her rhinoceros hide."

"Okay," Jeff said. "I'm going with you."

"No need. It's a thirty-minute round-trip, and if you come she'll start asking questions. I don't want to tell her anything until I have her back here. Then she can have her meltdown." I was talking too fast, sounding a little too frantic.

Jeff gripped my shoulders. "Think about it. What if Kate calls your cell and none of us is with you? What will you do?"

I put a hand to my forehead. Closed my eyes. Why couldn't I think straight?

"We will get her back, Abby, but you need to keep focused on that goal. Now, let's pick up your aunt Caroline."

"But what if the bank calls? Won't I need to talk to them?"

"White or DeShay can handle that. They know we're on this, and anyway, you're not releasing any funds. We have to provoke this guy out of the shadows—get him to make direct contact with you."

"Then let's hurry so we can get back," I said.

We took my car, but Jeff drove. I'd left my gun on the passenger seat after my last trip to Aunt Caroline's house, and now I held the Lady Smith in both hands. I never knew a gun could offer comfort, but it did. Yes, a gun could provide what was probably a false sense of hope when you felt powerless and out of control, like I did.

"Um . . . we've got a tail," Jeff said. We were at a light, and his eyes were fixed on the rearview. "Use the cosmetic mirror and see if you recognize those two guys in the SUV. Right lane, two cars back."

I did. "Damn. I think that's Kravitz and the cameraman, Stu Crowell."

"Obviously they were hanging around your place and saw us all arrive," Jeff said.

"I called Kravitz to put a man outside Aunt Caroline's house, and he must have decided I wasn't being straight with him, even though I was at the time."

"Losing them is pointless," Jeff said.

I turned the gun over and over, my throat tightening even more. "You can't make them stay out of this?" But I knew it was a stupid question, and Jeff, thank goodness, ignored it.

"I'd feel a whole lot better if you'd put your Lady away." Jeff nodded at the gun.

"You don't want a jumpy girlfriend with a loaded gun sitting next to you?"

He rested a hand on the back of my neck and rubbed at the tension residing there. "I wouldn't put it past you to take a warning shot at those guys behind us."

I opened the glove compartment and did what he asked. "Happy now?"

"Just looking out for you."

I smiled, grateful that he was here with me and not in Seattle.

"Here's the plan," Jeff said. "We get Aunt Caroline out of her house and we don't talk to those guys, okay?"

"Okay," I said.

Ten minutes later we parked in my aunt's driveway, and Kravitz pulled up behind the guard's car across the street.

But the guy who was supposed to be protecting Aunt Caroline didn't seem to be in his car. *Great protection, Kravitz,* I wanted to shout when I saw him and Stu get out of their SUV. Stu hoisted his camera and pointed it at me.

Kravitz was headed toward the guard's car.

Then, before I could take another breath, Kravitz shouted something I didn't catch—didn't catch because Aunt Caroline's front door opened at the same moment.

Harrison Foster stood in the doorway—and he had a gun.

I froze.

"Get down," Jeff yelled.

I fell to my hands and knees, but I was on the side of the car without protection. I crawled around to the back of the car, fully expecting a bullet to flatten me.

Then I heard the shot, but he must have missed.

I made it around to the driver's side and realized he hadn't missed.

Jeff was down.

I scrambled to him and gently turned him onto his side. He was grimacing in pain, and a crimson stain was spreading on his chest. I fought the panic threatening to take me over. I needed adrenaline, not fear, to be in charge here.

"Kravitz," I shouted. "Call nine-one-one!"

Then I put my mouth to Jeff's ear. "Is it bad?"

"I-I don't think I can get up." His words were halting, like he didn't have enough air to speak.

Foster shouted, "Abby, look who I've got."

I pried Jeff's gun from his fingers and stood up just enough to see through the driver's-side window. Foster held Kate in front of him. He had had a far better shot at me a few seconds ago and hadn't taken it. He wanted his money, and probably figured out he needed my help with the account.

I'd trade myself for Kate in a minute if not for Jeff. Would he bleed to death while I got this bastard what he wanted?

My heart, already beating crazily, felt like it might come out of my chest. What did I do? Stall for time?

Foster's arm was around Kate's chest near her throat. Her mouth was duct-taped, and so were her hands in front of her. He held his gun to her head.

I glanced right, hoping to see Kravitz with a phone to his ear. But I couldn't find him. Stu Crowell must have ducked for cover, too.

Foster said, "Join us, Abby. Your sister seems to have decided we need your help with something."

Since we'd been taken by surprise, help was at the very least minutes away. But I had to call 911 now. Jeff might not have minutes.

I was about to reach in my pocket for my phone, but then I saw Crowell with his camera behind the wide trunk of the live oak in Aunt Caroline's front yard. Then Crowell stepped out to tape the horror unfolding.

His sudden appearance distracted Foster, and his gun swung away from Kate's head toward the camera.

This was my chance. I stood, my hands amazingly steady when I raised Jeff's Glock with both hands. I aimed for Foster's left shoulder and hit the mark, just as I'd hit so many bull's-eyes with Daddy admiring every shot. Foster crumpled to the ground without firing a round.

He might still be able to use his weapon—but Kate took care of that problem by kicking the gun away. Then she put her foot on Foster's throat.

I shouted, "Crowell, help us, for God's sake."

He was no more than fifty feet away and yet was willing to let Jeff bleed out so he could capture the drama on tape.

Jeff's eyes were closed, but he was still breathing. I pressed a hand against his chest wound and fumbled for the phone clipped to his belt. I flipped it open and started to press the number pad with my bloody thumb—God, there was so much blood—when I felt someone grip my shoulder.

I looked up and saw the investigative reporter who worked for God knew who—Mary Parsons.

"The police are coming," she said. "Should be here any minute. And they're sending an ambulance."

"Thank you. Thank God." I rested my face against Jeff's cool cheek. My sister needed me, but I couldn't leave him. I had to keep him warm, keep my hand tight against the hole where his life was leaking out. "My sister? Can you see her?"

Parsons, who was crouched near us, raised her head and looked through the driver's-side window. "The man is still lying there on the grass. Your sister has her foot on his neck. And that asshole is still taping every second of this."

The police came then. But not with sirens blaring. The SWAT team was upon us so quietly I nearly cried out in surprise.

After they assessed the scene, one of them radioed for patrol and homicide. But when I told them one of their own was down, the officer got back on the radio and said, "Where's the fucking medics?"

The ambulance must have already been coming down the street, because it seemed like only seconds later when the paramedics pried me away from Jeff and began their work.

Then that helpless, hopeless feeling, the same one I'd had when I knew my sister was in danger, hammered down on me again.

I think I heard someone say, "Ma'am, are you all right? Have you been injured?"

I didn't answer. I couldn't speak.

27

There had been no hospital vigil when my daddy died. His heart attack had been brutally quick, with no chance for good-byes. *Maybe that's better,* I thought, as I sat and waited for word on Jeff.

I wasn't alone. In fact, so many other officers had come to wait, come to give their blood for their brother, that the hospital had put us all in a conference room; either that or we would have taken over the regular waiting area.

After Kate had given her statement to police, she insisted on staying with me. I held her cold hand tightly in my own as we sat in padded chairs around the long table, cold cups of coffee in front of us. Kate should be in the ER getting checked out, just like Aunt Caroline was. They'd both been bound, perhaps even hurt by Foster. But Kate had refused to be anywhere but here. We'd been told we'd get word on Aunt Caroline as soon as she was evaluated, but the Hermann Hospital ER we'd all been brought to was very crowded.

DeShay was pacing like a parrot on a perch, and White was with Harrison Foster at Ben Taub Hospital, where they'd taken him. Foster's wound turned out to be minor. He was doing fine. Just *fine.* Had my decision not to shoot to kill been correct? Or would this be a regret I'd carry with me to my grave? It all depended on one thing—the one thing I did not know yet: whether Jeff would live or die.

"Why is this taking so long?" I said.

I'd been asking this question probably every ten minutes since they'd taken Jeff into surgery—like some terrible aberration of the "are we there yet?" children's chant.

Kate squeezed my hand, and DeShay grazed his fingers across my shoulders on one of his passes. Earlier, Kate had told me what little she knew of Foster's motive—something to do with his wife's mental state after their baby was born fifteen years ago. But she'd been too terrified to listen carefully to his ramblings—and he had rambled, mostly about how it was over, how he'd be leaving behind plenty of money for his family, and that was why Kate had to transfer the funds to support his new life in someplace far, far away. A definite fairy tale, was all I could think.

"There may be more you don't remember," I said.

"Probably," she answered. "Maybe he talked so much because we'd . . . shared a lot beforehand." She'd gone silent then, lost in her own guilt. I wanted to tell her she had nothing to feel guilty about, but knowing her, she wouldn't have agreed.

Someone knocked on the door, and everyone not already on their feet stood silently in one motion—like we'd all gotten orders from our drill sergeant.

A volunteer opened the door, not the doctor we were awaiting. "There's someone out here named Emma Lopez," the woman said. "She says she's not the press, that—"

"Let her in, please," I said.

All the other men and women waiting with Kate and me had no interest in this visitor. They returned to pacing or drinking coffee or resting their heads on the table.

Emma ran into the room and embraced me, pulling Kate into the hug as well. "I am so sorry," she whispered. "This is all my fault."

I withdrew and held her by the upper arms—too roughly, I suppose. "Don't you *ever* say that. Don't you ever blame yourself for wanting the truth."

These were the words I wanted to say to Kate and couldn't. Because that was what Jeff would have told them both. He hunted down the truth and made sure people paid for their crimes. For him it was simple, yet so important. And victims or family members taking responsibility for the crimes in any way? Well, that was simply wrong in his book.

I let go of Emma and apologized. "It's just that Jeff wouldn't want you saying that."

DeShay mumbled, "You got that right, sister."

One of the uniformed officers silently brought a chair over so Emma could sit by us.

She did. "I came here to Hermann Hospital as soon as I heard, but it was chaos in the emergency room waiting area, so many police and reporters. Someone from a TV station spotted me, started asking questions. I had no answers, and that's when she told me this man Foster had exchanged my sister for a dead child, that he killed my mother. She said he'd been shot and was taken to Ben Taub Hospital, so I went there."

"Why would you ever do that?" Kate asked.

"I don't know—at least, my conscious mind didn't know. I guess I thought I could walk in and ask him why. That's all I wanted, really—to know why. Kravitz must have been hanging around there, because he found me. Before he could talk to me *she* walked in with her . . . daughter. A police officer whisked them away pretty quickly."

"Who are you talking about?" I asked, even though I was pretty sure I knew.

"Foster's wife . . . and his daughter. She looks like Shannon. And so much like my mother." Tears welled. "That one glance may be all I'll ever get of my sister. And then I thought about you again and I had to come back here. You've paid such a high price for—"

I put a finger to her lips. "Quit that. Jeff's the strongest person I've ever met, and he'll pull through."

Nods in the room, like silent amens.

Minutes that seemed like hours later, a woman in surgical scrubs appeared in the doorway. "Next of kin?" she said solemnly, scanning the grim faces in the room.

I felt sick, felt like I was falling off the earth.

DeShay took my elbow, lifted me from my chair, walked me over to face this tired-looking, sober messenger. "This is Jeff's next of kin," he said.

She didn't question whether that was true or not. She

just started talking. "We had to remove the spleen. And repairing his lung was delicate, but my team and I believe we have a decent outcome. The bullet passed between the ribs and lodged near the heart, so the length of the surgery—"

"Is he going to be all right?" I sounded impatient and harsh and maybe a little crazy. I didn't care.

Her smile was small and tight. She had no laugh lines and I imagined that smile was probably difficult for her to produce. "Yes. I believe he will make a full recovery."

The room erupted in whoops. There were hugs and high fives, and despite the clamor, I heard the doctor say, "He'll be in recovery for at least an hour before being transferred to ICU. You can visit him once he's settled. Don't be alarmed by all the tubes. We're giving him blood, draining his lung, monitoring every part of him." Then she got out of there as fast as she could.

Kate and Emma wrapped their arms around me. We swayed with joy, my face wet with tears. Then DeShay joined us. He buried his face in my hair, and his strong hand on my back felt wonderful. I put an arm around his waist, and then suddenly the room grew quiet again and we released one another.

The chief of police had arrived. He said, "Don't let me stop the celebration. We've had wonderful news about our fellow officer, Sergeant Jeffrey Kline. I want to personally thank all of you for being here for your brother, for giving your blood, for offering your free time, for comforting Jeff's partner and his good friends. Carry on." He looked at me then.

I never thought I'd hear a damn speech in a hospital. The chief walked over and picked up my hands. "Abby Rose, correct?"

I nodded, wondering how he knew.

"I understand you and Sergeant Kline are very close," he went on. "This has been a horrendous day for you and for the rest of your family—the women this criminal took hostage. On behalf of the city, I want to thank you for your assistance in bringing this man to justice. Do not entertain any fear that charges will be filed against you."

Charges? I couldn't believe this. I take down a bad

guy and he's talking about charges? And somehow this all felt rehearsed, insincere.

"There is one more favor I ask on behalf of Houston. It is my understanding that a television program has been following this case, that they even lost one of their investigators—a man who was guarding the home where the hostage situation took place."

I hadn't even asked what happened to Kravitz's man, had totally forgotten about him. I swallowed hard. "Oh, no. He's dead?"

"Apparently when Mr. Foster brought your sister to the house, he . . . he *eliminated* him before this investigator could call for help."

I looked at Kate. "Why didn't you tell me?"

Her lips were trembling, her face streaked with tears. "I-I couldn't think about that. Couldn't have *you* thinking about that. Not until we knew if Jeff would be okay."

"But . . . but you watched him *kill* someone, Kate." I looked at the chief. "That's what you're saying, right?"

He nodded. "Paul Kravitz is currently in the media room we've set up. He called nine-one-one and—"

"No, the other reporter, Mary Parsons, did that," I said. "That bastard Kravitz disappeared."

"Seems you're unaware we had two emergency calls about the incident. Kravitz called from his man's car, stayed with him, hoping he could be revived. Help was on the way as soon as Sergeant Kline went down, but you acted swiftly, probably avoided a prolonged and dangerous hostage situation. We all admire your courage, not to mention your marksmanship, Ms. Rose."

But he was about as genuine as a furniture salesman. Why? What was going on?

Kate sniffed, and I found her hand, grasping Emma's with my other.

"That said," the chief continued, "we would like you to cooperate with the television crew. Their program will bring positive publicity to Houston. As I understand it, the parent production company has already agreed to assist one very special family. Their arrival in town set the wheels in motion that helped Sergeant Peters and Sergeant White close several cases with your assistance. Please cooperate with Paul Kravitz, if you would."

Ah, now I understood. The TV connection again. I wanted to tell him I wouldn't be talking to anyone, that I would be sitting by Jeff's side until he was well enough to walk out the hospital door. Then another thought pushed everything else away. I turned to Kate. "Oh, my gosh. Doris. We have to phone Loreen and tell her Jeff will be gone for a while. When I called her, she promised not to tell Doris anything until . . . well, you know."

Kate rested a hand on my shoulder. "We'll take care of all that."

How could she be so calm? But I knew this would hit her hard soon enough. And I would be there for her.

The chief extended his hand. "Thank you, Ms. Rose. We are in your debt."

We shook hands, and then he was gone.

As the chief mentioned, the media was camped out at the hospital in their own conference room. They'd already been on high alert because Hollywood had come to town, and now everything had exploded into front-page news—hostages, another murder, a wounded officer fighting for his life and the suspect himself injured. Yeah, stuff like that drew plenty of reporters.

To avoid them, Kate and I had to sneak up the stairs to visit Aunt Caroline after we were told she'd been admitted for observation.

She sat propped in her hospital bed with probably half the pillows on this ward. Her hair was a mess, and the dark circles under her eyes coupled with her pale skin reminded me of a panda. I could tell she was in pain despite the lack of facial expressions due to her latest round of Botox injections. The discomfort showed in her eyes.

Kate told me Foster had tied Aunt Caroline to a dining room chair, and the chair had fallen over when she struggled—and I could certainly picture her struggling. She'd been through the wringer forward and backward today.

Aunt Caroline's first words to us were, "What took you two so long? No one's told me anything, and it's given me a giant headache."

I don't think I'd ever been so happy to hear her being

her usual cranky self. Kate and I explained where we'd been and that Jeff would be okay. I kept a careful eye on my watch during this conversation, anxious for the time when I could get into ICU to see him.

When we were finished explaining, Aunt Caroline said, "Kate, I hope you understand why I had this man investigated. I didn't like him from the minute I set eyes on him and my instincts were correct."

"Um, can we save the gloating for later? You've both been through hell today." I glanced at Kate, but she seemed to have cut off any emotion. Her face was impassive.

Aunt Caroline said, "It's not gloating; it's . . . it's . . ."

She's at a loss for words? Don't tell me she might be having a small epiphany?

"Abby's right, and I'm sorry, Kate," she went on. "You were very brave and very calm, and I drew strength from you today."

Kate said, "Thank you. And I'm sorry I put you in harm's way."

Aunt Caroline reached out a hand, and Kate took it. "I love my girls very much. Love them enough to get involved in their lives. Now. As for that very excellent young man, Terry, you have foolishly abandoned. I think—"

"Not now," I said firmly. Jeez, I felt like my aunt's conscience.

I glanced again at my watch. I hated to leave Kate here to take a verbal beating, but I wanted to see Jeff.

Kate noticed I was fidgety and said, "Go. Then come back and let us know how Jeff is."

I kissed Aunt Caroline on the cheek, and this seemed to ease her out of her snit. Her meddling had proven useful for once, and I should be grateful. Or maybe I simply loved her despite her flaws. After all, I had a few of those myself.

As I left, I heard Kate say, "Have they given you anything for your headache?" I knew my sister would keep herself occupied playing nurse, and that Aunt Caroline would milk Kate for every ounce of sympathy she could get.

Minutes later I arrived at the double doors to ICU.

The unit lay beyond a door marked, DO NOT ENTER WITHOUT AUTHORIZATION. PRESS BUZZER FOR ASSISTANCE. I followed instructions, and a female voice came over a small speaker above the door, asking if she could help me.

"Has Jeff Kline arrived from the recovery room yet?"

"The police officer?"

"Yes."

"And your name?"

I told her, and she said, "He's been asking for you. Please wait there."

A few minutes passed before a man in scrubs came to the door. "Abby Rose?"

"Yes."

"I'm Sergeant Kline's nurse, Joey. Come with me."

We passed a long counter with a bank of monitors for each room. I immediately spotted Jeff on one of the screens. He seemed small lying there with tubes coming out from him like tentacles. My stomach tightened at the sight.

The door to his room was filled with so much equipment, they must have been checking every cell in his body. Blood hung from an IV pole attached to the bed, and its dark red tubing snaked down and over Jeff's body, led to his forearm and disappeared under adhesive tape.

Joey said, "His chest tube is on the left side. Please come around to the right."

Even though the nurse spoke softly, Jeff's eyes opened, and he tried to smile when he saw me.

"You look wonderfully . . . fuzzy." His *fuzzy* came with about ten Zs.

Hearing his voice made the knot in my gut begin to unwind. I wanted to touch him, but I feared I'd knock something loose. His mouth seemed safe and splendid territory, and I planted a kiss on his lips.

"Did you meet Abby, Joey? Abby is soooooo hot." He moved his head back and forth—the only part of his body he probably could move—and said, "Hot, hot, hot."

"Yeah, we met," Joey said. "I'd say you are one lucky dude."

"You got that right." Jeff closed his eyes, smiling.

I kinda liked Jeff on drugs. They should have passed around morphine in that conference room so the rest of us could have been as mellow as he was right now.

"They say you'll be fine," I said.

He didn't open his eyes. "Was there any doubt?"

"No," I said quickly.

He looked at me. "You still have my weapon? I know I let you borrow it, but I *will* need that back."

"I don't think I need your gun anymore. I guess I can return it."

"Come closer. I need to tell you something." He was grinning like a friendly wolf.

I put my ear near his mouth.

He whispered, "You better still need my other gun."

Yup. Jeff was gonna be just fine.

28

I left Jeff about five minutes later, after DeShay arrived to take my place, and started for the stairs back to Aunt Caroline's room. I checked my watch. Eight o'clock. I hoped I could get an officer to take Kate and me home. We could pick up Subway sandwiches, then get some rest. Though I wanted to stay here in case anything unexpected happened to Jeff, I didn't want to leave Kate by herself. Not tonight. I'd already given Joey all my phone numbers, and he said he would pass them on to the night nurse and notify me if Jeff's condition changed. But Joey assured me that everything seemed to be going well. Jeff was a fit man with a strong will.

I reached the stairs, and when I opened the door I nearly shouted out in surprise. Paul Kravitz was leaning against the wall in the stairwell.

"Sorry, Abby. Didn't mean to scare you." His voice seemed to bounce off the walls. "How's your friend?"

"He's . . . okay. He'll recover completely." I had to admit Kravitz was smart. I should have known he'd find me.

"Good. Even our bad guy will be okay. They patched him up and transferred him to the police station—what do they call it? Travis? Took him there for interrogation."

"Really? Thanks for telling me." I swallowed, met Kravitz's stare. "I'm sorry about the man who worked for you. Really sorry. What was his name?"

"Cooper. Bill Cooper. The police say he probably never knew what hit him."

"I-I still feel terrible."

"Why? Foster's the one who killed him." Kravitz sat on the stair closest to him.

"Thanks for trying to let me off the hook, but he's still dead, and I still feel awful."

"I'm not letting you off the hook. I think you owe me an interview, Abby. Can we talk about that?" He patted the concrete next to him.

Maybe I did owe him, but the last thing I wanted was to show my face on a TV show that millions watched. I sat beside him, hoping a conversation would be enough.

"Stu videoed the whole thing today, the shooting, everything," Kravitz said, "but the police took the tape. I want it back. You have strong connections to them. Maybe you can accomplish what I couldn't."

"The chief of police told me to cooperate with you and Venture, said you'd bring good publicity to the city. I'm not sure I understand why they're withholding the video."

"They say they need it to prosecute Foster. That it's evidence," he said.

"Their best evidence. But they can copy it for you. I'll see what I can do."

Kravitz nodded. "Thanks."

I was puzzled. "If they're asking *me* to cooperate with you, why won't they?"

"You want my guess? Because you took that guy out, not them. And what's on the tape is not what they want the world to see."

I turned to look at his profile, again amazed at how old he looked in contrast to what we saw on TV. "I'm wondering if this is the story you want to tell. That SWAT didn't arrive until a few minutes after I shot Foster? That HPD was late to the game?"

"I'm pissed off about them shutting me out all of a sudden, so maybe yes. Maybe that *will* be my slant." His neck was reddening and his jaw was taut.

"Can I offer you some advice?" I said. "Don't do that. This case is about so much more. This is about how you can never really bury the past. This about three families all touched by Foster's crimes."

"Three families? Who else besides Emma's family and the Fosters?"

"Emma has two half brothers she's never met. She has a half sister she may never meet, either. But what she *does* have is the truth. She knows what happened to her mother now. And all the hard work she put into raising her brothers and sister will be rewarded. This is a story about horrible crimes that led to a happy, if not so perfect ending. Isn't that a whole lot more important than a tape in an evidence locker?"

Kravitz sighed. "I'll have to think about it. Meanwhile, you still owe me a formal interview—you promised your cooperation, right?"

Guess stairway conversations didn't count as cooperation. "Interview, yes, but I don't want to show my face on TV."

"Why not? You've got a great face." He smiled.

"I run a very small business and am extremely selective about my clients. Just the mention of my name on a local TV show brought Chelsea Burch to my doorstep."

"You got a problem, then. This story was syndicated. UPI, Reuters, all of them have it. And when the *Today* show calls tonight or tomorrow, I hope you tell them no and give me an exclusive agreement in writing, especially since we lost one of our own to help your solve this thing."

"The *Today* show won't be calling me. That's ridiculous."

"Not ridiculous at all," Kravitz said. "Seems you're a damn hero, Abby Rose."

Jeff's fellow officers and the hospital administration continued to shield Kate and me from the herd of reporters still waiting to talk to us. We heard that even Aunt Caroline's name was big news. She was now the "socialite hostage" and had her own guard at the door, I guess to keep the press out. My sister and I would never be allowed to forget her important role in all this.

Before Kate and I could be escorted through a back exit of the hospital, the phone in Aunt Caroline's room rang. She was so knocked out, the noise didn't wake her. She'd had some strong medicine—maybe a sleeping pill the staff begged her doctor to order to shut her up.

I picked up quickly and said, "Hello?"

It was DeShay. "I'm still with Jeff, and—"

"Has something happened? Is he all right?" My heart went into overdrive again.

"He's sleeping like a baby. No problem there. But White called. He wants you and Kate to come with me to Travis. We need formal statements. But there's something else."

"What?"

"Foster says he'll confess to everything on the record—and we love confessions—but only with Kate present. She doesn't have to do this, but I'm relaying the message."

I glanced at my sister. This had to be her choice. "Hang on a minute." I motioned Kate away from Sleeping Beauty and relayed what DeShay said. "You're under no obligation, and, in my opinion, you should pass. They have plenty on him."

Her brown eyes darkened with anger. "I'm not passing. I can't think of anything I'd rather do."

"You're sure?"

She nodded.

"I'm going with you, then." I spoke to DeShay again. "We haven't got any wheels, planned on bumming a ride with one of the officers downstairs. Can you come up to Aunt Caroline's room and get us?"   •

Don White and Kate sat facing Harrison Foster in a small interrogation room, while DeShay and I watched on a live feed in the next room. Foster's arm was in a sling, and dried blood on his orange jail jumpsuit marked the spot where the bullet had struck him.

White told Foster they had his *almost* ex-wife in another room and they'd be checking Foster's story against hers.

Foster offered his dimpled smile. "Good. What about my daughter?"

"She's being taken care of," White said. "But she's not really your daughter, is she? You want to tell us about that?"

Foster ignored the question, had eyes only for Kate. "I wouldn't have killed you. If you'd given me the money, I would have disappeared forever."

I didn't believe him, and sure hoped Kate wouldn't buy his bullshit either.

Kate leaned forward in her familiar therapy mode. "You've harmed a lot of people when the truth would have been simpler. I'm not sure I understand why you felt the need to do so much damage."

"You don't know what I've had to overcome to get where I am. I had two dollars when I came to this city."

Kate said, "Did your family throw you out? Maybe after you repeatedly hurt someone close to you— probably for fun? Maybe more than one someone?"

He kept smiling. "That's why I needed you to come here—to help you understand."

"And you're helping us *understand* without a lawyer present?" White said.

Foster stared at White for a second and then calmly said, "I've already waived those Miranda warnings twice. You want me to write it in blood?"

His attitude, his creepy smile made chill bumps rise on my arms. How had this man masqueraded as Mr. Nice Guy? But sociopaths *are* chameleons, and Foster had convincingly camouflaged his true self.

"Tell me how all this happened," Kate said. "That's what you want to talk about, right?"

"Yes. Because my wife and my child have nothing to do with this."

"The wife who kicked your ass to the curb?" White said.

Next to me, DeShay groaned. "Why you doing that, man? Let the turd talk."

Foster ignored White, but I, too, hoped White would keep his attitude out of this.

Kate broke the tense silence that followed. "How did you find out your life was about to be turned upside down? When the house came down and reports of infant bones were broadcast on the news?"

"I was at work and saw the bulletin on a local TV Web site. I went to the O'Mearas' house, talked to a neighbor hanging around the scene and heard all about the television show. Quite a knowledgeable woman. I learned Emma's name, heard the whole story about how her mother had abandoned her and her siblings. The

O'Meara name was very familiar to me. Yes, this was about the baby—the one I knew about."

"Knew about? Let's not fool around. Your baby had been buried under that house, right?" Kate said.

"Of course." Another cold smile.

Jeez.

"And you couldn't let anyone find out, so you followed Emma Lopez that evening and ran her off the road," White said. "Did you think that would accomplish anything?"

He smiled and kept his unwavering gaze on my sister. "*That* was a mistake. Panic leads to mistakes, and I've made too many—that first day and now today. But that's not what you really want to know, is it, Kate? You want to know why I came after you."

"You're wrong," she said evenly. "I want to know what happened to your baby. That's the only reason I'm here."

"You're kidding yourself, but I must say, you are probably the first genuine person I have ever met. I truly regret we didn't meet under different circumstances."

Kate didn't flinch, didn't allow her emotions to take over even though Foster probably hoped she would.

He sat back in his chair. "In the end, you won me over, Kate. That's why I promised the truth, and I'll deliver. My wife, Beth, began behaving oddly after our daughter was born. I understood this better after that mother who killed her kids was all over the news a few years ago. Beth was like her. Postpartum depression. She kept saying she was evil, that she didn't deserve a child so perfect. That maybe she should kill herself. I took her to a shrink and they doped her up good."

"But something happened anyway?" Kate said. "She harmed your baby?"

"No." Such a simple word, and so devoid of emotion coming from his lips. "I was the one."

"You . . . you did it?" Kate couldn't hide her horror this time.

"You know, you're overly sensitive, Kate. Too pampered, maybe." He spoke in a mocking tone, and I wanted to get her out of there, give Foster a swift kick in the groin while I was at it. But I didn't. White's goal was to learn if this man's wife had been complicit in his crimes.

"Keep going," Kate said calmly. I was relieved to see that she'd regained her composure.

"Beth was sedated, and I was exhausted the night it happened. I never heard any sound through the baby monitor. Nothing. I thought the baby had slept through the night for the first time. But she was dead when I went into her room that morning. Cold . . . blue . . . dead. I wrapped her up and was holding her when the cleaning lady came. Just so you know, that woman was despicable."

"Despicable enough that you made a deal with her?" White asked.

"Am I talking to you?" Foster snapped. Then he looked at Kate again. "She realized the baby was dead, and her wheels started turning right away. See, I stupidly wondered out loud how I'd explain this problem to Beth when she was finally with it enough to understand."

"You were worried about Beth?" I could hear the skepticism in Kate's tone.

"Oh, you are a smart one—you and your sister both." His tone was hard now. "There were things in my past I'd managed to hide up to that point. I couldn't have any fucking investigation over a dead kid."

I nodded and noticed that DeShay was getting it, too. We were now seeing the real Harrison Foster, the man who'd held a gun to my sister's head today, shot Jeff and shown no mercy to his other victims. This had never been about anything but protecting Harrison Foster—or whoever Harrison Foster really was.

"Did Christine O'Meara take the baby's body off your hands?" White asked.

"Yes. That day. Said she'd bury it. Said she could get some herbal medicine and induce her labor. She was eight and a half months along and could provide me with a brand-new healthy baby right away for a price. Beth would never know the difference; that's for sure."

"Even if it was a boy?" White again. He'd probably never heard anything like this—had any of us?—and I couldn't have kept my mouth shut either.

"Beth wasn't a problem," he said. "I mean, the

woman was damn psychotic—still is, if you ask me. I could have convinced her of anything. But a boy would have required a forged birth certificate and probably a quick relocation away from her friends. Her family lives in Oregon, and I figured that if the O'Meara woman delivered a boy, I could always explain later that Beth got it all wrong when she called them, that she'd had a breakdown and was under treatment. Turns out, I didn't have to worry."

Kate nodded. "You *bought* a new baby?"

"Yes. And I took care of her until Beth was well enough to function again. Took months. I considered my actions an investment in my future."

I wondered how his *actions* had affected that poor kid. Having this sicko for a father must have had some negative impact.

"Let me get this straight," White said. "Your wife had no knowledge that your daughter Amy wasn't her biological child?"

"Interesting question. A man who's been 'kicked to the curb,' as you put it, might want a little revenge on an ungrateful wife, might tell you Beth was the one who forced me to switch the babies. But you know, I like Amy. I don't want to damage her by leaving her without both her parents. She'd end up in foster care. The truth is, Beth and Amy do not know the truth."

Damage. That word meant something to him. Another chill crawled up my arms. This man's wife might never know how lucky she was that he'd be locked away until they put a needle in his arm.

"Your actions made sure Emma and Christine's other children were left without a parent and ended up in foster care," Kate said.

"Better them than Amy. If O'Meara hadn't demanded more money from me, she'd still be alive. Stupid woman thought she could run a business. When she failed at that—and she would—I knew she'd be back. I couldn't have that." He shook his head. "Nope. Couldn't have that."

"So you shot her," White said.

Foster blinked several times, his face impassive. "Yes."

"You killed two other people," Kate said, "or two that we know about."

He smiled. "All out of necessity, sweet Kate. Billings was easy. A weak man. He told me he already had a buyer for his information, but that if I could offer him more, he'd be happy to help me out. That buyer was your sister, of course. I'd watched her hand him cash earlier in the day. No matter how much I paid him, he'd never keep his mouth shut. He chose his own fate by being greedy."

I couldn't believe this guy.

"That's how you found him? Following Ms. Rose?" White asked.

"Yes. When the man got off work that day, I was right behind him," he said.

"And behind him when you slit his throat," White said.

I saw Foster's lips tighten, saw his posture stiffen. He kept his focus on Kate. "I resort to violence only when necessary."

"Did you even know if Billings had any information worth selling?" White asked.

"Didn't matter. That man would be trouble, might mention me to Abby. She'd want a description, and I do have distinctive features. He had to go. Kate understands, don't you?"

Kate closed her eyes for several seconds. When she spoke, her voice was so soft I could hardly hear her. "Oh, yes, I do understand. I understand everything now."

29

DeShay and I helped Jeff walk to the wheelchair in his hospital room. He was going home after only ten days—or, rather, heading for my house. He didn't complain as he took each slow step, even though I could tell he was hurting. "Pain is comforting," he'd told me while he recovered. "Pain means you're alive." That was as close as we'd gotten to discussing how near he'd come to dying. Knowing him, we might not ever talk about it again.

I'd done the interview for Kravitz two days after Foster was caught. Makeup was provided by the very talented Sandy Sechrest, who made all of us look like movie stars—all of us being Kate, Aunt Caroline, Emma and me. Loreen had absolutely refused to be interviewed, much less taped.

With cameras and lights taking up most of my aunt's living room, we answered Kravitz's questions for several hours. At times the crew dragged chairs from different rooms, moved tables and lamps and had us sit in other spots—sometimes together, sometimes apart, depending on who was talking about what. I was told this would keep the audience from getting bored with the set. I didn't really care. I wanted to be done.

I was sure most of what Stu taped would end up on the cutting room floor, and thank goodness for that, but I had the feeling Aunt Caroline might be disappointed. She'd lapped up the attention like a cat with a saucer of cream. The deal with Kravitz included a clause that Mary Parsons could air her own interview on the late news after the *Crime Time* episode was finished. Kravitz was concerned she'd leak something, so the plan was to

tape my interview with her on the same morning the
Crime Time episode aired in November.

A nurse's aide arrived and wheeled Jeff to the elevator and out the lobby door to the car that DeShay had
parked at the front entrance. A security guard was lurking, perhaps ready to call for a tow truck, but when
DeShay flashed his badge, the man understood who the
T-bird was waiting for. Everyone knew the story.

The ride home was blessedly quick, and Loreen and
Doris were waiting for us at my place. I'd moved them
from Jeff's apartment once Loreen finally believed that
Jimmy the pimp hadn't been outside her house that
night. Maybe no one had been outside.

Loreen and Emma had reunited the day after Foster
was caught. Emma's gratitude was obvious, but Loreen
didn't want any credit for doing "what any decent
human would do." She said she'd finally gotten something right for the first time and she was the one who
should be thankful.

After ten days, Diva and Webster still weren't sure
about Doris's aggressive approach to pets, but Loreen
was working with her on that.

"Jeffy's better," Doris chanted over and over when
we came in the door. She did a little clapping, too, and
I agreed his arrival was worth the applause.

When Doris held her arms out, ready for a run at her
brother to offer one of her infamous hugs, Loreen
stopped her by placing a gentle hand on Doris's arm.
"Remember how Jeffy hurt himself? You can't squeeze
him like you do me."

"That's right." Doris hit her forehead with the heel
of her hand. "Jeffy's got a hole in him. I don't know
how you get a hole in you, but if it makes you walk like
that, I don't want one."

Jeff and DeShay were moving through the foyer, and
he smiled and held out his hand to Doris. "Help me
over to Abby's . . . is that a recliner?"

I nodded. "Thought you might be more comfortable
there."

Doris forgot about helping. She ran to the recliner,
ready to show Jeff all the chair's bells and whistles—the
remote compartment, the massage options, the little

table that you could flip up for your drinks or snacks. She'd been playing with the chair for a week and was quite the expert.

Jeff looked at Loreen. "I can't thank you enough for taking care of her. She seems so comfortable with you, so happy."

"She's sweet. Like the kid I never had."

"I really appreciate your help," he said.

I raised my eyebrows and looked expectantly at him. "Loreen lost her job at Purity Maids, hint, hint."

A bigger smile from Jeff. "Really? Would you consider staying on? I don't know what your salary was, but—"

"But you'll get more. Plenty more," I finished.

Jeff shot me a look, but then he smiled again. He knew we'd work it out.

Epilogue

Kate and I joined Emma and her brothers and sister on a chilly November evening to watch what *Crime Time* had done with Emma's story. How would Christine O'Meara fare? Would the slant Kravitz took make HPD look bad? I sure hoped not, considering I got him that copy of Stu's tape. The confession and Foster's guilty plea to all the murders probably had more to do with that than my request.

I finally met Scott, Emma's oldest brother. He seemed reserved with Kate and me, unsure whether he liked all that had gone on and our role in it.

The new home was spectacular, and there had been other gifts besides the landscaping and the houseful of furniture. There were college scholarships for the kids, enough money for Emma to finish her master's in business, an apartment for Scott at college. *Reality Check* and Erwin Mayo had kept their word and didn't skimp. I had to admit, I might have been wrong about them. Perhaps they did want to help people, even though they came across as fake and self-centered.

The place smelled like the new carpet and the lemon-oiled built-in entertainment center. Shannon and Luke were sitting on the floor, busy with their laptops—more of Venture's generosity. Kate and I sat on the sofa to wait out the twenty minutes until showtime. My TiVo was set to record back home. Loreen and Doris had gone to a recently released preholiday animated film. Doris did not need to see or hear what had happened to her brother.

Jeff had insisted on returning to work, to desk duty

that he hated, but it was better than the recliner he'd grown tired of. He and DeShay had plenty of paperwork piling up.

Scott paced in the space connecting the living and dining areas, a longneck Bud Light in his hand. With his mother's history of alcoholism, I wondered if Emma worried about him. He wasn't even legal drinking age yet.

Emma came into the living room with chips and salsa, set them on the coffee table and sat in one of the new tub chairs. I'd already grabbed a Diet Coke from the kitchen, while Kate stuck with water.

"One of my half brothers called me today," Emma said. "Raul. He and Xavier Junior want to meet me."

"How do you feel about that?" Kate asked.

"I feel wonderful," Emma said. "I'd love to see my new dining room table filled with brothers and sisters."

A short, awkward silence followed. We knew that might not include one sister. Beth Foster and the daughter her husband had stolen seemed to have disappeared. Probably fleeing the media, if they had any sense. I may have unearthed the truth, but I'd fallen short. Emma wanted to meet the child she'd help bring into the world, but Amy's place at the table might never be filled.

"You look rested, Emma," I finally said, wanting to change the dark mood that had descended on the room.

"I am at peace, because of you and Kate. Thank you again so much," she said.

We spent the time until the show started talking about Shannon's good grades, Luke's successes on the football field and Emma's plan to return to school. Finally Scott, a few minutes before showtime, came and sat with us.

He looked at me and said, "I want to thank you, too. For helping my sister. You and Dr. Rose risked your lives. I'm sorry I didn't come here and, like, be here for everyone. I didn't think she was doing the right thing."

"Takes a strong person to admit they were wrong, Scott," Kate said. "I believe that's even more proof what a fantastic job Emma did raising the three of you."

"The show is starting," Shannon said.

We all turned our attention to the TV.

Kravitz began the narrative on an airplane, said he

was heading to Houston, Texas, to cover an amazing and complex story of deceit, murder and a family who wouldn't give up until they learned the truth about a sister lost to them years ago.

Truth, I thought, smiling to myself. *You did do the right thing, Paul.*

I hadn't been aware of the tension in my shoulders, but once he spoke those words, I sat back and enjoyed every minute of *Crime Time.* He presented the story concisely and with plenty of those cliffhanging questions before each commercial break. The demolished house and the tiny grave made it on the air; so did much abbreviated interviews with Kate, Emma, Aunt Caroline and me. Don White spoke for the police and was more charming than I imagined he could be, maybe because his partner was amazing everyone in rehab. When the clips of the hostage situation were shown, Kate bowed her head, but then footage of a shackled Harrison Foster being transferred to court for arraignment followed, and she watched intently. But her back was ramrod straight, her hands joined a little too tightly in her lap.

We learned new information as well. Harrison Foster wasn't his real name, and he did have a secret past, as Kate and I had suspected. He was Howard Nolen, and the unsolved murders of his parents in a small Nebraska town were added to his terrible résumé.

I glanced again at Kate when this was revealed. She was blinking back tears. I hated this, hated seeing her in so much pain. I'd heard her pacing in the night one too many times and guessed she had delayed moving into her new house because she didn't want to be alone. Not yet. The wounds Foster had inflicted were perhaps too fresh, too raw.

When the show ended, Emma said, "That wasn't so bad, was it?"

"They did a decent job." I welcomed a chance to talk about their take rather than analyze Kate's reaction in front of everyone. "Now you can talk to the *Today* show or *Good Morning America.* You said they've been calling."

"Oh, no," Emma said. "No more television for me."

"I'll do the talk-show rounds," Luke offered.

"You will not," Emma said. "None of you will. Haven't you learned anything from my mistakes?"

Scott rose. "I've got to drive back to school tonight. Paper due."

"Not after you've been drinking," Emma said. "Get up early tomorrow."

I thought I caught a look of relief on his face before he said, "Whatever."

He started toward the hall that led to the bedrooms, but a knock on the door stopped him.

Shannon, who'd been lying on her stomach on the floor typing on her laptop, sat up. "More reporters?"

Emma sighed. "Probably."

"I'll get rid of them," I said.

But when I cracked the door, I saw Beth and Amy Foster standing on Emma's front porch.

"Is . . . is this where Emma Lopez lives?" Unlike Emma, Beth Foster looked like she hadn't slept in weeks. Amy, Shannon's clone, seemed dazed. These two probably felt like they'd been sitting in the middle of a stampede for weeks.

"Emma," I said. "You've got visitors."

She cocked her head, reluctant to go to the door. "Who?"

"See for yourself." I widened the door and said to these brave souls who had come calling, "I think both of you are welcome here."

Kate and I left an hour later, but Amy and Beth remained. They had begun to warm up to everyone only after awkward introductions. No one spoke about Beth's husband, and I didn't think they would. Not now, anyway.

"You did what you promised," Kate said, once we were on the road. "You found their sister."

"Yeah. That feels good. This case has been all about sisters, hasn't it?" I was giving her an opening to talk.

But what she said surprised me. "I'm not running back to Terry, even if you and Aunt Caroline think I should. The safest option isn't always the best."

"You think that's what I expect?" Her defenses were still up.

"I-I don't know what you expect," she answered.

"The answer is no, okay? You ready to talk yet? About . . . him?"

"Not really."

I reached over, found her hand and squeezed it tightly. "That's okay. I can wait."

And I could.

Read on for an excerpt from

PUSHING UP BLUEBONNETS

the next Yellow Rose Mystery
by Leann Sweeney
available from Signet
in January 2008.

My daddy used to say there's news and then there's sit-down news. When I received the call from a small-town police chief named Cooper Boyd asking me to help him identify a car wreck victim, I was glad I was already seated in the big leather chair in my home office.

"Oh my God," I said. "Is it Kate? Or Jeff? Or—"

"Ma'am, the victim is female. Who is Kate and when did you see or speak to her last?"

My heart was racing now. "Kate Rose is my twin sister. She has dark brown hair and brown eyes. She went to work this morning and I talked to her before she— Oh God, what happened?"

"Okay. Take a deep breath. Obviously this woman is not your sister. The accident happened last night and I should have told you that first."

Now that my thoughts were no longer focused on worst-case scenarios, I noticed Boyd's voice sounded like he'd gargled with axle grease this morning.

"This wasn't exactly an accident," he went on. "I've come from Pineview near where the wreck occurred. They had to life-flight the young lady to the Texas Medical Center. She's in a coma."

"W-will she pull through?" My pulse slowed a little

but the coffee I'd just finished was still sloshing around after being stirred by panic.

"Doctors aren't saying much," he answered.

"You said Pineview? I've never heard of it."

"It's in far northwest Montgomery County. You know anyone up that way? A client? A relative? A friend?"

The word *client* caught my attention. "You must know more about me than my name. Why do you think I can help you identify this person?"

"The victim had your business card in her possession, ma'am. Yellow Rose Investigations, right? And adoption reunion is your specialty?"

"Yes," I said.

"See, her having your card is one of two things we know about her."

"And the other?" I asked.

"Someone wanted her dead."

I closed my eyes, pictured a young woman—not her face of course, since I'm no psychic—but I could imagine her body tangled in the wreckage of an automobile. It didn't help the swirling in my gut. "And she had *my* card?" was all I could manage in response.

"Yes, Ms. Rose."

"Okay, I'm worried she might be one of my former clients, even though I'm pretty sure I've never done a search for anyone from Montgomery County. But she could have just moved there or—"

"Listen, I need your help now," he said. "This young woman probably has relatives who should know she's in critical condition. Think you could meet me in the hospital lobby?"

"I—Yes. Sure. Which hospital?"

"Ben Taub."

"Of course." Ben Taub has one of the best trauma centers in the country. "I can be there in fifteen minutes. How will I know you?"

"I'm in uniform. Brown and gold." He disconnected without a good-bye.

Since it was August and hotter than hell's door handle, I was dressed in shorts and a tank top. I decided that wasn't suitable hospital attire and hurried upstairs, my cat, Diva, on my heels. I quickly changed into lightweight capris, a sleeveless cotton blouse and summer clogs.

"What the heck do you think this is about?" I asked Diva as I applied lipstick. No time for any other makeup to cover my usual crop of summer freckles, which had appeared despite the gallon of sunscreen I'd gone through since May.

Diva answered my question with several insightful meows. Too bad the cat whisperer wasn't around to interpret her answer.

As I stepped outside and went through the back gate to the driveway, I wondered if I'd ever had so much as a letter from a client from Pineview. I sure couldn't remember, but there were times when I couldn't even remember the Alamo.

Using the remote on my key chain, I turned off the car alarm on my new silver Camry. I'd had a superduper special-order car alarm installed; it beeped a reminder to engage it whenever I parked. No one got near my car without that thingee making enough noise to embarrass thunder. I'd had a little trouble on a case last year with a very bad man sticking GPS devices under my bumper every time I wasn't looking, and I wasn't about to have that happen again.

Five for Fighting's latest CD started playing as I turned the key and started the ignition. The drive took only ten minutes, and that meant I had five minutes to find a parking place in the Medical Center—a definite challenge. But since it was nearly noon, most of the morning appointments were over, and I located a spot pretty fast. Then I walked the long path to the hospital.

The air-conditioning made the lobby almost as cold as my ex-husband's heart. Guess hospitals have lots of stuff that might smell a whole lot worse without AC. I spotted the man in the brown uniform with gold trim and approached him. Then we shook hands.

"Abby Rose," I said.

"Thank you for coming." Boyd reached into his pocket and pulled out a folded sheet of paper and handed it to me. "This is a copy of what we found under the woman's front seat. We sent the actual card to the crime lab for fingerprinting."

It was my business card, all right—front and back. Someone had scrawled the words _adoption search_ and _do this today_ on the back. The card appeared smudged and wrinkled, and this condition made the copy a poor one.

I looked at Boyd, who was average height with a red-blond crew cut. He was graying at the temples but didn't look much older than fifty. "Can you give me more details? I could have had some contact with this person in the last few years, but as I said, I don't remember your town."

"What kind of details do you want?" he said. His drawl had to be East Texas. Very pronounced.

"You're sure this was a murder attempt?" I asked.

His jaw muscles tightened. "Yes, ma'am, I'm certain."

He then took me up to the fourth-floor waiting area for the neuro ICU, which was across the hall from the forbidding doors that would allow us in. Boyd told me to have a seat and he'd arrange for us to visit the victim.

A few minutes later, we were admitted, and Boyd took me to the mystery woman's room. She was covered with a white thermal blanket and was so tiny she seemed lost in the small space crowded with medical machinery, all of which was either beeping or blinking. An IV dripped slowly into tubing that fed down to her bruised arm. But that wasn't all that was bruised.

Her thick black lashes rested against the dark purple crescents under her eyes. She had a battered forehead and a split lip, and her blond hair had been shaved away for stitches above a large lump on her forehead. She was as pale as the sheets.

"Heck fire," I whispered. I blinked several times, wondering how anyone would recognize this woman, even someone who knew her. She was lucky she wasn't already pushing up bluebonnets.

Penguin Group (USA) Online

What will you be reading tomorrow?

Tom Clancy, Patricia Cornwell, W.E.B. Griffin,
Nora Roberts, William Gibson, Robin Cook,
Brian Jacques, Catherine Coulter, Stephen King,
Dean Koontz, Ken Follett, Clive Cussler,
Eric Jerome Dickey, John Sandford,
Terry McMillan, Sue Monk Kidd, Amy Tan,
John Berendt…

You'll find them all at
penguin.com

*Read excerpts and newsletters,
find tour schedules and reading group guides,
and enter contests.*

Subscribe to Penguin Group (USA) newsletters
and get an exclusive inside look
at exciting new titles and the authors you love
long before everyone else does.

PENGUIN GROUP (USA)
us.penguingroup.com